BASHKIM

Benjamin Walker

ISBN: 979-8-9883069-0-0
First Edition
Developmental Editing: Kathrine Snow of "Prolonging the Prologue"
Copy/Line Edit: Tanya Grenier
Cover Art (dragon): Breandan Scott-Arbuckle
Logos and Icons: Robyn Walker
Book Design: Me (and I had no idea what I was doing)
Independently published by Benjamin Walker (that's also me)
kesshonitelegends@gmail.com

I would love to dedicate this book to certain people. However …

No matter who I do, or do not pick for this specific moment will most likely, undoubtedly, not be approved by someone, somewhere.

And for that very reason, I've decided to instead make everyone angry and dedicate it to my neighbor's dog. The dog had absolutely nothing to do with the book, but she was nice enough to come bark at my front door almost daily so I would take a break and play fetch.

She was so concerned about me overworking myself that she would even check on me at two in the morning to make sure I was sleeping.

Multiple times a week.

BASHKIM

A Kesshonite Legend

Benjamin Walker

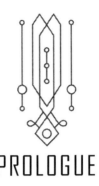

PROLOGUE

Datori hid behind the massive tree that had managed not to catch fire yet. He held his breath in fear. The entire forest surrounding him continued to burn. He wanted to escape, but more horrors awaited him in every direction. The heat from the fire reached out and whipped against him. Sweat poured down his face, half from the rising temperature and half from terror. He could feel his skin slowly starting to burn, but he dared not attempt to use his own magic to cool himself down. Such a thing would surely get him caught.

Just on the other side of the tree he hid behind stood a man with powers like he had never seen before. The stranger had torn his friends apart simply by waving a hand. With a single flick of his wrist, he had slammed one of Datori's friends onto the ground. Something that could not be seen forced his legs to twist in ways they were never meant to bend. They cracked and snapped, and his friend cried for help. The others were too confused to process what took place directly in front of them. Instead, they stood there, unable to react. Before they knew it, their friend's limbs were pulled from his body and tossed to the side.

Datori closed his eyes and shook his head as he tried to keep the vision from replaying in his mind. He had to act. He had to escape. But how? The mysterious man wasn't the only thing waiting for him. Something else lurked in the burning forest. Something that Datori feared even more than the stranger and the fires combined. A hideous monster covered in white scales. Datori had seen it with his own eyes. He saw it twist and slither between the trees as it towered over his friends before snatching one of them up into its jaws.

Datori nearly threw up as the image came back to him. The monster chewed his friend as blood and innards squeezed between its teeth. He grabbed his stomach and covered his mouth, trying to keep his last meal down. The screams of his last remaining friend echoed and begged for his help. Datori closed his eyes and tried to hold his tears back. He couldn't help him, even if he wanted to.

What am I supposed to do against a man with that kind of power? he thought. *Or one that can control such a beast?*

Nothing. No matter how much he may have wanted to help, his hands were tied.

"Datori! Help me!" his friend pleaded, sounding as though he were in immense pain.

Datori didn't dare look from behind his tree.

"Are you going to let him die, Datori?" the stranger asked.

Datori's eyes widened in fear.

He thought he had gotten away without being seen. He continued to hold his breath and ignore the blazing heat surrounding him as his heart thumped against his chest. A gradual thud against the ground approached him slowly. Each step the beast took could be felt in Datori's body, and the fear stabbed him like a knife as the monster drew closer.

Against his own wishes, Datori began to breathe rapidly in short breaths as he pressed himself against the tree's wide trunk. The head of the monster slowly slid around the tree and faced him, its yellow eyes nearly level with Datori's. A deep, resonating growl came from the monster that vibrated Datori's entire body. His hair stood on end as the beast snarled just enough to show its many teeth.

"It's time to come out, Datori," the man called again. "I would like a word with you."

Datori started to slowly scoot away from the beast as it stared him down. Once around the tree and onto the other side, Datori got to his feet and quickly put some distance between him and the massive creature. Unfortunately, doing so also put him closer to the stranger. The man seemed to be nothing more than a regular eshan. He stood no taller, no stronger, and no different than even Datori himself. The pointed ears on his head were the same as everyone's, and the strands of white in his lengthy hair even suggested he had more than a few years under his belt.

Next to the stranger hung Datori's friend, suspended in the air by nothing more than the man's magic. His arms and legs stretched out as though they were being pulled by something, but no ropes could be seen. Datori's friend looked at him with wide and terrified eyes. Datori couldn't bring himself to look at his friend, for he knew he could do nothing to help him and had chosen to leave him.

"Would you like to save your friend?" the man asked.

"Yes," Datori said quietly.

"Then try."

"I…I can't."

"And why can't you?"

Datori's mouth moved silently as he tried to form words. His eyes fell to the bloody remnants of his other companions. He tried to look away, only to see the gigantic creature sitting on its hind legs before him, eyeing him hungrily.

"Because," Datori said, looking back to the stranger as he tried to correctly word the obvious, "your magic. It's far beyond my own or anything I've ever seen. And your…dragon."

Datori's voice trailed off.

"Are you saying you're powerless to save him?" the man asked.

Datori stared at his own feet. "Yes."

"And how do you think I felt when I came home to find my wife and child dead on the floor?"

Datori said nothing and continued to stare downwards.

"How do you think I felt?" the man bellowed.

Datori's friend suddenly burst into flames. He screamed as loud as he could, begging for it to stop. The fires burned his skin to a crisp and left nothing more than a charred husk. The man let the burned corpse fall to the ground with a thud. With his voice still raised, he repeated his question.

"How do you think I felt as I listened to my wife draw her final breath?"

Datori cowered as the man spoke. The white-scaled dragon stepped behind him, its giant head looming over him as it stared down with hungry eyes.

"Powerless," Datori blubbered through his fear.

The man remained silent and watched Datori squirm.

"I'm sorry!" Datori cried. "It wasn't supposed to happen. Nobody was supposed to get hurt."

The man looked down at his hand. To Datori's surprise, the man's hand looked as though something had stained the skin and turned it black. The stranger paused before slowly tucking the hand underneath his robe.

"Yes," the man said calmly. "That is exactly how I felt. But I am not powerless against *you*."

The entire forest fire instantly snuffed itself out with a sharp but short hiss and left nothing but smoke. The man turned from Datori and walked away with the dragon following behind him. Datori watched with wide eyes as the two left him and waited for what he knew would be his end.

Even after they had left his sight, Datori still doubted his existence. He patted himself repeatedly and made sure everything remained in one piece. He collapsed to his knees and took a much-needed breath. Somehow, someway, the stranger had chosen to let him live.

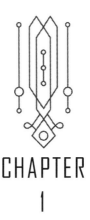

CHAPTER

1

Forceful winds swept across the cave's jagged entrance and howled through its interior. Snowflakes skittered farther across the stone floor with each gust. As they drew closer to the fire within, they turned to water and collected in a puddle. Bashkim groaned as he grabbed his furs, trying to wrap them tighter around himself. The warmth from the small flames did little more than melt the snow that dared approach.

He gazed into the fire with tired eyes, watching it hover slightly above the floor. The flames swayed from side to side, burning silently and without fuel. The light they provided flickered against the barren stone walls of the hole he called home for the night.

Underneath his furs, Bashkim crossed his arms. With another groan, he admitted he needed a bigger fire. A single, slow wave of his hand forced the flames to grow. Up they went, their tips just brushing the ceiling.

Too big, Bashkim thought.

With another motion of his hand, the flames slightly lowered.

Bashkim leaned against the stone wall and tried to enjoy the heat. He had endured a long, cold hike from the village at the bottom of the mountain and had yet to reach his destination.

She's doing this on purpose, he thought, scoffing to himself.

He reached over to his pack and retrieved a small piece of dried meat. Bashkim bit into the bland dinner, looking towards the bones of a small animal at the opposite end of the cave as he chewed. They were completely stripped of all their meat and left to dry, suggesting that whoever, or whatever, had done so some time ago and moved on. Bashkim shoved the rest of the dried meat into his mouth and stood up. He made his way to the bones and rolled them over one by one with his foot before squatting down for a closer inspection. He saw no signs of teeth marks from a larger animal. Instead, the bones looked like they had been hacked with a dull blade, crushing them more than slicing. Next to the bones lay a collection of small stones, as well as scorch marks on the floor, suggesting that whoever had been here at least knew how to make fire.

Goblins, Bashkim sighed, recognizing the barbaric butchering.

Swallowing the remainder of his dinner, Bashkim grabbed the stones and used them to make a circle around his own fire. He then started to feed the flames an assortment of twigs and branches he had collected earlier in the day. One by one they went in, fueling the fire so that it could survive on their own.

Satisfied that the heat source no longer required his aid, Bashkim slid his sword to the head of his bed to keep it close and lay down. He used his backpack as a pillow and pulled his blanket over him. No longer having to keep a magical grip on the flame, Bashkim drew in a slow and much needed breath. The fire began to crackle and pop, and the branches glowed red hot. Passing wind sucked the smoke outside the cave. Bashkim watched as the fire slowly consumed the broken limbs. The occasional spark jumped from the wood as it split and collapsed on itself.

The sounds seemed to grow louder as he watched. They echoed in his head. His hands gripped the blanket, and a heavy frown formed on his face. Despite the fire remaining a consistent size, he felt trapped. Bashkim whipped around, almost snarling as he turned his back to the flames. A single pulse came from the fire. The brief but sudden rush of intense heat in the flames reduced the branches to embers.

Bashkim closed his eyes and sighed, pacing his breathing.

Do I need to have a fire? he wondered. *Maybe between the furs and the blanket…*

Outside, the wind continued to howl as a reminder. Admitting that the night would only get colder, Bashkim grabbed a few more of the thicker branches he had gathered and set them into the pile of glowing embers. Between the hot coals and a little help from his magic, the fire sprang back up in no time.

Once content that the fire would burn on its own *again*, Bashkim rolled back over to face the stone wall.

Rays of morning sun slipped into Bashkim's cave, bouncing off the smooth stone. Grumbling, he rubbed his face and looked at the remains of his campfire. The fire had run its course, leaving nothing more than ash and coal. With a yawn and a decent stretch, Bashkim rose to his feet.

He packed his belongings and made sure his boots, jacket, and furs were all tied and properly secured. For breakfast, he served himself another piece of dried meat, paired with a piece of rather stale bread. Still chewing the meat, Bashkim put his backpack on and approached the cave's exit. He squinted as his eyes adjusted to the sun bouncing off the newly fallen snow.

Before fully stepping out of the cave, Bashkim turned back, taking one more look at the campfire's remains.

It's fine, he tried to convince himself but failed.

Bashkim spread the ashy remains out with his foot, thoroughly checking for any remaining embers. A dust cloud formed and covered his boot.

"Humph," he grunted, heading back to the narrow entryway and pulling his hat down over his ears.

Bashkim tucked his arms underneath his furs and took his first step outside the cave. A satisfying crunch came from under his boot as it flattened the snow. The morning sun felt good beaming down on him. Its rays provided a small amount of comfort as he observed the still scene.

The wind had stopped at some point in the night, allowing the snow to pile. The pine trees scattered across the mountain held the snow, undisturbed, in their branches. Several rocks and boulders protruded from the white blanket as well, trying their best to keep from being buried. It all would have made a beautiful painting if not for the tracks nearby. Unlike the bones in the cave, these tracks were fresh and plentiful.

Bashkim calmly continued up the winding path, pretending to ignore the tracks, as well as the occasional grunt from behind the large rocks.

How many? Bashkim thought as he walked. *Three? Five? Is it merely the scouts, or have they already mustered their friends?*

Bashkim stopped walking once he assumed himself to be in a proper line of sight. He feigned a yawn, stretching his arms out high above his head, fully exposing his back. The twang of a taut bowstring broke the stillness. Bashkim's hands sprang open, and a thin wall of ice shot up from the ground behind him, throwing snow.

An arrow struck the ice but failed to fully pierce. As the snow fell back to the ground, Bashkim stepped out from behind the wall. A goblin archer stood on top of a boulder, his small body adorned with various animal parts. Below him, creeping out from behind several rocks, came more goblins. Bashkim held his left hand close to the wall he had made. The ice started to move, forming itself over Bashkim's forearm and creating a small shield.

As the goblin tried to ready another arrow, Bashkim charged forward and drew his sword. The goblins readied their own weapons, which consisted of large animal bones, iron skillets, and a few rusty blades. The archer fired another arrow before Bashkim could fully close the distance, but his frozen shield protected him.

He swiped his sword across the chest of one goblin and smashed his shield against another. As the archer attempted to draw a third arrow, Bashkim rushed him with his shield. Once in range, a thin spike jutted from Bashkim's shield and drove through the goblin's neck. Twisting his wrist, Bashkim broke the spike from his shield, and the archer fell into the snow with a muffled thud.

Another goblin came at Bashkim, swinging a rusty blade overhead. Bashkim put his frozen shield in the way, meeting the blow full force. The goblin's sword chipped partly through the ice. Before it could pull the blade free, the ice shifted and formed itself over the goblin's weapon, locking it in place. Bashkim yanked the goblin forward, driving his sword through the goblin's heart.

The remaining goblins shrieked, circling Bashkim. A strong wind swept through before they could close in. Bashkim and the goblins shielded their faces as the flurry of snow beat against them.

"Who dares to disturb my *slumber?*" a voice boomed down the mountain.

As the gust faded, Bashkim and the goblins looked up. Before them stood a massive creature adorned with light-blue scales and an array of spikes and horns that trailed its spine. The creature folded its gigantic wings back and stared down at them, stomping forward on all four legs.

The head on its lengthy neck lowered to the ground and slithered between them like a giant serpent, eyeing every one of them.

"You step foot on *my* mountain," the dragon said, the voice rumbling within Bashkim's chest. "Yet you present yourselves empty-handed."

The goblins began to shake, slowly stepping backwards as the dragon's head moved towards them.

"I smell not a single gold coin on these caterwauling goblins," the dragon said. "Perhaps they hope their pots and pans will pass as an offering?"

The dragon spiraled around, facing Bashkim. "Or perhaps *you* are the offering?"

Bashkim remained in place, showing little to no concern. The dragon brought its head even closer to Bashkim, to the point of being within arm's reach. A low, slow growl came from the dragon, as did an icy cold breath.

"A little over the top, don't you think?" Bashkim whispered.

"Oh, come on," the dragon said in a much softer, feminine voice.

Bashkim chuckled quietly, motioning with his head for the dragon to continue. The dragon scooped Bashkim into her massive hand and stood on her hind feet.

"I accept your offering," she said, her voice booming again as she turned to the goblins. "But I will *not* accept your disturbance!"

The goblins began to flee, but the dragon blew her icy breath down on them, freezing several in place. A wide swipe of her tail shattered the frozen goblins into pieces and crushed several others that attempted to run. The dragon's tail continued through the goblins and into the trees and rocks, creating a wave of snow and debris.

The few remaining goblins scattered in a blind panic. The dragon roared and spewed more of the frozen storm after them. She held Bashkim gently in her hand all the while. Bashkim politely cleared his throat, catching the dragon's attention. She sighed in disdain and let the rest of the goblins run as she took to the sky, flying up the mountain.

A large opening higher up on the side of the mountain waited for them, inviting them into a spacious cavern covered in ice. The dragon landed in front of the frozen cave and gently laid her hand down on the ground. The clawed fingers spread apart, allowing Bashkim to step out.

"That'll do, Rin," Bashkim said once he had his feet on solid ground and patted the giant, scaled hand.

"You know I have to keep up *some* kind of appearance," Rin said.

Though she chose to use the softer tone, Bashkim could still feel the resonance of her voice vibrate in his chest.

"You keep me up here on this mountain all alone," she said dramatically. "I can't have something as simple and vile as goblins believing I'm a weak-willed creature that bows to the whims of a man."

"I don't keep you up here," Bashkim argued. "You left me to come back and add to your horde."

"You say that as though it were a bad thing."

Bashkim rubbed a hand across his face. "Anyway. I'm here to talk about your eating habits."

"The audacity!" Rin gasped in feigned shock. "I save you from those nasty creatures and take you into my own home. And for that, I deserve this?"

"It's about what you're eating," Bashkim said, waving the dragon away. "Not how much. I wouldn't know what a dragon's waistline is supposed to look like anyway."

"My diet has remained free of humans, and eshans for that matter," she said, only slightly more serious, then added with a mocking tone. "Two legs bad, you said. Unless it's the goblins, because apparently those don't count. Which is unfortunate because they're rather foul tasting."

Bashkim crossed his arms and tapped his foot against the icy floor, staring the dragon down.

"Well, they are nasty," Rin said. "If you don't believe me, wait and see if a vulture will eat one. I suggest you get comfortable, though, because you'll be waiting a while."

Bashkim continued to tap his foot.

"Oh, alright," she said, rolling her eyes. "One! One single human and it was far from here. You should be happy about it anyway. He was running from the law. I did the world a favor by getting rid of him, and imagine the tales the soldiers will tell about a dragon eating their escaped prisoner."

Rin stared past Bashkim as if recalling a fond memory. "Ah, what a find it was," she sighed. "Apparently sitting in a dungeon does little to tarnish the taste of a human, because I assure you, he was *delicious*."

Bashkim stopped tapping his foot, frowning as he continued to stare.

Rin turned to face Bashkim, speaking with a more serious tone this time. "You have my word, Bashkim. I promise you; it is only the one. No more, no less."

"You haven't been to Telscara?" Bashkim asked.

Rin arched her neck back in surprise. "Goodness, no. Why would I go there? You know I steer clear of villages and cities, especially when the fools decide to roost at the bottom of my mountain. No need to give them a reason to come up here trophy hunting."

"One of their farms was destroyed, and some of the people were taken. Supposedly by a dragon."

"And I suppose Bashkim, the white knight and doer of good deeds, readily came to their aid?"

"I was in the neighborhood."

"Indeed. And what did the hero find? Was he convinced a dragon attacked them?"

"It definitely looked like it. A farmhouse was crushed, giant ruts in the ground, and the description seemed close enough."

"Oh?" Rin asked, eyes wide and voice curious. "And how did they describe this dragon? Beautiful? Elegant? Mythical and gorgeous?"

"Terrifying," Bashkim stated. "Unfortunately, the dragon attacked at night. The people said it had white scales."

"White scales?" Rin bellowed, standing up on her hind feet and spreading her wings wide to show her glorious body in full. "Do these scales look *white* to you?"

"They are a lovely shade of light blue," Bashkim said without hesitation.

Rin sat back down on all fours, satisfied with the answer. "And they're beautiful."

"Each and every one of them, and no other dragon can even hope to compare. However, I would imagine when there's no sunlight and one is running for their life, it might be difficult to appreciate such beauty."

Rin pointed her nose up, looking down at Bashkim. "I can accept that."

Bashkim shook his head and Rin lowered hers, getting closer to him. "I was only away for a few days," she said with a devious grin. "Just how much trouble do you think I could get into?" Bashkim only looked at her, unamused. "Fair enough," she said. "But do you *actually* think that was me?"

Bashkim sighed. "No, but dragons don't normally attack villages, so I'm not sure what's going on."

The playful grin on Rin's face slipped away. Bashkim felt the air from her nose as she sighed softly.

"A *proper* dragon wouldn't, no," she said.

"Proper?"

Rin nodded. "If the people really did see a dragon in white scales, then I'm afraid the hero may have gotten himself into more than he bargained for."

"What do you mean?"

"I saw a dragon in white once, or, at least, something posing as a dragon. It may have looked the part, save for the extra set of hands on the crook of its wings, but never have I felt a presence so twisted and perverse. I've watched your kind for some time, Bashkim, and I've seen them practice some unusual and disturbing things. But none of that compares to what I felt radiating from that creature. The feeling it stirred within my own bones was like none other."

Rin shrugged her massive shoulders as if shaking something off. "Vile, disgusting thing. With eyes like that, I refuse to believe it was an actual dragon. I was fortunate to only see the one, for I've heard there were more, and they caused quite the stir."

"When?"

"I saw it a couple hundred years ago. I heard word from other dragons that they encountered them as well, but all chose to steer clear. I'm afraid I know little of this beast, and I don't care to know more."

"I've never even *heard* of one until now," Bashkim admitted. "You'd think something dangerous enough to push dragons away wouldn't go unnoticed for two hundred years. If it attacked Telscara then surely that's happened elsewhere before. At the very least, there should be stories and rumors going around the local taverns."

"I agree. Humans do love their storytelling."

"Humans aren't the only ones."

"Perhaps, but they do tell some of the better ones. A shame most of them come from exaggeration or complete fabrication."

"And just when have you had the chance to listen to these stories?"

"Come now, Bashkim," Rin said with a proud smile. "You know dragons have exceptional hearing. I can hear a couple's argument in Telscara from here."

"I think that exceptional hearing may also be exaggerated."

"I would never," Rin said, feigning offense. "I am shocked you would insinuate such a thing."

Bashkim shrugged. "I would think if you could hear so well then you would have heard me coming up the mountain a lot sooner. Surely you wouldn't let me climb that far on my own just to get to you."

"I would if I liked to play hard to get," Rin said, her smile stretching across her scaled snout.

Bashkim gently pushed her head away, chuckling. "Let's be serious for a moment. If these things are as bad as you say, we have a real problem on our hands. I'm not exactly thrilled about hunting something that is not only the *size* of a dragon, but apparently worse than one."

"Well," Rin said softly. "You don't *have* to."

"I can't accept that, and you know it."

"Perhaps you should, Bashkim. You'll never fly with the shackles you've bound yourself to."

"What difference does it make to you?" Bashkim asked, his voice rising slightly.

Rin reared back with widened eyes and a look of shock. Bashkim felt the instant shame of his reaction and fumbled for words to apologize.

"Was it bad last night?" Rin asked, letting the incident slide.

Bashkim stared down at the floor. "Yeah. It wasn't great."

Rin slowly brought her head down closer to Bashkim again, speaking softly. "Are you sure you want to help this time? It might be too much for you to handle."

"I have to try."

"Then, if the hero insists, I know of an...acquaintance we can talk to. He may know more of these creatures. At the very least, he can point us in the right direction."

"Where is he?"

"If I had to wager, I'd say he's still keeping near Nennossen."

"That's not exactly close. Would you be willing to take me?"

"Of course."

"*Without* leaving me behind again?"

"Oh, you didn't have to go *that* far. And I came back before those goblins could do anything, didn't I?"

Bashkim slid both his hands down his face, groaning.

"I will take you." Rin chuckled and stood up. "And I will not abandon you."

Rin walked deeper into her cavern with Bashkim following behind. As the sunlight failed to reach them, Bashkim stepped on something that clinked. Curious, he held his hand out with the palm facing upwards. Magic moved in his chest then swam through his arm and up to his hand. A small sphere of fog appeared slightly above his palm. Hundreds of tiny shards of ice swirled within the magical sphere, causing micro bolts of lightning to strike between the frozen fragments.

The flickering light from the sphere gradually became more stable. It bounced off the ice, giving the floors and walls a slight sparkle. The light also gleamed off several golden coins scattered across the floor. Bashkim lowered the ball of light and held it outwards, revealing Rin's hoard. Swords, armors, jewels, crowns, and coats piled up on even more coins.

"Your stash has grown significantly since I was last here," Bashkim said.

"What?" Rin asked with her back still facing him. "Can't a woman have nice things?"

"You have several nice things by the look of it."

Rin returned with a tangled mess of straps attached to a saddle and set them before Bashkim. "Are you calling me greedy?"

"Never in a hundred lifetimes," Bashkim replied while trying to make sense of the leather catastrophe.

"Good. I'd hate to think you forgot who gave you your sword."

"Your generosity is only exceeded by your beauty."

Bashkim released the small sphere of light and let it hang in the air, where it shone down on the many straps. He slowly untangled them and began running them through their correct hooks and loops.

"Such an overly complicated trick for making light," Rin said, her head moving around the ball. "Especially when fire is so much easier."

"It's not so bad once you get the hang of it. Just need a bit of practice. Besides, it provides better light than fire."

Rin pulled away from the lightning ball and watched Bashkim. He kept focus on the straps and saddle, but he had already started to pace his breathing.

"So it does," she said, moving towards the entrance of the cave. Having untangled and corrected the straps, Bashkim got up and lifted the saddle. As he did, he heard a jingling from one of the saddlebags. "What's this?" he asked, dismissing the light as he approached Rin and shook the saddlebags again.

"I can't leave empty-handed," Rin said playfully. "What if I want you to buy me something nice while we're out?"

Bashkim carried the saddle up onto Rin's back and ran the straps between her spikes, latching the hoops where he could. He tightened each one down, securing the saddle in place and making sure Rin remained flexible and comfortable. Only when she nodded in approval did Bashkim sit down in it. He reached into the bag and pulled out a pair of goggles and put them on his head.

"Onward, my mighty steed," he said with an uncontainable chuckle and gave Rin's sides a light tap with his heels.

Rin curled her neck back until her snout rested in front of Bashkim's face and squinted. "You're not out of reach, you know."

"I would never be out of your reach." Bashkim smiled, patting her on the nose.

A small, chilling snort escaped Rin as she rose to her feet.

"The things I do for you," she sighed.

Rin spread her wings wide and squatted down on all fours. Her claws gripped the ground as her muscles tightened, ready to jump. Bashkim grabbed the goggles and slid them down over his eyes.

"And that's why you'll never get rid of me," Bashkim said.

Wind swept under Rin's wings as she soared through the sky. Bashkim remained safely secured in the saddle, holding the leather straps tightly as the force of the wind beat against him. Thankfully, the goggles kept his eyes protected so he could enjoy the view. He could see all the way down Rin's mountain, spotting Telscara at the base. Despite the constant wind noise, Bashkim still found a certain peace and comfort in leaving all his problems beneath him.

"This is nice," Rin said. "You should take me out more often."

Bashkim chuckled, patting and rubbing her armored hide.

"Would you like to take a detour and savor the moment?" she asked.

I'd like to keep going and never stop, he thought, giving her offer some serious consideration.

He couldn't deny his reluctance to see the big city of Nennossen, but he couldn't forget his reasons for going either.

"I'm afraid we can't," Bashkim shouted over the wind. "We should stay on task."

"As you wish." Rin thrust them forward with a strong push of her wings.

Bashkim remained silent while she flew, picturing the city and all its inhabitants. Citizens, soldiers, royal figures, it didn't matter. He could see each of them looking down on him.

Immundrid, they would say, pointing a judgmental finger.

Bashkim shook his head. As he dismissed the negative thoughts, he felt Rin's muscles tighten underneath him.

"Something wrong?" he asked.

"I don't think we're alone anymore," Rin said, the playfulness in her voice absent.

Bashkim held the straps a little tighter and looked around him. Rin flapped her massive wings repeatedly, thrusting herself forward as if fleeing. Bashkim looked behind and underneath them but saw nothing.

"Do you still feel it?" Bashkim asked.

"I do."

Confused, Bashkim looked up just in time to see a dragon emerge from the clouds high above them. Its wings spanned much wider than Rin's, nearly enough to wrap around her entire body. Spikes and horns reached out from all over its massive frame, some broken and jagged while others curved out to a sharp point. The dragon closed the distance between them in an instant. Bashkim's eyes widened in terror once he saw the scales.

"White dragon!" Bashkim shouted.

The monster's jaws shot forward, its hundreds of pointed teeth hungry for flesh. Rin spun around and countered with her icy breath. The white dragon roared in anger as it tried to shield itself. Rin lunged forward, ramming her body against the iced-over dragon.

"What are you doing?" Bashkim asked as his body flung around in the saddle.

"I'm not waiting to see what comes out of its mouth," Rin snarled.

Rin drew another breath and blew her icy storm against the white dragon as hard as she could, forcing it down. Bashkim could feel her sides rapidly expanding and contracting as she drew in air for more breath attacks.

If she's this scared, I can't just sit here, he thought.

"Get us above it!" Bashkim shouted, drawing his sword.

Rin flapped her wings and thrust herself over the dragon as it scraped the ice off itself. Bashkim unhooked the straps securing him to the saddle and held his breath, preparing himself. Sword in hand, he jumped from Rin's back and dove towards the dragon.

"Bashkim!" Rin cried.

Bashkim reached out with his off hand, pointing his palm towards the dragon. As he got closer, a surge of magic shot through his body, and the ice covering the white dragon shattered into thousands of tiny shards. With another jolt of magic, the ice spun rapidly around the beast, forming an electrical charge between the shattered fragments. As the charge built, it jumped through the white dragon and connected with the ground below, forming a massive lightning bolt. Thunder echoed in the sky, and the white dragon roared in pain.

As Bashkim approached, he could see the web of scorch marks across its scales. He gripped his sword with both hands, pointing the blade downwards and driving it into the monster's side. The blade sunk into the flesh and locked in place. The sudden stop ripped the blade from Bashkim's grip as he smacked against the dragon's hide and continued his freefall. Black blood dripped from the wound, and everything seemed to slow while Bashkim spun in the air.

He looked up at Rin and the white dragon, their movements dragging. A whisper came to him in a faint voice, sounding as though it spoke from inside his head.

"Bahntu farrandemzime, Bashkim."

Bashkim's eyes widened in shock. The magic inside of him began to spiral violently, as though it were trying to jump out of his body. Just as time had seemed to slow, it suddenly returned to normal pace. Down Bashkim fell towards the world below as Rin swooped after him. She snatched him with her hand, knocking out what little wind he had left.

"You're a damned fool!" she exclaimed.

"Maybe, but there's no way we're outrunning that thing," Bashkim wheezed.

Rin growled and held Bashkim close. She turned around and thrust herself back towards the dragon, spewing her icy breath over him once more. Once she got closer, she snapped at one of its wings, puncturing it with her teeth. The white dragon started to grab her, but she swung her tail over her shoulder. One of her many spikes struck the white dragon's face, gouging its eye. The white dragon pulled back, snarling as more of the black blood seeped from its wounds. With a wide swipe of her free hand, her claws tore away a strip of its scales as she turned to flee, using her feet to both push the monster away and thrust herself forward.

As they fled, Bashkim tried to look back between Rin's fingers. The white dragon shook its head violently, clearly hurt from the tail strike. Despite the white dragon not coming after them, Bashkim heard the voice again.

"Delso nacht indulsa mesh, Bashkim," it whispered inside of his head. "Mesh jah frunwah mich delso,"

"What is that voice?" Bashkim asked.

"What are you talking about?"

"Do you not hear it?"

"I hear nothing but you and two angry dragons," Rin answered.

The mysterious voice chuckled softly. Its words came through more clearly. "Mahn tu, Mykenebres."

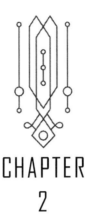

CHAPTER
2

Bashkim watched from between Rin's scaled fingers as the white dragon retreated.

What was that voice? Bashkim wondered, staring in disbelief.

Rin didn't look back, nor did she slow down. The sharp winds beat against her hand and tunneled between her fingers.

"Is it gone?" she asked.

"I think we're safe for now," Bashkim gasped, trying to catch his breath.

Rin swooped down onto the side of a mountain. "Oh, thank goodness," she said, collapsing with a loud thud.

She stretched her arms and legs out wide, pushing the many rocks away and opening her hand to release Bashkim. Bashkim only managed a couple steps out of her palm before collapsing onto a patch of grass. The two of them lay on the ground, their lungs filling with air. Bashkim started to pat himself down, ensuring all his limbs were still attached.

"Are you okay?" he asked when content with his limb count.

"I think so," Rin said between breaths. "Just a little winded. You?"

Bashkim sat up, rolling his shoulders and groaning. He started to untie his gauntlets to check his arms and hands.

"Bruised," he said, taking note of the black blood on his gauntlets. "But not broken."

Rin chuckled. "Such is the life of the hero."

"All day every day. Bastard still has my sword though."

"I'll buy you a new one."

"Deal," Bashkim said, letting the loosened gauntlets slide off his hands and fall to the ground.

Alternating between each hand, he massaged his palm with a thumb. The soreness he found reached through to the back of his hand. As the adrenaline left his body, his bruises began to throb, and he discovered he had more than he realized. His shoulders hurt, his wrists ached, and his chest felt as though it had been hit with a hammer. *Must have slammed against that thing harder than I thought.*

Rin's head slowly slid across the ground, moving closer to Bashkim. She watched him grimace as he moved. "We've barely begun this adventure and you're already massaging your wounds. Are you sure you want to do this?"

Bashkim reached down and grabbed his gauntlets. "We're still going to Nennossen. I'd like to think there's only the one white dragon, but that's probably just wishful thinking. We'll need all the help we can get."

"If you insist."

"I do," Bashkim said, tying the gauntlets down. "Though I'd like to have a new sword *before* we got to Nennossen."

"I'm certain I've heard the strikes of a smith's hammer from Telscara."

"You did. I saw her making a sword while I was there."

"Oh?" Rin said with a smile and widened eyes. "Took notice of her, did you?"

"I did. I thought it was a bit strange for a village smith to be making swords instead of tools."

"I'm sure you did. Shall we take a detour to Telscara then?"

"I think so," Bashkim said, crawling up Rin's side to get back in the saddle. "With any luck, maybe we can clear your name and warn them of what's *really* attacking them."

"As if they would bother to notice the difference between two dragons," Rin said as she got to her feet.

"It's worth a shot."

Bashkim reached up to pull his goggles down but found only hair. He ran his hand over the top of his head then patted it several times. When he felt nothing, he scanned the ground on both sides of Rin.

"Something wrong?" Rin asked.

"I lost the goggles during the fight," Bashkim said, then added with a groan, "and my hat."

Telscara rested between the bottom of Rin's mountain and a river. A modest village most would miss in their travels that sheltered only a handful of guards. Unsurprisingly, two of them were posted at the village entrance. They sat in their chairs, leaning against the wall of logs that protected the homes within.

The two guards jumped to their feet when they saw Rin above them, and the townspeople ran for shelter. Rin landed outside the wooden walls, allowing plenty of space between her and the guards.

"It's alright!" Bashkim shouted from Rin's back, waving his hands in the air. "Don't be alarmed! She'll do you no harm."

"Bold claim," Rin whispered.

The guards kept a firm grip on their spears but didn't take a single step forward.

"Is that the dragon that attacked us?" the first guard asked.

"She is not," Bashkim said, filling a small purse with riches from Rin's saddlebags. "But we did find it."

"And?"

Bashkim tied the purse shut and crawled down Rin's side. "And it's more dangerous than your average dragon," he said, trying to fix his hair from the windy flight. "I'm going to Nennossen to see what I can learn and hopefully get some help."

"Very well," the same guard said, keeping his eyes on Rin. "And as much as we appreciate *your* help, I'm afraid you'll have to do something with your dragon. You're terrifying the village."

"I understand," Bashkim said, lifting his arm to reveal the empty scabbard on his belt. "All I require is a sword. I lost mine in the fight."

The guard motioned Bashkim forward, keeping his eyes on the scaled beast before him. "You're lucky that's all you lost. Follow the main path about halfway through. Cynthia's shop will be on the right. Just follow the hammering."

"Thank you."

The guard stepped to the side to allow Bashkim an easy pass, but something caught his attention as Bashkim got closer.

"Hey, wait a minute," the guard said, putting his hand out.

The guard eyed the pointed ear protruding from Bashkim's shoulder-length hair, then glanced back at Rin.

"Are you an eshan?" the guard asked quietly.

"No, sir," Bashkim answered, his voice softer and his head lowering.

The second guard looked at Bashkim's ear, confused, then stepped over to look at both of his ears at once. "Blue blazes of holy fire, he's got one of each. He's an—"

A low growl came from Rin, vibrating the bones of the soldiers.

"You're a hybrid," the first guard corrected, motioning for his partner to step back. "Nothing wrong with that. Just don't think we've ever seen one out this far."

"Please," Bashkim said. "I just want to get a sword and be on my way."

"Absolutely," the guard said, moving Bashkim along. "My apologies. Please, go on through. And when you reach Nennossen, be sure to speak with Captain Simon about our situation and what you've learned."

Bashkim stepped past the guards and through the gate, brushing his hair down again and trying to hide his pointed ear. He grumbled to himself once out of earshot of the guards, longing for his hat so he didn't have to deal with any of this.

One by one, the villagers poked their heads out from their homes as their curiosity grew. They stared at the beast outside their walls, whispering amongst themselves and trying to figure out why it hadn't eaten them yet. Considering a portion of their protective walls and the farmhouse debris still lay crushed on the ground, Bashkim could hardly blame their suspicions.

I'm surprised that's all the white dragon destroyed, Bashkim thought, observing the damage. *As big as it was, it could have flattened this village easily.*

Despite most people hiding in their homes, Bashkim still heard a hammer striking metal. It grew louder as he made his way through the village, and just as the guard had said, he found the smith about halfway through. She stood next to a stone pit full of fire. The large bundle of sweaty hair she'd tied behind her was nearly as orange as the glowing coals. Her back faced Bashkim, and she showed little concern for the dragon outside her village. She continued to hammer at the heated metal, sparks flying from her work with each blow.

"Watch your step," she said when Bashkim approached, not bothering to turn around. "I'd hate to set those furs of yours alight."

Bashkim stopped and took a half step back. "Yes, ma'am. I was wondering if I could buy a sword."

"One minute, please," she said, still hammering.

Alright then, Bashkim thought, frowning slightly.

Bashkim glanced over his shoulder to make sure Rin remained in place. Her head extended well above the village's wooden walls, and she gave him a small nod. Bashkim returned his focus to the smith and watched her form the glowing steel. Her muscular arms swung the hammer with ease, beating the metal into the rough shape of a blade.

"Did you pass any rain on your way in?" she asked.

"Rain?" Bashkim repeated with raised eyebrows. "No. It's a clear day."

"That's what I thought, though I could have sworn I heard thunder."

Bashkim kept silent, watching her work. The metal's glow began to fade. Once it had become too hard to form, she stuck it back in the pile of glowing coals.

"There," she said, removing her leather gauntlets and tossing them over her broad shoulders. "Now. Something about a sword?"

Bashkim nodded. "Yes, ma'am. I've lost mine and require another."

"Your friend over there eat it?" she asked, nodding towards Rin.

"No. Actually, I lost it to another dragon. The one that attacked your village."

The smith placed a hand on her hip, looking Bashkim directly in the eyes. "So you're the one that went dragon hunting? I reckon if you got a pet dragon of your own, then you're the man for the job, aren't you, green eyes?"

"Hardly a pet," Bashkim said, removing the scabbard from his belt and handing it over. "Do you have something of similar size to this?"

"Not a very large blade, is it?" she asked, taking the scabbard.

"I like to keep nimble."

The smith studied the scabbard carefully, rubbing her thumbs along its carvings. She rolled it over a couple times, checking both sides.

"Your sword had a small curve to it," she said, looking down into the scabbard. "And only a single edge."

"Yes."

"This was an eshan sword, wasn't it?"

"It was."

"Interesting," she said, smiling. "Not many eshans around here. I've rarely gotten to see their craftsmanship up close. It's a shame all I have is the scabbard to look at, as nice as it is."

Bashkim nodded his head carefully, making sure his hair stayed in place.

"Oh, you're not fooling anyone, green eyes," she said with a grin, pointing to the side of Bashkim's head with the scabbard. "Not even I have enough hair to hide an ear like that."

"Please, ma'am," Bashkim said, slightly raising his hands. "I just want a sword."

"Oh, come now," she said, giving him a gentle poke with the tip of the scabbard. "I don't care what you are so long as you have money to pay with."

Bashkim tried not to groan as the scabbard drove into his bruises. "I have money."

"Then step inside. My name is Cynthia, and I think I have exactly what you're looking for."

Bashkim followed Cynthia into her home and discovered a small armory. Racks upon racks held spears and swords. Swords that couldn't find a home in the racks stood propped in a corner, leaning against one another. Shields hung from hooks on the wall, and piles of leather gauntlets with metal strips rested below them.

"I'll admit," Bashkim said, eying the arsenal, "I'm surprised to see a weaponsmith in a small village. I expected you to be making tools, not preparing for a war."

"I'm sure my father would be much happier if I did," Cynthia said, stepping into another room. "But Telscara already has somebody taking care of that. I help him from time to time, but I find making weapons for Nennossen's soldiers far more enjoyable than hammers and shovels."

"Then why not live in Nennossen where the work is?"

"Because it's peaceful here," she said from the other room. "Fewer people. Though there has been a problem with dragons showing up of late."

Bashkim chuckled and continued to observe the weapons. He certainly couldn't argue with the appeal of being around fewer people. While waiting, he pulled one of the swords from the rack.

Too heavy, he thought, lifting the double-edged weapon up and down.

As he placed the weapon back, Cynthia returned with an armload of sheathed swords. She laid them on a table with a clatter and carefully spread them out for Bashkim to see.

"That's quite the collection," Bashkim said. "Did you make these as well?"

Cynthia crossed her arms, trying to keep herself professional as the smile across her face grew. "I did. I've only ever seen eshan swords in passing or on the rare occasion one gets found. As you can imagine, there's not much of a need for them around here. But I love to make them anyway. It's such a beautiful style, but without a teacher, it's awfully hard to replicate."

Bashkim grabbed the swords one by one, halfway sliding them out of their sheaths for inspection. Most of them weren't as wide as the blades she made for Nennossen's soldiers, and the grips were made entirely of wood. The degree of curve in the blade varied from sword to sword, with some even being completely straight.

"I doubt even an eshan could tell these were human-made," Bashkim said.

Cynthia's cheeks turned red. She cleared her throat and grabbed a sword from the pile. "I don't have any fancy scabbards like yours, but I think this blade is fairly close to what you had."

Bashkim took the sword from her and stepped back to fully unsheathe it. He moved the blade through a series of slow-cutting motions and extended his arm to check the weapon's reach and balance.

"Yes," he said, sliding it back into the sheath. "I like this one. I think it will do nicely."

"Perfect for taming dragons?"

Bashkim snorted. "No. I don't think a sword is much good for taming anything."

"Headed into dangerous territory then?"

Bashkim hesitated, considering his destination. "Dangerous for some."

Cynthia raised an eyebrow, picking up on his discomfort. The distant look on his face didn't help hide his feelings.

"Do you have any spare cloth?" he asked, gently rubbing his eshan ear.

"Cloth? Yeah, I've got a few scraps and whatnot. What'd you have in mind?"

"Scraps will be fine. I'll pay for what I use."

Cynthia left the room and returned with a pair of small wooden crates filled with scrap material and hand tools. Bashkim dug through the random scraps for the longest piece he could find and started to wrap it around his head.

"What are you doing?" she asked.

"I'm travelling to Nennossen. If I cover my ear, I can usually get around unnoticed. I figure if I make it look like a head wound then they'll be more apt to leave me alone."

"Well, if you want it to look like a wound then at least use something with blood on it, even if it's not yours."

Cynthia left the room again, this time returning with a blood-stained cloth.

"Smithing isn't the kindest to your body," she said, handing the cloth over. "Lots of burns and cuts. Maybe you can find some benefit from my accidents."

"Thanks," Bashkim said, removing the cloth on his head and checking the fit of the dirty one.

Cynthia took the scrap cloth and stacked the crates, sliding them out of the way. "Is this a common trick amongst hybrids?"

"I wouldn't know," Bashkim said, content the faux bandage would work and rolled it up for storage. "Most hybrids are holed up in Handleson. It's the only place I know of where they're allowed to live a decent life."

"I've never been there."

"It's a town between the human and eshan capitals. Serves as a middle ground for trade. Makes sense that hybrids would live there."

"So why not stay there? Surely that's better than running around with somebody else's dirty bandage on your head and trying to hide."

Bashkim grabbed his new sword and paused, pursing his lips as he searched for an answer.

"Hey," she said with a hand on her hip. "You asked me why I don't live in Nennossen. It's only fair, green eyes."

A grin found its way onto Bashkim's face. He secured the new sword to his belt and a distant stare replaced his smile. "I don't think it's for me," he said quietly.

"Have you ever tried giving it a chance?"

Even though Bashkim already had his sword in place, he adjusted his belt again, avoiding the question.

"Sorry," Cynthia said, holding a hand up. "Maybe I'm overstepping. I ask because I never would have thought smithing was for me, much less weapons. Now look at me. If I hadn't given it a chance, I wouldn't have found my love for the craft, and you wouldn't have that sword hanging at your hip. I'd hate for anybody to miss out on something so beautiful simply because they made up their mind before trying."

Bashkim grabbed his purse and pulled some coins out. "It's alright. Will this cover the cost?"

"That will do just fine," she said, taking the payment.

"You can keep the scabbard if you think it'll be useful."

"Oh, I can certainly make use of it."

Bashkim reached into his purse again, pulling out a small, green jewel. "I'd also like you to have this."

"Whatever for?"

"Something extra for your kindness," he said, placing the jewel on the table. "I appreciate being treated like a normal person."

"I'm not sure I can accept such a gift simply for being nice."

"Then consider it payment for your advice," Bashkim said, tucking both his purse and the bloodied cloth underneath his coat.

"Well, it is good advice," she said with a smile, taking the jewel and lifting it up to look at it.

"I have some red ones if you prefer a different color," Bashkim offered.

"Nope. I like this one," she said with a wink. "You be careful out there, green eyes."

Cynthia returned to her work outside at the anvil, and Bashkim waved goodbye as he headed back down the road towards the town's gate. Rin waited patiently outside the walls for his return, randomly giving the guards a quick look to keep them on their toes. Shaking his head, Bashkim climbed back up onto Rin's back and secured himself in the saddle. Rin squatted down and prepared to leap upwards but looked towards the guards once more.

The guards smiled nervously, eager for her to leave. A sharp snort from Rin made them jump. Chuckling, Rin thrust herself upwards and flapped her wings, taking her and Bashkim away from the village.

"You're terrible," Bashkim said as she brought them higher.

"Perhaps. But at least I don't go around giving away other peoples' money as gifts."

Bashkim smiled, patting Rin's side. "Only one gem. And I think she deserved it."

"Perhaps. Though as nice as she is, I still give you better swords."

Rin carried Bashkim until the sun had set. With darkness on their side, they chose a thick forest to hide Rin and set up camp for the night. Bashkim sat on the ground with his legs stretched out, looking around them and trying to see into the darkness of the woods. Rin, on the other hand, remained seated calmly as if she had no further plans for the evening.

"Are you sure this friend of yours will help us?" Bashkim asked.

"*Acquaintance*," Rin corrected. "And he won't eat you, if that's what you're worried about."

"It had crossed my mind."

Rin chuckled. "Believe it or not, Bashkim, even if other dragons fancied the taste of two-legged creatures, they'd be shunned for partaking. Eating people is highly frowned upon."

"That explains why you don't socialize with them much."

"I happen to be a rare case of sophisticated taste," Rin said with a hand on her chest and holding her head high.

Bashkim lay down on his back, staring up at the top of the forest. "Lucky me," he sighed. "Do you think he knows we're here?"

"Oh, he's been watching us for some time now, and I think we've waited long enough."

Rin then spoke in words that Bashkim could not understand. Curious, he sat up straight and looked around, then jumped to his feet in shock. The head of another dragon had emerged from the darkness. The dragon slowly stepped forward, weaving his way between the trees. He stood before Rin, slightly taller and with dark-red scales. They hadn't the sheen of Rin's, and many of his spikes came to a broken tip, suggesting either more age or a less luxurious lifestyle.

The red dragon squinted at Bashkim as he snarled his words to Rin in short sentences. Bashkim could not understand the language, but the narrowed eyes and tone of voice married to the sharp head movements suggested disapproval. Rin ignored the abrasive behavior and remained calm and unbothered in her replies.

With each word she spoke, the red dragon seemed to ease more. He eventually stopped staring Bashkim down and turned his full attention to Rin with widened eyes. To Bashkim's surprise, Rin stood up. Her words were spoken more clearly now with a much bolder tone. The red dragon pulled back slightly, tilting his head as though Rin's words had confused him. He glanced back down at Bashkim briefly, then returned to Rin.

A silence fell between the two creatures, and the next few seconds felt like an eternity for Bashkim. The dragons stared each other down, narrowing their eyes almost enough to close them. Bashkim looked repeatedly from one dragon to the next, watching what appeared to be a silent conversation. Finally, a long-winded sigh came from the red dragon. After a few more words from each, the dragon lowered his head and turned to leave. However, he paused to face Bashkim on the way.

"Delso Trakear zime, Bashkim," the red dragon said, bowing his head. "Gondo es."

The red dragon turned his back to the two of them and disappeared into the trees.

"I'm afraid I'm not fluent in dragon," Bashkim said once they were alone.

Rin turned to Bashkim and smiled. "No two-legged mortal is."

"What did he say?"

"A lot, believe it or not, and several words that I won't repeat. But as far as your white dragons are concerned, they apparently chipped more than a few scales. A white dragon terrorizing the populace doesn't quite give the rest of the dragons in the world a good look, does it?"

"I wouldn't think so."

"Hence their initial disapproval. Their attempts to speak with the white dragons only resulted in death. Due to the white dragons' blind hostility and the fact no one had ever seen them before, there is talk that these things aren't even true dragons but instead some sort of abomination created in their image."

"What about you?" Bashkim asked, crossing his arms. "What do you think?"

"I think you and I are flesh and blood of *this* world, Bashkim. That thing is *not* like us."

Bashkim scratched his chin. "Considering it bleeds black, I'm inclined to agree. But even so, if that's true, that doesn't tell us what they are."

"Unfortunately, that part remains a mystery. After my kind lost some of their own, they decided to steer clear. The truth was never revealed to them."

"Did he have anything else to say?"

"It would seem Nennossen has some history with these creatures. Apparently, they had knights that were able to fight back, and they could do so quite well. So much so that the knights became the hunters and the white dragons the hunted. How they were able to do such a thing, I'm afraid remains a silent secret even to the ears of dragons."

"Of course it does," Bashkim sighed. "I hate to say it, Rin, but I don't think we could have finished that fight with the white dragon. I'm surprised it chose to leave us alone. And if magic and a whole other dragon can't stand up to one, I can't help but wonder what Nennossen had to give them such an advantage."

"Whatever it was, it included eshans."

"Pardon?"

"He said when Nennossen fought against the white dragons, both humans and eshans stood together."

"Are you sure?"

Rin nodded. "He claimed to see one of the hunting parties with his own eyes."

"I don't guess he saw a battle take place?"

"He did not."

Bashkim rubbed a hand through his hair. "Well, good to know humans and eshans can put aside their differences long enough to fight a common enemy, I suppose."

"Oh, it seemed to be a little more than that," Rin said with a smile.

"What do you mean?"

"The eshans were sharing a roof in Nennossen."

"They lived there?"

Rin nodded. "Though it wouldn't seem for long. Whether they were thrown out or left on their own is unknown. But if I were a gambling girl, I'd wager each theory played equal parts."

"I wouldn't doubt it, but that's...interesting," Bashkim said and stopped to think, scratching the side of his chin. "But still...even with humans *and* eshans working together, I'm not convinced that'd be enough to stop those things. Maybe one, but definitely not multiple."

"One would think if they had such a power, they would be eager to put it on display. Or, at the very least, boast of it."

Bashkim nodded. "I agree, and that makes this all the more interesting."

Rin brought her head down next to Bashkim, slowly curling around him as the excitement in her voice rose. "So, what's more mysterious? This strange, unknown power? The white dragons? Or the unlikely alliance?"

"Honestly?" Bashkim asked, rubbing the tip of her snout. "I'm not sure. I think we'll have to look into all of them."

"A wise choice, hero. But how?"

"We'll go to Nennossen as planned. I'll keep a low profile and try not to ask too many questions. Surely they have something there that can point us in the right direction. Old stories or records. If all else fails, I can at least inform the captain about Telscara, but *something* of the past has to remain. I'd bet your entire stash on it."

"Laying hands on a dragon's stash is a dangerous game," Rin said in a low voice.

Bashkim chuckled. "Come on. Let's get some rest."

"As if one could in these conditions," Rin groaned as she curled up on the ground. "I long for the cold of my cave and to be surrounded by ice."

"You'd wake up in a puddle if you did that out here."

Bashkim unpacked his bedroll and placed it next to Rin. He lay on his back, staring up at the trees and watching the few stars he could see through the forest canopy. He pulled his blanket up to his chin, trying to keep himself warm.

"No fire tonight?" Rin asked, looking down at Bashkim.

"I don't need one."

Rin frowned as she watched Bashkim wrap the blanket around himself tighter. With a small sigh, she got back up to her feet.

"Have I ever told you the meaning of the words Jinkear Deneelsah?" she asked, standing on her hind legs to tear several large branches from the trees.

"You have not. What do they mean?"

After she collected the branches, Rin used a single claw to dig a small pit near Bashkim. "Through family and fire, the soul will live on. Or at least, that's what can be translated to your tongue. There is a ritual dragons believe in that once our time here has come to an end, our bodies must be purified through fire so our souls may pass on. In the simplistic words of man, it would be called The Final Flame."

Rin stuffed the branches into the pit, snapping and crushing them as she pushed. She brought her head down, and with the gentlest breath she could muster, fire came from her mouth and set the broken branches ablaze.

"That is why all dragons are given the gift of fire," she continued. "For only through the fire of another dragon can one be purified and turned to ash."

Bashkim rolled over and watched the branches crackle and pop in the fire. "What happens if you're alone? If you're away from the others?"

"I've been told that when a dragon faces their final moments, they are given tremendous strength. They must choose to use that strength either to flee or to defeat their enemies. Arbiters willing, the dragon will have the chance to find their kin. Now, whether any of that's true or not, I don't know."

Rin curled up and laid back down, closing her eyes.

Bashkim slid his blanket down slightly as the fire warmed him. He watched the flames slowly consume the branches, processing what he had just learned.

"Why are you telling me this?" he asked.

"Because there is a fire in all of us, Bashkim, and I'd hate for you to condemn yours before it was given a chance to breathe."

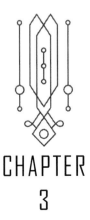

CHAPTER
3

Bashkim traveled alone for the majority of the following day while Rin remained hidden in the forest. By the time he reached Nennossen's reinforced doors, the sun had just started to touch the distant treetops. The guards at the entrance looked him over thoroughly, eying him from head to toe and taking note of the sword at his hip, as well as the bandage on his head.

"Do you require a doctor?" one of the guards asked.

"No, sir." Bashkim handed his backpack over for inspection. "Just a small scuffle with some goblins is all. What I need is some food and rest as I've been on my feet all day."

"Nasty little bastards," the guard responded. "Don't you worry, though, we've plenty of food and water here. Just mind where you swing that sword of yours, or I'll throw you out myself."

"I'd rather not swing it at all," Bashkim said honestly.

"Good man. The doctor is down the main road if you'd like a fresh bandage. You'll find him near the marketplace."

"Thank you," Bashkim said, taking his backpack once the guard finished his inspection. "I'll keep that in mind."

The guard nodded and turned to bang his armored fist against the wooden doors while shouting to the other side for passage. Metal rubbing against metal could be heard from within as the giant latches slid apart. One of the doors groaned and slowly opened just enough to let a single person through. The guard motioned with his head for Bashkim to proceed, and into the city Bashkim went.

No turning back now, he thought, as the door shut behind him with the chilling clang of the latches locking in place.

Bashkim looked at what felt like the entirety of Telscara's population merely in Nennossen's entrance. People walked in pairs, groups, or by themselves. Others pushed wooden carts filled with various goods. The foot traffic disappeared into the narrow alleyways between structures, only for more people to appear from the same alleyways a second later.

Bashkim gazed up at the city's towering walls as he double-checked the bandage on his head. He knew he had to be careful. One wrong move and he may never see the other side of those walls again. A growl from his stomach interrupted his thoughts and got him back on track. He looked down the main road, watching the people pass. Bashkim squinted, half expecting somebody to call him out before he could take a step, but nothing happened. They ignored him.

So far so good. They think I'm one of them.

Instead of taking comfort in blending in, he became uneasy and his shoulders tensed.

They think I'm one of them, he told himself again. *They think I'm...like them.*

Something about the idea didn't feel right. He had blended in with humans more than once before, but this time it felt...*wrong.*

I'm probably just hungry, he told himself and approached a random stranger.

"Excuse me," Bashkim said, but the man didn't hear him and kept pushing his cart.

I'm definitely not like you people, he thought, gritting his teeth.

Bashkim tried his luck again, this time approaching a pair of women that crossed paths with him.

"Excuse me, ladies," he said, but his voice couldn't be heard over their own conversation.

"Ma'am!" he barked, grabbing one of the women by the arm.

Both of them jumped and gasped, drawing some unwanted attention.

"I'm sorry," Bashkim said, quickly letting her go and stepping back. "I've been trying to ask for directions but I'm getting ignored."

"Not from around here then, are you?" she asked, waving the onlookers away. "The city is a busy life. You got to speak up if you want to be heard. Grabbing folks sure isn't the way to go about it."

"I apologize."

The woman smiled. "Ah. It's alright. Can't help what you don't know. Seems you got manners enough anyhow. Now. What were you looking for?"

"I'm trying to find food and water, maybe even a place to sleep for the night."

"Well, you're in luck," the second woman chimed in. "There's a tavern not far from here."

The two women proceeded to give directions through a series of rights and lefts to navigate the city's streets. Bashkim nodded while listening but found himself growing aggravated with the women.

What's wrong with me? he wondered.

"Thank you," Bashkim said immediately after the women finished and stepped away.

Bashkim ran a hand over his face as he walked down the street, blinking his eyes several times.

Something isn't right. I've travelled farther than this. I've been hungrier than this before. Why am I so angry?

Bashkim shook his head and tried to clear his mind. The more he tried, the more the strange feelings came back to him. Something inside him twisted itself into a knot, and wave after wave of negativity came over him as he looked at the citizens. They nodded and waved to him, unaware they were causing his anger to grow. Bashkim's hands tightened into fists, and his fingers drove into his own bruises.

I'm not one of you. You've never let me be one of you.

His breaths quickened.

Fools. All of you. You're all...

Bashkim put his hand to his chest. He could hear his heart thumping inside of him, each beat getting louder. His magic started to swell within him as if being summoned. He tried to force it down, but it fought against him and attempted to bite its way out. The harder he shoved it down the more aggressive it seemed to get. It felt as though it might tear him from the inside out. A voice came to him, speaking in his mind through a whisper of unknown, drawn-out words.

"Delso nacht indulsa."

Bashkim gasped and froze in place, terrified at the possibility some of his magic had slipped out. People continued to walk all around him and seemed to not even notice he existed.

Where am I? he wondered, shocked at the sudden unfamiliarity of the road he stood on.

He turned around to find he could no longer see the city's gate he had come through. Paths stretched out to the left and right, but he failed to recall which one had brought him here.

"Easy," a voice said suddenly as a hand rested on Bashkim's shoulder. "You alright, son?"

Son? Bashkim thought, wanting to snap back but caught himself before a jolt of magic could escape him.

"Yeah," Bashkim said, catching his breath. "I'm not sure what happened."

"I think it might be time to get that head wound looked at. You were marching through here with a purpose then stopped as if you completely forgot where you were."

Bashkim looked at the man. He clothed himself in a large brown robe, and lengthy white hair dripped from its hood. The wrinkles on the man's face suggested he had more than a few years behind him.

"Are you a monk?" Bashkim asked.

The old man laughed. "Not with the sins I've committed, but that doesn't mean I can't help. The doctor isn't far from here. Do you think you'll be alright?"

Bashkim drew a deep breath and slowly let it out, the magic inside of him finally calming. "I think so."

"You sure?" the man asked.

"Yes. Thank you for your concern."

The man patted Bashkim on the back. "Alright. Have it your way. Best of luck to you, son."

The old man waved goodbye and made his way down the road. Bashkim rubbed a hand across the top of his head, pulling his hair back.

What the hell just happened?

His stomach growled, again reminding him of the task at hand.

Right, Bashkim thought, patting his stomach as he studied his surroundings. *I'll need more directions.*

Bashkim managed to make his way to the tavern this time, finding several round, unoccupied tables inside. The establishment's few occupants paid him little mind as he stepped across the stone floor. Bashkim noted that, save for a couple daggers, he seemed to have the only weapon. A man with an apron behind the bar watched Bashkim find his seat at an empty table near the end of the room. He walked over to Bashkim, wiping his hands on the towel he carried.

"Hey, stranger," he said from beneath his bushy beard. "What can I get for you?"

"Water will be fine," Bashkim answered. He eyed the large cuts of meat hanging from hooks behind the bar. "And some food. Whatever you have ready will do."

"The hunters have had a good haul of late. Ribs, tenderloins, steaks, you name it. We even got a lovely batch of venison stew hot and ready to go if you'd like. Bread too. Day's coming to an end, and everybody will be looking for dinner soon."

"Stew would be great, as well as some bread and water," Bashkim said before reaching into his purse. "Will this do?"

Bashkim placed a few gold coins into the man's hand.

"You must be some kind of adventurer," the man said, studying the currency. "I've not seen coins such as these."

Just take the damned money, Bashkim thought but took a small breath to calm himself.

"I am," he replied. "I have others if you need."

"Nah," the man said with a friendly smile and slid the coins into his pocket. "It's all gold at the end of the day and spends the same. It'll do just fine."

The man left through the doorway behind the bar, leaving Bashkim alone. Bashkim closed his eyes and put the bridge of his nose between his finger and thumb.

Get a hold of yourself.

The faint hint of a whisper swam through his mind, its words jumbled and stacked on top of one another.

No, he thought. *Stay away.*

Bashkim shook his head and sank into his chair. *What's going on?*

The man returned a moment later with a large glass of water and a steaming bowl of stew. The scent of fresh food went straight to Bashkim's nose, and he nearly forgot what had just happened.

"So what brings you around, adventurer?" the man asked, wiping his hands on his towel again after setting Bashkim's meal down.

"Just passing through and needed a place to rest," Bashkim said, taking a much-needed drink of the water. "Though there's a small hobby I entertain. When I visit cities for the first time, I like to learn about them and their history. Would Nennossen happen to have a library? Or something similar?"

The man rubbed a hand across his bald head. "There is a library not far from here. When you leave, take the first right you come across. Down that way a bit and you'll spot it. Stone building with a tall wooden door. Hard to miss. Got two stained glass windows on the front."

The man rubbed his hand across his head again, hesitating. "But...I'll be honest. I'm not the best at reading, so I can't tell you exactly what's in there. But Wesley is a good man and can help you out. He takes care of the place. Old soul, that one. Does a lot of scribing for the king, too. If he doesn't have anything, I'd bet good money he could point you in the right direction."

"That sounds promising, thank you."

The man nodded and left Bashkim to his meal. Not long after, more people began to fill the room. They came in one by one, taking their seats and waving to those they knew. Bashkim watched the barkeeper pour drinks for everyone, greeting most by name and making sure each of them had dinner to eat, all while happily taking their money. A faded whisper returned to Bashkim. He tightened his grip on his spoon. The words swam from one side of his head to the other, causing the hairs on his body to stand. Suddenly, a second voice came to him, overpowering the strange whisper. His eyes widened, surprised by the familiar words of the second voice.

"Have you ever tried giving it a chance?" he heard Cynthia ask.

Bashkim paused, staring down at his bowl of stew. For just a brief second, everything became silent. He looked up at the patrons and watched. The sounds of the tavern slowly came back to him. He could hear the people speaking about their days, their children, even their goals and plans in life.

"Sir?" a voice asked. "You need these?"

Bashkim looked over to realize he had completely missed the stranger approach him. The man had his hands on the two empty chairs at Bashkim's table.

"We're short a couple chairs," the man went on. "I seen you were already eating and assumed—"

"It's fine," Bashkim said, cutting the man short. "They're yours."

"Thank you, sir," the man said and slid the chairs across the room.

Bashkim rested his hands on the sides of his bowl, staring at his empty table.

I already had my chance.

With a much happier stomach, Bashkim made his way down the street to the library. He gently pushed the tall, wooden door open and stepped inside. The two stained glass windows the barkeeper had mentioned let the remainder of the setting sun spill inside with the orange rays slipping through the other small windows. Several bookcases filled the large room, stuffed with leatherbound books and rolled-up scrolls.

A few tables stood in the center of the library, accompanied by chairs and a single old man. He hunched over the table next to a small lantern and a pile of papers, dabbing a pen into an inkwell. The old man repeatedly switched between looking at the open book propped in front of him and writing carefully on the pages under his hands.

He was so absorbed in his work that he failed to notice Bashkim sneak in. Bashkim made it all the way to the table without catching the man's attention. Bashkim waited for the man to fully take his pen away from the paper before announcing his presence.

"Wesley?" Bashkim asked quietly.

As Bashkim had feared, the old man jumped, nearly spilling his ink.

The man quickly cleared his throat and slid his circular glasses down to look over the top of them. "Yes, I am. Can I help you?"

"I hoped to find some information on Nennossen's history. I'm told you might be able to help me."

The old man observed Bashkim, alternating between looking over the top of his glasses and through them. His eyes trailed down to Bashkim's sword, then back to his eyes. "I'd take you more for an adventurer than a historian, but yes. We have some things here, depending on what you're searching for."

"Nothing too specific. I'm just passing through and like to read up on the places I visit. How it's developed over the years, important events that have occurred, that sort of thing."

"A traveling scholar?"

Bashkim frowned and tilted his head. "Not quite. I just enjoy getting to know a place."

"Interesting. While I find it impressive a swordsman can actually read, I'm afraid you're not very good at lying."

"Excuse me?"

Wesley sighed, gently putting his pen down on the table away from his papers. "I've been around a long time, young man. I've met and come to know plenty of people, and sadly I've outlived a fair share of them. I think I know an adventurer when I see one, and I've never met an adventurer who cared to read a city's history that he only planned to visit briefly. So, what is it you're really looking for?"

Bashkim pursed his lips and held his breath, keeping his eyes locked on the old man. Wesley had caught him. He'd have to choose his words carefully moving forward.

"Very well," Bashkim said. "I'm studying dragons, but I didn't want to cause any alarm."

"You're a dragon hunter?"

"No. Not at all. I find it much safer to study them from a distance. A very *large* distance."

Wesley chuckled. "Well, you're smarter than the average adventurer, I'll give you that. But why Nennossen? I wasn't aware we had more history with dragons than other cities."

"There's a specific type I'm interested in. They're a bit...different than anything else I've seen before. From what I understand, Nennossen might have encountered them in the past."

"Different?" Wesley asked, scratching his lengthy white beard. "I don't guess I understand what you mean."

"They're much more dangerous, for starters, and aggressive. I encountered one near Telscara. I need to learn what I can about it so I can properly warn others of what might be coming. I'd like to get all my facts together first before causing any panic."

"Smart," Wesley said, giving his beard another couple of strokes. "Very smart. And appreciated."

The old man looked Bashkim over again and gathered his thoughts. With a couple of grunts and nods, Wesley got up from his chair. "Fair enough. I might have a thing or two around here. Come, come. Follow me."

Wesley slipped past Bashkim and up a few stairs with a small groan. He stood about a head shorter than Bashkim, making the bookcases seem that much taller as he walked past them. He grabbed from nearby a small, three-stepped stool. He pushed the wooden booster down the aisles with his foot, the sound echoing in the library as it dragged against the stone floor. He grunted with each step up and down the stool and slid his index finger across the tops of books. Every so often he would stop, nod his head, pull a book out, and plop it down into Bashkim's hands, crushing the bruises in his palms.

"You alright?" Wesley asked, noticing the winces on Bashkim's face.

"I'm fine."

"Good," Wesley said, adding rolls of paper to Bashkim's growing stack.

Dust flew upwards with each book dropped onto the stack, causing Bashkim's nose to twitch.

"Are these all about dragons that attacked Nennossen in the past?" Bashkim asked.

"No," Wesley said, bringing Bashkim back to the tables in the center of the room. "You wanted information about dragons. This is what I have."

Bashkim unloaded the literature onto the table, and Wesley took one of the scrolls. He unrolled it, spreading it wide across the table and revealing many sketches of different types of dragons.

"Do any of these look like what you're after?" Wesley asked.

Bashkim shook his head. "Not really, no."

"Does it have any distinguishing features? Something that would help narrow our search?"

"On the crook of its wings, it had hands."

"Hands on the wings?" Wesley asked, stroking his beard. "Interesting. But still two arms and legs?"

"Yes, sir."

"What color was it?"

Damn it, Bashkim thought.

The old man had him cornered. He had already given more information than he wanted to. Worse yet, Wesley had already caught him in a lie. If Bashkim didn't tell the truth, he risked being caught again. Or, at the very least, given the wrong information concerning his search. On the other hand, if Nennossen had kept the white dragons a secret intentionally and he admitted to searching for information about them, things could go from bad to worse.

Bashkim almost winced as he spoke. "White...ish."

"A white dragon?" Wesley asked, giving his head a slow scratch. "That seems an odd color. Are you sure?"

"I saw it myself. I'm pretty sure."

Wesley grabbed one of the many books and flipped through the pages. He skimmed over the sketches and notes that filled it, occasionally asking Bashkim if anything resembled what he had seen. Bashkim shook his head each time and grabbed his own book to look through.

"You *can* read, right?" Wesley asked, watching Bashkim skim the pages.

"Yes. I was fortunate enough to be taught at a young age."

Wesley closed his book and sat it on the table. "Very well then. As exciting as all this is, I'm afraid you caught me at the end of my day. I was about to head out for some dinner, but by all means, stay here in the meantime. I'll run down to the tavern and be back in just a moment. Would you like anything?"

"No, thanks," Bashkim said, holding his hand up. "I just had my dinner before coming here. But thank you."

Wesley smiled and nodded, wishing Bashkim all the luck, and left him alone at the table. While grateful for the old man's help, Bashkim couldn't help but feel more grateful for being left alone. He found it much easier to concentrate without Wesley trying to pry information out of him.

It's not that strange an adventurer can read, is it? he wondered.

Bashkim continued to flip through the books, studying the few mentions of dragon sightings near Nennossen.

Most of this is just speculation and guesswork, he thought, nearly chuckling at the inaccuracy of the tales told by those foolish enough to hunt dragons and lucky enough to come back alive.

Some writings suggested that the dragons watched the city from afar for one of two reasons: One theory suggested that the dragons were waiting for an opportune moment to attack the city. The other stated that the dragons acted as the city's protector, watching from afar. Bashkim considered the red dragon Rin spoke with. Rin knew he would be there. Perhaps the red dragon *had* been watching the city for whatever reason.

Why would he protect it, though? These people would kill him if they were able. Bashkim snorted at the irony of his own thoughts. *As if Rin hasn't asked me the same thing.*

Bashkim reached for a random scroll and unrolled it, revealing a detailed drawing of a dragon. A note at the bottom of the paper explained that the drawing had been sketched from a dragon killed near Nennossen, allowing the artist to get an accurate representation by studying the corpse. Bashkim recalled what Rin told him about the Final Flame and wondered what became of this dragon in the afterlife.

If there even is one, he sighed.

While an impressive drawing, it had nothing to do with what he sought. Bashkim grabbed another book and flipped through it. He found little difference between it and the others he had already skimmed. Aggravated, he closed the book and tried his luck with another roll of paper. This one had more drawings, but they paled in comparison to the last. The drawings appeared as though they had been sketched from a blurry memory, or even the words of someone else. The dragons' features were exaggerated, disproportionate, and quite frankly didn't look anything like Rin or the red dragon.

Bashkim rolled the paper back up and added it to the growing pile of discarded literature. Only a couple more books remained, and his chair had grown uncomfortable. He shifted around, drumming his fingers against the table as he sighed. The outside light creeping in had disappeared by this point, causing Bashkim to get up to borrow Wesley's lantern.

He didn't seem fond of adventurers, Bashkim thought, considering the old man might have decided to eat at the tavern instead.

Before Bashkim took the lantern, he stopped momentarily to look over Wesley's work area. The inkwell remained open, and the current piece of paper he had worked on had but only a few lines written.

Seems like he had quite a bit left to copy, Bashkim thought, noticing that the book Wesley copied from only had a few pages turned.

A large stack of blank papers sat nearby, ready for use.

Wait a second, Bashkim thought, studying the librarian's work. *He said it was the end of his day and time for dinner.*

The old man's workspace suggested otherwise, appearing as though he had just started working.

Bashkim lifted a piece of paper draped over something. *Son of a bitch.*

Lifting the paper revealed a plate covered in breadcrumbs and the small corner of a sandwich. The old man had played him. No wonder he had so many questions. He had sniffed out Bashkim the minute he walked in. But where did he go? To get a guard?

Bashkim paced back and forth, gripping the handle of his sword. The beat of his heart thumped against his chest. If Wesley had gone for the guard, he might be able to slip out of town before they returned. The gate couldn't be that far away.

No. It's probably too early to change shifts. The guards will recognize me. I told them I needed food and rest. A side gate, perhaps? But where?

If Wesley came back with a guard, he could just play dumb. He had already explained to Wesley that he had encountered the white dragon and merely wanted to help. He could tell the guard the same thing. It'd be the truth. He didn't have to tell them *everything* he knew or that he suspected Nennossen was keeping secrets.

Maybe he was just scared and wanted to leave. Maybe he's getting a guard for his own safety.

"Shit," Bashkim said aloud as he paced.

He should have lied. He should have made up something, *anything* but specifically mentioning white dragons. He should have let Wesley believe he was just some illiterate adventurer looking to hang a random dragon's head as a trophy.

Why? Why didn't I do that? What was I thinking?

It didn't matter why Wesley left. Bashkim had made his way into a densely populated city with no way out. If they revealed his disguise, no courtroom would care for his innocence. They'd hang him for sure for poking his nose around.

Bashkim decided to take his chances and head for the gate, or maybe just lose himself in a crowd. He could choose later. Right now, he just needed to *not* be in this library. He made his way over to the door, grabbing the handle and pulling it open.

Not locked in at least.

He opened the door, revealing a city guard looking directly at him. The guard held his hand out, motioning for Bashkim to stop.

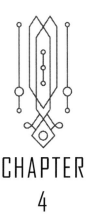

CHAPTER
4

"Stop right there," the guard said, holding his hand up.

"Is something wrong?" Bashkim asked.

"You need to wait inside. The captain will be here in a few minutes."

"Yes, sir."

Bashkim made his way over to the tables in the center of the library and slid a chair out.

The captain? he thought as he sat down. *Why the captain?*

Bashkim set his arms on the table. His hand repeatedly tapped against the wooden surface as his mind raced.

Should I run? It's just the one guard. A little magic and he'll be taken by surprise. Maybe lock his feet in place with ice.

A tempting thought.

No. If I don't make it out after that, they'd know what I am. No court would hear the pleas of a hybrid. Especially not from one that just assaulted a city guard.

Bashkim looked over at the guard. He remained by the door, blocking the library's only exit.

"I also need you to remove that sword and slide it over," the guard said.

Well, shit.

Bashkim slowly reached down, unhooked the sheath from his belt, and sat the weapon on the ground. While still holding the sword, he looked back up at the guard. The soldier watched him carefully, keeping an armored hand near his own sword. Bashkim let go of the weapon and sat back upright in his chair. He used his foot to shove the sword forward, sliding it across the floor. The soldier picked it up and held onto it. He kept his eyes on Bashkim and stuck to his post by the door.

And now I have no weapon, Bashkim complained to himself.

Bashkim drummed his fingers against the table, trying to calm himself while his eyes scanned the library repeatedly.

I didn't do anything wrong, he tried to convince himself. *All I did was ask about dragons. White dragons, maybe, but what difference does it make? Do they know something? Do they think I know something?*

Bashkim's mind raced, and his heart began to beat loudly. Every time he tried to flush out a question, two more took its place.

Is Wesley even a librarian? Did the bartender set me up?

Bashkim couldn't stand it. He sat in the library, trapped and unarmed. Magic brewed inside of him, begging for release while he waited for a fate he had no control over.

Maybe I should just try to stay in Handleson with the others.

The thought calmed him for only a second before a harsh truth set in.

No, I can't. Not there anyway.

Bashkim continued to drum his fingers against the table, waiting for what seemed an eternity. Several distorted figures could be seen passing by through the library's stained-glass windows, but Bashkim couldn't make out the details. Every figure that walked by sent a surge through his body, causing his eyes to widen and his back to straighten as he tried to look.

A firm knock abruptly broke the silence, and the door swung open. In came another soldier, followed by Wesley.

"Is that him?" the new soldier asked.

The guard inside nodded. "Yes, sir."

"Very well. Would you wait outside, please?"

"Yes, sir," the guard said again, handing Bashkim's sword over to the new soldier.

The guard stepped outside and closed the door behind him. Bashkim remained silent and watched the guard's replacement turn to face him. The new soldier stood slightly taller with much broader shoulders. Spots of grey dripped throughout his once black hair. A well-polished breastplate covered his torso, contradicting the rest of his otherwise worn exterior and clashing with the small scars on his face. The armor's sheen failed to hide the worn look in his eyes from the many years of service.

"My name is Captain Simon," the solder said, still standing by the door. "You'll have to pardon the inconvenience. I like to keep my city safe."

"I'm Jonus," Bashkim lied, hoping to keep his name out of it. "I assure you that I mean no harm."

"Unfortunately, words aren't worth much," Simon sighed. "I'm sure you can imagine why."

Bashkim nodded in agreement, keeping his hands visible. Simon stepped forward and stood on the opposite side of the table. He snapped Bashkim's sword halfway out of its sheath, exposing the eshan blade. Bashkim held his breath and waited for Simon to speak. The captain's eyes remained focused on the weapon, his facial expression suggesting some admiration.

"Nice sword you've got here."

"Thank you," Bashkim said. "It's brand new. For me, at least."

Simon let the blade sink back to the bottom of the sheath. "A freshly forged eshan sword? Where did you get it?"

"Telscara."

"Cynthia?"

"Yes, sir."

"That girl's talent never ceases to amaze me."

"She does seem to have a gift."

A small smile grew on Simon's face, and he shook his head slightly. He set the sword down on the table and paused for a moment. Hand still on the sheath, he slid the weapon over. Bashkim looked down at the sword, then back up at Simon. The captain nodded and released the weapon, pulling his arm back. Bashkim slowly took the sword and latched it back onto his belt.

Interesting move, Captain, Bashkim thought.

Simon removed his armored gloves and plopped them down on the table as he pulled up a chair and sat down across from Bashkim. His bare hand rested on the table with a thud, and his fingers drummed against the wooden surface in a smooth and slow motion. Following his lead, Wesley took his own seat, only he put a small amount of distance between him and the two swordsmen in the room.

"So," Simon said with a small grin. "Dragons, is it?"

"Information mostly," Bashkim nodded. "Telscara was recently attacked by a dragon. I was told by the guards there to speak with you, but first I wanted to do some research, as I'm sure you've already been informed."

"Yes. Wesley told me. Apparently you were a bit reluctant to come forward with your intentions. Why?"

"I didn't want to attract attention to myself."

"How's that working out?"

"Not well," Bashkim admitted.

"Then tell me, *Jonus,* what do you know about white dragons?"

"Very little, I'm afraid," Bashkim sighed, his shoulders drooping. "That's why I came here. I know they made an appearance once before but were dealt with somehow. I was hoping to figure out how exactly that happened and, with any luck, do it again before this thing causes any more harm."

"Do you think there's more than the one you saw?"

"I don't know. So far, it's the only one I've seen or know of."

"Is that what happened to your head?" Simon asked, nodding towards the bandage.

Bashkim retreated into his seat. "No. I'm afraid that comes from something far less adventurous than a dragon attack."

"Have a run-in with some goblins?"

"Yeah."

"Nasty little things," Simon grimaced. "Always causing a problem. So, what did happen then? With the dragon, that is."

"The encounter was brief. I was being honest when I told Wesley that I'm no dragon hunter."

Simon glanced over at Wesley, smirking. "*Somebody* wasn't quite convinced."

Wesley crossed his arms and scoffed. "Some swordsman walks into my library requesting books about dragons. What else am I to think?"

"I think Jonus here might actually want to help us," Simon said, turning his attention back to Bashkim. "Or at least I hope so."

"I do," Bashkim nodded. "Unfortunately, I don't have much to share other than that I saw one and that it bleeds black."

"Black blood?" Simon asked. "You fought it then?"

"Only because it came after me. I managed to wound it in my escape. Strangely enough, the dragon spoke when I wounded it."

Simon's eyebrows raised. "A talking dragon?"

"Yes, but I couldn't understand the words. The only one I could make out clearly was 'Mykenebres'."

"My word, son," Wesley gasped. "Are you certain?"

"Pretty sure. I take it you know what that word means?"

Wesley started to speak, but Simon held his hand up. "Before we get sidetracked by religion and mythology," Simon said. "Let's keep focused on the physical side of things. This white dragon you saw; how does it compare to other dragons?"

Bashkim desperately wanted to bring Rin into the story to properly contrast the difference between the two dragons but felt as though he had to leave her out for the sake of his own credibility. Simon already seemed shocked enough that the white dragon could speak in its own language. How much stranger then, would he find another dragon that could speak clearly? A dragon that he had learned to call a close friend and travel with?

No, Bashkim decided. *Now is not the time.*

"It's a bit bigger," Bashkim said. "Or at least this one was. From what little I've seen of dragons, this one seems to be more...animal-like. More wild. More violent. If that makes sense."

"Are all dragons not wild animals?" Simon asked.

If only you could see Rin, Bashkim thought while he collected his words. "I believe there's more to dragons than most people think, but I didn't come here to convince you two of anything. If you remember, I was trying to keep to myself."

"Fair enough," Simon said as he leaned back into his chair. "Did you find anything in these books that could help?"

"No. Nothing even comes close."

"What made you think Nennossen had information?"

"I have it on good authority that Nennossen dealt with these things the last time they came around. If it's true, then that suggests they had something in their possession to help them turn the tide. I was hoping to find a trace of whatever that was."

"Do you still believe that? Even though you haven't found anything?"

"I do."

Simon crossed his arms and remained still in his chair. He tapped his finger slowly, watching Bashkim. Wesley glanced over at the captain, also anxiously waiting for a response.

"Come," Simon finally said and rose to his feet. "Both of you. I will escort you to the king."

"The king?" Bashkim asked, his voice almost cracking. "What for?"

"We have more we need to discuss, but he needs to be present." Bashkim swallowed hard.

If I wasn't trapped before, I am now.

Bashkim awkwardly got up from his seat, revisiting his thought of making a dash for it.

"Oh, and Jonus?" Simon said. "Do make sure that bandage is good and tight, will you? I'd hate for the king to have to see any open wounds tonight."

Simon took Bashkim straight to the castle and led him through several hallways. Bashkim kept his head low, trying to avoid eye contact with the guards. The attempt proved itself an effort with little success, for an individual being personally escorted by the captain seemed a unique occasion. Wesley trailing behind the two of them didn't help Bashkim blend in, either.

Bashkim eventually found himself at another table, only this time in a much smaller room. Wesley left to collect some more books while Simon sent a guard to retrieve the king. Bashkim looked around the room as he waited but found nothing of interest. There were no windows and the floor stretched out just enough to accommodate the round wooden table and chairs. If anything, the room could have served as a closet.

Simon sat at the opposite end of the table, just as he had at the library, watching Bashkim shift around his seat.

"It'll be alright," Simon said. "I just want to get to the bottom of this."

Bashkim nodded. "Sure. I'm just not in the habit of having an audience with royalty."

Simon chuckled. "You aren't missing anything. Just make sure to be respectful and everything will be fine."

It'll be fine as long as you think I'm human, Bashkim thought.

Wesley returned a moment later, placing a few books and scrolls on the table.

"I believe these are what you were hoping to find at the library," Wesley said and passed a scroll over to Bashkim. "Does that look at all familiar?"

Bashkim unrolled the scroll, revealing another dragon sketch. Only this time it actually looked like a white dragon. A small shiver ran through Bashkim as he recalled his encounter. "That's much better. Surely you two can see the difference between this one and a normal dragon?"

Simon studied the picture. "I'm no dragon expert, but yes. Even my eyes can see that this creature is...different."

A soldier interrupted the conversation by knocking on the door and peering inside. "Sir. The king is here."

Simon and Wesley quickly rose from their chairs as the king walked in. A quick glance and a small head motion from Simon signaled for Bashkim to do the same. Bashkim jumped to his feet and tried to follow their lead.

Does he even know how to use that thing? Bashkim wondered, taking note of the ornate dagger hanging from the king's belt.

Judging by the gemstone embedded in the weapon's handle, Bashkim assumed it to be nothing more than decoration and an ego booster.

"Your majesty," Simon said with a quick bow. "I'm sorry to disturb you. I know you have already retired from your duties for the night, but I assure you this is important."

"We shall see," the king said, looking Bashkim over. "You have a visitor with you."

"Yes, my lord," Simon said and pulled a chair out for the king. "Please. Have a seat. There is much to discuss."

The king took his seat and waited for an explanation. Simon gently closed the door to the small room and motioned for the others to sit while he grabbed his own chair next to the king.

"My lord," he started. "This is Jonus. Jonus, this is our king, Lord Omar."

"Sir," Bashkim said with a nod of his head.

"Sir?" Omar scoffed with furrowed eyebrows.

Bashkim looked at Simon, hoping for a clue as to what he had done wrong.

"He's..." Simon tried to explain. "Not from around here. He's not a city dweller and being in the presence of a king is new to him."

"I see," Omar said, then leaned onto the table. "Then allow me to help you. You refer to Simon and his soldiers as "sir". You'll address me as your lord, your king, or your majesty."

"Yes, sir, majesty," Bashkim said, quickly catching his mistake.

A small sigh left Omar, but he seemed willing to let it go. Most of his facial expressions hid behind a large, white beard and his baggy coat did little to reveal any helpful body language.

Prick, Bashkim thought.

"Jonus came to our city looking for information on white dragons," Simon began, but the king shot him a sharp look.

Bashkim watched with slightly widened eyes as Simon took in a small breath and held it. The captain had apparently crossed a line.

"He's *seen* one, my lord," Simon said in a lower tone. "And he knows they're not normal."

Omar looked over at Bashkim. "You're sure of this? You're absolutely certain of what you saw?"

"Yes, king," Bashkim said. "I'm more than sure of what I saw."

Bashkim retold his tale of the encounter in detail, sparing Rin from the story and making the rest up as he went.

"You're lucky to be alive," Omar said once Bashkim finished.

"I won't argue with that," Bashkim said. "But I might not be so lucky next time, nor anybody else that crosses paths with that thing."

"A fair point, but why our city? Why come here?"

"Jonus knows that Nennossen has *some* kind of history with the white dragons," Simon interjected.

"Some?" Omar asked, giving Simon a look of disapproval.

"Yes, my lord."

"On that note," Wesley said, getting his turn in the conversation. "Jonus, you mentioned the word 'Mykenebres' before."

Bashkim nodded. "I did, yes. I heard it from the dragon."

"And you don't know what that word means?"

"No," Bashkim admitted. "Should I?"

"I wouldn't think so," Wesley said, shaking his head. "It's an ancient word for Umbra. Scarcely used, even in the oldest of texts. Or at least the ones that I've been fortunate enough to read."

"Umbra?" Bashkim asked. "As in, *the* Umbra?"

Wesley nodded. "The very same. Evil, sin, wickedness, darkness, whatever name your religion has given it."

"I'm afraid I don't have one."

"Then it's a good thing my job is to teach and not judge. Those who follow the teachings of the Light believe that Umbra is the source of our sins. It is he who tricks us into our temptations and corrupts and blinds us. He is the sin that destroys our world."

"And it's those knife-eared bastards you can blame," Omar interrupted. "Them and their so-called Arbiter."

"I don't understand," Bashkim said, looking to Wesley.

"There is some debate regarding how Umbra came to be," Wesley said once Omar relaxed back into his seat. "There's a theory that our world lived for a time without such sin and violence. It's believed that all of that changed when an Arbiter went astray and eventually fell from the heavens."

"Fell?" Bashkim asked.

"Cast out!" Omar interrupted again.

"He's not wrong," Wesley sighed. "The Arbiter of the eshan people, Forrandi, was cast out of the heavens. During the time of peace, Forrandi was unsatisfied with the position of her people. She thought they deserved more, and to accomplish this, she sought to take the power of the other Arbiters in order to give them what they needed. In the end she was caught and ultimately banished, leaving us mortals to wonder if Umbra existed all along, or if Forrandi's fall is what brought sin into our world. Personally, I believe there was sin long before—"

"The eshans are a godless people," Omar said with narrowed eyes, cutting Wesley short. "Their witchcraft brought this evil into the world."

"Witchcraft?" Bashkim asked. "You mean the magic they're *born* with?"

"It's an abomination!" Omar snarled.

Bashkim slowly slid his hands under the table, letting them tighten into fists.

If only you knew there was magic right in front of you.

"Before we deviate too far," Simon said before tensions could rise. "Jonus, what else do you know about these white dragons? Clearly you've been getting information from *somewhere.*"

"There isn't much I know about the dragons themselves," Bashkim admitted. "But I know there were knights from here that fought against them. And they weren't just defending themselves. Somehow they were able to turn the tide so much that they were the ones hunting the white dragons down. The problem is, I have no idea what gave them such an advantage."

"And where have you heard all of this?" the king asked.

"If I were the type to reveal my sources, they wouldn't trust me with such information. But if it helps put you at ease, they aren't citizens of Nennossen."

"It does little to ease me. For it seems there are people outside these walls spreading lies and rumors of our city."

"I would have to disagree, your majesty. My sources remember what they saw with their own eyes."

"Their own eyes?" the king scoffed. "This was over two hundred years ago. Anybody who saw it is long gone."

"My sources live longer than humans and eshans. A *lot* longer."

"And just who, or what, have you been conspiring with?"

"My lord," Simon interjected. "There's no sense in pretending Nennossen has no history. I believe we should share what we know. It's in our best interest if we wish to stand a chance against what might be returning."

The king crossed his arms and kept his eyes locked on Bashkim. "Very well."

"In that case," Wesley said. "Allow me to inform you that you are correct. There were indeed knights who sought to eradicate the white dragons, but I'm afraid we are also in the dark as to how they did so. I'm also a bit embarrassed to say there are no records of these knights. Not a single indication as to who they were. No ties to family, friends, or if they were even Nennossen's soldiers to begin with. Truly, an insult to scribes everywhere. But not all is completely lost. We have a single name at least. A man by the name of Ascura led them."

"A name is a good start," Bashkim said.

Wesley sighed. "You would think, but unfortunately in all of Nennossen's records, the name appears nowhere."

"There's a bit more," Simon added. "The source of the creatures and why they might be returning."

"They were summoned by one of the devil's children," Omar blurted.

"Devil's children?" Bashkim asked.

"An eshan," Simon said, a small frown forming on his face. "A powerful wizard by the name of Telanos."

Bashkim's eyebrows raised. "How do you know this?"

"Because Telanos has been kept under our guard in Nennossen for the past two hundred years."

"He's still alive?" Bashkim gasped. "And here?"

"Alive, yes, but...maybe not here anymore."

"How do you keep a wizard imprisoned? Or alive for two hundred years for that matter?"

Silence filled the room. Wesley and Simon both looked over at the king and waited for his approval.

"If magic is involved," Bashkim said. "I'm already aware there were eshans in Nennossen back then. They helped with fighting the white dragons."

Omar's eyebrows furrowed slightly. "You seem to know a lot for someone not from around here."

"And you seem to really hate magic."

"I'll have nothing of it in my city!" Omar said with a rising voice. "It's eshan witchcraft and the works of their fallen god!"

"Then that probably explains why the eshans didn't stick around," Bashkim said, the words slipping from his mouth before he could catch them.

Ah, damn it, Bashkim thought, instantly realizing his mistake.

The king leaned onto the table, lowering his tone and speaking slowly so that each word could be heard clearly. "Magic is evil. You'd do well to remember that while you're in *my* city."

Bashkim held his tongue, silently reminding himself that the castle's dungeons were probably just a few hallways away.

Stay focused.

"Let's all take a step back," Simon said, holding his hands up. "Remember, the white dragons are the enemy here. Not us."

The king took a slow breath and leaned back into his chair. He waved his hand, motioning for the other two to continue the story.

"Right, well," Wesley said, clearing his throat. "Back when the white dragons were originally a threat, they had deemed a man named Telanos responsible. The man was eventually found, and in what I would imagine was an attempt to cheat death, he sealed himself within a magical barrier. The eshans constructed a special sarcophagus to contain him, locking both him and his own magical barrier away. We are left to assume the incident happened here in Nennossen and they deemed it too risky to move him."

"And he's not in there anymore?" Bashkim asked.

"We can't tell," Simon admitted. "But there's reason to believe he's escaped."

"How so?"

"Just a few days ago we discovered a...leak from the sarcophagus."

"A leak?" Bashkim asked. "I don't understand."

"There's a plant the eshans use," Simon explained. "The nectar within it can negate their magic. It's no myth. I've seen it used in their bindings."

"I've heard of this nectar," Bashkim said, all too familiar with the concept.

"His sarcophagus was filled with it before being sealed. Apparently the stone has eroded over the years, allowing it to drain. I can only assume that someone who has magic powerful enough to summon dragons only needs a small crack to escape through. I have my doubts as to whether or not the nectar actually slowed him."

"Can one really use magic to control dragons?" Bashkim asked. "Or shapeshift?"

"I don't know about shapeshifting," Wesley said. "But onto how he was controlling the dragons...that has been a question for a long time. We've long known that eshans only have some control over fire and ice, which is a far cry from summoning dragons or wiggling through cracks in a stone sarcophagus. But after what you've told us, we might have a new theory."

"And what's that?" Bashkim asked.

"If this dragon really was calling on Umbra's name, then it's probably safe to assume they are tied to him somehow. Whether that means they actually are from the underworld or just creatures that are now bound to him, I can't say. However..."

Wesley hesitated for a moment. A smile came across the king's face that put Bashkim on edge.

"If," Wesley continued. "These creatures are tied to Umbra in whatever way *and* Telanos was controlling them...then I'm afraid we may be dealing with a man of darkness. Someone who has turned to the greatest evil of this world and now wields an extremely unholy power."

"See what I mean?" the king asked, pleased with what he had heard. "They are the devil's children."

Bashkim tried to hold his tongue. Every ounce of his being wanted to call the king a fool. He wanted to tear the bandage off his head and show the king he had been speaking to a hybrid devil child the entire time.

It's not worth it, he told himself. *The old fool is too far gone. He couldn't change if his life depended on it.*

As Bashkim tried to argue with himself, he could hear the voice coming back to him. Only this time it laughed. Bashkim's heart pounded against him and his vision shifted randomly.

No. I can't lose it here. Not now.

Bashkim breathed in deeply and held it in place, trying to calm himself. His eyes remained locked on the king who continued to sit proudly in his chair, perfectly content with his mockery of the eshan people. As he observed the king, Bashkim couldn't help but sense something about the old man. A strange feeling came from him, as if it were reaching out. Some tangible source that he might be able to take hold of.

What is that? It feels almost...familiar. Is that...? No. It couldn't be.

"Something wrong, boy?" the king asked.

"Yes," Bashkim said, his tongue betraying him once again. "I'm trying to understand the logic in ignoring such a massive problem. You've had Telanos under your watch for years, noticed a leak in the sarcophagus, and yet you remain here in silence. You ignore the danger that's in your own home."

"Don't get ahead of yourself," Simon said quickly. "Pointing fingers won't do any good for anyone. What's done is done."

Bashkim sank back into his seat. The whole thing felt wrong. How could these people just sit here when they knew the danger? Part of him wanted to scream, but he failed to see what good it would do other than relieve some tension in his chest.

I have no power here, he admitted to himself.

"I'm sorry," Bashkim said. "Is there no way to tell if Telanos is still in the sarcophagus or not?"

"The only way to be sure would be to break it open," Simon said. "The eshans might be able to tell, but the rest of us are blind."

"Has anybody reached out to them yet?"

"No," Simon said before the king could answer. "We have not. Considering our differences, I can't imagine they'd be receptive to a plea for help."

"With what might be at stake, I think it's worth the try," Bashkim insisted. "The white dragons threaten all of us. Not just humans. I don't believe it's a coincidence that one has been spotted only days after you discovered the leak."

"And you think they'd help?" Omar asked. "Or better yet, just let you waltz right into their city?"

"I don't plan on waltzing," Bashkim said, his hand gripping the edge of the table. "I'm just going to ask a few questions. With any luck, they'll remember a few things of the past that's been lost to the rest of us and understand the situation we're in."

"I don't envy you," Simon said. "But I can offer a horse if need be."

"That won't be necessary," Bashkim said. "I have transportation of my own."

"Then I believe we're finished here," Omar said, getting up from his chair.

Simon and Wesley quickly rose to their feet, and so did Bashkim. The king opened the door and left the room, letting Simon sigh unnoticed.

Simon stepped over to Bashkim and put a hand on his shoulder. "Come. I will escort you out."

Simon walked beside Bashkim as they walked through the city's streets. The sun had completely set, and the citizens had all returned home for the night, leaving the streets empty. Lanterns mounted on tall posts brightened their path, if only by a bit. It felt strange to Bashkim, to stand in the middle of a city with so little noise.

"Can I ask you something?" Bashkim asked, breaking the silence.

"Of course," Simon answered.

"Why does the king carry a dagger? I wouldn't expect someone in his position to feel the need for personal protection considering he's surrounded by guards."

Simon snorted. "Maybe it makes him feel a little safer."

"And the guards don't?"

"I've always assumed it was sentimental. I've never seen him without it. But, on the subject of the king, while I appreciate your cooperation, I must ask that you do better at holding your tongue next time."

"I'll try," Bashkim said. Though he hoped that there wouldn't be a next time.

A small sigh escaped Simon and he put a hand on Bashkim's shoulder, gently bringing him to a stop. "I know it's hard to sit back and do nothing when you're looking straight at something you know is wrong. I was young once too, believe it or not, and my mouth almost cost me my head on more than one occasion. It's only by the Light's good grace that it's still attached to my body. But unlike you, I'm only human."

"What do you mean?"

Simon smiled and patted him on the back. "I know who you are, Bashkim. I knew it had to be you the moment I walked into the library. Somebody in my city asking about white dragons and carrying an eshan sword? Who just happened to have an ear covered? I've no qualms in admitting I'm a fan of yours. I've heard several tales of you and had always hoped to catch you in Nennossen."

Bashkim scratched the side of his chin, unsure of what to say. "I appreciate you letting me remain hidden. That's not usually what happens."

"I can't pretend to know what it's like being in your position. But I *can* relate to being in unfortunate situations you have no control over."

"You don't agree with the king, do you? About eshans and magic."

Simon sighed, choosing his words carefully. "It'd be a damned shame if the circumstances of your birth laid the road for your entire future. I'd like to believe it's your choices that do that, with each choice being one more stone in the road you build each day."

Bashkim let the words sink in. He knew the captain would never speak against his king, but he came awfully close.

"And besides," Simon continued. "Who is to say eshan magic is a cursed thing? Their Arbiter falling was not their doing, so who are we to treat them as lesser?"

"Talking like that will get you in trouble," Bashkim joked.

"I told you my mouth has gotten me in trouble before."

"What happens to those who attempt to do anything with magic here?"

Simon's eyes lowered, staring at the ground. "By the king's decree, they are hauled away to prison, or worse. You would think the threat of a lifetime in prison coupled with humans' inability to even use magic would deter them from trying, but it doesn't. I've still had to bring people in."

"And you lock them away simply because your king believes it's evil?"

Simon raised his head and looked directly at Bashkim. "I never said I liked it, or agree with it, but I'm a soldier. My job is to carry out the orders of the king and make sure this city stays safe. Sometimes that means doing things you don't want to do."

"Doing something you don't want to do and doing something you know is wrong are two completely different things."

"Just because the king doesn't care for eshans and their magic doesn't mean the rest of us here feel the same way."

"But if you keep supporting his views then what difference does it make how you feel?"

Simon kept his eyes on Bashkim, taking in a long breath and letting it out in a huff through his nose. "I'm just a soldier. Bound by an oath to serve *this* city. Not all of us have the same freedom you do. I suggest you take advantage of it. Now come. It's late. I can set you up with a room at the inn for tonight. I assume tomorrow you will start your journey?"

"Yes." Bashkim nodded. "And thank you. I'll head straight to Teasvanna."

"Right to the eshans' main city? Can't say I envy you."

"It has to be done. One way or the other."

"Maybe you'll have better luck not drawing attention to yourself there," Simon said, then motioned for Bashkim to follow. "Come. The inn is this way."

CHAPTER
5

Despite starting his morning early, Bashkim found Simon waiting for him outside the inn's front door. Bashkim made sure to express his gratitude once more for the warm bed and meal, as well as keeping his identity a secret.

"Don't mention it," Simon said, then added with a more serious look on his face. "Seriously. Don't."

A small snort escaped Bashkim.

"I wanted to give you this," Simon said, unrolling a piece of paper in his hand. "It's an official letter from Nennossen. Written by me and signed and stamped by the king."

Bashkim looked down at the bottom of the letter and took note of the stamp along with both Simon's and Omar's signatures.

"Did you have to steal the stamp?" Bashkim asked.

Simon grinned, handing the letter over. "No. But it did take more convincing than I care to admit. Hopefully my troubles will benefit you in Teasvanna."

Bashkim read over the letter carefully. He found it almost hard to believe the elaborate letter came from the captain of the guard. The soldier certainly knew how to present himself politically when a situation called for it, such as officially requesting assistance from the eshans.

"It should at least prove my intentions are honest," Bashkim said, rolling the paper back up. "Hopefully."

"You seem hesitant."

"To be fair, Simon, I was hesitant to come here too."

Simon crossed his arms over his armored chest. "Yes. But there's something else, isn't there?"

"No offense but when it comes to hiding it's a little easier to fool humans. Eshans can often sense the magic in others around them and hybrids give off a different...smell, for a lack of better words."

"Do you think it'd be beneficial to bring some guards with you?"

"I can get there faster on my own. A lot faster."

"Then I'm afraid all I can do is pray for your safety and wait for your return."

"That's more than what most do," Bashkim said, his own comment causing his head to droop.

Simon reached out and put a hand on Bashkim's shoulder, giving it a slight squeeze. He motioned with his head for them to start walking and escorted Bashkim out of the city. From there, Bashkim spent the rest of the day travelling on foot back to Rin. He informed her of everything that had happened and they both agreed they would head to Teasvanna first thing in the morning.

Despite their several stops for breaks, Bashkim and Rin made it to their destination within a single day of flying. Bashkim silently wondered to himself if all dragons required so many stops. Considering how long it would have taken him on horseback, he deemed it wise not to ask and instead thanked Rin for her assistance.

The two made their camp in another forest, this time next to a small flowing stream. The sun still floated just above the horizon, providing its final rays of light before retiring for the night. Rin sat by the stream, dunking the tip of her face in while she drank. Bashkim sat farther upstream, occasionally tossing small rocks into the water.

Rin eventually stopped drinking and got herself comfortable. "So...Teasvanna tomorrow?"

"That's the plan. Should be able to get there on foot in about two days."

"We could cover some more ground so you wouldn't have to walk so far."

"I don't want to risk getting you any closer."

"My hero," Rin said playfully. "But you know you haven't had luck in the past with eshans. What's your backup plan this time?"

Bashkim tossed a small stone into the water. "I'll head out in the morning. On the second night, I want you to do a quick flyby near the city. Use those wonderful dragon ears of yours to listen for my signal."

"And if you're in need of help, what am I to do?"

Bashkim watched the ripples from the last rock slowly fade. "Whatever you have to."

Rin remained silent. She watched Bashkim grab a handful of more stones, picking them one at a time and gently tossing them into the water.

"You've been quiet all day," she finally said. "Something on your mind other than Teasvanna?"

I'm hearing voices in my head, he wanted to say.

"You could say that," Bashkim said.

"And what would that be?"

Bashkim rolled a single rock around in his hand and stared at it. *What would she think?* he wondered. *I'm not sure I should tell her. Not yet anyway.*

Bashkim took in a large breath and let it out in a short huff while attempting to change the subject. "Why do they lie?"

"Who?"

"Omar. His people. Why do they keep everything a secret? White dragons are a danger to everyone, yet they want to pretend nothing happened. Do they hate the eshans so much that they'd willingly put their entire city at risk to avoid working with them?

"Maybe it's jealousy?" Rin asked. "Humans can't use magic, after all. Perhaps they feel inferior."

A small groan came from Bashkim. "How stupid would that be."

"Regardless of their reasoning, are either one of us surprised?"

Bashkim closed his hand on the rock he held and squeezed it. "No. I just...I was just hoping, you know? Part of me hoped they didn't know about the white dragons at all. I thought maybe if they didn't know...then maybe they'd be more willing to help."

Rin tilted her head slightly. The single tear sliding down Bashkim's cheek did not go unnoticed.

"Bunch of damned idiots," Bashkim muttered, squeezing the rock. "All of them."

Bashkim lowered his head and whispered to himself. "I hate them."

The whispered words did not escape Rin's ears. She raised her head up and watched him curiously. Bashkim tossed the small stone into the water and steam rose from where it landed. The hissing noise from the water cooling the heated rock broke the silence. Bashkim sank his head into his hands in defeat.

Bashkim arrived at Teasvanna's entrance on the second day as planned with the sun already brushing the tips of the trees in the distance. *Not a lot of time left,* he thought. *But that might be for the better.*

He patted the bandage on his head, once more checking he had the human ear covered this time as he approached the gate. Two eshan guards stood by the closed doors, both dressed in steel and holding a spear. One of the guards held his hand up and motioned Bashkim over towards him. Bashkim approached slowly and made sure not to make any sudden movements or to get his hand too close to his sword.

"Name and business?" the guard asked routinely.

Bashkim handed Simon's paper over. "My name is Bashkim and I've come on the behalf of Nennossen. At least one white dragon has been spotted and there's reason to believe that Telanos may have escaped. Nennossen is—"

"Woah, woah, woah," the guard interrupted, waving his hand as he read the document. "Easy there, killer. One thing at a time. Let me read this first."

"White dragons?" the second guard asked and stepped up. "What makes a white one different than any other color?"

"Have you seen a white one?" Bashkim asked.

"Well, no," the second guard admitted. "But I'm not exactly the type to go looking for such things either."

"They're much worse, and that's why I've come here. I've already spoken with Nennossen about it."

"With the humans? Bloody hell, that was probably a treat, wasn't it? Surprised they gave you the time of day."

Bashkim held his tongue and shrugged his shoulders in response.

"This is quite the letter," the first guard said once he finished reading. "It definitely looks like Nennossen's stamp alright, but I'd be a liar if I said I believed it."

"Pardon?" Bashkim asked.

"Nennossen? Asking for our help? It's a little strange, don't you think?"

"Desperate times call for desperate measures. I can assure you that the danger is real."

The first guard eyed the bandage on Bashkim's head then looked him directly in the eye. The lack of expression on the soldier's face told Bashkim nothing, other than he had probably already been sniffed out.

"Right," the guard finally said. "Wait here."

Keeping the paper, the guard shouted to the other side of the door. "Send for Fandul. His presence is needed at the gate."

Bashkim waited as patiently as he could, leaning over the stone railings that lined the path towards Teasvanna's front door. The two soldiers remained at their post. One of them kept a close eye on Bashkim while the other questioned the occasional traveler entering to the city.

Despite feeling like it had taken forever, the city's door opened again only a few minutes later. Another guard came through, this one taller than the others. He wore no helmet and allowed his lengthy blonde hair to flow down to his shoulders. Bashkim could see the sternness in the eshan's eyes but he found himself slightly less intimidated due to the cleanly shaven and youthful face.

"What is it?" the man asked as the door shut behind him.

"Master Fandul, sir," the guard said with a sharp salute and handed over Bashkim's letter. "This man wishes to speak with the king. His name is Bashkim and claims to be here on the behalf of Nennossen. Something about white dragons, sir."

Fandul unrolled the paper and began to read while the guard spoke too quietly for Bashkim to hear. Fandul glanced over at Bashkim for a brief second before returning to the document. His eyes ran over each word carefully and he squinted once he got to the king's stamp.

"Thank you," Fandul said, motioning for the guard to return to his post.

Fandul rolled the paper back up and joined Bashkim by the stone railing. "White dragons, is it?"

The eshan stood tall enough to easily see the top of Bashkim's head, causing him to bend down to look Bashkim in the eyes. Bashkim could sense the magic within Fandul, radiating from his body, ready to fire off at a moment's notice.

"And what are you?" Fandul asked. "You seem a little short for a dragon hunter."

"I am nothing of the sort," Bashkim said, looking up at the eshan soldier. "Do you know of white dragons? Or perhaps their history with the eshans?"

Fandul stood up straight and crossed his arms. "Enlighten me."

"Alright," Bashkim sighed. "About two hundred years ago, there was an eshan sorcerer by the name of Telanos. Somehow he either brought these white dragons into the world or made them himself. They terrorized both humans and eshans alike. There was a man named Ascura that gathered knights from Nennossen and convinced the eshans to help fight alongside them. Together, they overpowered the white dragons and sealed Telanos away. That's all I know of the story. I'm here because at least one of those dragons has returned. I saw it myself."

"Ascura?" Fandul asked, scratching his bare chin. "That sounds like an eshan name. It's hard enough to believe that humans would work alongside eshans, but to be led by one? I don't think that's likely. Now tell me. What makes these white dragons so special?"

"It's hard to describe without showing you," Bashkim admitted. "I crossed paths with one recently. I can assure you that it is not to be taken lightly. If there is more than one of them, then Teasvanna is in just as much danger as Nennossen."

"So you've come to warn us? You don't need an official letter from Nennossen for that."

"I've come to warn *and* find information. The knights of Ascura had something that allowed them to overpower the white dragons. I was hoping Teasvanna could shed some light on what it was or perhaps share more details to the story that seems to have been forgotten by Nennossen."

"Did they forget?" Fandul asked with a raised eyebrow. "Or did they just not wish to tell you?"

"I..." Bashkim started to say but caught himself freezing. "I can't know for certain. But they at least shared that Telanos's seal might have been broken."

Fandul nodded his head and leaned against the stone railing. "An interesting story for sure, but why do you hide, hybrid?"

"Excuse me?"

"There may be blood on your bandage but I'd wager it isn't yours."

Both Bashkim's heart and head sank.

"I could sense you the minute I stepped through the gate," Fandul added.

Shamefully, Bashkim slowly undid his bandage to reveal himself. "I don't want to cause any trouble. I'm just trying to do what's right."

Fandul lowered his head and sighed. He leaned over onto his elbow and looked the defeated hybrid over. Bashkim felt the magic from Fandul subsiding while he relaxed.

"Do you honestly think the king will hear your stories?" Fandul asked. "Or believe them? You're trying to tell us that one of our own is responsible for unleashing some sort of monster on the world."

"I don't know the whole story," Bashkim said, rolling up the bandage in his hands. "But what I do know is that I saw the white dragon. If you knew the truth was somewhere between humans and eshans, wouldn't you try to find it? Even if it was just for the benefit of Teasvanna?"

"I would, yes. But for you, who benefits? Are you here to protect Handleson?"

Bashkim took a breath and held it before admitting the truth. "No," he said. "I have no home."

"Yet here you are."

"Yes," Bashkim nodded, squeezing the bandage in his hand. "Here I am."

Fandul tapped his fingers against his armored gauntlet and studied Bashkim. Determination burned in the hybrid's eyes, but it couldn't hide the sound of defeat slowly gnawing away at his voice. Fandul stood up straight up and placed both hands on the rails. The soldier sighed and stared out into the distance. Bashkim waited silently while Fandul tried to figure out what to do with him.

"You can turn your back now and be on your way should you so desire," Fandul said without looking at him. "No harm, no crime. We'll let you go without trouble, and if need be, we can even supply you with some food for the road. But if you insist on continuing in this endeavor, then you must know that I am bound by the king's word and have no say against what he may choose to do with you. Also, the bandage stays off. I will not smuggle a hybrid into my city, nor attempt to trick his majesty. You *will* come as you are."

Bashkim considered the offer carefully. He *could* turn back. He could walk away and not deal with any of this. Why *shouldn't* he walk away? The issues between the two cities had nothing to do with him after all. If white dragons wanted to come back and destroy them, why should he care? He could take Rin and fly far away from the whole mess while the fools sorted things out themselves.

They figured it out two hundred years ago, he told himself. *They could probably do it again. Why should I be the one to save them this time?*

Hearing his own words in his head gave him pause. *Is that really what I think? Or is that you, white dragon?*

Bashkim handed the bandage over to Fandul. "As I am. No more hiding."

Curious, Fandul took the dirty bandage. "Are you sure?"

"Yes. I already have enough trouble sleeping at night. I can't imagine how hard it would be knowing I turned my back today."

"Very well," Fandul said and motioned for Bashkim to follow. "We might be able to catch his majesty before he retires for the night if we move quickly."

Before entering the city, Fandul ordered the guards to search Bashkim. He handed over his bag, allowing one of them to search it while the other patted him down for hidden weapons. Fandul also required that Bashkim hand over his sword. Bashkim did as instructed and unhooked the weapon from his belt and placed the sheathed blade in Fandul's hands on top of the bloodied bandage. Content Bashkim had nothing concealed, the guard handed the pack back over, and Fandul motioned for Bashkim to follow him. The door groaned as it opened and granted passage.

The busyness of the streets in Teasvanna were comparable to Nennossen, but the structures within the city walls had their differences. The eshans clearly favored wood over stone. Homes with rounded and curved roofs proudly displayed the eshans' advanced abilities to bend and shape timber. Were Bashkim not currently being escorted, the eshan architecture would have been more thoroughly enjoyed.

Fandul stayed close to Bashkim during their march through the city, keeping one hand on the hybrid's arm. Even though Bashkim shared their heritage, he couldn't help but feel like he had been put on display once the city noticed *what* Fandul escorted. A few individuals stood over a large workbench and used a combination of their fire and ice magic to produce large amounts of steam to bend a lengthy piece of timber. One of them quickly patted his partner on the arm and nodded towards Bashkim. They paused their woodworking and scratched their heads as they tried to figure out exactly what the guard had brought in.

The curiosity seemed to flow through the city as Bashkim's presence became more known. They would look over and get their friends' attention, pointing in his direction and whispering to one another. Bashkim tried to ignore them, but he couldn't. The more he tried to, the more he seemed to be drawn to them. The white dragon's voice came to him. It started off subtle enough, but it didn't take long to get worse. Bashkim stared down at his feet. He squinted his eyes and tried not to listen. Still the voice continued to speak. Its voice rose so it could not be ignored. As the voice spoke, Bashkim could feel himself being drawn back to the citizens that watched him. Oddly enough, their voices became clear enough to hear as if they were right next to him.

"A human?" one of them asked. "In our city? Wonder what that's all about."

"Oi. That's no human," another voice said. "Look at his ears. It's an immundrid."

"Disgusting," a third voice snarled. "What eshan is desperate enough to bed a human?"

"You, probably," another voice joked. "I've seen human women before. Can't say I blame you."

Bashkim turned his head away as he tried not to listen. The white dragon's voice grew even louder as it tried to pull him back.

Don't make me listen, Bashkim begged.

"Ay, look there," he could hear someone say. "Looks like the guards found themselves an immundrid."

Please stop.

"Handleson not good enough for them? What's he planning to do here?"

Why? Why are you doing this to me?

More voices from the citizens filled his head and swarmed in his mind like a tornado. They grew both louder and in number. He could hear the white dragon, buried beneath them, laughing.

Shut up! Bashkim wanted to scream.

He shook his head to try and tether himself back to reality.

Not this time, he said, realizing he had almost lost himself again.

"Are you alright?" Fandul asked.

Bashkim looked around. None of the citizens seemed to pay him any attention since they were all preoccupied with their own lives.

"Yeah," Bashkim said, rubbing his head with his free hand. "Just...a chill is all. I'll be fine."

Fandul escorted Bashkim through the castle's interior, passing several other armed guards. The soldiers eyed Bashkim curiously, some of them even sneering and asking Fandul what he had managed to "catch" today. Fandul seemed uninterested and brushed them off as he hurriedly made his way to the king.

After passing through a few more doors, Fandul brought Bashkim into a large, spacious room. A wide, red carpet with golden trim lined a path through the center. At the end of the room and a few steps up sat two large wooden chairs, each sculpted from wood in an elaborate design. An older man with white hair and beard sat in one of the tall-backed chairs while a much younger woman sat in the other next to him.

The many guards in the room stood at attention and saluted Fandul as he approached. Fandul signaled for a specific guard to come forward. The biggest eshan that Bashkim had ever seen answered the order and came to Fandul. The armored house of a man stood taller than Fandul and strapped to his back rested a sword that Bashkim could only assume weighed more than himself. Bashkim couldn't help but look the man over from top to bottom. Armor covered his entire fortress of a body and from his belt hung a golden trimmed red cloth with Teasvanna's emblem. The soldier removed his helmet and revealed a head with short, spiky black hair and a scarred face.

"Hang on to this guy for a moment, will you Dasc?" Fandul asked and handed Bashkim over.

"Aw he's a tiny one, isn't he?" the giant said with a growly voice and a smile that showed all of his teeth.

"Yes," Fandul said before stepping away. "Please try not to crush him."

"I'll do my best, sir," Dasc said, then handed his helmet to Bashkim. "Here. Hold this."

Confused, Bashkim took hold of the helmet. As he did, Dasc turned him around to properly face the king then grabbed both of his arms. Before he knew it, Bashkim felt himself being lifted from the ground and held in place. Bashkim winced under the more than necessary grip strength of the new guard.

Ignoring the humility of feeling like a toddler as his feet dangled beneath him, Bashkim looked over at the eshan king. Physically he didn't see much difference between this one and the human king, aside from the pointed ears. They were both old men in robes living in castles. Judging by the way the king looked down upon him, he couldn't help but feel that Omar and the eshan king would hold the same cold heart. The young woman next to him, however, Bashkim couldn't quite figure out.

A daughter, perhaps? he wondered.

"Lord Orenzen," Fandul said when he approached but stopped before getting too close. "May I have a word?"

The old man motioned Fandul forward and leaned to the side of his chair as Fandul approached. Fandul came to the king's side and whispered something into his ear as he handed Bashkim's document over. Orenzen unrolled the paper and read it over carefully, frowning. When he finished, he rolled the paper back up and looked down towards Bashkim. His face wrinkled in such a way that made his displeasure easily visible.

The reaction from the woman had been much different. Her eyebrows instantly shot up when Fandul spoke, but she tried to hide her reaction by quickly brushing some of her lengthy brown hair behind her ear. Barely catching the brief moment of surprise, Bashkim continued to watch her as she tried to casually lean over to better hear the whispered words.

Both Fandul and Orenzen seemed to either not care about the younger woman or failed to notice as they exchanged more of their whispered words. Eventually, Orenzen did glance over at the woman. She smiled at the king who then smiled in return. Orenzen looked back over at Fandul and motioned him away. Fandul returned to Bashkim and ordered Dasc to put Bashkim down and return to his post.

"All yours, sir," Dasc said, taking his helmet back.

Fandul grabbed Bashkim's arm, though much gentler than the armored giant, and took him out of the king's throne room and into a much smaller room. Very similar to Nennossen, Bashkim found himself yet again in a stone room that could have been a storage closet with a small table and a few chairs. Two guards stood outside the door to the back room and only a few minutes later did the king arrive. He entered the room calmly and closed the door behind him.

"My name is Lord Guero Orenzen," Orenzen said and took a seat on the opposite side of the table. "But there is no need for your introduction, Bashkim, for you have quite the reputation. Anything from saving damsels in distress to fighting dragons. Some say you've even managed to tame one for yourself. Truly, a man's man and a hero of the ages. But I'm curious about what brings you to my city."

"I have news from Nennossen about Telanos," Bashkim said, ignoring the feigned praise. "I've also encountered one of the white dragons myself."

"So I'm told," Orenzen said, leaning onto the table. "An experience few would live to talk about. Assuming you are telling the truth and this letter wasn't forged for some mysterious reason, then I believe it's safe to assume the humans have allowed Telanos to escape, have they not?"

"They don't know for sure if he's escaped, but yes, they did notice a leak in the sarcophagus. I don't think it's a coincidence a white dragon has made an appearance."

"And what did you hope to find here? Did you think we would come running to assist? Dear boy, Telanos's power isn't forgotten to us. Our best scholars still study his works to this very day. I can assure you that if there is even the slightest of cracks in his prison then he is already out, assuming the sarcophagus could even contain him to begin with."

"Are you prepared then? Are you able to hold back the white dragons?"

"Teasvanna's defenses are none of your concern."

"So you're not ready?" Bashkim asked, his tongue betraying him once more. "You've done nothing to prepare for this?"

"What do you want, Bashkim? A secret weapon? Some magical device from heroes past that you can use to save the day? Or perhaps we should summon the ghost of Ascura himself?"

"No," Bashkim pleaded. "I'm sorry. I just...I don't think the knights of Ascura would have been able to fight back against the white dragons without *something*, let alone wipe them out. Nennossen doesn't know what it is that allowed them to do that, which is why I'm here. I was hoping to find some new information."

"They don't remember?" Orenzen asked with a raised eyebrow. "By the Arbiters, the hell they don't. They would never forget such a thing. We gave them the power of the gods."

"I don't understand."

"They lied to you, child. The humans played you for a fool."

"So you do have something then? Something that can help defeat the white dragons?"

Orenzen remained silent and stared across the table at Bashkim, slowly drumming his fingers.

"Take him away," Orenzen finally said, the chair squealing when he stood. "I'll decide what to do with him tomorrow."

"Eshans helped in the past," Bashkim said quickly. "I don't know what happened back then, but if Telanos is back with his white dragons, then you have to help again."

Orenzen stopped at the door before opening it, holding his hand up to stop Fandul from hauling Bashkim away.

"I *have* to?" the king asked with his back still to Bashkim.

"I think it's pretty clear that eshans and humans had to work together in the past," Bashkim said. "Unless you want Teasvanna and Nennossen to be destroyed, then yes, you have to help."

Orenzen tapped his fingers against the door handle and paused. Bashkim held his breath, waiting for the king's response.

"You save women," Orenzen said. "You bring home lost children. You go out of your way to find those in need and you put your own life at risk." Orenzen turned around to face him. "And do you know why you are this way?"

Bashkim started to answer but chose to hold his tongue, assuming the king would answer for him.

Orenzen stepped up to the table and leaned over, speaking in a lower tone. "It's because you're on the outside, Bashkim, and you always have been. You yearn to be accepted, but neither human nor eshan will have you. The world doesn't want you, immundrid, and that's how it will *always* be."

The verbal knife cut through Bashkim's chest. He wanted to fight back, but Fandul gently placed a hand on his shoulder.

Orenzen straightened himself and returned to the door. "If you're so inclined to worry about other peoples' affairs, then go watch over your own kind and stay out of my city."

The king left, again ordering Fandul to take Bashkim away. Bashkim's head dropped as he sank back into his chair.

"I saw one," Bashkim said quietly. "I promise."

Fandul sighed softly. "Come on," he said gently, patting Bashkim's shoulder. "Let's go."

CHAPTER 6

Bashkim's head hung low as Fandul escorted him through the castle's many halls. Fandul kept a firm grip on Bashkim's arm but hadn't the need to jerk him around for Bashkim offered little resistance. The two of them walked in silence until Fandul finally decided to speak up.

"For what it's worth," Fandul said. "The harshness of the king's words wasn't needed."

"You disagree with him?"

"I believe hybrids have an unjustified difficulty in life and that words such as his will do little to alleviate that burden."

"Kind of walking a fine line, aren't you?"

"Everyone is allowed to have their own thoughts and opinions," Fandul said. "It's what you do with them that will get you in trouble."

Fandul suddenly stopped walking and lifted Bashkim's sword into both their views. "Speaking of. Where did you get this?"

"I bought it in Telscara."

"That's a small village near the mountains is it not? Southwest of Nennossen?"

"It is."

Fandul looked down each end of the hallway, making sure they were alone. He leaned in closer to Bashkim, whispering, "You needn't lie to me. This is the sword of a Senguan Knight. Either it was given to you or you stole it."

"A what? No," Bashkim said, shaking his head. "There's a smith in Telscara that makes eshan style weapons."

"What for?"

"She appreciates the style. She said she only sees them in passing or when one is found."

Fandul looked down at the sword. "If your story is true, then this smith is rather talented. I almost didn't recognize the design at first. I thought perhaps it was an older one I wasn't familiar with. But...a human? Odd she would want anything of ours."

Bashkim raised his eyebrows, looking at Fandul. "Surely it's not that hard to believe."

"My experiences with humans haven't been the most inviting."

Strange, Bashkim thought as he listened to the distance in Fandul's words. *Wouldn't think a guard behind eshan walls would care much what humans think.*

"Well cry *me* a river," Bashkim said, trying to smile through his own misfortune.

A small snort managed to escape Fandul before he could properly compose himself. "Yes, well," he started, gently pulling Bashkim along while walking down the hallway, "I suppose my experiences fall a little short compared to some, don't they?"

"If it helps, I don't think all humans are the same."

"Clearly," Fandul said, waving the handle of the sword in Bashkim's view. "But there just doesn't seem to be enough of the good ones to make a difference, does there?"

Bashkim's head sank again. "No."

"I don't think eshans are all the same either. If it helps."

Bashkim glanced back over at Fandul. The eshan kept his eyes forward but a small grin could be seen. Before Bashkim could think of anything else to say, the lady who had sat next to the king rounded the upcoming hallway intersection and blocked their path.

"Lady Treydola," Fandul said in surprise, taking a step back to avoid colliding into her and gave a quick bow.

"Where are you going?" she asked.

"To the cells, milady," Fandul answered. "As ordered by your father."

Treydola put a hand on her hip and looked Bashkim over. "A hybrid?"

"If you worry for his safety, he will have his own cell."

"No. I think a hybrid should be in the underground."

"With the old man?"

"Yes. Is there something wrong?"

"No, milady," Fandul tried to say, "but your father—"

Treydola shot Fandul a look with narrowed eyes that caused him to stop short. She stepped forward close enough for him to feel her breath against his face. Treydola stared at Fandul's eyes and raised a single eyebrow.

"Do all soldiers question their orders?" she asked. "Or just you?"

"No, ma'am," Fandul said. He tried to bow, but Treydola refused to move out of the way. "I'll take him to the underground."

"Good," she said, stepping back.

Fandul bowed now that he had enough room and stayed lowered as Treydola looked them both over again. Bashkim remained standing until a firm tug from Fandul told him he shouldn't be.

"Well," Treydola said once Bashkim bowed. "Maybe there's still hope for you."

Her lengthy brown hair swung when she turned around to leave. Fandul remained bowed until she rounded the next corner.

"She seems nice," Bashkim joked quietly.

"Easy," Fandul said, tightening his grip on Bashkim's arm.

Fandul obeyed Lady Treydola's new orders and brought Bashkim down to the underground level of the castle. The hallways were narrower and lit only by the few torches along the wall that Fandul had to light with a wave of his hand. Bashkim remained silent as Fandul escorted him. Fandul held his own tongue and let Bashkim walk what might be his last steps in peace.

A single door waited for them at the end of the hall, groaning as Fandul opened it and led them inside. Several iron bars came from the ground and reached to the ceiling, forming the prison cells inside. Fandul set Bashkim's sword and backpack in the corner of the room away from the cells.

"I'll assume you've been a law-abiding citizen your entire life and are unfamiliar with the process," Fandul said, grabbing a pair of leather straps from the wall. "These will restrict your magic. It stings a bit when you first put them on so brace yourself."

The leather straps had a light-blue glowing line from one end to the other on their underside. Bashkim winced slightly when they wrapped around his forearms, the sensation similar to several small bugs biting him all at once.

"It'll pass," Fandul said once the straps were tightened.

He then grabbed a pair of wide iron shackles that covered half of Bashkim's forearms. Fandul locked the iron shackles shut, preventing Bashkim any and all access to the leather straps.

"Should the king see fit that you live and are allowed to leave," Fandul said, motioning for Bashkim to step into the cell. "Your belongings will be returned to you. Considering your judgement is in the morning, I'll leave them here in your sight."

"Thank you, but are these necessary?" Bashkim asked, holding his arms out. "I'm behind bars."

"Only for the eshan half," Fandul smirked.

"Fair enough. At least I'm not chained."

"Only because you've been cooperating so well," Fandul said and locked the cell door in place. "Unfortunately, that is the most I can reward you with. Tomorrow the king will decide your fate."

Fandul reached his hand out, lighting a single torch on the wall in front of Bashkim's cell.

"I'll leave this one burning," Fandul said and made his way to the door. "It should last for about an hour."

"Before you go," Bashkim said, stopping Fandul at the door. "That woman, Treydola. Was that behavior normal?"

"What do you mean?"

"Does she normally circumvent the king's instruction?"

Fandul opened the door to leave but paused as he considered the question.

"No," he finally said, closing the door behind him as he left.

Bashkim let out a long, slow sigh as he sat down on the stone floor of his prison cell. The torch Fandul had left for him provided little light, barely reaching the bars of his cell.

Still more than most would have done I suppose, Bashkim thought.

He listened to Fandul's footsteps moving farther down the hallway, eventually leaving him in silence. Bashkim held his hands out and attempted to harness his magic in hopes of more light. He could feel it inside of him, making its way through his arms and trying to reach his hands. As the magic flowed through him, he could feel something squeeze *inside* his arms, choking his magic. The more he tried to push, the more intense the pressure became. It slowly made his way up his arms, eventually crushing his chest.

Bashkim let his hands fall down, the metal shackles clanging against the ground. He finally took in several breaths as the pressure in his chest lifted.

"Let me help you with that," a voice said from the next cell over. Bashkim heard something metal slide across the ground. Unable to see, Bashkim used his hand to feel around on the floor and discovered a key. He took it and much to his surprise it fit the locks of his bindings. The iron shackles squeaked open and he quietly set them on the ground. As Bashkim undid the leather straps, he squinted to try and see in the adjacent cell.

"If a prisoner has the key to their own bindings," he asked, setting the straps with the shackles. "Then why are they still in prison?"

"Are you asking me?" the voice answered. "Or yourself?"

Bashkim held his hand out and made another attempt to use magic. This time it flowed freely through his body, and he summoned a small sphere of swirling ice bits. The tiny storm sparked repeatedly, progressing from a flickering light source to a steady glow. As the light reached out, Bashkim could see an old frail eshan in the other cell, thin from improper nourishment. Torn rags covered his body, as did lengthy and unkempt white hair from both his head and face.

Bashkim moved the ball of light closer to get a better view, allowing him to see the piece of cloth wrapped over the man's eyes. The cloth sunk in slightly, suggesting that the eyes were missing entirely.

"You're blind," Bashkim said.

"But not completely without sight. For I can tell that you are a hybrid."

Bashkim sat the ball down, letting it hover in place just above the floor. "I am. But all you had to do was listen to me and the guard talking to figure that one out."

"True," the old man agreed. "But I can also sense the magic in you. It's strong. Very strong. Not everyone can conjure what you just did. But...there is also something else. Something familiar. Something I've felt before. Something...dark."

"Probably just your eshan pride getting in the way. That or you're hungry."

The old man chuckled, holding his ribs in discomfort. "Maybe so."

Bashkim remained silent, gently pushing the ball of light back and forth to keep himself distracted.

"So," the old man said after a moment. "Treydola sent you here?"

"She did. Apparently she didn't want me in the other cells."

"What did you do to deserve that?"

"Asked the wrong questions, I guess. It seems people don't like it when you ask about the past."

"The past?" the old man asked. "I've got quite a bit of that."

Bashkim snorted. "So, what are you down here for?"

"Messed with the wrong woman."

Bashkim looked over into the cell and pushed his ball of light over so he could make sure he had indeed seen an old and frail man.

"You must have been down here for quite some time then," Bashkim said.

The old man cackled, slowly sliding down the wall he leaned against and laughing as much as his worn body would let him. He slowly propped himself back upright again and brushed his hair out of his face.

"A very long time," the old man said. "But what about you? Your shackles are open. Surely you won't let simple iron bars hold you?"

"For the moment they will," Bashkim said, getting himself more comfortable. "I've a friend that will come for me if I don't return."

"If I'm not mistaken, I heard the guard say your fate will be decided in the morning. Hopefully this friend of yours will come before then."

"She'll be here tonight."

The old man smiled. "Well then. Since you're going to be here for a little while, what is your name?"

"Bashkim. And you?"

"The people around here call me Ishmonyae: a prisoner of time."

"You seem fine with the idea."

"It matters little to me what they call me. A name is a name and nothing more. It cannot change who I am."

"Fair enough."

A silence came between them. Bashkim watched the swirling ball of light in front of him and reduced its size a little to keep from wearing himself out. Pacing his breaths, he started to contemplate his next move for when Rin showed up.

"There are easier ways to create light," the old man said.

"I prefer this way."

The old man slowly crawled over to the bars closer to the light. He held his hand over the glowing ball, carefully hovering around it.

"Thousands of shards of ice," the old man said in a lower voice. "All jagged and sharp, spiraling around in what you believe to be contained chaos. But what happens when you can no longer control it?"

Bashkim raised his eyebrows, unsure of how to answer the question. To his surprise, the old man tapped the tip of his finger on the glowing orb. The light instantly vanished, and the tiny fragments of ice flew across the room in every direction, stinging Bashkim as they struck his exposed skin.

"Eshans, as well as hybrids, were given a gift," Ishmonyae continued. "We have means of making light in the darkness."

Ishmonyae held his hand out and summoned a small flame in his palm. With his free hand he motioned for Bashkim to come closer. Bashkim slid over slowly, watching the fire.

"Hold out your hand," Ishmonyae said.

Begrudgingly, Bashkim carefully held his hand out. Ishmonyae started to move his fire closer, but Bashkim pulled back.

"It's alright," Ishmonyae said, gently taking Bashkim's hand. "Use what you were given, trust what's inside of you, and you will shine even brighter."

The fire slid from Ishmonyae's hand into Bashkim's palm. As it touched Bashkim, the flames briefly turned blue. Just as quickly as it had appeared, the fire returned to a normal orange. However, the light it provided nearly lit the entire room. Bashkim looked around the room in awe, then back at the small flame in his hand.

"How?" Bashkim asked. "How does such a small flame provide so much light?"

"When you're surrounded by darkness, even the smallest light shines bright."

Ishmonyae slid himself over to the wall and leaned against it. Bashkim continued to stare at the flame, carefully laying it down on the floor. He could feel his connection to it. The magic gently swirled inside of him, though this time it felt more...free. He could breathe easily, no longer feeling like he had to force the magic in the direction he wanted.

"So...Bashkim," Ishmonyae said after a while, "what were you asking about that got everyone's feathers ruffled?"

"White dragons," Bashkim answered, joining the old man at the wall. "And a man named Ascura."

"Ascura," the old man echoed. "If that's what you went around town asking about, then I'm surprised you lived this long."

"I take it the king isn't fond of Ascura?"

"It's something he would rather his people forget. Or the world for that matter."

"And why is that? Why does everyone want to forget what happened?"

"I can think of a few reasons. But why don't you spare this old man some air and tell me what you already know? Or at least, what you've been told."

Bashkim took a deep breath and recalled the events of the past several days. He included Rin in his storytelling this time, figuring it safe to give the old man all the details whether he believed them or not.

What's the worst he can do? Tell the guards I know a dragon? They're all going to find out soon anyway.

Ishmonyae listened intently, nodding his head as Bashkim spoke. A smile would come across his face every so often out of his control. Bashkim paid it little mind, figuring the old man had been desperate for someone to talk to.

"Gave them the power of the gods?" Ishmonyae cackled once Bashkim finished. "What a pompous little man."

"I take it that's not how it happened."

Ishmonyae leaned towards the bars that separated them, getting closer to Bashkim. "Come here. Let me tell you what *really* happened."

Bashkim also leaned over towards the bars, eager to hear what the old man had to say.

Ishmonyae cleared his throat with a dry cough. "The humans weren't completely honest with you either. Seems they left out a few details. They were right about Forrandi falling from the heavens, but she wasn't the only thing that fell."

"There was another Arbiter?"

Ishmonyae shook his head. "No. Not an Arbiter. Her belongings. Forrandi *was* trying to capture the powers of the other Arbiters. Eshans have long theorized that she was successful and trapped their powers in devices she had created. This theory also states that those devices fell *with* her when she was cast out."

"I'm guessing that's not just a theory anymore."

"Indeed. Eshans searched for those devices of hers for who knows how many lifetimes. But they finally found them. Not that it did them much good."

Bashkim's eyebrows raised slightly. "Oh?"

Ishmonyae laughed, seemingly recalling an old joke. "They couldn't figure out how to use them! You see, the powers of the Arbiters, they were trapped inside of crystals."

"Crystals?"

"Who would have thought? Though it's not very convenient for mere mortals like us, is it? Those who discovered it called it kesshonite, and they were more than convinced that it contained the powers of the Arbiters. Problem was, no matter how hard they tried, they couldn't seem to extract it. Couldn't do it through physical means or magic. That's where the humans came in."

"How so?"

Another smile came across Ishmonyae's face. "Turns out the humans could use the kesshonite just fine. Apparently us high and mighty eshans are walled off from it. As far as I know, nobody ever found out why either. I had always suspected it was our own magic that negated it somehow."

Ishmonyae started wagging his finger in the air. "But the humans! Oh no. They had no problem at all with it. Not in pulling the power *out* of the kesshonite anyway. Stopping it was another issue. Turns out, not only is kesshonite extremely powerful, it's also a bit unstable."

"So how did they contain it?" Bashkim asked. "Or did they?"

"They did. The eshans may not have been able to use the kesshonite themselves but turns out they were pretty good at negating it. With a balance between human and eshan, the kesshonite's power could be controlled."

Bashkim slowly shook his head. "So that's why they were working together. Unbelievable."

"That's not the part that's hard to believe," Ishmonyae said, wrapping his hands around the bars while he leaned forward. "The humans that were exposed to kesshonite...they could use magic."

Bashkim pulled back in disbelief. "What? No. You're lying."

"I have nothing to gain from lies. The kesshonite is changing our world, Bashkim."

Humans using magic, he thought, barely able to process it. *Does anybody know?*

Bashkim remained silent. One question after another raced through his mind. What if the people of Nennossen learned they had the ability to use magic? Or did they already know and that's why Omar put laws in place? Did the eshans know all of this too, or were the secrets reserved for those in power?

"How do you know all of this?" Bashkim eventually asked.

"I'm old," Ishmonyae said with a cough and let go of the bars. "The history you seek to learn wasn't so ancient when I was younger."

"That's why you're really in here, isn't it? You were making sure people didn't forget."

The old man nodded his head slowly before leaning back up against the wall. "Something like that."

Bashkim pulled himself back up to his feet and made his way over to the door of his cell. He wrapped his hands around the bars, resting his forehead against them as he digested all of the new information.

Why does everyone lie? Why hide the past? For pride?

The whole thing seemed stupid. Two old men hiding behind their walls and pointing fingers while everyone around them suffered the consequences.

Are they kings or children?

A whisper of the white dragon's voice came to him, but faintly. Bashkim closed his eyes, trying not to listen. The words were unknown to him, but he could feel the emotion they carried. They were angry. Bashkim's grip on the bars tightened as it spoke, and the small flame on the ground started to stand upright and stiffen.

"There's something brilliant inside of you," the old man said. "It's fighting, trying to stay alive. But there is something else. Something that seeks to extinguish that light."

Bashkim loosened his grip on the bars and took a breath. The flame softened, returning to its original wavy state. Bashkim turned to look at the old man, but before he could speak, a loud ring from a large bell echoed throughout the castle.

"I think your friend has arrived," Ishmonyae smiled. "We are under attack. It's time for you to go, Bashkim. You have the key. Don't let something as simple as iron bars hold you back."

Bashkim grabbed the key from the floor and unlocked his cell door. He grabbed his belongings, securing them to his body as he looked back at the cells.

"Will you come with me?" Bashkim asked as he hooked the sword back to his belt.

"I would only slow you down," Ishmonyae said. "And besides, I have a role to play here. It might not look like much, but you'll just have to trust me on this one."

Bashkim held the key in his hand, watching Ishmonyae. He wanted to open the door and free the old man anyway, despite what he had told him.

This is wrong, Bashkim thought when he stepped over to Ishmonyae's cell and slid the key back to him.

The old man crawled his way over and got to his feet, using the bars to hold his frail body up. He reached an arm through and put his hand on Bashkim's shoulder.

"Remember," he said. "Your fight is not against the flesh and blood." Ishmonyae tapped his finger against Bashkim's chest over his heart. "It's against the darkness. Now. Go."

"Thank you," Bashkim said as the old man sat back down. "For telling me the truth."

Bashkim opened the exit door just enough to see out of. The hallway appeared empty and dark, for the guards had run to answer the bell's call. He could hear faint shouting in the distance as the guards bellowed their orders and mustered the rest of the soldiers. Exceptional hearing or not, Bashkim knew Rin wouldn't be able to hear him all the way down in the castle's dungeons.

I need a window.

Bashkim made his way through the halls, retracing his footsteps from being escorted by Fandul. He stepped into a large room filled with a mixture of civilians and passing soldiers. Bashkim tried to keep his head low, hoping to blend in with the panic taking place while people ran through the room to get to safety. Much to his dismay, he saw a particularly large and familiar eshan herding the civilians to safety. The giant of a man saw Bashkim, recognizing him immediately.

"Hey!" Dasc shouted, getting the attention of the other soldiers. "What are you doing here?"

Bashkim wasted no time. He waved his hand and ice came up from the ground, rooting the soldiers' feet in place.

"I'm sorry!" Bashkim shouted and ran past them before they could break free.

Bashkim ran through another series of doors and hallways, finding himself back in the throne room. Along the walls were tall, open windows. The soldiers had already started closing the bulky defense shutters to seal the openings.

"Rin!" Bashkim shouted as loud as he could. "Help! In the castle!"

The soldiers spun around at Bashkim's cry and those he had passed before were already catching up to him. He couldn't run this time. He would have to wait it out until Rin came for him. The eshan guards drew their blades and began to approach Bashkim. He held his hands up, showing he meant no harm.

"Please!" he said. "Please stay back. I don't want to hurt anyone!"

The soldiers ignored his pleas and continued to step forward. He waved his hand wide and summoned more ice around their feet. There were far too many soldiers for him to catch at once. By the time he tried to freeze the others in place, the firsts were already using their own magic to break free. Worse yet, he could hear Dasc and the guards from earlier approaching from behind.

Bashkim tried to make his way around the soldiers, getting himself closer to the center of the large room while trying to put some distance between them. The eshans started to form a circle around him, keeping their shields up high as they closed the gap. One of them made a waving motion with his hands and ice reached up from the ground and locked Bashkim's feet in place. The white dragon's voice suddenly came to Bashkim. It didn't whisper this time. It spoke loudly and clearly.

No, Bashkim thought, trying to break his feet free. *No! No! Not now!*

The voice didn't let up. Bashkim could feel the magic surging through his body and out towards his hands. Fire began to form in his palms. Panicking, Bashkim attempted to hide them.

No, no, no, Bashkim pleaded internally. *Go away!*

The fire in his hands only grew and the voice got louder. The eshans tried to disarm Bashkim by summoning ice around his hands, but the fire instantly turned it into water and steam.

"Ulsa!" the voice roared in Bashkim's head. "Zuntrineer, Mykenebres!"

"Shut up!" Bashkim shouted.

The fire in his hands erupted in size, covering half of his forearms. His body strained against the magic flowing from him, pain starting to stab his chest. The frozen bindings on his feet shattered, causing the eshans to slow their approach.

"I said shut up!" Bashkim screamed, throwing his arms out wide.

The flames flung from his hands and created a wide, burning ring of protection around him. The flames stood upright and stiff, burning brightly enough that Bashkim had to shield his eyes. The eshan soldiers jumped back, but not before the fire could catch some of them. The intense flames did more than just heat their metal exteriors. Their armor turned orange, softening and deforming from only a second of contact with the fire. The soldiers panicked and tried to throw the burning armor off their bodies. Their comrades came to their aid, summoning ice on both the burn wounds and the heated metal as Dasc practically threw them out of harm's way.

"You!" a familiar voice said from across the room.

Fandul had arrived, his eyes burning with a justified fury. He drew his sword and stepped towards Bashkim without hesitation.

"Just stay away," Bashkim pleaded, gasping for air and clutching his chest. "Nobody else has to get hurt. Just let me go."

Fandul ignored the hybrid's pleas and approached the edge of the fire. Using his foot, he slid one of the soldiers' dropped swords into the fire. The blade turned orange and melted into a puddle within seconds.

"What magic is this?" Fandul barked.

"Please," Bashkim gasped. "Just let me go."

Fandul raised his fist up, the back of his hand pointing towards Bashkim. Ice formed around his forearm and grew outwards and down towards the floor. The ice took the shape of a large tower shield wide enough to curve around Fandul's body. Once the ice touched the ground, Fandul ordered his men for backup. More ice formed on the floor, attempting to part the flames enough for Fandul to step through.

To Bashkim's disappointment, Fandul stepped forward without hesitation. The ice spread from under his feet and the frozen shield slid across the ground. Surprisingly, the flames gave off no heat themselves and instead only consumed that which they touched, including the path the soldiers tried to make. The flames were quickly closing in on him, and he struggled to keep his shield intact.

Steam rose up from the frozen shield as the flames nicked it and cracks began to form. Fandul gritted his teeth, forcing more magic out of his body and into his shield, doing everything he could to keep it solid. He made it through the burning barrier with one final step, gasping for air from the magical strain he had just endured. Keeping the shield in front of him, Fandul peered from behind it. A few steps ahead of him was Bashkim on his knees, coughing violently.

"Please don't do this," Bashkim said between breaths. "It doesn't have to be this way."

Fandul let the frozen shield fall to the ground with a crash, breaking into large pieces.

"You made it this way," he growled, keeping his sword ready.

Bashkim coughed again, blood spattering against the floor this time. Fandul couldn't help but notice the darkened color of the blood against the white stone, causing him to halt his movement forward. Before Fandul could decide what to do next, a crash filled the room as the floor beneath him shook. One of the walls burst open and dust and stone went flying across the room. The head of a dragon shot from the wreckage, roaring loudly as it spewed an icy cold wind from its mouth. The eshan soldiers held their shields up in defense, blocking both the debris and the chilling winds. Ice formed along the floor and walls, growing upwards into spikes that pointed towards the soldiers.

Fandul stepped back in panic, almost stepping right into the fire behind him as the dragon's arm reached forward. The giant scaled hand wrapped around Bashkim, grabbing him and pulling him away. Rin retreated through the newly made hole in the wall and pushed herself against the castle, launching herself as she caused more wreckage to come tumbling down.

The flames around Fandul shrank as though they were being swallowed by the floor, allowing him to move freely. The eshan soldiers hacked and burned their way through the ice blockade, approaching the massive hole in the wall with bows drawn. They summoned fire at the tips of their arrows and pulled the bowstrings taught.

"Enough!" Fandul shouted as he held his hand up to stop them. "They're leaving. Don't bother wasting the effort."

Fandul stepped over the edge of the opened wall and watched silently as the dragon flew away.

"Are we not going after them?" Dasc asked once he came to Fandul's side.

"No," Fandul sighed and sheathed his sword. "I'm not sure how far he'll even make it."

Fandul stepped over to the blood Bashkim had coughed up and kneeled for a closer inspection.

"What do you mean?" Dasc asked.

"That magic...that fire was more intense than anything I've ever seen. That puddle over there used to be a sword. No eshan I know has that level of magic. That kind of power comes at a cost."

"You think he pushed himself too far?"

"I do. Possibly enough to cost him his own life."

CHAPTER
7

Rin fled Teasvanna quickly, carrying Bashkim all the way to the forest where he had left her. She landed near the stream again, taking in a massive breath as she carefully opened her hand to let Bashkim out.

"Are you alright?" she asked.

Bashkim merely rolled out of her hand and onto the forest floor, lying on his back and looking up at the treetops.

"I think so," he said, despite the trees spinning.

Rin let out all of her air at once, the sudden gust of wind pushing many of the trees' branches back. "Good," she said, her massive chest expanding when she drew another large breath. "I take it we won't be shopping in Teasvanna anytime soon?"

"Not likely," Bashkim said, rubbing a hand through his hair, a small cough escaping him.

He tried to remember the flight back but realized that he couldn't recall anything after leaving the castle.

"Did I pass out?" Bashkim asked.

"You weren't moving much," Rin said as she moved over to the stream for a drink. "It's probably safe to assume you were asleep."

Bashkim looked over at her, still lying down as he tried to get his bearings. He felt like he had been interrupted from a deep sleep, but also like he had been running for hours. He put his hand on his chest, feeling his heartbeat.

Seems fine, he thought. *I have my breath...no blood from the cough.*

"What about you?" Bashkim asked, picking himself up to stand with a groan. "Were you hit anywhere?"

"Oh, I doubt it," Rin said, turning away slightly as she continued to drink. "They were all taken by surprise."

"Well let me look anyway."

Bashkim looked Rin over from horn to tail, making sure her prized scales remained intact. Rin groaned slightly, sitting down and crossing her hands over themselves.

"There's no need, Bashkim," she said with a small huff. "I am fine. It will take more than a few eshans to hurt me."

"You were in a pretty dangerous spot," Bashkim argued.

"As were you."

"Yeah, well...I'm a lot smaller than you. Harder to hit."

Bashkim made his way to the front of her and saw her crossed hands. "Let me see," he said, pointing at the hand on the bottom.

Rin hesitated, staring down at Bashkim.

"What?" he asked.

"When I saw you in the castle, you were surrounded by fire. Whose magic was it?"

"Mine," Bashkim said, his eyes trailing down to the forest floor. "It...it was an accident. I was trying to protect myself until you showed up. All I wanted to do was keep them away, but I might have lost some control. Why? Did I hurt you?"

"There was something different about that fire. I thought nothing of it when I first saw it, but when I reached for you..."

Rin's voice trailed off as she tried to find the words. Bashkim could feel a lump forming in his throat as he looked at the large hands in front of him.

"Let me see," he said in a whisper.

"Are you sure?"

Bashkim nodded his head, bracing himself. Rin lifted her hand, revealing the other underneath it. What were once beautiful light blue scales were now charred and deformed. Some had even melted away completely, exposing the soft tissue underneath. Bashkim's eyes widened in horror, tears welling within them.

"Rin," he said, barely audible.

"It will heal," she said calmly, "and it's not as though you did it on purpose."

"That doesn't change what happened." A tear slid down his cheek. "It doesn't change what happened the first time, and it doesn't change it this time."

"Don't go there," Rin said with sternness in her voice. "It will only make you condemn the fire inside of you."

Bashkim shut his eyes and clenched his fists, his fingers digging into his palms. He could feel the magic suddenly swelling in his body as he recalled the fire he had summoned in the castle. His teeth gritted against one another, and he shut his eyes, squeezing them tightly.

Emotions swirled inside of him without direction. He grew angry with himself for what he had done while being sad at the same time for hurting his friend. Confusion tagged along, holding hands with shame. The magic inside only grew, digging and cutting at every part of him.

"Let your fire shine, Bashkim," Rin said again, though more softly this time.

Bashkim's body started to shake.

"Bashkim!" Rin said, loud enough to make the forest creatures flee in fright.

Bashkim's eyes popped open, and he took a sudden gasp of air. His heart raced, and he could feel it pounding away inside of him. He put his hand against his chest and took long, slow breaths.

"I'm here," he finally said, tilting his head back and looking up towards the sky. "I'm here."

"Good. I went through all the trouble of bringing you here, the least you could do is stay a while."

Bashkim tried to laugh, but only a tiny snort made it out of him.

"You know," Rin said, getting herself more comfortable and laying down. "It's quite rare that one would possess enough magical strength to harm a dragon. Not that I would encourage such behavior, but to have that kind of power is quite the feat."

Bashkim removed his pack and let it slide down to the ground. "I don't know where it came from," he said, sitting down and leaning against her side. "Ever since we started this whole white dragon nonsense, things have been...different."

"How so? Your magic has always been a step above most."

"I've felt strange a lot of times. Sometimes I'll get so angry that I can't see straight. Sometimes I forget what I'm doing or where I'm going. And when that happens I can usually..."

Bashkim paused. He knew he couldn't hide it from her anymore. He had to tell her.

"I can hear it talking to me," he admitted.

"It?" Rin asked, bringing her head closer.

"The white dragon. I heard it the day we encountered it."

"Yes. You mentioned you had heard something, though my ears heard nothing."

Bashkim nodded his head. "Yeah. I was hoping I had been mistaken, but I've heard it more than once since then. I heard it both in Nennossen and Teasvanna. It feels as though the white dragon is right there."

"I promise you I am the only dragon here. What does this voice say to you?"

"I don't know," Bashkim sighed. "It speaks in a different language. One word that stuck out was Mykenebres. When I was in Nennossen, Wesley said it was an ancient word for Umbra."

"Indeed, it is," Rin said, a look of concern growing on her scaly face. "A word used sparingly, I might add. Do you recall any of the other words it spoke? Even if not in order?"

Bashkim scratched his head. "Maybe? In the castle it said...sun. Soon? Soon tree?...maybe. It's hard to understand."

"Zuntrineer?"

"Yes. That. It said 'Zuntrineer, Mykenebres'. Do you understand it?"

Rin lifted her head, pulling it back. "Loosely, it means 'the power of'."

"Oh," Bashkim said, his voice trailing off. ". . .oh."

The two sat in silence, unsure of what to make of the new information. Bashkim moved his mouth to speak several times but failed to find his words with each attempt. He drew a breath in and lifted his hand as though he had finally found it, only to remain silent.

"If those are the words you hear," Rin said while Bashkim's struggle continued. "Perhaps it is not dragon slaying knights you are in need of, but a priest."

Bashkim rubbed his hand against his face.

"What else happened since the day we met the white dragon?" Rin asked.

"Today it was the magic. There was so much of it. It felt like I couldn't hold it in. It *hurt* to hold it in. I had to let it out, and when I did...well, you saw it."

"The fire?"

Bashkim nodded. "Yeah. That."

"I've never seen fire burn that hot before," Rin said. "Not unless it's a dragon's fire. Is it possible that it came from whatever it is that speaks in your mind? Perhaps it is manipulating your magic as well as your thoughts."

"It came from me. I felt every bit of it. Felt like my chest had been cut open."

"Was that the only time this has happened?"

"I felt it earlier too, just a moment ago when I saw your hand."

"But nothing came out," Rin said. "So you *can* contain it."

"*That* time I could. Who knows about next one."

Bashkim sighed and looked over at Rin. "We need to do something about that wound."

"Do you have bandages large enough for dragons in that pack of yours?"

"No," Bashkim said, getting to his feet. "But we're next to a stream and surrounded by plants and trees. Surely we can get it cleaned and covered."

"My hero," Rin said, rolling over onto her side.

Bashkim ignored the comment and started collecting a series of large leaves from the trees as well as the thinnest twigs he could find. The twigs were broken down into thinner strips and braided together, creating a small makeshift rope. Rin blew some of her icy breath over her wound in an attempt to cool the burns while she watched him work. Once he felt he had enough rope and leaves, Bashkim told Rin to dip the wound in the stream to remove any castle debris. She stuck her hand in the water, wincing slightly as it touched the burned skin.

"I was doing fine," Rin whined.

"Maybe, but it'll be worse tomorrow if we don't do something about it."

Thanks to her massive size, Rin easily split open some trees so that Bashkim could extract their sap. Bashkim used the sticky substance to cover the entire area of her wound, causing her to wince even more. Bashkim started to make a joke about her size and being such a wimp but one look at the burn only filled him with guilt. Instead, he kept quiet and used more of the sap to stick the leaves to her hand. He then used the makeshift rope to secure the many leaves in place.

"It's not much," he said, tying off the last knot. "But it'll have to do. It's better than nothing."

"I feel better already," Rin said, curling up and laying back down. "Now, tell me what all happened in Teasvanna and how you managed to get arrested *again*."

"I didn't do anything wrong," Bashkim said while rolling out his bed. "I presented Simon's letter and was honest about why I was there. They didn't like it and hauled me away. It's not like I make a habit out of getting arrested."

"So you *did* get arrested!"

"Yeah, you just…" Bashkim's voice trailed off when he realized what Rin had done to him.

A large grin stretched from one side to the other of Rin's scaled snout as her chin rested on the ground.

"Clever girl," Bashkim said, reaching into his pack for a late-night snack.

Rin's tail almost began to wag. "Now that we have *that* sorted, what did you learn while you were there?"

"Quite a few things, honestly," he said, taking a bite out of his food. "How surprised would you be if I told you the king wasn't very helpful?"

"Not very."

"Yeah. Me neither."

Bashkim paused for a moment, remembering Orenzen's parting words. A small shiver ran through his body as he tried to flush the thoughts out.

Old fool, he told himself, then sighed before continuing his story. "But there is some good news. I met somebody else there. He seemed to know quite a bit about what we've been looking for."

"Oh?" Rin asked, sliding her head closer. "Do you think you can trust him?"

"Considering they had him locked up like me, probably. Seems to be what happens to people in the know."

"And what did he tell you?"

"A lot. Turns out a few details were conveniently left out when I spoke with Omar and the others."

"Do you think Simon knows?" Rin asked, her head tilting slightly as she eyed Bashkim.

Bashkim paused, considering the question carefully before answering. "No. I'm inclined to think Omar has him in the dark too. Who knows? Maybe he has *everyone* in the dark."

Bashkim stopped chewing his food and his eyes trailed off into the distance, staring emptily.

"Can you imagine?" Bashkim asked, still staring into nothing. "Lying to an entire city that you rule?"

"What do you mean?"

"Kesshonite," Bashkim muttered, only half answering her question. "And magic."

"What are you talking about?"

Bashkim didn't answer. Instead his eyes remained locked, looking down into the forest as if something were there. His mouth moved slowly, trying to form words, but sounds failed to come out.

"Bashkim?" Rin asked.

"Liars," he said quietly in a bored tone. "All of them. Just a bunch of liars. All they do is lie, lie, lie."

Bashkim casually reached his hand out and made a small fire pop into existence next to him. Rin flinched and jerked her head back, looking at both Bashkim and the stiff flame. Bashkim's eyes refused to move and continued to stare into the darkness of the forest.

"Bashkim!" Rin said again, with enough resonance to rattle Bashkim's bones.

Bashkim jumped slightly, his fire instantly vanishing but not before he could catch a glimpse of it. He stared at the ground in disbelief.

"Was that you?" Rin asked. "Or something else?"

Bashkim laid down on his bedroll, rubbing his hands over his face. "I don't know anymore."

"Let's go to bed," Rin said, using the tip of her claw to dig a small hole near Bashkim. "We can talk in the morning."

Rin grabbed some branches and crushed them in her hands, shoving them down into the hole she had just made. With a small breath of fire, she set the broken branches ablaze. Bashkim only laid there, watching while the flames consumed the fuel.

Is it me? he wondered.

Morning came the next day the same way it always had before. The sun rose and woke the two, causing them both to stretch and yawn. Bashkim stood up and groaned once he saw his pack on the ground.

"Damn it," he muttered.

He had forgotten to secure his things before falling asleep, and at some point in the night the local wildlife had taken the rest of his food. A squirrel darted out of his pack as he grabbed it, leaving behind crumbs and a few other "presents". Bashkim growled under his breath, letting the pack fall back to the ground. He had been careless, and because of it, he had no food.

Not how I wanted to start my day.

Bashkim felt something brewing inside of him when he looked down at the backpack. The magic in his body started to swirl and worm through his body, trying to escape.

Bashkim took a slow breath and forced the magic back down. *No. It's just food. I can get some more.*

Bashkim quietly stepped over to the stream and looked down into the water. He could see a few fish swimming around, all of them plenty big enough for a morning meal.

One of those will do just fine.

As a single fish swam a little too close to the edge of the bank, Bashkim quickly lifted his hand up. A small spike of ice shot upwards from within the bottom of the stream, skewering the fish and raising it above the water. Bashkim removed the fish from the frozen spike and glanced over at the remnants of the campfire. He could bring the fire back to life with a simple flick of his wrist, but considering the events of the previous night, he decided not to. Instead, he laid the fish down on a nearby rock large enough to hold it.

"Hey, Rin," Bashkim said, causing his large companion to roll over.

"Yes?" she asked, not bothering to lift her head from the ground.

"I bet you can't cook this fish without burning it."

Rin narrowed her eyes and considered the challenge. "How much?"

"Well, I don't exactly have much on me at the moment, but I tell you what. First gem I find is yours."

Rin shook her head and got up to her feet. "Gambling away what you don't even have."

Rin stepped up to the fish and lowered her head to get closer. "The first gem you find?" she asked.

Bashkim nodded. "It'll be yours."

"You have yourself a bet."

Rin drew in a small breath and exhaled slowly. A thin stream of fire came from the tip of her mouth. She blew the flames down to the base of the rock, causing the entire stone to heat up. The fish began to sizzle as the surface it laid on grew hotter, for not even a solid stone could resist the dragon's fire. Rin pulled her head back, looking down at her work with a grin. The fire continued to burn, but it refrained from spreading into the rest of the forest.

"I want the first *green* gem you find," she said.

"Why green?"

"Because you owe me one, *green eyes*," Rin said in mocking tone.

"How'd you know that's the one I gave her?"

"Oh, dear Bashkim," Rin chuckled. "I know *exactly* how many coins and jewels are in my bag. Should one go missing, I will know."

Bashkim shook his head.

"Now," Rin said, lying back down. "Where are we off to next?"

Bashkim took his sword out and used it to flip the fish over. "Back to Nennossen. I think I learned a little more than Omar intended while I was in Teasvanna."

CHAPTER 8

Bashkim returned to Nennossen's front door two days later and told the guards that he wished to speak with Simon. The guards instructed him to wait outside while sending another soldier to fetch the captain. Bashkim agreed to wait and stepped out of the way so that other travelers may pass unbothered and go through their inspections before entering.

Bashkim sighed and brushed his hair out of his face and over the bandage. Hiding normally didn't bother him so much, but the past few days had worn him thin. He had told Fandul no more hiding, but here he stood, hiding behand a faux bandage once more.

I should take it off. Just march through the city for all to see.

His lips formed a small grin when he imagined the stupid look on Omar's face if he were to do such a thing.

Nah. Simon doesn't deserve that.

Simon had already stuck his neck out for him and kept him safe. Keeping the bandage on for his sake only seemed fair. As the thoughts continued to float around in Bashkim's mind, Simon arrived at the door. The captain smiled once he saw his visitor.

"You've returned!" he said heartily. "Either you've changed your mind or that's one hell of a steed you've got."

"I went," Bashkim said. "My method of transportation is a bit faster than horses."

"I'll say. Did you learn anything in Teasvanna? Were the eshans willing to assist?"

"I learned quite a bit, but getting any help from them was...less fruitful."

Simon shook his head. "That's a shame. Though I'd be a liar if I said I was surprised. Disappointed, sure, but not surprised. Come then. I imagine you have news that needs to be shared with the king?"

"I do," Bashkim answered, motioning with his hand for Simon to proceed. "Please. Lead the way."

Simon took Bashkim through the main gate and escorted him through the city's streets. As they walked, Bashkim couldn't help but notice something troubling the captain. Simon had clearly shown his excitement for Bashkim's return, but he kept silent as they hurriedly made their way to the castle.

"Is there something wrong?" Bashkim asked.

"Yes," Simon answered plainly, then pulled Bashkim to the side once they passed the busier sections of the city. "Your white dragon has been spotted."

"Where?" Bashkim gasped.

"To the west of Nennossen. One of our patrols found it—" Simon turned his head before finishing.

"They didn't make it, did they?" Bashkim asked.

"Only one. He just made it back yesterday. Poor kid is still shaken up about the whole thing."

"I can understand why."

"There's something that doesn't make sense though. Those that weren't devoured started attacking one another."

"Your soldiers were fighting themselves?"

"According to him, yes. Does that at all sound like something this dragon would do?"

Bashkim paused. The white dragon tormented his mind since he met the damned thing, but to draw a sword against his own brothers in arms?

I've been angry, he admitted to himself. *But to kill my own? I don't think I could go that far.*

"I'm not sure," Bashkim said. "But we also don't know everything this dragon is capable of, so anything is possible."

"That's what scares me," Simon sighed. "Come on. Let's go talk with the king. The sooner we can deal with these things, the better."

"Wait," Bashkim said, grabbing Simon by the arm to keep him from leaving.

"Yes?" Simon asked.

Bashkim hesitated before speaking. He had to choose his words carefully. "Do you trust Omar?"

"What do you mean?" Simon asked, slightly taken off guard by the question. "It would be rather difficult to serve someone you did not trust."

"I get that, but does he have *all* your trust? Do you think he tells you everything?"

"I might be the captain of the guard, but at the end of the day I am still just a soldier. It isn't my place to know everything, just that which I need to know. The king is the one who rules this city, not I. He will tell me what he sees fit to tell me."

"And if he had something this entire time that could have been helping us? If he had been lying to you? To everyone?"

Simon leaned in closer, speaking in a lower voice. "I'm not sure what you learned over there, or what you think you've learned, but it sounds as though you aim to make a villain out of my king. Last time you were here you struggled to hold your tongue. While I can understand your frustration, do know that not everyone will take to it as kindly as I have. Now, can I trust you to behave in the king's presence? Or should I merely relay a message for you?"

"You can trust me," Bashkim said.

"Good," Simon smiled. "I had a feeling I could."

Simon escorted Bashkim into the castle and took him straight to the throne room. There they saw Omar sitting in a large chair, dealing with the citizens of Nennossen that had requested an audience with him. One by one they stepped forward with their questions and concerns, and one by one Omar dealt with them.

The king took notice of Simon and Bashkim and motioned them to come forward ahead of the others. Simon nodded towards the throne, signaling Bashkim to follow him. Bashkim followed behind Simon and made his way up the few steps towards the king in his royal chair.

"Back so soon?" Omar asked quietly once they stood next to him.

"Yes," Bashkim nodded. "I'm a fast traveler."

"And here I thought maybe you had given up. Now tell me, boy, did you learn anything of importance from those devil worshipers?"

Simon let out a small cough to get Bashkim's attention. The captain's eyes locked onto him, silently telling Bashkim to hold his tongue. Bashkim ignored the glare and instead focused on something else in the room.

There it is again, Bashkim thought. *That feeling. If what Ishmonyae said is true, then...*

Bashkim's skin began to crawl as he considered the possibility. Had it really been in front of him this entire time? His eyes trailed down to the small dagger hanging from the king's hip. He could hear the white dragon speaking to him.

"Krist desser," it said.

Bashkim's fingers began to jump back and forth. He could feel the magic building inside of him. It grew at a rate that he struggled to control.

Omar lied to me.

"They will not help us," Bashkim said quietly, trying to hide his internal struggle.

"I thought so," Omar huffed. "It would be of no surprise to me if they helped bring those creatures back. But enough of the obvious. Did you learn anything else of use?"

"Krisssssst," the voice in his mind hissed.

Bashkim felt his eye twitch. "Yes, I believe so. But this might not be the best place. Can we talk somewhere else?"

"I agree," Simon said. "Your majesty, we'll wait for you in the side room to finish addressing your people."

"Very well," Omar said, waving them away.

Simon and Bashkim bowed and left. As they reached the steps to go down, the magic in Bashkim intensified to what seemed ten times over. Time itself slowed to a crawl, and what felt like knives sliding across his skin spanned across his entire body. The magic had become too much, and that feeling coming from Omar still taunted him.

I can't hold this in, Bashkim thought, then saw the frosty air forming on the floor around his feet. *I don't want to hold this in.*

As Simon took his first step down, Bashkim shoved him from behind. The sudden force threw Simon forward and sent him tumbling down to the ground. Bashkim spun around to face Omar and raised his arms high. Large icicles sprung up from the ground, twisting and writhing like vines as they wrapped around one another to form a barricade that separated Bashkim and Omar from the rest of the room.

More of the frozen vines rose from the ground, this time around Omar's chair. They moved with a life of their own. Their sharpened points reached towards Omar and trapped him in place. Omar pushed himself back into his chair, trying to create as much distance as possible between him and the frozen spears.

"What is the meaning of this?" Omar bellowed once the ice froze in place.

"Krist desser," the white dragon said again, laughing.

"You lied to me!" Bashkim yelled, trying to drown out the voice and ignore the pain in his body. "You knew about the kesshonite!"

"It was of no concern to you!"

Bashkim felt like one of his own frozen spikes had pierced his body, causing him to cough.

"No concern?" Bashkim asked, wiping the spit from his mouth, not believing what he had just heard.

Simon had already gotten back to his feet and joined his men in trying to hack away at the frozen barrier between them and Bashkim. However, as they chipped away the ice, the frozen vines only thickened and wove themselves tighter together.

Bashkim ripped the bandage off his head and pointed to his eshan ear, hunching over and clutching his chest as he gasped for air.

"Look at me!" he said between breaths. "I come to you with news of white dragons returning, a threat that you are *clearly* aware of. I risked my neck to help you. Me. A hybrid! Helping *you* of all people! And you have the *audacity* to sit there and tell me that the very thing that was used to destroy white dragons is of no concern to me?"

Simon stopped trying to break the frozen barrier and held his hand out to the side, ordering his soldiers to halt.

"There's a power that can save people," Bashkim continued. "And where is it? Do you keep it hidden all to yourself? Because that's the real threat for you, isn't it? It's not white dragons. It's losing control of your power. I can only imagine how much easier it is to control something when nobody even knows it exists."

"We have no kesshonite here," Omar argued. "The eshans took everything back with them when they left. They have it all!"

Bashkim took in a long, slow breath through his nose as he straightened his posture and stood up properly. He rolled his shoulders and stretched his neck. Several pops and cracks could be heard as he moved. His eyes fell upon the dagger on Omar's belt. Bashkim stood almost as still as the frozen barricade, and a small smile started to form on his face.

"They missed one," Bashkim said softly. "Didn't they?"

Omar remained silent and locked his eyes with Bashkim. Simon held his breath as he watched, as did the other soldiers. They looked back and forth between one another, waiting for their captain to give an order. Simon stood quietly and watched with narrowed eyes for Bashkim and Omar to make a move.

Omar suddenly reached for the dagger at his hip, but one of the many ice vines surrounding him instantly came to life. It snapped out of its frozen state and shot towards Omar. The sharpened point went straight into Omar's palm and out through the back of his hand, pushing it away from the dagger and holding it in place while he screamed in pain.

"You almost had me fooled," Bashkim said as he stepped forward.

The other frozen vines surrounding Omar came to life as Bashkim approached, curling out of the way as he reached forward to pull the dagger from Omar's belt.

"I sensed it the first time we met," Bashkim continued. "But I just couldn't quite place what it was. But now...now that I know what really happened so many years ago, I can sniff you out just like the eshans can me."

"I have no idea what you're on about," Omar snarled.

Bashkim took a few steps back and let another frozen vine slowly grow forward, its point barely touching Omar's neck.

"Simon," Bashkim said calmly, but loud enough to be heard. "I'm going to break these walls. I need you and your men to stand down. You said you trusted me, right?"

"I did," Simon said. "But that was when you were willing to help us and not holding the king hostage."

"I have no plans to kill him. I wouldn't dare deprive his people that pleasure. However, should you try anything, I'll make sure his body hits the ground before mine."

The frozen vines surrounding Omar curled back towards him, each and every one of them ready to strike. Simon looked at Bashkim through the small gaps between the frozen vines, sighing in defeat.

"Stand down, men," Simon said quietly.

The soldiers looked at Simon, unsure of what to do.

"I said stand down!" Simon repeated more loudly and with a growl in his voice.

The soldiers sheathed their weapons and stepped away from the ice.

"You have what you asked for," Simon said. "Now please, let the king go."

Several of the icy vines in front of Simon suddenly cracked. Simon jerked back in shock, and the cracked vines crumbled into pieces.

"You can have him," Bashkim said, motioning to Omar with his hand. "But he has something to show you first."

"What does he mean?" Simon asked, looking at Omar.

"This man has lost his mind!" Omar growled. "Strike him down!"

The soldiers hovered their hands over the handles of their weapons, but Simon made sure they all remained in their sheaths.

"I'm inclined to agree," Simon said, giving Bashkim a stern look. "But at the same time, I cannot, and will not, deny the words I heard you speak."

"You will do as I say and strike this man down!" Omar yelled, making sure to hold still. "Do not forget who you serve, Captain."

"I know who I serve," Simon said loudly, his voice completely overpowering Omar's and echoing through the throne room. "It is the city and its people, and if you're putting them in harm's way by denying them a power to save themselves, then it is *you* who I must protect these people from."

"You will hang for this," Omar said.

"And I'll die a soldier loyal to his people. Bashkim, if you have a point to make, the sooner you make it, the better."

"Magic," Bashkim said, turning his eyes back to Omar. "It's *in* you."

"Preposterous!" Omar blurted.

Bashkim narrowed his eyes, and the frozen tip against Omar's throat quickly pricked him, drawing a small amount of blood.

"You're not exactly in a position to argue," Bashkim said.

"You'll never make it out of here alive," Omar said through gritted teeth.

"I think that decision belongs to Simon. Now. Show them."

Omar snarled at Bashkim and gritted his teeth. Bashkim grew impatient and forced the ice impaling Omar's hand to quickly retract.

"Today," Bashkim said over Omar's whimper.

The frozen vines pointing towards Omar curled back to give him space. Omar reluctantly held his unwounded hand out, and to the amazement of everyone in the room, a small flame appeared on his palm.

"You can do better than that," Bashkim said.

With a small grunt, the flame in Omar's hand doubled in size.

"You see?" Bashkim asked loudly, motioning towards Omar. "Eshans aren't the only ones that can use magic. It's not witchcraft. It's a gift that your king would rather you not know you can have!"

Simon slowly stepped up to them, staring at the flame in Omar's hand. Lips quivering, he struggled with the reality that stood before him.

"Is that your fire?" he asked.

"It is," Omar answered.

Simon closed his eyes and a tear slid down his cheek.

"Put that magic away," Simon said quietly in such a way that caused both Bashkim and Omar to obey.

The fire vanished and the many frozen vines quickly retreated into the ground, leaving puddles of water behind. Simon stepped closer to Omar, towering over the old man in the chair and looking down at what he had once called his king.

"Magic was forbidden by your decree," Simon said, leaning in closely so that Omar wouldn't miss a word. "If anyone tried to practice it, if anyone tried to study it, if anybody simply had the idea of it, they were to be taken away. By your word was this law made, and by my hand was it carried out. I've taken mothers and fathers both from their children, and not even the young were safe from your law. By your word, and by my hand, some of them were even put to death."

Bashkim couldn't help but notice Simon's hand clutching the handle of his sword as if he planned to draw it.

"And here you are," Simon continued. "Practicing that which you have condemned and ordered me to purge from your city."

"I am your king," Omar said through a thick lump in his throat as he held his bleeding hand. "You will do what I say. I have my reasons for my actions."

"If I were to continue following your orders as the loyal soldier I am, then I would remove the heresy that sits before me."

"Guards!" Omar shouted. "Take Simon and this immundrid away immediately!"

The guards didn't move. Instead, they looked at one another, waiting to see if anyone else would take the first step forward. One by one they turned to Simon and stood at attention.

"You might be the king," Simon said, taking a step back and standing up straight. "But I'm still captain of the guard."

Omar deflated and sank back into his seat. The look on his face showed that he finally realized he had lost any and all control of the situation. His power had been taken.

"Take him away," Simon said, motioning his men forward with his hand. "Treat his wound and chain him up in the darkest cell you can find. Release the innocent and bring them here. I will speak with them in a moment."

"Yes, sir," the guards said, grabbing Omar and hauling him away.

Bashkim watched the soldiers take the royal figure away. The old man squirmed and cursed the entire way, refusing to accept reality as he bled all over his coat. Simon remained still, staring at the empty chair that once held a king.

"Was this confrontation the only reason you returned?" Simon asked after a while.

"No," Bashkim answered. "I honestly did learn a lot about our white dragon issue."

"Then come with me. Tell me the entire story so that I might be able to save what's left of this city before it's too late."

Bashkim and Simon left the throne and made their way to a side room. Inside stood a rectangular table with an odd number of chairs and some cabinets filled with an overflow of dishes from the castle's kitchen. Simon motioned for Bashkim to take a seat and inform him of the events that had taken place in Teasvanna. Bashkim did just so, and Simon got to hear the story in full, complete with Rin's participation.

"So that's how you made it there and back so fast," Simon said, rubbing a hand over his hair. "Amazing."

"It's doubtful I would have made it out alive without her," Bashkim said.

"Indeed. She's a great companion to have. But still, everything you have learned came from a prisoner. Are you sure that's reliable?"

"There's a king in your own prison, is there not?"

Simon nodded. "I suppose there is, and clearly your man was right. I can't help but wonder if the soldiers that locked him away knew what they were doing."

Simon stared at Omar's dagger that rested on the table between him and Bashkim.

"Perhaps we aren't so different after all," he said distantly. "I suppose there's some solace to be found in the fact that despite our differences, we can find common ground in our faults."

Bashkim didn't respond. Instead, he watched Simon, whose eyes remained focused on the dagger.

"Something wrong?" Bashkim asked.

"I'm scared of it," Simon admitted. "If what you say is true, that little dagger can kill a dragon. All because of that kesshonite jewel."

Both of them looked down at the dagger, waiting as if they expected something to happen.

"All these years," Simon finally said after a while. "Omar had this power hanging from his hip and not a single one of us knew. I had my own suspicions of the king...of Omar...and those suspicions only increased tenfold after your first visit, but never did I expect *this*. As glad as I am to have him exposed, what you did was reckless. Gambling with your life is your own business, but you cross the line when you start gambling with somebody else's."

Bashkim held his tongue. Part of him wanted to apologize, but another part of him failed to feel even remotely sorry for what he had done. That same part felt almost proud of what it had accomplished with Omar.

I'm no child to be scolded at, Bashkim thought. *I knew what I was doing. Omar was a terrible person and will finally get what he deserves.*

Just the thought of Omar's lies got him worked up. His heart began to beat heavily, and he could feel it thumping against his chest. The sudden shift gave him pause. He started to question himself and his mental state at the time.

I was in control...right? Bashkim wondered, remembering the white dragon spoke to him during the confrontation.

He recalled the feelings that flowed through him when he approached Omar, as well as the pain that had rippled through his body when using his magic.

Just like in Teasvanna. But I was in control this time...yeah. I was in control. There was no fire this time.

He reassured himself repeatedly. He knew Omar had lied to him, and he knew the scurvy old fool needed exposed. Why not? Simon had even told him that being a loyal soldier limited him. He said he lacked the freedom that Bashkim had and that he should take advantage of it.

And I did. The city is better off for it. What I did here was a good thing.

"I'm sorry," Bashkim said, only half meaning it.

"I reckon it doesn't matter much anymore," Simon sighed. "What's done is done. But do know that you've put me in a very difficult situation."

"Omar has been exposed. Surely that will lead to a better future, right?"

"Eventually, yes. But what about right now? There were more than enough witnesses there, so there's no denying what took place. By the laws Omar made himself he would hang for what he's done. But, if humans really can use magic and we don't want to discourage them from it, then hanging Omar for that very reason wouldn't be in our best interest, would it?"

"Then let him hang for his treachery to Nennossen. He's been putting the entire city in danger for his own gain."

"If only it were that simple. He has family that will defend him, as well as family that would encourage such a hanging so that they might acquire the throne for themselves. As I've said, you've put me in a difficult position. To make matters worse, not only do we have no king at the moment, but we also have a white dragon problem to deal with. Not to mention a certain wizard that's escaped. Two more issues that the citizens of Nennossen aren't even aware exists."

"Then you lead Nennossen," Bashkim said.

"Excuse me?"

"You lead the people. Be the leader this city needs. You're aware of the dangers out there, and it's clear you care about these people."

"It doesn't work that way. Kingship falls on the royal bloodline. Not to mention you can't just arrest a king and assume authority yourself. I'm just a soldier, and one that will probably hang when this is all said and done."

"You honestly think they'll come for you? Omar was a fraud. Surely the people can see that."

"Sometimes it doesn't matter what the people see," Simon said. "But even if it ends for me, I've made my peace."

"Your soldiers still follow you. Why not keep yourself in charge until the white dragon situation is dealt with?"

"A coup?"

"Call it what you will."

Simon crossed his arms and leaned back into his chair. "I think you've done enough for Nennossen for one day. Now tell me what *you* plan to do next."

"I need to talk to that lady I told you about. Treydola."

"You're going back? After what you did in your last visit, a visit that I requested by the way and signed off on, I can't imagine that's going to end well for you."

"I'm not going inside the city," Bashkim said. "I'll have to get her to meet me somewhere else. I'm certain she put me in that cell with Ishmonyae for a reason. Convincing her to meet shouldn't be hard. Getting the message *to* her...that's going to be the trick."

"How are you going to manage that?"

"I'm going to need that dagger," Bashkim said, pointing to the weapon on the table.

Simon looked down at the dagger. It remained sitting between them, undisturbed.

"Humans can't stop it," Simon said. "And eshans can't unleash it. So where does that leave hybrids?"

"The old man didn't say."

"Are you sure you want to take that chance?"

Bashkim paused for a moment, staring at the weapon. It had only the one jewel imbedded into the bottom of the handle. Other than that, it seemed nothing more than an ordinary dagger save for the overly ornate scabbard it rested in. Yet at the same time, he could feel the power radiating from it. It felt like an eshan stood next to him, full of magic and ready to burst at any moment.

"Do you?" Bashkim asked.

"Honestly, I want nothing to do with that thing. Arbiters only know what it's capable of."

"Then I'll take it," Bashkim said. He reached for the dagger, but Simon held his hand out and made him stop.

Bashkim waited for Simon to speak, but the captain said nothing. His hand remained out, and his eyes continued to focus on the blade.

"Be careful," Simon finally said, taking his hand back. "If I'm still alive, Arbiters willing, I will eagerly await your return."

CHAPTER 9

Bashkim got up from his chair and reached for the dagger. He paused and silently questioned whether or not he should lay a hand on it. Due to all the adrenaline from the confrontation with the king, he didn't really remember holding it before. Now that things had calmed down, he had the opportunity to stop and consider the danger.

It's just a dagger, he tried to tell himself. *But I can feel something coming from it. Something...similar to magic, but much stronger.*

"Everything okay?" Simon asked, seeing the hesitation as he got out of his own chair.

"Yeah," Bashkim said, taking the dagger and quickly putting it in his backpack. "It's just a bit strange."

"Even for a magic user like yourself?"

"I might know a thing or two about magic, but kesshonite is just as much a mystery to me as it is you."

"About that," Simon said, a small frown on his face. "The magic, that is, not the kesshonite. I was wondering if I could ask a favor of you."

"What is it?"

Simon motioned with his head towards the door at the end of the room. "Just on the other side of that wall is a group of people waiting for an explanation. People that my men have arrested. People that *I* have arrested. We have labeled them "magic offenders", and now I am to set them free. I would like to give them a proper explanation, but I'm afraid I know nothing of magic."

"You want me to talk to them?"

"No," Simon answered quickly, a small grin on his face. "I've a feeling you'd rather chase dragons than suffer that fate. I will talk to them, but any knowledge you can give, or assistance, would be of great help."

"What would you like to know?"

Simon ran a hand over his hair, scratching his head. He stood silent for a moment, unsure of what to even ask.

"I don't even know where to begin," he said with shrugged shoulders. "How does it work, I guess?"

"With practice. You're not born knowing how to use it, or at least I wasn't. If you don't know what you're doing..."

Bashkim's voice trailed off for a moment. "Well. Bad things can happen."

The pause in Bashkim's answer didn't go unnoticed, but Simon chose to ignore it. "Is the training difficult?"

"Are you considering giving it a try?"

"No, no," Simon said, holding his hands up. "I've nothing against those who want to, but I don't think it's for me."

Bashkim smirked. "I'm not the best to ask about training since I didn't have anyone to teach me. I had to learn on my own. It was a struggle, but with practice and a hard enough head, one can make their way through."

Bashkim reached his hand out and hovered it just above the table. A cold fog formed beneath his palm, and a small block of ice rose from the wooden surface.

"Summoning the magic is the easy part," Bashkim said, sliding the ice down towards Simon. "Controlling it is what's difficult."

Which is not what I did earlier, he reminded himself.

Simon grabbed the ice and held it in his hands, rubbing his thumbs across its surface. "Strange," he said. "It's the first time I've seen magic up close. Or at least when not being in danger."

Simon's eyes trailed off as he stared into the ice slowly melting in his hands. "It feels real."

"It is real," Bashkim reassured. "It's just ice brought into existence with magic."

"How does one summon something out of nothing?" Simon asked, placing the ice block back on the table.

"I wouldn't call it nothing. It comes at a price."

"How so?"

"Using magic puts a strain on the body, much like doing something physical, and everyone has their limits. Similar to one's own strength, some people just naturally have more than others, while some have to work to grow that limit. Use too much magic and you can really hurt yourself. Enough to even kill you."

"I had no idea magic was so taxing."

"It's not if used within reason. A little magic practice can even feel refreshing."

But not what I did. What I did earlier should have killed me.

Bashkim paused, considering just how far he *had* pushed himself. *How did I survive that?* he wondered. *Even in Teasvanna I got away clean. No sign of permanent damage even if it did hurt like hell. But still...I should be dead, or at the very least, severely wounded.*

Simon put a finger against the ice and gave it a gentle push, watching it slide across the table. "I bet you can make a nice cold beverage with magic."

Bashkim tried to chuckle. "It definitely has its advantages when it comes to food and drink."

"Honestly," Simon sighed. "I'd love to see that kind of thing in Nennossen."

Simon held his left arm out and began to undo the straps on his gauntlet, removing it and setting it on the table. He rolled his sleeve back until it scrunched up against the next piece of armor on his arm. A lengthy scar could be seen that covered most of the higher end of his forearm.

"That's left over from a burn," Simon said. "Got it from an eshan's magic. Damned fool couldn't have been more than twenty."

"What happened?"

"We were patrolling the border," Simon said as he slid his sleeve back down. "Came across an eshan patrol, which wasn't unusual. One of them was young and hot headed. Tried to start a fight. One thing led to another."

Simon stopped talking and focused on strapping his gauntlet back on.

"It was a long time ago," he finally said. "But I'll not soon forget how it felt. From what I've seen, magic can be a bit wild and hard to control, even for an eshan."

But what are a hybrid's limits? Bashkim wondered. *I had no teacher, no guidance. By all means, earlier should have killed me.*

Bashkim started to consider that maybe he had more power than he gave himself credit for. Why shouldn't he have more power? He had been adventuring for most of his life. He had faced danger countless times and used his magic to save himself frequently. What better teacher than experience itself?

Maybe I've reached new levels. Maybe I've achieved new heights that others merely wish they could achieve. Or maybe...maybe I've stepped up to Telanos's level.

It shouldn't be impossible. If an eshan could reach such magical power, why couldn't a hybrid? Maybe a hybrid could even handle kesshonite? It required both humans and eshans to handle safely, so why not?

I'm both human and eshan. Maybe I have the ability to handle it on my own.

Bashkim nearly forgot about the conversation currently taking place with Simon and rested his hand on his backpack.

If I can use this level of magic and survive, then I can handle the kesshonite for sure.

Just the idea of hybrids wielding the kesshonite when humans and eshans couldn't almost put a smile on his face.

What are you doing?

Bashkim snapped back to reality, realizing that his hand had moved itself closer to his pack for the dagger.

You're losing control. Remember what happened at Teasvanna with Rin?

Bashkim pulled his hand back, almost shaking as the memory came back to him.

Is that you, white dragon? What have you done to me?

Bashkim rubbed a hand down his face. "Yeah. Emotions definitely play a part with magic. You have to be careful, else you'll hurt yourself...or others."

"And humans don't have magic on their own?" Simon asked. "Unless they're exposed to kesshonite?"

"That's what the old man said."

"Don't guess he gave you instructions."

"Sadly, no."

Simon nodded his head a few times, twisting his lips as he weighed the situation. "I'm not exactly eager to hand them all magic. It's a recipe for disaster."

An irritated sigh left Simon. He tapped his knuckles against the table. "Starting to feel like there's no winning this, Bashkim."

"What do you mean?"

"I have a room full of released prisoners that risked their lives trying to get their hands on magic, and I have the key to it right in front of me. If I give them the magic, they'll probably burn the city down, either by accident or out of rebellion. On the other hand, if I *don't* give them their magic, then am I any better than Omar?"

"Omar was lying to them and hoarding the magic for himself. You are not."

"I know. But it doesn't make it feel any better. Arbiters only know what kind of effect this ripple will have on the city."

"You think there will be an uprising?"

"Hard to say," Simon admitted. "There's enough people in the city that don't care about magic nor want anything to do with it. Enough to tip the scales in my favor, anyway. However, an entire city finding out their king was putting them all in danger...that's something they can all rally behind despite their moral differences."

"Is that something you can handle?"

Simon chuckled. "Bashkim, with all this talk about magic and kesshonite, an angry mob trying to tear the city down is the *only* thing I have enough confidence to handle."

Bashkim stood at a loss for words. The weight of the situation finally hit him as he fully realized the position he had put Simon in.

Maybe I was the fool after all.

"Something wrong?" Simon asked once he saw Bashkim's hesitation to speak.

"What are you going to tell them?"

"Everything."

"Even the kesshonite that I'm taking with me?"

"Do you think I shouldn't?"

Bashkim paused again, trying to choose his words carefully and avoid more damage.

"I'm surprised you're even considering telling them otherwise," Simon said before Bashkim could piece together an answer.

"I don't *want* to lie to them, or hide anything, but you've got me thinking about the city and everything else."

"Quite the burden, isn't it?"

Bashkim could feel himself deflate and let his head drop.

"The prisoners have been released," Simon explained once he saw the defeat in Bashkim. "First, I have to explain why, and the answer is because they were locked away for unjustified reasons. That reason being Omar said magic was outlawed despite there being no threat of them ever having any magic. Then I have to explain *why* there is no threat of them having magic, which is the kesshonite Omar kept hidden. But if they learn that, then I have to tell them they can't have it, and they can't have it because you're taking it with you, and you're taking it with you because we have a white dragon issue."

"What are the odds of the prisoners keeping all this to themselves for the time being?"

"Low."

What have I done?

"I'm sorry," Bashkim muttered. "I didn't mean for all this to happen."

"That's what happens when you act without thinking, but what's done is done. And who knows, maybe we can turn this whole thing around in our favor before you turn *all* my hairs grey."

Bashkim nodded his head, unsure what to say.

"If you want to make up for it, you can help me address these people. I'll do most of the talking, but I would greatly appreciate it if you were by my side to help with any questions they may have about magic."

"I can do that."

"Good. Then let us go speak with them."

Simon opened the door and led Bashkim back into the large throne room. In the center stood a group of about thirty or so people. Some of them wore clothes that were nothing more than torn rags while others' attire remained more intact. All of them, however, sported dirty hair and grime on their skin and were in dire need of cleaning.

An equal number of guards stood in the room as well. They were posted in groups of three by all the room's exits while the rest remained close to the prisoners. The ex-convicts continued to look around the room curiously, anxiously waiting to learn why they had been summoned.

Simon made his way up the few steps towards the king's empty chair and faced the people, motioning for their attention. Bashkim stood to his left, a single step behind him.

"Good luck," Bashkim whispered.

"Is that something you can summon with magic too?" Simon asked as the people came forward and gathered around.

"You have to pray for that one."

Disappointed, Simon took one step forward and took in the scene before him.

"There's no easy way to say this," Simon started. "So I'm just going to get straight to it. Omar is no longer king of Nennossen. It was revealed he was a magic user and stripped of his power."

Several of the prisoners lifted their heads in surprise and began to mumble amongst themselves.

"Hold your words for now," Simon said loudly as he held his hand up. "There's a lot more to this so I need you all to pay attention. Omar was not stripped of his power because he used magic. He was removed because he has been putting this entire city in danger. As of today, and so long as I stand, magic is no longer a crime."

The prisoners couldn't contain themselves. They cheered loudly and clapped their hands, smiles stretching across their dirty faces. Simon took in a slow breath and held it. Bashkim knew the captain wanted to deliver more good news to the wrongly convicted, but instead he had to do something far less enjoyable.

"I'm afraid it's not all good news," Simon said when the crowd settled down. "As the light has been shed on the injustice you've been served, it has also revealed knowledge about magic and humans. Knowledge that some of you might find hard to accept. Magic is...magic is out of your reach. It's just not possible on your own."

"What do you mean?" somebody from the group blurted out.

"Let me explain," Simon said sternly. "It's not possible *on your own*. Yes, a human *can* wield magic, but there's a tool required. Something that came from the eshans called kesshonite."

"Well how does it work?" another person asked.

"That's what we don't know and want to find out," Simon answered. "We only have the one piece of kesshonite, but it is needed elsewhere."

"Keeping it for yourself?" a man from the crowd asked.

Simon frowned. He had expected nothing less from the people.

"You," Simon said, pointing to the man that had spoken out. "Come here."

The man didn't move, hoping that Simon had pointed to somebody else instead. Simon looked towards one of his soldiers and motioned towards the man with his head. The guard stepped into the crowd to grab the man and brought him to Simon.

"Thank you," Simon said, signaling for the guard to release the individual.

The soldier nodded his head and stepped away to return to his post.

"What is your name?" Simon asked.

"James, sir," the man said, swallowing.

Simon drew his sword out of its sheath, causing the crowd to gasp. "You don't like me, do you, James?"

What the hell? Bashkim wondered with wide eyes.

Bashkim's hand hovered over his own sword, unsure of Simon's intentions. He started to intervene, but instead decided to wait it out. James remained silent, staring down at the ground.

"At this moment," Simon said. "I don't like myself either. I learned that I willingly served a man who dared to call himself king while endangering all of those around him. I followed his word, for it was law. I locked away innocents like you, James. I locked away those that I swore an oath to protect. By all accounts, I am guilty and deserve to be stripped of my rank."

Simon held his sword in open hands in front of James as though he were passing it. "If you would like to take my place, then by all means, take my sword. But before you do, know this. It will be your sworn duty to protect this city and its people from enemies both within and outside these walls. The lives of hundreds will depend on you, and every step you take, every word you speak, and every action you make, will be judged by citizens, your soldiers, and the gods above us. And you, James, must be willing to lay down your life at a moment's notice for the safety of this city. A task that is bound to come sooner rather than later, for right now a threat that plagued our city two hundred years ago has returned. I've already lost good men to this beast, and I've no desire to lose more."

James refused to look at the sword or Simon's face, and instead took a step back.

Simon sheathed the sword and put his hand gently on James's shoulder, lowering his head so that he could look him in the eye. "Then let me speak."

Simon motioned for James to return to the crowd, patting him on the back as he left. James let his head hang low and disappeared back into the group of people.

He cut me more slack when I mouthed off to Omar, Bashkim thought, crossing his arms and watching Simon with interest.

"I'm sorry," Simon said to the people. "For everything. You've been served an injustice unlike anything I've ever seen before. To make matters worse, it was I who carried out this injustice. I know there is nothing I can do to atone for what I've done. But believe me when I say there is a danger out there even greater than Omar. A white dragon, a creature that our ancestors fought two hundred years ago, and they did not fight alone. They fought alongside eshans, and together they won. Kesshonite was the key back then, and I believe it can be today too. But right now, our relations with the eshans are rocky at best. If we want to beat this thing, we'll need their help. If you want magic, *you* will need their help. And if we can't get along amongst ourselves, then what hope do we have in ever fighting by their side?"

The people exchanged looks with one another waiting to see if anybody else would speak up. Several heads nodded and murmurs could be heard. Eventually, a woman towards the front of the group raised her hand.

"Yes, you," Simon said, pointing to the woman. "You've a question?"

"Yes, sir," she answered. "What's the plan?"

Simon reached back and brought Bashkim up closer to his side, patting him on the back. "Bashkim here has been helping us with this white dragon problem, along with a few other issues this city has. He'll be travelling to Teasvanna to try and recruit some help, as well as hopefully learn how to use this kesshonite."

"Do you think they'll help us?" one of the people asked.

"They'll have to," Bashkim said before Simon could answer. "If they want to survive, that is. If we don't work together we're all as good as dead. Eshans can't use the kesshonite without humans and humans can't control it without eshans. And since we need it to stop the white dragons, our cooperation is mandatory."

"What about the kesshonite then?" the same person asked. "What's going to happen to it? Simon said it was how we could get magic."

"It is," Bashkim answered. "But how that works we don't know yet. I imagine Omar would know if you saw fit to interrogate him, but in the meantime I'll be taking it with me to Teasvanna. I believe it can help in getting us some eshan support."

"Do we have anymore?" another person asked. "If that's all we have and something happens to it, and what you say is true, then we'll never have another chance at magic."

"Again," Simon said, taking a small step in front of Bashkim. "I apologize for the wrongs that I have done to you but hear my words and hear them well. Bashkim is on a mission, and if any of you so much as lay a finger on him, I will personally take you right back to prison and make sure you share chains with your previous king. Do I make myself clear?"

The people avoided eye contact with Simon, nodding their heads and mumbling their acknowledgements. A sigh left Simon and he stepped down towards the group to get closer to them.

"I know it's a tall order to ask you to trust me," Simon said softly. "you've been betrayed by your king, by me. But if I didn't want what's best for this city, for you, then you would not be standing here right now. That throne would not be empty. Unless you plan on burning Nennossen to the ground, then I've no desire to keep magic from you. So please, I'm asking for your cooperation. Let us save our city from these dragons, and then you can have your magic."

Again, a silence fell over the group as they looked amongst themselves. Eventually a voice came through.

"What else have we got to lose?" a woman asked. "We're being set free. If you want to be hard-headed and go back to prison, be my guest, but I'm doing what the captain says."

"Aye," a man agreed. "I can't say I like the idea of letting the kesshonite go, but free is free. Can't say I'm fond of the idea of dragons either."

Others began to nod their heads and offer their agreements, though a few in the crowd still crossed their arms and scowled. However, the unconvinced did not argue.

"Thank you," Simon said. "Now, let's talk about how we can get you all back on your feet and try to right the wrongs you've been dealt."

Later that evening, Bashkim found himself in his own private room in the castle with guards posted outside his door. As if it didn't feel strange enough just getting to enter the castle, getting to stay as a welcome guest was something else entirely. He also couldn't help but feel a bit guilty about the arrangement.

I put Simon in a hard spot, he thought, lying on the bed and staring up at the ceiling. *Yet he defends me. Even the first time I was here, lying to his face and pretending to be somebody else.*

A small sigh left Bashkim as he tried to relax.

Almost doesn't make sense, really.

Not much of it did. Not anymore. It seemed like each new day threw something new at him. White dragons, kesshonite, a voice in his head, uncontrollable magic, he could only guess what tomorrow would bring. One thing, however, stood out the most tonight. While grateful that Simon had made it out of this mess unscathed, he had said something during his speech that stuck with Bashkim.

I know there is nothing I can do to atone for what I've done, Bashkim thought, repeating Simon's words in his mind.

He tried not to think about it, but much like the white dragon, the thought seemed to enjoy playing with his mind. A small shiver ran through his body, and he rolled over to his side.

Nothing I can do, he repeated to himself. *Nothing I can do.*

Bashkim shut his eyes and tried to think of something else.

I have to talk to Rin tomorrow. I have to tell her what happened.

The new line of thought hadn't improved much from the previous.

I don't think she's going to be very happy.

Of course she wouldn't be. Bashkim had left her in the woods without telling her a single thing about his plan to out the king. He didn't tell her because he didn't *have* a plan. He went in blind. He learned about the kesshonite from Ishmonyae, and he knew humans could use magic because of it, but what did he actually hope to accomplish by returning to Nennossen?

She'd just as soon eat the king anyway, Bashkim told himself, rolling over to his other side.

You should have at least planned ahead. This way there'd be no surprises. What if it hadn't worked out in your favor?

What difference does it make? The deed is done, and it looks like it worked out for the better.

I'm sure Simon feels the same way.

Bashkim rolled over again, back to his original position. The scene played through his mind once more, showing him the magic he had summoned. Omar sat trapped in his chair, pinned by the ice and terrified.

You enjoyed it, didn't you?

Bashkim stared at the wall in front of him, his eyes refusing to stay shut and let him sleep.

Yes.

He could hear a faint chuckle in his mind, followed by a familiar voice.

"Bagrash zeen, Bashkim."

When Bashkim woke up the next morning and left his room, he found Simon waiting outside the door. Bashkim thanked him for the room, and Simon wished him much luck on his second journey before escorting him out.

Bashkim then made his way back to Rin, taking most of the day to get there. Part of him wanted to slow his pace so he wouldn't get there so soon, for guilt had started to build in him after struggling with the previous night's thoughts.

Did I really enjoy it? Even if I can control this new power of mine, I shouldn't be throwing it around like that.

Fallen twigs crunched under his feet as he entered the forest. *But maybe it's time to. Maybe it's time to be more aggressive with these people. Surely Rin can understand that.*

Rin remained in the forest where he left her, anxiously waiting for him to return and tell his story. Her eyes glowed during Bashkim's recap, but when he got to the part about trapping the king, the smile from her scaled snout faded, and her eyes grew concerned as she waited for him to finish.

"You took the king hostage?" she asked loudly once the story had ended. "What were you thinking?"

"It worked, didn't it?" Bashkim asked, holding his arms out as if presenting himself.

"And if it hadn't? Then what would you have done?"

"I would have gotten out just fine."

"And then where would you be? You'd be wanted for attempted assassination of the king! How would that help you with anything? And *how* would you have gotten out? Do you expect me to tear down the walls of another castle?"

"Why not?"

"I just broke you out of one city, Bashkim. I can't do that again. Dragons get enough of a bad reputation as it is. I can't continue to make them look like villains."

"Why do you care?"

"Because I'm a dragon!" Rin snarled.

"You would have just eaten him!" Bashkim fired back, also raising his voice. "Maybe I should be more like you and just finish the job myself!"

"Like me?" Rin bellowed, standing up.

"You do what you want. You take what you want. Seems to work out for you just fine. Meanwhile, I'm down here spending all my time trying to help these fools."

Rin pulled her head back slightly and silenced her snarl. She looked down at Bashkim, considering his words.

"That time you spent helping people is what led Simon to trust in you," Rin said, softly this time. "A trust that is quite possibly broken now. Arbiters only know who else has been secretly looking up to you. Is that something you really want to throw away?"

Bashkim crossed his arms and a huff of air shot out of his nose. "I doubt anybody other than Simon does."

Rin relaxed a bit, laying back down and lowering her head. "I think you'd be surprised. Though, on another note, I believe it's high time we finally talked about *why* you've been playing hero for so long."

"What do you mean?"

"You're running, Bashkim."

Bashkim uncrossed his arms and held his hands next to his sides, tightening them into fists. "I'm not running."

"Yes, you are," Rin said, holding her ground.

"Stop."

"I will not. I am your friend, Bashkim, and what kind of friend would I be if I did not confront you? You didn't become a hero because it was the right thing to do, you did it because you were running away, and you've been running all your life. And now? I think now you're starting to realize that no matter what you do, nothing will atone for—"

"Shut up!" Bashkim yelled, cutting her short.

"Nothing will bring those people back!" Rin bellowed over Bashkim, causing her voice to growl as she stood back up and gripped the ground with her claws. "They're gone, Bashkim! And you're running out of places to run."

"I said shut up!" Bashkim yelled again, a brief flash of fire bursting from both of his hands.

Rin drew back, and her head rose. She looked down at Bashkim, watching the grass around him begin to wilt and fade to black. Small strands of smoke rose from the forest floor, slowly swirling around him. Bashkim brought a hand to his chest and clutched his heart. Small hints of fire randomly flashed in and out of existence around his body and he fell to his knees.

Bashkim started to gasp for air, staring down at the ground as he tried to contain the magic swelling within him. The smoke eventually dissipated while he caught his breath, and the small fires failed to come back.

"What am I supposed to do?" he asked quietly between breaths, still on his knees and staring at the ground. "What *was* I supposed to do?"

Bashkim hunched over, looking as though he could no longer lift his own head. "There was so much fire. I tried to save them. I *could* have saved them."

Rin lowered her head down and tried to get a better view of her friend. She could see the tears slowly sliding towards the bottoms of his cheeks.

"They just..." Bashkim sobbed, trying to hide his face. "They kept burning...all of them."

A slow breath left Rin as she observed the man before her that she had broken. He refused to look at her and remained in the grassy area he had ruined. Rin looked at the sky, a pretend frown forming on her face as she groaned. She brought her head back down and extended one of her wings out, holding it over Bashkim.

"I never did like the rain," she said gently.

Bashkim turned to hide his face and wiped a hand across his eyes.

"Do you still hear the voice?" she asked, keeping him shielded with the massive wing over him.

"I do," Bashkim said quietly.

"Then I think it might be time for the hero to get help for once."

"And who is going to help me? A doctor, or a priest? If they don't throw me out for being a hybrid, then they sure as hell will when I tell them what's wrong with me."

"Then what do you plan to do?"

"I don't know," Bashkim sniffed.

Rin remained silent, keeping her wing over Bashkim while she waited.

"How long do you think it's going to rain?" Bashkim asked after a moment.

"Could be a while," Rin said, glancing up at the clear sky. "It's quite the storm. We should probably lay low for the rest of the day."

Bashkim nodded slowly. "I agree."

Keeping her wing in place, Rin carefully sat down on her hind legs, waiting for Bashkim to regain himself. Bashkim drew in a long, slow breath and closed his eyes. A single tear slid down the side of his face as he tried to hold his head up.

"If it really is the white dragon's voice I keep hearing...then that seems all the more reason to kill them."

"And if that doesn't work?"

"Then at least people won't have to worry about white dragon's anymore."

Try as he might, Bashkim found little rest that evening. He tossed and turned through the night, and Rin kept an ever-watchful eye on him. Groans and mumbles escaped him, followed by the occasional bead of sweat dripping down his face. Rin kept her lengthy body curled around him while he slept, trying desperately to shield him from whatever troubled him.

Bashkim remained in his bed even as the sun rose, finally getting what looked to be some peaceful sleep. Grateful, Rin decided to let him lie undisturbed so that she might finally steal a few minutes herself. As the sun continued to rise, it eventually began to pour down through the treetops, spilling over Bashkim's face and waking him up.

"If I didn't know any better," he groaned and rubbed his eyes. "I'd say the sun is up earlier than normal."

"It's actually been up for a few hours now. You might have been asleep last night, but I doubt you got much rest."

Bashkim blinked his eyes several times, forcing them to stay open and shading them with his hand to look at the sun's position. "Sure doesn't feel like it."

"Well, now that you're awake, do you still think Treydola can help you? Or have you changed your mind after sleeping on it?"

"It's not that I think she can help us, it's just the only thing we have left. If she can't help, then we're back to asking the eshans for support, and I think we both know how well that will go."

"We certainly didn't leave on good terms. Which begs the question: how do you plan to talk with her?"

"I'll have to get a message to her. Convincing her should be easy enough but getting her somewhere we can talk will be tricky. Handleson would be ideal, but I'm not sure yet how she'll get there. I doubt a king's daughter can just simply leave the city whenever she wants."

"A safe assumption."

Bashkim slowly got to his feet and attempted to pack his things. Rin watched him slowly roll up his bed and pause once he had reached the end. He blinked his eyes again, shaking his head as he fumbled to tighten the bedroll's straps. Bashkim looked around, trying to find his pack.

Rin slowly reached out with a single claw and slid the pack in front of him. Bashkim didn't even process what had happened. Instead, he reached down and began strapping the bedroll to his backpack. When finished, he paused as if he didn't know what to do next.

"Breakfast?" Rin asked.

Bashkim didn't respond. He simply reached into his backpack and retrieved some food, chewing it in silence and staring out into nothingness.

"Do you hear the voice again?" Rin asked.

"No. It's quiet now."

"Is that unusual?"

"Not really. It only speaks at certain times."

"Have you noticed a pattern?"

"At first I thought being angry made it show up, but when I really think about, I'm not so sure that's what it is."

Rin waited for Bashkim to continue, but he only stood there.

"Then what is it?" she finally asked.

"It happens when I'm scared."

CHAPTER 10

Thanks to a late start and a lack of good sleep, Bashkim and Rin failed to cover much ground. Rin flew slower and required more stops than usual. Feeling indifferent about the lost time, Bashkim decided to call it in early so they could make a second attempt at getting some rest.

Since they didn't make it to their originally planned destination, the two had to make a slight detour to find a different forest to hide in. This one found itself not far from a small village, but at least far enough away for them to remain hidden and clear of trouble. Even if anybody had seen them come down, Bashkim doubted anyone from the village would be bold enough to come looking for them.

Rin made another campfire for Bashkim for the night and watched him as he got himself comfortable. Bashkim laid out his bedroll near the open flame and sat down, grabbing a stick to gently poke the burning branches.

"Something on your mind?" Bashkim asked once he noticed the two large eyes watching him.

"No," Rin answered. "I'm going to go hunt for some food. I will return shortly."

"Don't go eating any villagers that might have wandered too far off."

"Honestly," Rin groaned in an attempted playful manner, but her delivery came off preoccupied. "The things I do for you."

Bashkim chuckled to himself, grinning as she flew off. She clearly had something on her mind, and clearly, she didn't feel like sharing at the moment.

But at least you still have your spirits. We're both probably just tired.

He quietly watched the flames sway back and forth and used his stick to make sure the branches stayed in the center of the fire.

*Although...*Bashkim's thoughts wandered as Rin's attempted joke set in. *You really do a lot for me. You build my fires. You carry me around everywhere. You're there during my lows, and you were there when I lashed out at you. Hell, you even broke me out of jail.*

As much as he wanted to smile at the image of Rin breaking him out of the castle, he couldn't help but remember how his magic had burned her in the process.

You're here even after I hurt you.

The thought weighed heavy, and the guilt cut deep.

Not sure why you bother sometimes, really. But...that's what friends do, right? They stick together. Even in the bad times.

Bashkim's eyes stared into the fire and watched it consume the branches.

I hope I can be there if things ever get bad for you.

He shrugged his shoulders and wondered if dragons could even have bad times.

Surely even a dragon has bad days, he told himself while sinking back into his bed.

Hunting normally only took Rin a few minutes, for her keen eyes could easily spot her prey. One strong flap of her massive wings and she could swoop down and catch a meal in her jaws. He had witnessed it several times before, but tonight seemed different. Several minutes had passed already, and she still hadn't returned.

Maybe she is having a bad day after all.

Rin eventually returned, and with her the carcass of two deer and a rather large bear.

"That's quite the hunt," Bashkim noted.

"You should have some," she said, dropping her kills and motioning him over with her head. "You need to eat too."

"I'm not very hungry."

"Eat," Rin said, somewhat sternly.

"Alright, alright."

Bashkim got up and made his way over to one of the deer. He tried to hold it in place while Rin used the tip of her claw to cut it open.

"I'm sure glad I don't have to feed you," Bashkim joked, using his sword to cut off a small slice of meat.

"You know dragons don't have to eat that often."

"Yeah, but when you do, it sure takes a lot to feed one."

"Someone used to feed me when I was a pup, you know."

"So you've mentioned," Bashkim said and returned to the fire to sharpen a stick to roast the meat on. "But you've never really told me much about him."

"You never asked," Rin said, pushing her kills into a pile.

"I wanted to, but I thought maybe it was a sensitive subject since you never volunteered the information. I figured you'd tell me when you were ready."

"Such a gentleman."

Bashkim smiled. "Does that mean you're ready?"

Rin tilted her head to the side, looking down at Bashkim with a frown.

"I can only contain my curiosity for so long," he said.

Rin snorted. She stayed quiet for a moment and watched Bashkim as he cooked his food. She had a distant look in her eyes, and Bashkim could see her sides swell as she took a large breath to tell her tale.

"He was a farmer," she said, pushing her food away from her as she waited for Bashkim to cook his. "He found me when I was but a hatchling of a dragon. No more than a pup I was, though I suppose it was more so me that found him, for I was the one that stumbled across his land. Without hesitation he took me in as if I were just one more animal on the farm under his care. He provided food and shelter, and he made sure I was healthy the best he knew how. Looking back, I do realize that he kept a closer eye on me than the rest of the animals."

"Probably worried you were going to eat them," Bashkim joked.

"Most likely."

"Did you?"

"I did not," Rin said, holding her head up with pride. "I only ate what he provided. I may have been young and without parents, but even I knew better than to bite the hand that feeds you."

"A wise dragon child."

"Indeed, and I followed that man around everywhere he went and helped where my little dragon hands could. He would talk to me each day while he worked, which he did with most animals under his care. He had no wife or children, so I imagine he found some solace in speaking with us. Though the other animals were only capable of understanding simple commands and had little to say otherwise. He knew I could understand what he said, but I was unable to give anything back to him. So, I tried to learn the farmer's language. Speaking your words is difficult, Bashkim, if not painful. A dragon's tongue is not meant for the words of man."

A small chuckle escaped Rin as she recalled the memory. "You should have seen the look on his face when I tried to speak for the first time."

"I can only imagine," Bashkim said. "I was pretty surprised myself the first time I heard you talk."

"Yes, but you hadn't already spent years with me. This man fell over when he heard me mutilate your language. Through many years and several long nights, he managed to teach me your words. Not once did he give up on me, even if there were times when I did."

"Sounds like a good guy."

"He was," Rin said with a distant sigh. "Though I suppose nothing is forever, is it?"

"What happened?"

"Dragons live a lot longer than most beings. It was only natural that I would bear witness to his final days. Though I am happy to say he did live a long and full life. His final moments were spent in the presence of a dragon that he himself had raised. A deserving death, I would think, for a deserving man."

Rin paused to collect herself. Bashkim focused his attention on cooking his dinner to give her some space. However, curiosity eventually got the best of him, and he attempted to steal a glance at her. He didn't know if dragons could cry, but he could easily see it in her eyes that she wanted to.

"The Final Flame," Bashkim said, remembering what she had told him before. "You gave it to him, didn't you?"

"I did." Rin nodded. "Hey may not have been a dragon, nor did he even know of such things, but he deserved it all the same in my eyes. And as both a dragon and probably the closest thing he had to family, I feel as though the right to make that decision was mine."

"I agree, and I think it was a good choice."

Rin looked down at the animal carcasses in front of her. "He often warned me of the world and what it had to offer. Every time I left to hunt for food, he told me of those that would take my head as a trophy. He spoke of the world and its troubles, of the people that I might see, both good and bad. Having been raised by that man, the standard for what was good had been set awfully high."

"It certainly sounds like it," Bashkim said and took his dinner out of the fire.

"Of all the things he tried to warn me about, he never did quite prepare me for other dragons. I can only assume he thought me meeting others of my own would be a good thing. Little did he know that dragons have an abundance of their own problems."

Bashkim stared at the cooked meat, unsure of what to say while he waited for his dinner to cool. Instead of responding, he chose to wait and see if Rin would continue the story on her own. She tilted her head back, her nose pointing to the sky as she closed her eyes.

"I'm really glad you shared your story with me," Bashkim said after waiting. "But may I ask why you chose tonight?"

Rin took a breath in slowly. "I miss that man, Bashkim. Truly, I do. You remind me a lot of him in your own little way, and while it does sadden me greatly to think that one day I will outlive you as well, there is something else on my mind."

"What's that?"

"I knew that man's heart," she said, opening her eyes and looking down at Bashkim. "I knew it through and through, and not once did he falter. And yours, Bashkim, is just as great. But lately I fear that you may have lost something. Something that has separated you from the rest of the world since I've known you. We spoke one night, and I'll not soon forget his words. He said it's not the flesh and blood we fight against, but the powers and rulers of darkness. A fight that I fear you have been losing of late."

She had caught Bashkim off guard, causing him to take a sharp breath and hold it. The old man in Teasvanna had told him the same thing, and the familiar words made him pause. He knew she meant his recent outbursts, particularly with Omar, but he didn't know how to make her feel any better. Truth be told, he didn't know how to make *himself* feel better and partly agreed with her. He knew things had been different with him lately. Hell, he even told her as much. But what could he do about it? He did the best he knew how, but the fight between a mere mortal and a white dragon had proven to be more than difficult. Still, he felt he had done a pretty good job of it so far, all things considered.

"Don't worry," he said, trying to reassure her, and thumped himself on the chest. "I'm still the same Bashkim you've always known and loved! No white dragon can take that away."

"See that it doesn't," Rin said, taking her food and turning away from him.

The burning branches inside the small fire pit continued to snap and crackle. Their orange glow stayed bright and kept Bashkim warm. He lay on his back, listening to the sounds as he stared up towards the treetops. Rin had long ago finished her dinner for the night, her large breaths louder than the crackling fire, yet more soothing. At one point her back legs even started to move as though she were running in her sleep.

I wonder how many people she's terrorizing in dream land.

Try as he might to fall asleep, he remained wide eyed and awake. His mind wandered in circles around the kesshonite dagger in his backpack. He wanted to know how it worked and how it would react to a hybrid's touch. At the same time, he wanted nothing to do with it.

What would happen if I just tried?

His curiosity stirred, as did hope. What if hybrids didn't need eshans *or* humans? What if a hybrid had the best of both worlds and could use it on their own?

Even if they could, you're not exactly a normal hybrid anymore. There's something else in you in case you've forgotten. How do you think the kesshonite will react to this new magic you have?

The thought didn't set well with him. What if he had gone through all this trouble only to find out he couldn't use kesshonite? He'd have to sit the battle out while everyone else fought the White dragons. He would be ignored, and his work would be forgotten.

It's not about the fame. It's about...them. The one's back...

A shiver went down Bashkim's spine as the unpleasant memory started to come back to him.

Home...the ones back home.

For a moment, Bashkim couldn't tell which disturbed him more. Remembering the past events that had pushed him down into the lifestyle he chose, or the life he had spent thus far meaning nothing. When it came time to fight, would he just have to sit and watch? Would he not be able to help?

No. I don't think I can rely on humans and eshans to work together. Not yet, anyway. I'll still have my chance.

Bashkim put his hands to his face and let them slowly slide down. Things didn't seem to be looking very good. He had come so far and uncovered so many secrets. Secrets that otherwise may never have been revealed. He had freed an entire city of its treacherous king. The future for all humans had potentially changed because of him now that they knew the truth about magic. Yet, despite having done all this, none of it quite felt like a win.

Hybrids still hide. Will anything I do ever actually help them?

A quiet sigh left Bashkim as he stared into the campfire.

Perhaps a walk would do me good. I don't think I'm going to be getting sleep anytime soon.

A nice stroll through the woods sounded like a good idea. The moon glowed brightly, and the trees stood far enough part to let the light through.

Ah. Why not?

Bashkim carefully got up from his bed, making sure not to wake Rin.

I won't go far, he thought as he quietly stepped away. *I'll just walk out this way a little bit and do a few laps around camp.*

Bashkim silently stepped through the forest farther away from Rin so she could continue to sleep.

Guess those wonderful dragon ears don't work so good when you're passed out, he thought, taking a deep breath once he felt he had gotten far enough away.

He proceeded to walk at a normal pace while still taking some precautions not to step on any loud twigs. The trees around him all stood strong, though there weren't quite as many as the last forest they had landed in. The animals seemed to pay no mind, for they had made their homes in them all the same. The owls resting on the scraggly branches above him hooted as they watched him casually stroll by.

Apparently, the owls had more interest in the stranger walking through their wooded home than the massive dragon sleeping in it. Bashkim let them be and kept walking while trying to keep his head clear and ignore a question that kept nagging at him.

What if I can't use the kesshonite? What if I can't help them?

The question repeated in his mind several times over, and the whisper of the white dragon faintly came to him.

No. I'm not in the mood for you, Bashkim said in his mind, quickening his pace without realizing.

His mind continued to focus on the kesshonite and the dagger he had left at camp. The thought of not being able to use it and being forced to sit the fight out haunted him.

It wouldn't be fair. To go through all of this trouble only to have to sit on the side and hope others can carry through.

The white dragon continued to speak in its unintelligible whispers.

What do you want from me? Bashkim asked. *Do you want the kesshonite? Are you using me to get it?*

No. That couldn't be right. The white dragon should be afraid of the kesshonite. They were killed off by it two hundred years ago. It's supposed to be their weakness, their downfall.

Then perhaps you are afraid? Maybe you fear the idea of me with that kind of power in my hands?

The white dragon laughed in response.

So you doubt me? Or are you trying to convince me to abandon this quest?

"Kungrast delso gorotto mannaneeresh, Bashkim," the voice said.

I'm not afraid of you. I've faced you once before and survived. You were also defeated two hundred years ago. What makes you think it can't happen again, and by my hand?

Bashkim could feel the magic start to slowly build inside of him as he argued with the voice. His pace quickened to a jog, proceeding in a straight line *away* from Rin before any of his magic could escape. She already had enough concerns about him. He didn't want her to worry any more than she already did. More importantly, he didn't want to *hurt* her again.

Got to get away from her. Got to get away from the kesshonite.

Bashkim's eyes widened briefly, followed by a short gasp.

The kesshonite, he told himself again, oblivious to how far from the camp he fled. *This new magic...what will happen if they interact? What will...no. Think about something else. Anything else.*

His jog progressed to a full-on sprint, his mind racing alongside him.

Have to be able to use it, he thought, unable to ignore it. *Can't count on humans and eshans working together. I won't sit by and do nothing.*

Too dangerous. If you try to use the kesshonite and destroy it or yourself, what will happen to Teasvanna and Nennossen?

What will happen to them if I don't try to use it?

Bashkim continued to run through the forest, blindly pushing the brush out of his way while he charged forward. The magic swelled inside of him and filled every part of his body as the white dragon's voices grew louder.

Leave me alone, Bashkim pleaded.

Bashkim put his head down and ran as fast as he could. His lungs began to burn, and the muscles in his legs grew stiff. No matter how fast he went, he couldn't seem to outrun his mind. It kept pace with him, always one short step behind and able to grab him.

Magic, he heard in his mind, the thoughts becoming jumbled.

Don't use the magic. Not safe.

Kesshonite.

Kill the white dragons.

Use your magic against them.

His mind felt like it had split as multiple thoughts ran alongside one another and swirled around in his head.

No.

My magic is too strong.

The magic isn't right. There's something wrong.

Control it. Keep it down.

Don't let go.

Bashkim focused on trying to run even faster, hoping that burning out physically would keep the magic from escaping. Thoughts began to overlap one another and became harder to make out clearly.

Kill the white dragon.

Embrace your magic.

Don't use the kesshonite.

Hold it in.

No! Don't hold it in. Let go!

Don't let go. Don't let go.

Bashkim didn't know what to do anymore. Part of him wanted to explode and let out all his magic and destroy everything around him however he saw fit. Another part of him wanted to cower and hide until the whole thing went away.

Save them, a small thought cried out as it tried not to be buried under the rising storm in his mind. *Save them. All of them.*

You can't save them.

Yes, I can. I have to.

You don't have that kind of power.

Yes, I do.

Bashkim's head began to ache, and he wanted to scream. He could feel the sweat dripping down his face, but he refused to stop running. He had to. He had to keep going. He had to get away.

What are you running from?

Keep running. Don't stop.

He didn't stop. His head stayed down, and he panted for air as his feet pounded against the forest floor. As he ran, other voices started to come to him. Voices that were not his own.

The world doesn't want you, immundrid, he heard the eshan king tell him.

Magic is evil! Omar said. *It's witchcraft!*

You're wrong, Bashkim tried to argue with them. *Both of you! You're wrong!*

He couldn't escape it. The voices spoke too loudly, and they chased him like demons. They trailed behind him and reached out to grab him with their jagged claws. If he just kept running, he could stay one step out of their reach.

I can never atone for what I've done, he heard Simon say.

Yes, you can. Bashkim fought back. *And so can I!*

You're running, Rin chimed in. *You've been running your entire life.*

I have to. I can't stop.

Don't stop.

His heartbeat thumped against his chest and echoed in his head loud enough to drown out the noises of the forest. The owls had grown silent, and his feet stomping against the forest floor could no longer be heard. The last beam of moonlight faded from his view and left him in darkness. He could no longer feel his own body, and the voices grew louder and more intertwined with one another.

Just as he felt as though he had completely lost his grip on reality, one voice stuck out among the rest. A familiar voice. One that had previously brought him unsuspected comfort.

Have you ever tried giving it a chance? He heard Cynthia ask.

Bashkim's eyes widened and forced him to realize what had happened. He had blacked out again. His legs continued running forward, but how far had he gone? Where did he go?

Why don't you stop?

I can't.

The thoughts and voices in his head suddenly went silent, leaving room for a certain voice he had grown much more acquainted with the past few days. It spoke clearly, its words easily understood as they came directly into his mind.

"Stop running," the white dragon said.

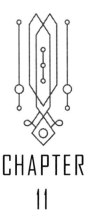

CHAPTER
11

Bashkim came to an instant halt once he heard the voice in his head and nearly toppled over himself. His eyes stretched wide open at the realization he had understood the white dragon's words. He hunched over and put his hands on his knees, gasping for air. The white dragon had gone silent and left Bashkim alone for the moment.

What was that? Bashkim asked himself as he tried to catch his breath. *I understood it. It spoke my language.*

As his lungs filled with air to recover his body from its run, Bashkim could hear the faint sounds of people in the distance. He got down to the ground and slowly moved his way forward to investigate. The voices sounded like they came from men, and he assumed it to be nothing more than some travelers making their way to the nearby village. However, as he got closer, he could hear the muffled cries of someone struggling.

Somebody needs help, he thought, quickly trying to catch his breath while attempting to stay quiet at the same time. *It might be a good thing I came out here after all.*

As Bashkim got closer to the new voices, he could see the flickering light of a small campfire. Keeping low to the ground and staying behind the trees, Bashkim eventually made his way up to the scene. The voices he had heard didn't belong to travelers, but mere thieves and kidnappers. There were three male humans, one of them holding a woman captive. Their positions were a bit farther apart than Bashkim cared for.

I need to catch my breath, Bashkim thought to convince himself to wait before jumping into action. *She doesn't seem to be hurt yet.*

One of the men stood a good bit shorter than the others and spent his time rummaging through a leather satchel. His little hands threw random items out of the bag, and he scoffed once he had reached the bottom. He held the bag upside down and shook it in hopes of finding something more.

"What's the matter, Liam?" asked the man holding the woman captive.

"Bah," Liam said, tossing the bag to the side. "She ain't got nothing. You'd think somebody out and about at this hour would have *something* interesting. There's not even any food in there."

Liam scratched the scraggly hair patches on his face and looked down at the bag. The woman squirmed and tried to break free, but the large man behind her held her still. It took only one of his burly arms to hold both of hers behind her back, which allowed him to cover her mouth with his free hand. The brute chuckled as the woman attempted to break free of the relentless grip.

The third man, however, remained close to their campfire and appeared to struggle with watching the whole thing unfold. He continuously looked back at the fire, seemingly trying to hide his face in shame. Yet, every time the woman tried to scream, he couldn't help but turn to look.

He's young, Bashkim thought when he saw the youthfulness of the thief's face. *Maybe his first time?*

Bashkim watched the boy, taking note of the concern in his eyes. *Doesn't matter. He made his choice.*

"Well, so much for that," Liam said, putting his hands in his pockets and stepping over to the woman. "Just what *are* you doing out here so late, anyway?"

The woman cried as loud as she could and tried to pull herself away from the approaching stranger, but the large, hairy brute behind her kept her silent and still. As she squirmed, Liam seemed to take notice of something on her. He tilted his head, narrowing his eyes as he looked at her.

"Hold up," he said, and reached out and to brush back the hair on one side of her head and revealed a bandaged ear. "Looks like you've already gotten into some trouble."

The woman kept still this time, breathing rapidly as tears streamed down her face.

"I think I know what's going on here," Liam said, casually undoing the bandage.

The cloth wrapping fell to the ground and revealed a pointed eshan ear on the side of the woman's head.

"So *that's* what you're doing out here so late." Liam chuckled. "*And* alone. Sneaky little immundrid."

"Doesn't that mean she has magic?" the younger man by the fire asked.

"Ha!" the bigger one laughed. "What's the matter, Nathan? You scared?"

"Just being cautious."

Before the bigger man could make a retort, fire started to appear in the woman's hands. The flames burned her captor and made him jump back and let her go. The woman started to make a break for it, but the brute grabbed her before she could even take two steps. His beefy hand grabbed the back of her neck with his fingers wrapping around her throat and squeezing firmly.

The woman tried to scream, but sound failed to leave her when the man tightened his grip. Bashkim slowly reached down for his sword, ready to make his move. He could feel his own magic swirling and building inside of him.

She's too vulnerable right now, Bashkim thought, convinced that the thieves didn't want to kill the woman yet. *He could snap her neck if I make a move at the wrong time.*

"Now, now," Liam said, unfazed by the attempted escape. "Let's not do anything hasty."

The large man brought the woman back in front of Liam with her arms behind her back again. His hand remained around her neck and throat, keeping a firm grip.

"That's enough, Joe," Liam said. "I need her to be able to breathe."

"She's going to scream," Joe argued.

"Are you?" Liam asked, looking at the woman. "Do you really think that's the wisest decision right now?"

More tears streamed down her face, but after facing the reality that surrounded her, she slowly shook her head.

"That's a good girl," Liam smiled.

Joe released her throat and instead used both his hands to keep her arms behind her back. The woman gasped for air but did not scream.

"Much better," Liam said. "We've gone through all this trouble, and yet you have nothing of value to us."

Liam's eyes trailed down the woman's body and slowly made their way back up to her face. "Well...not in the bag, anyway. I think there might be something *else* you can offer to make up for it."

Liam drew the short sword from his belt and started to slowly cut the woman's blouse open, starting at the top and working his way down. The woman started to scream, but the brute behind her tightened his grip on her arms. She then closed her eyes and turned her head as the man exposed her.

That's enough, Bashkim thought and got up to his feet.

Bashkim stepped out from hiding and made himself visible to the thieves. Joe saw him approaching and nodded in his direction. Liam whipped around and jumped back slightly when he saw Bashkim.

"Just walk away, friend," Liam said after he regained himself. "None of this concerns you."

"It doesn't," Bashkim said. "But I'm going to ask you to let her go anyway."

Liam looked at his two companions, then back again to Bashkim and started to laugh. "Are you on the drink? There's three of us and one of you."

"Sounds like bad odds," Bashkim said, holding his ground. "Maybe you should ask the hybrid for help."

"Oh, ho, ho! You're a sassy son of a bitch, aren't you? I like it!"

Bashkim drew his own sword, his facial expression unchanged. "I'm a tired son of a bitch. And you're keeping me awake."

"You want me to take care of him?" Joe asked.

"Nah. I'll handle this one," Liam answered. "Maybe Nathan can learn something."

Liam lunged forward to attack, but with one simple step, Bashkim slid to the side and swiped his own sword in an upward motion. The blade's edge cleaved through the man's wrist and removed the hand entirely. In one fluid motion, Bashkim struck the back of Liam's neck with the pommel of his sword and sent him tumbling down to the ground. Liam screamed in pain as his severed hand fell to the forest floor with a small thud, still clutching the weapon.

Joe decided to assist and threw the woman to the ground. He drew his own sword and charged forward. Bashkim swept his free hand upwards, and up from the ground shot several frozen vines. The ice grabbed the man's arms and legs, wrapping around his limbs and holding him place. He tried to move, but the vines solidified themselves and refused to budge even the slightest. Bashkim could feel the drain on his body as the vines rooted themselves in place, and his heart began to beat wildly. He brought his hand to his chest, his fingers trying to dig into his own body as he kept the magic under his control. Bashkim narrowed his eyes and glared at the younger man.

"I wouldn't make any sudden movements if I were you," he said between breaths.

Nathan held his hands up and kept them there, refusing to move a single step. Bashkim released his grip on himself and took a slow breath in.

The magic is still growing inside of me.

It moved throughout his entire body as though something physical crawled around beneath his skin. The frozen vines coming from the ground felt as if they were his own extra limbs. He could feel all of them, even the ones that had formed underground and remained hidden.

I won't be able to stop it.

I don't want to stop it.

Bashkim grabbed the leather satchel and started to hurriedly throw all the items back inside. The woman remained on the ground, covering herself as she watched the stranger take her belongings and oblivious to the real fight taking place inside of him. The vines wanted to grow. They wanted to move and consume everything around them. Keeping them contained felt like holding his breath, and right now, he just wanted to breathe.

Wait until she's gone. After that...it doesn't matter.

As he grabbed the last couple of items and stuffed them inside the satchel, he realized just what he had been collecting.

"Who is sick?" he asked, handing the satchel of medicinal ingredients over to the woman.

"My husband," she answered, keeping herself covered as she took her belongings back.

Bashkim turned to the younger man, pointing at him with his sword. "You. Give me your jacket."

Nathan followed the order without question and quickly removed his jacket. Refusing to step closer, he tossed it over. Bashkim caught the jacket and handed it over to the woman while helping her up to her feet.

"Can you make it to the village?" Bashkim asked, barely able to hear himself over his own heartbeat.

"Yes. I believe so." The woman put the coat on and retrieved her fake bandage from the ground. "It's not far, and I have friend there I was to meet. She can keep me hidden."

"Then go," Bashkim said, placing his hand on his chest.

"What is your name?"

"Go!" Bashkim said loudly, followed by a grunt as he tried to control his breath.

The woman flinched and took a step backwards. She quickly regained herself and nodded. "Thank you, hero," she said and ran away.

Bashkim turned back to face the thieves once she had gotten far enough away.

No...there's no hero tonight.

Liam had slowly tried to make his way back to his severed hand to retrieve his weapon but froze in place once Bashkim turned around. Bashkim took his hand off his chest and held it out with his open palm facing the thief. A large bolt of lightning shot forward and lit the entire forest with a brilliant flash of light. A thunderous crackling noise followed, and the other two thieves closed their eyes to shield themselves.

The thunder echoed through the forest, causing many animals to stir and flee in the distance. The rumbling slowly came to a stop, and only a faint sizzling sound could be heard. The two thieves opened their eyes, readjusting to the darkness. In front of them laid the remains of Liam. Smoke rose from his corpse. His clothes had completely disintegrated and nothing but a charred body beyond recognition remained.

The ice holding the larger man suddenly came alive again. The vines slowly grew in length and wrapped themselves farther up his limbs.

"I can't stand you people," Bashkim said between breaths as he sheathed his sword. "You're just...so damned stupid."

Bashkim's body shook as he tried to control the magic. "All of you!" he said, his voice rising. "It doesn't matter what you are! Kings. Thieves. Peasants. Soldiers. You're just...you're all the same!"

The frozen vines tightened their grip, and snapping could be heard as they crushed the man's bones. He screamed in pain and begged for mercy.

"Are you afraid?" Bashkim yelled. "Don't you think this is how she felt?"

The vines reached out farther, several of them starting to wrap around the man's torso.

"Is this how she felt?" Bashkim bellowed.

"Yes!" Joe whimpered.

"For Arbiters' sake, what is *wrong* with you people?" Bashkim ranted. "All of you! You didn't even know she was a hybrid when you took her. You thought she was human. One of your own! If you can't prey on others, you fools would just as soon consume yourselves!"

The vines started to squeeze the man's chest, causing him to gasp for air and beg for his life.

"Help me!" Joe pleaded.

"Help you?" Bashkim yelled. "How can I help you?"

The vines gripped tighter, and more bones snapped as the man tried to scream.

"You're beyond the help this world can give you! You need divine intervention!"

Nathan watched in horror while the frozen vines twisted and pulled away from one another. In the blink of an eye, they ripped Joe into pieces. The remnants of his torso fell to the ground with a thud while his blood and entrails slid down the vines. Slowly, they frozen vines slithered down into the ground and let the bloody remnants pile on the forest floor.

Bashkim took several breaths, clutching his chest. "You!" he shouted, pointing to Nathan who remained by the fire.

"I didn't want to hurt her, I promise!" Nathan pleaded.

The fire next to him suddenly burst in size, catching him off guard and throwing him to the ground. Several frozen vines shout out from within the stiffened flames. They wrapped around his ankles and slowly pulled him back.

"You stood there in silence!" Bashkim growled, gasping for air. "You did *nothing!*"

"Please!" Nathan cried and clawed at the dirt to pull himself forward.

"You could have stopped them!"

"I wanted to! Please! Let me go!"

Nathan's ghastly cries echoed through the forest as the vines jerked back and pulled him into the center of the raging fire.

"All you had to do was say something!" Bashkim yelled, falling to his knees as he watched the fire consume Nathan. "Anything!"

His chest felt like it was being stabbed. He could feel the frozen vines writhing underground as his muscles spasmed. His hands shook from the intensity of the magical flame, and his head started to spin. Bashkim put his hands down to the ground, digging his fingers into the dirt as he tried to control the magic.

The vines beneath him slowly dissolved into water, one by one, and the fire eventually snuffed itself out. A small strand of smoke rose from the remains of the young thief. The boy's bones had become brittle from the intense heat, collapsing in on themselves. A shiver went through Bashkim as he laid eyes on the skull, watching it crumble as the orange sparks jumped from it.

Bashkim could feel the magic subsiding ever so slowly inside of him, its hunger finally satisfied. The pain started to leave him and let him finally draw long and much-needed breaths. He felt as though he had finally broken the chains of massive weights bound to him.

As his senses returned to normal, he realized the temperature had dropped considerably since he left the camp and felt as though it were still dropping. A phenomenon that he had felt more than once before.

"Rin?" Bashkim asked, looking around him.

Rin hid behind the trees with her head kept down low. She snarled and bared her teeth as Bashkim locked eyes with her. Her claws dug into the ground, and she looked as though she were about to pounce at a moment's notice. Bashkim started to get up and step towards her, but she jerked back.

"What's wrong, Rin?"

"What have you done?"

"Those men were robbing that woman. You had to have heard what was happening here. They were about to do far worse to her until I intervened."

"You did more than just intervene."

"They deserved it."

"And so it is your place to cast such a judgement? Since when did it become your job to deliver the fate you've deemed fit for others?"

"I did what I had to do."

"No," Rin said, only slightly relaxing her posture. "You did what you *wanted* to do."

"And just what does that mean?"

"It means you've become that which you've wanted to destroy. You are no longer the man I once knew."

"I'm not the farmer that raised you, no matter how much of me you see in him. I never have been, and I never will be."

"No!" Rin said, her voice stern. "I once knew a man named *Bashkim.* He was kind, courageous, and everything a hero ought to be. I thought I had rescued him from the eshans of Teasvanna, but clearly, I was mistaken. For you, I know not. You are an imposter. A two-legged creature that I do not recognize, and one that I *fear.*"

"What are you getting at?"

"You curse both the humans and the eshans. You call them fools for their segregation, yet there is no discrimination from you, is there? For in your eyes, *all* are guilty."

Rin raised her head all the way up and took a deep breath. Bahkim couldn't help but notice the similarity of the look in her eyes when she had told him of the tale of the farmer, and now.

"And that is why I must take my leave," she said. "For I fear the day may come when you will deem me a sinner and put me to the blade."

"No," Bashkim said. "It's not like that and you know it."

"I'm going to search for Bashkim," Rin said, turning her back to him. "Should you choose to end me, then all I ask is that you let me die in my own home so that my friend may find me one day, for I had chosen him as the bearer of my Final Flame."

Before Bashkim could speak, Rin pushed herself upwards and took flight, forcing him to shield his face with his arms. Once the gust had passed, he reached out with an open hand. He kept his hand in the air, barely able to process what had just happened as he watched her fly away. Her silhouette soon faded from view, and he found himself accompanied only by the mutilated remains he had created.

For years Bashkim had considered himself alone in the world. He knew the humans wouldn't have him, nor would the eshans. He cursed them for that, just like she had said, claiming they had abandoned him. He *thought* he knew what that felt like. Now, for the first time in his life, he truly felt the crushing and empty feeling of being left alone. Not even the white dragon's voice chose to haunt him. The silence did a good enough job of that.

Bashkim slowly made his way back to his camp by following the tracks Rin had left behind. He dragged his feet the entire way while letting his head hang low. He cursed himself with every shuffled step he took.

"Damn you," he said aloud. "Is this what you wanted? Was the goal to drive Rin away all along?"

Nobody spoke.

"And now you keep silent," Bashkim growled. "What are you, a coward? Are you hiding? Do you fear me? Are you afraid of what I might become with the kesshonite and these new powers?"

His own words caused him to stop walking. Images of Simon and Fandul, as well as their soldiers, flashed through his mind. He could see the scared looks on their faces when he used the new magic. They were shaken, terrified of the thought that they might be next to fall victim to his uncontrollable wrath.

"I'm afraid," he whispered. "And so is everyone else."

The realization hit him like the kick of a horse and kept him silent as he wondered if he had become a worse threat to the world than the white dragon itself. He found his bed where he had left it at camp, and the small fire still burned. Next to the bed lay Rin's entire saddle and harness. He knelt down in front of it and slowly rubbed his hands over the teeth marks where Rin had pulled it off by herself.

She already knew she was going to leave...before she even caught me out there.

Bashkim grabbed the bag on the side of the saddle and gave it a small shake. He could hear the jingle of gold and gems inside. She had left him with a parting gift so that he might finish his plans.

With a sinking heart, Bashkim carefully removed the bag from the saddle, and tears began to form in his eyes. He tried to hold them back, but as the straps came undone and he stepped away from the saddle, the pain became too much. It hurt worse than uncontrollable magic ever had. The tears stood no chance against it and streamed freely down the sides of his face. He fell to his knees, clutching the bag and pressing it as hard as he could against his chest. He slowly rocked back and forth, holding the bag as reality pulled him down like an anchor. Down he sank towards the bottom of the depths of his own mistakes where he had to face an unsettling truth.

Rin was gone.

CHAPTER 12

Several days passed after Rin's departure, and Bashkim did everything he could to avoid contact with the living. He kept off the main road to stay as far away as possible from any travelers. He didn't care that it added significantly more time to his journey.

It's safer this way, he tried to convince himself.

It made sense, mostly. Most of his solo journey had been in eshan territory so far, and he wanted to avoid the possibility of any eshans sniffing him out and giving him a hard time. He didn't need any more accidents.

The morning after Rin's departure, Bashkim had exchanged some of her leftover riches for a horse from the nearby village. The horse's help paled in comparison to the convenience of a dragon's wings. Each day he found himself longing for the sound of her voice, even if the words were filled with sarcasm. He didn't care. At this point, he would have gladly welcomed a scolding from her. It could be anything, just so long as he got to have her around again.

The horse shook its head and snorted when Bashkim brought it to a stop. He continued to spend his nights in the forests, even though he had no need to hide a dragon. If he couldn't have Rin anymore, he could at least try to feel at home. He needed the comfort, for every night since her departure haunted him. The nights were lonely, empty, cold, and when his mind wandered, terrifying.

It felt like he hadn't slept a single night since Rin left. Even before that night, he had struggled enough trying to get some decent rest. More than once he had nearly fallen from his horse from sleep deprivation. Dark circles formed under his eyes, and he could feel the weight pulling against his face.

Even though the horse had stopped moving, he continued to sit on it. He remained still, staring blankly up at the treetops.

I should make it to Teasvanna by tomorrow afternoon.

A long and tired sigh left him. Part of him just wanted to stop. No more travelling. No more adventuring. No more...anything. He just wanted to stop and breathe, but he couldn't.

Have to keep going, he told himself and dismounted the horse. *I've come this far. Might as well go the whole way. If anything, maybe it'll at least make up for how badly I screwed up Simon's life.*

Bashkim wrapped the horse's rope around a nearby tree, making sure his steed didn't wander off in the middle of the night. He shook his head, trying to wake himself up enough to at least make his bed.

Maybe after this, he thought while spreading out his bedroll. *After the white dragons and all that, if I'm still alive...maybe I'll put this life behind me.*

Bashkim went on to collect several dead branches and sticks. He set them in a pile and started to prepare a fire for the night. Instead of lighting it, however, he only stared at it. He sighed and sat down on his bedroll, silently hoping, like he had every night, that Rin would suddenly reappear.

She's gone. And you've nobody to blame but yourself.

Bashkim closed his eyes at the thought and pulled his knees up to his face. He wrapped his arms around his legs and tucked himself into a ball, trying to stay warm.

Look at you. You can't even light a fire on your own.

I can.

Then do it.

I don't need to. Not yet, anyway.

Yes, you do. Now light it.

Bashkim slowly held his hand out and faced his palm towards the sticks. He could feel a small amount of magic start to swim around in his chest. It slowly flowed through his body, down through his arm and out to his hand. Before it could reach out, Bashkim drew his hand back.

No. I can't. Not yet.

Bashkim stared at the sticks, a part of him hoping they would simply light themselves. Naturally, that did not happen. Instead, the sticks remained in their pile, undisturbed and cold. His hands fidgeted with one another, and he started to slowly rock back and forth.

She's not here. You don't have to worry about hurting her with your magic.

Bashkim pushed his head into his knees.

I can't. I don't want to use magic again. It's too dangerous. Clearly, I can't control it. Not even...back then.

That was years ago. You more than know how to control fire now. It shouldn't be this big of a deal.

It is to me.

A muffled growl came from within Bashkim's ball. He started to crawl around on his knees, searching for dead grass and leaves he could use as tinder. He even used his sword to peel off small shavings from the larger branches and stuffed them underneath the pile of sticks. Bashkim struck the pommel of his sword repeatedly against a rock, trying to create a spark. Cynthia's once beautiful creation had become worn and scarred from the repeated nights of abuse, destroying the work of art she had forged.

A spark jumped from one of his strikes and landed in the pile of tinder. Bashkim quickly dropped his tools and brought his face close to gently blow. The glow faded within seconds, and the almost fire vanished. He had blown too hard.

You're making this more difficult than it has to be.

Humans have to do it this way. I'll be fine.

Bashkim grabbed the sword again and started striking it against the stone. After several attempts, one of the sparks finally lunged from the stone and into the tinder. Again, he quickly got down to blow, except more gently this time. A glow from within the pile of tinder could be seen, and it steadily grew in intensity. A small strand of smoke began to rise, and a fire slowly started to form.

He could feel the fire in front of him. Not the heat, but the connection through the magic within his body. It wanted to reach out and take control of the fire to keep it calm and in check.

No. Let it burn on its own.

Bashkim took a slow breath and laid down on his bedroll. He remained silent and watched the fire continue to grow. Eventually it started to crackle and pop, and the tips of the flames reached towards the top of the pile.

That'll do just fine.

He looked over at the horse, waiting for a moment as if he had actually expected it to say something. The horse remained silent and continued to graze on the grass within its reach. Bashkim groaned in aggravation and looked back up at the treetops.

While grateful to have a steed that could carry him, it still left a lot to be desired. The creature could never be left alone and smelled awful. Its understanding of Bashkim's words was limited to simple commands and offered nothing in return in the form of communication. A decent enough steed, but far from a companion.

Nothing like Rin.

Nothing like her at all. Nothing could compare to what she offered. Bashkim snorted as he recalled when he had first met her. Telscara had reported a dragon sighting on more than one occasion, but nobody wanted to step up to the challenge. Understandable, as dragons were not something one should mess with. A much younger Bashkim, however, didn't know any better. People were in danger, and that's all he knew.

He at least knew enough to be afraid, for he recalled the gradual sinking feeling as he hiked up the mountain for the first time. Each step he took he asked himself what he had gotten himself into.

Fighting dragons? He remembered thinking to himself. *What the hell was I thinking? I don't know anything about dragons.*

It didn't stop him. He continued to climb up the mountain, ready to face whatever lay at the top. A heroic victory, a bloody death, or perhaps the beast wouldn't even be home. He thought he had pictured every possible scenario, but Rin had thrown him for quite the loop. At the top he found a cavern made entirely of ice, and within it stood piles of riches.

"Who dares to set foot in my chamber?" a voice echoed through the room, its boldness thumping against his chest.

Terrified, Bashkim answered the strange voice. "My name is Bashkim."

"And what does Bashkim want? Have you come for my gold?"

"I have no desire for your treasure."

"No desire?" the voice asked, sounding surprised. "A mortal without greed? Then why have you come? Are you here to take my head as a trophy?"

"I'd rather not," Bashkim admitted. "But the people of Telscara are afraid."

"As they should be."

"So long as I'm being honest, I'm afraid too, but I can't just stand by and do nothing."

"You have no desire for my gold, and you are willing to lay your life down for mere peasants. What does one gain from such a task?"

"What would you lose if you left them alone?"

"Are you proposing a bargain?"

"I haven't much. But I would much rather give what I have than fight when it's not necessary."

A small smile found its way on Bashkim's face as he recalled that day. He remembered the silence that came at that moment, and how he thought his end would surely come as he heard the giant footsteps approaching him. Out of the darkness came the face of a dragon, causing him to take a step back. The dragon slowly extended its head forward and put its face directly in front of him. He could feel the dragon's cold breath pushing against him. It chilled his entire body. The beast looked him over, sniffing him with its large nostrils.

"A hybrid," the dragon said, this time in a more feminine voice.

"That was you? You can talk?"

"I can. And beautifully I might add."

"I..." Bashkim said but found himself at a loss for words. "I didn't know dragons could talk."

"Have you ever asked one?"

"Well, no. Honestly you're the first I've seen."

The dragon chuckled and pulled her head back and placed a hand on her chest. "I'm honored to be your first dragon. Though I'm afraid I must be the bearer of bad news and inform you that not *all* dragons can talk. Not your language, anyway."

"That must make you pretty special then."

"Oh, stop," the dragon said, waving him away as though she were embarrassed.

Bashkim rolled over on his side and stared at the campfire, fighting back a tear as the memory replayed in his mind. The two hit it off immediately that day, joking with one another like old friends. It didn't take him long to forget that before him stood a beast that could swallow him whole, for he saw only Rin and nothing else.

It's quiet, he thought, realizing how still things were without her. *It's just...so damned quiet.*

Even the voice in his head seemed to have little interest in him. He hadn't heard it a single time since Rin left, despite him cursing it and calling it a coward. He had even tried challenging the voice the previous day, demanding it face him. Despite his cries, the voice made no return.

Instead, it left Bashkim to swim in his own late-night thoughts. He wanted to blame the voice in his head for what happened to those men in the forest, as well as with Omar. Though the more he thought about it, the more he started to consider the idea that those actions were his own and the voice merely a bystander. An antagonizing bystander, perhaps, but the choices made still belonged to Bsahkim.

Is this really who I am? Have I always been this way?

He thought back on his past adventures. Confrontation had led to blood before, and he knew that it would more than likely happen again if he were to continue this line of work. It's just the way things were. It's how the world worked. There were bad people, and somebody had to deal with them, one way or another. Even Rin agreed to that. Hell, both of them had taken lives in the past. He didn't *want* to, but sometimes he didn't have a choice.

*But what if...*he thought, his mind taking him all the way back to a much earlier memory in his life. *What if...I'm the one that's bad?*

He had asked himself this question before, and more often than not he could convince himself he would be okay if he kept moving. Tonight, however, brought different feelings and different thoughts. The memory played vividly in his mind, and he could hear their screams clearly, begging for his help as they burned alive.

If I'm the bad one...then who is going to deal with me?

A sudden shiver ran through his body.

No, he thought, closing his watering eyes. *That wasn't me. I didn't want that to happen. It wasn't my fault.*

Despite his attempts, convincing himself of his own innocence proved to have little effect. His mind seemed intent on blaming him for what had happened that night.

What if this voice has been in my head all along? Maybe it's been using me since the beginning.

A terrifying thought, but it might mean he had *some* innocence to him. Perhaps he had been a puppet in some otherworldly being's plan beyond his control.

But why would it be coming out now? Am I just now starting to get some sense of control in my life, instead of losing it?

He wanted it to make sense, but it didn't.

That's just what I want to be the truth. The fire was mine. I can't blame anyone else for that. That was my sin.

Figuring it would be another long and uneasy night, Bashkim formed his hand into a fist and struck the ground in aggravation.

"Damn it," he growled and sat up straight.

A single tear slid down his cheek, causing him to wipe his face as he stared into the fire.

I'm a lost cause.

"You don't have to be," a familiar voice whispered in his mind.

"You," Bashkim said aloud in a tired voice, recognizing the white dragon.

"Teeus mon deela," the voice said, sounding pleased to hear from Bashkim.

Bashkim's hands tightened into fists as he listened to the words, quickly forgetting his earlier issues. "Why do you not show yourself? Why are you always hiding?"

The voice chuckled slightly. "Oh, Bashkim," it said clearly in words that he could understand. "It is not I who hides."

Bashkim narrowed his eyes and relaxed his hands, trying to decide whether he actually spoke to the white dragon or if his sleep deprivation had finally taken him.

"So you can speak my language after all," Bashkim asked, playing along. "What changed your mind?"

"The words of mortals are primitive and barbaric. Such genagwae is unfit for a tongue such as mine."

Almost not caring anymore, Bashkim chuckled at the voice's bravado. "You seem to have an awfully high opinion of yourself, white dragon."

"I am no mere dragon," the voice said, sounding almost amused at the idea. "I am a power beyond your comprehension. Grunaneer tumozen! Mortals refuse to even speak my name, and Arbiters cower in my presence. I am that which the Light fails to destroy. Ruler of the dark. Devourer of souls and this world. I am, Mykenebres."

Bashkim took a sudden and sharp breath and his eyes widened. All this time he had thought the voice in his head belonged to the white dragon, a mythical creature of days gone that could be defeated in theory. He thought at worst that Mykenebres merely controlled the dragon.

Bashkim stood up straight, trying to retain his composure as the truth set in. "If you're the one that's been haunting me, then were does the white dragon fit into all this?"

The voice in his head chuckled. "He was but a fool who thought he could defy me."

It was true. Bashkim hadn't challenged the white dragon. He had challenged the devil himself.

"You made him that way?" Bashkim asked. "Is that what you wish to do to me?"

"He brought that fate upon himself. But for you, Bashkim, I offer a gift."

"And what is that?"

"What you did to those thieves was merely a taste of what you want people to have. There are those who need to pay for their sins, do they not? Isn't it about time somebody brought some justice to this world that we call home?"

"And you want me to be that person?"

"Sin will exist with or without me, Bashkim. Man is a flawed creation with a corrupted heart. But with my help, you could have the power to change this world. You could do what the Arbiters clearly cannot. You can bring balance, Bashkim. The world needs you."

Bashkim remained silent. He could feel the strange magic inside of him slowly starting to grow. It seemed under his control for now, but he knew that wouldn't last forever. It hadn't in the past, and he couldn't think of why now would be any different. He knew being scared caused things to spiral out of control before, and right now, that's exactly how he felt.

"The likes of Omar and Orenzen?" Mykenebres asked. "Their fates could be whatever your judgement deemed fair. That power, Bashkim, could be yours, and yours alone."

"Perhaps. But having the power and having the right are two different things. What you call justice is nothing more than bloodlust. I've been down that road, and it cost me my closest friend."

"Was she your friend? She fled when she saw only a hint of your power. She was your friend only when she had power over *you*."

"Enough!" Bashkim snapped, ignoring his fears. "Torture me all you wish, but you leave her out of this."

"You can't hide forever," Mykenebres said, his voice rising. "Even the strongest will break if they deny themselves. Within you is the lust for blood. Those are your desires, not mine! If you fail to quench that thirst, you will descend into madness!"

"No! That's you making me that way. I was fine until you came along!"

"The world needs you, Bashkim! Do not hide from you true nature!"

The campfire began to grow, and its flames stood up straight as they reached for new heights. Bashkim could feel the piercing in his chest as the magic swelled inside of him and stole his breath. He ignored the pain and continued to stand against the voice.

"You're the one hiding!" Bashim yelled. "You speak in my mind, but you never show yourself. You're a coward hiding in the shadows!"

The voice started to laugh, pushing Bashkim to his limits.

"Face me!" Bashkim yelled.

Bashkim's emotional outburst caused the campfire to explode in size. The flames shot upwards towards the trees above him and stood upright and stiff. The branches that touched the flame instantly turned to ash. The light from the new fire lit the entire area around him, forcing him to shield his eyes and making the horse buck wildly in fear.

"No," Bashkim said. "You'll not have me this time."

Bashkim held both his hands out and faced his palms towards the blazing fire. He attempted to conjure his own magic, and he could feel it inside of him, cutting its way through the corruption that mutated his campfire. The pain in his chest started to loosen, and he could feel himself able to breathe more easily.

Not this time.

Bashkim stepped closer to the flame with his hands still out. His magic continued to push through. It flowed from his chest and out into his arms. Down the corrupted flame went, slowly back to Bashkim's height.

Not this time.

He fell to his knees, keeping his arms out as he pushed harder. His breaths became heavy and sweat started to drip down his face as he tried to bring the fire under control. Memories from before started to play in his mind, and the screams filled his head. They begged for him to stop the fire. They shouted for their lives, crying for mercy.

"Leave me, Mykenebres!" Bashkim shouted, pushing himself back up to his feet.

He swept both of his arms wide, crossing themselves over one another. The fire shrunk and retreated into the ground almost instantly. As his eyes readjusted to the darkness, he could see a thick strand of smoke rising from the campfire's remnants. The moon's glow poured through the hole he had made in the treetops and highlighted the ash raining down around him. His horse continued to neigh in fright and tried to break free from its rope.

"Easy, boy, easy," Bashkim said, catching his breath.

Bashkim came to the horse's side and rubbed its snout and patted its sides. "It'll be alright."

A small snort came from the horse who seemed more or less convinced that it would indeed be alright. Bashkim blinked his eyes several times, still trying to readjust to the darkness since he had removed the fire and its blinding light. He looked up, able to clearly see the stars through the hole he had burned all the way through the top of the forest.

Yeah, he thought, gently patting his chest. *It'll be alright.*

Bashkim closed his eyes for a moment and took a slow breath in and held it. It *would* be alright. He gave the horse a couple more pats and returned to the remnants of his campfire which had become nothing more than a pile of ash. Bashkim acquired more sticks and branches and built himself another pile within just a few minutes. He stopped once he had enough fuel for another fire but paused for a moment and stared at it. He could feel his magic inside of him calmly floating around in his chest, ready to obey his command.

This is my magic, he told himself, holding his hand out. *Not his.*

The magic gently moved through his body, coasting its way through his arm and out towards his hand. Things were different this time as he let it flow.

It feels...good, he thought, confident the magic belonged to him.

With a small wave of his hand, another fire came to life and started to burn the branches. He could feel his connection to the flame. The magic inside of him held onto it carefully. He relaxed, breathing normally as he loosened his grip on the fire instead of choking it. The fire gradually grew on its own and consumed the small sticks while working its way to the larger branches. Bashkim eventually let go completely of his magical grip and let the flames move completely on their own.

"There's a fire in all of us," he remembered Rin telling him. "And I'd hate for you to condemn yours before it was given a chance to breathe."

Bashkim wiped away a single tear falling from his eye.

Thanks, Rin.

Finally feeling somewhat rested, Bashkim started his day shortly after the sun had risen. He packed his belongings and double checked to make sure the kesshonite dagger remained in his pack before mounting his horse.

Still can't believe Simon let me take it, he thought, closing his backpack. *Either he really wants nothing to do with it, or he has even more trust in me than I thought.*

He spent the better part of his morning thinking about Simon, replaying their conversation in his mind. Part of him wished he could see how things were going back in Nennossen and how Simon faired with the shift of power. However, Simon had been correct in what he told Bashkim. He *would* rather chase dragons than have to deal with that.

Bashkim tried not to think about the discussion with Mykenebres, but he could only hold out for so long. He tried to fill his mind with nicer things, such as the time he and Rin had spent an entire afternoon attempting to make ice sculptures, but it didn't seem to be enough. Not even the memory of him and Rin attacking an entire pirate ship on their own could keep his mind occupied, for the offer from Mykenebres became too much *not* to think about.

The power to change the world...can't lie. It's tempting. And he made some good points.

Bashkim couldn't deny that he felt the Arbiters were slacking in their duties. Stepping up and doing the job himself seemed like a sensible enough thing to do. And if he could be given the power to do just that, then why not?

But why the white dragons? What role do they play? Why would he need the beastly pawns?

He could at least find it believable they belonged to Mykenebres, even if he didn't understand why. Ascura and his knights had used kesshonite to defeat them in the past. Kesshonite came from the Arbiters themselves, so if anything in the world could take down a pawn of Mykenebres, then kesshonite seemed the obvious solution.

Why not come out himself? Why use the dragons? Surely, they're much weaker in comparison.

The whole thing made his head hurt. He knew he didn't have much hope in understanding what beings of higher existence had planned, but he wouldn't have minded a hint.

"One of you Arbiters could come down here and help," Bashkim said aloud, looking up at the sky. "Isn't this your fight? Why am I the one getting caught up in the middle of this?"

Bashkim waited, expecting nothing, and getting nothing.

"No wonder your world is going to shit."

Bashkim heaved a heavy sigh and let his shoulders drop. Against his better judgement, he started to consider the offer.

What if I did have the power to make a difference?

What could he do? With that kind of power, what *couldn't* he do? The Arbiters weren't doing anything, assuming they even existed. He could be the change the world needed. He could make things right. He could balance things the way he thought they should be.

No more kings. No more hiding behind castle walls. All would be on a level playing field. All would be equal. No eshans. No humans. No hybrids. Just...people.

The idea only became more tempting the more he thought about it. He paused and weighed the possibilities.

No, he finally told himself, remembering his last conversation with Rin. *Arbiters or not, I'm only a mortal. That kind of power is not for me. If I can't control what I already have, then I've little need for more.*

He sighed and shook his head, staring ahead while the horse continued to carry him. He couldn't deny the appeal of having the power to put people like Orenzen in their place, but he couldn't ignore what the voice had told him either.

A thirst for blood, he reminded himself. *If that's true, then Rin was right to leave.*

A sinking feeling came over him, but at the same time he felt some relief. If the voice spoke the truth about him, then he didn't want Rin anywhere near him. She would be safer staying away. It didn't feel great, but if it kept her from getting hurt, then he'd do it without second thought.

Grumbling, Bashkim looked down at his horse. "Don't guess you have any input?"

The horse said nothing.

"Yeah," Bashkim sighed, patting the side of the horse's neck. "I didn't think so."

Later that day, Bashkim arrived safely at Teasvanna as planned. He remained outside the city so that he would *continue* to be safe. He made himself a small makeshift camp consisting of nothing more than a tent barely big enough to cover him, as well as a campfire. Bashkim kept himself just enough in sight so that the city's guards would still see him. It took a couple days of waiting, but eventually a pair of guards finally made their way out to him.

"What are you doing?" one of them asked once they approached him.

"Please," Bashkim said, remaining seated on the ground and holding his hands up. "I mean you no harm. My kind is not welcome in your city, which is why I choose to wait out here."

Bashkim slowly moved his hands towards his hair and pulled it back, revealing both of his ears. "I would like to speak with Fandul, but I am afraid to approach Teasvanna on my own."

"What do you need from Fandul?" the guard asked.

"I have a message for him, but I must deliver it personally."

The guards looked Bashkim over, unimpressed.

"May I move?" Bashkim asked. "I have something for you."

"Slowly," the guard answered.

"Of course," Bashkim said and got to his feet, making his way over to his horse.

He reached into one of the saddlebags and pulled out two small red gemstones. He held them in his open hand so that the guards could easily see.

"I can give you these for your troubles. But please, tell Fandul I need to speak with him."

"Are you trying to bribe city guards?"

"No, sir. Merely offering you compensation for delivering a message."

"Well...I suppose we *could* ask him if he wants to speak with you," the more talkative guard said. "Obviously we're headed back that way anyway, so might as well, right? Though I can't promise you he'll come out here."

"I'm certain he will," Bashkim said, tossing the two gemstones to the guards. "Tell him a hybrid has news of white dragons."

The guards pocketed their new gemstones. "Very well. But if he doesn't speak with you by the end of the day, you *will* have to pack your things and go. We can't have you loitering outside the city like you have been."

"The sooner I can leave the better."

Bashkim watched the two guards leave. They became smaller and smaller as they got closer to the city, causing Bashkim to squint as he watched them disappear behind the large doors. After a couple of hours, Bashkim could see two new figures coming towards him. One of them tall and slender, and the other a giant of a man.

CHAPTER 13

Bashkim silently watched the two figures approaching in the distance, taking note of the larger one.

That must be Dasc, he thought, watching the giant figure gradually grow as it got closer.

He didn't blame Fandul for bringing backup. How could he, considering what he had done to their castle last time? It didn't mean he had to like it, though. He wanted to give Fandul a chance to speak his mind without prying ears.

Unless he trusts this Dasc fellow. He could have brought any of the guards with him, or even several, but he chose only a single companion...interesting.

Bashkim did his best to wait patiently and continued to cook the rabbit he had been holding over his fire for the past several minutes. By the time the two soldiers arrived, the meat had nearly finished cooking. Fandul stepped up first, keeping a safe amount of space between him and Bashkim. Behind him stood Dasc with his massive sword on his back. The hulking brute wore a full suit of steel, sporting a grin that showed his teeth as he cracked the knuckles under his armored gauntlets. Bashkim remained seated on the ground, checking the rabbit for its doneness.

A small huff left Fandul as he crossed his arms. "I had a feeling it was you. Arbiters only know why you've returned," he said, eyeing the fire and taking note that it burned without fuel.

"Relax," Bashkim said, dismissing his fire. "I told you before that I didn't want to hurt anybody. I didn't then, and I don't now."

"You say that, yet your burned several of our soldiers and destroyed the side of our castle."

"And for that I am sorry, but what choice did I have? You know Orenzen would have left me to rot in those cells, assuming he didn't have me executed."

"And had you let me do my job," Fandul argued. "I could have pulled some strings and had you out within a day and on your way."

Bashkim held his tongue and stared blankly at the cooked rabbit. He had prepared himself for Fandul's judgement of his escape but learning that Fandul had originally planned to have him released blindsided him.

"I didn't think you would be able to," Bashkim finally said. "Or would be willing. Surely you can understand that, all things considered."

Fandul locked eyes with Bashkim and tapped his armored foot against the ground. "What is it that you want?"

"Honestly, I had hoped to speak with you alone," Bashkim said, glancing over at Dasc.

"I trust Dasc with my life. Anything you can tell me, you can tell him."

Bashkim looked over at the large man. Dasc stood tall with an overly confident smile on his face and thumped an armored gauntlet against his steel chest. The blow sounded like it had been hard enough to dent his own steel.

"Fair enough," Bashkim said. "The food is done if you would like some."

"Fresh rabbit?" Dasc blurted and stepped forward. "Of course I would!"

Fandul held his hand out and stopped Dasc in his tracks.

"Aw, come on," Dasc whined. "I've been stuck in the throne room all day watching the king. I'm hungry!"

Fandul kept his hand against Dasc, preventing him from stepping forward as he narrowed his eyes at Bashkim.

"Surely you don't think this little, tiny man is trying to poison us," Dasc said, lowering his voice and turning to Bashkim. "Because he'd need a lot more than that little rabbit can hold."

"I'll take the first bite if it makes you feel better," Bashkim said.

"It would," Fandul said, taking his hand back.

Dasc eagerly stepped up and laid his massive sword down on the ground and took a seat in front of Bashkim on the opposite side of where the fire had rested. Fandul remained standing but took the cooked rabbit himself and started to portion it out randomly as he saw fit. Dasc rubbed his hands together as Fandul tore him off a piece but refrained from taking the first bite.

Bashkim took the piece Fandul handed him and blew on it to cool it down. He bit into it, keeping eye contact with Fandul as he chewed and swallowed. Fandul watched Bashkim carefully, as did Dasc, who licked his lips in anticipation.

"He's not dead yet," Dasc said. "Satisfied?"

"Very well," Fandul sighed, taking his own seat next to Dasc, who immediately began to consume his share.

Fandul took a bite of his portion and chewed it slowly as he continued to watch Bashkim.

"I hadn't heard of you before your first arrival," Fandul said after finishing a bite. "Once Lord Orenzen made mention that he knew of you, I started to inquire on my own."

"Learn anything good?" Bashkim asked.

"You don't seem to stay in one place for very long, for starters."

"That's what happens when you don't have a home. Even more so when nobody will *let* you have a home."

"I suppose you're right. But what brings you back here?"

"I need your help. It's that simple."

Fandul snorted. "If you're coming to *me* for help, it can't be that simple."

"I need to speak with Treydola," Bashkim said.

"The king's daughter?" Fandul asked loudly. "Are you insane?"

"Don't you think it was odd she ordered you to put me in those cells with Ishmonyae? You even said it wasn't like her to do so when I asked."

Fandul held his tongue, narrowing his eyes. "Go on," he said after a pause.

"I learned a lot in there," Bashkim explained. "About humans. About eshans. About *us*."

Dasc stopped chewing for a moment, his mouth full and his eyes wide as he looked over at Fandul.

"Then what do you need her for?" Fandul asked.

"I believe she knows more about our white dragon problem," Bashkim continued. "I'd wager she knows even more than Orenzen."

"And you expect me to bring you into the city to speak with her? Have you forgotten what happened last time?"

"No. I want you to bring her to me."

"That's even worse!" Fandul growled. "Do you take me for a fool?"

"Somewhere safe," Bashkim said, keeping calm. "Somewhere public, where you can have plenty of eyes on her. Handleson would be ideal. It's home to both humans and eshans so you can have witnesses from both sides. Plus, it's far enough away from Teasvanna that nobody will recognize either of you."

"You must think I'm mad."

"Not at all. I think you want to know the truth."

"That may be so but you're still reckless."

"I did what I thought I had to do," Bashkim said, his voice rising. "I tried my best not to hurt anyone."

"Sometimes trying isn't good enough," Fandul said, pulling his lengthy hair back and revealing a bandaged ear on the left side of his head. "Do you see this?" he asked. "This is what Orenzen did to me after you left. He said if I loved hybrids enough to let them into his city, then I wouldn't mind looking like one. This is why I say you're reckless, Bashkim. Look around you. There's more than just you at play here."

"I..." Bashkim started to say, but the shock choked his words. "I'm sorry. I didn't...if I had known..."

"Didn't you say Bashkim risked his neck coming into our city?" Dasc chimed in. "Marched behind you right through the streets of Teasvanna just to try and help us. He might be reckless, but it takes a man almost as big as me to do something like that."

Fandul took in a long breath and let his hair drop, as well as his tone. "I suppose you're right," he said. "It's probably safe to say most people don't expect a king to go around cutting off the tips of their soldiers' ears."

A silence came between the three, and once Dasc saw that Fandul had calmed down, he went back to finishing off his portion of the rabbit. Fandul ate in much smaller bites, staring down at the ground. Bashkim on the other hand, stopped eating altogether and reached for his pack.

"Here," he said, reaching in and grabbing the dagger. "I want to show you something. When I was in that cell, Ishmonyae told me about something from the past. Something that was used against the white dragons."

"A dagger?" Fandul asked, watching Bashkim unravel a roll of cloth and reveal the weapon.

"Not just the dagger," Bashkim explained. "But the power that has been infused in it. Here. Do you feel it?"

Bashkim handed the dagger over, but as Fandul reached for it, his hand jerked back right before touching it.

"By the Light," Fandul gasped. "What is that? What's in that thing?"

"He called it kesshonite," Bashkim said, motioning again for Fandul to take the dagger.

Fandul carefully reached out, wrapping his fingers around the small handle and lifting it out of the cloth that Bashkim held it in.

"I feel...something," Fandul said quietly. "There's so much power here, and it feels like it's right in the palm of my hand, but at the same time, I can't quite hold it. It's like it's slipping between my fingers."

"He said eshans can't use it, only suppress it. Humans, on the other hand, can pull it out but can't control it."

"And that's why they worked together in the past?"

Bashkim nodded his head. "And there's more. Humans can use magic too. The kesshonite gives them the power somehow. I saw with my own eyes the king of Nennossen summon a flame."

"If that's true," Fandul said, handing the dagger back. "Then that rewrites everything we know about magic."

Bashkim carefully took the dagger and wrapped it back in the cloth. "I promise you, all of it is true."

Fandul snorted at the idea, leaning over and looking at Dasc. "How does the idea of humans using magic make you feel?"

"Magic isn't everything," Dasc mumbled.

Fandul's shoulders jerked as he quietly chuckled before turning back to Bashkim. "You think Treydola will help you?" he asked.

"She jumped at the chance before," Bashkim said. "I can't promise you she knows much but she at least knew enough to put me in that cell with Ishmonyae."

Fandul nodded. "We've gotten reports of your white dragon," he said. "Seems it has made its way close to Teasvanna. One of our patrols went missing. No bodies, no weapons, nothing. A witness saw the dragon near the last known location of the patrol, so I'm inclined to believe it's responsible."

"Nennossen lost one of their patrols as well," Bashkim said. "Their captain said the dragon caused the soldiers to fight one another."

"A dragon that can bend the wills of soldiers?" Fandul asked. "That makes this thing even worse than I thought, but it could also mean our men are still alive."

"Maybe, but I don't think I'd count on getting them back. Nennossen's patrol fought themselves to the death."

"What kind of monster can control the minds of men?" Dasc asked.

"I don't know," Fandul said, looking over at Bashkim. "But if Treydola knows anything about it, then we should probably ask her, shouldn't we?"

"We should," Bashkim nodded. "And right now, you're the one with the power to make that happen."

Fandul took a slow breath, tapping his fingers against his armored knee. "Handleson isn't exactly close."

"That's about three days solo on a soldier's horse if you're lucky," Dasc said. "Probably a week with Treydola. I can cover for you while you're gone."

Fandul nodded his head and frowned as he looked at Bashkim. "The Arbiters must want to punish me, for they keep making me cross paths with you."

"I'm just trying to do the right thing," Bashkim said.

"Yes, well, this is definitely a step up from destroying castle walls, isn't it? But there's one more question that still lingers."

"What is that?"

"The magic," Fandul said, locking his eyes with Bashkim's. "*Your* magic. I haven't forgotten what I saw back at the castle. How did you manage that and survive? I saw the blood."

"I..." Bashkim tried to explain but struggled to find his words. "I'm working on it, but it's...complicated."

"That level of magic could kill a man. An *eshan* man."

"I realize that," Bashkim said, "and I wish I could explain, truly, I do."

Fandul stayed silent, keeping his eyes focused on Bashkim as he continued to tap his knee.

"Can you keep it under control?" Fandul finally asked.

"I believe so," Bashkim said.

"Then it's settled," Fandul said, rising to his feet. "We'll do it. Clearly, we're dealing with more than an ordinary dragon, and it would seem the king's daughter is more willing to help us than her father. Where in Handleson would we find you?"

"It's been several years since I've been there," Bashkim said. "But if it still stands, I'll wait for you at the Crossbreed Brew. If not, then whatever took its place."

"Very well. Dasc, come on. It's time for us to return."

"One more thing," Bashkim said. "A bit of a favor."

"You're asking me to deliver the king's daughter to you," Fandul said sternly. "What other favors could you possibly need?"

"A message. To Nennossen."

"Nennossen?"

"Yes. The captain's name is Simon. He's probably expecting me back already and wondering what's taking so long. Is it possible to get a message back to him?"

"Communication between our two cities isn't the best," Fandul admitted. "But it's not impossible. It wouldn't the first time we've passed word through our patrols, and I've men I trust all along the way to see it through. But why not just ride your dragon out there and tell him yourself? I would think you could make it back before we reach Handleson."

Bashkim held his tongue and stared down at the ground.

"Is that complicated too?" Fandul asked.

"Yeah," Bashkim said quietly, keeping his eyes down.

"We'll have it done," Fandul sighed, motioning for Dasc to follow him. "The message will say Bashkim is alive and well and continuing his quest."

"Thank you," Bashkim said quietly.

Dasc started to get back up to his feet but stopped halfway and pointed at the remaining rabbit on the stick. "Are you going to finish that?"

"Go ahead," Bashkim said, handing it over.

Dasc grabbed the rest of the rabbit as well as his massive sword and happily got to his feet. As he marched back to Teasvanna with snack in hand, Bashkim couldn't help but notice Dasc sharing half of it with Fandul.

Bashkim made good time reaching Handleson, despite his subconscious efforts *not* to. He stalled all he could, taking more stops than necessary along the way. Mykenebres kept surprisingly quiet during the trip, allowing him to drown in his own thoughts all by himself.

He hadn't been to the city for several years, and he had hoped not to return for many more. The fact that it had barely changed since his last visit seemed to only make it worse. The streets were still made of the same stone, all of them wide and allowing plenty of room for people to pass through, as well as the loads being hauled. Each street eventually wound its way back to the circular plaza in the center of the city.

In the middle of the plaza stood a large statue. It looked just the same as he had remembered. Two figures posed, carved from a single large stone. One human, one eshan, each of them bowing to one another serving as a reminder that all were equal within Handleson. In front of it, carved in a stone tablet were the following words:

> *Greater than neither are we, but equal in our sins*
> *May Handleson forever be the home for those that remember this,*
> *And forever the bridge between those that forget*

Bashkim rubbed his hand across the stone tablet, observing the date.

Founded almost two hundred years ago, he thought. *That's close to when the white dragons first attacked. Wonder if they even knew it was happening at the time.*

Bashkim took his hand back and sighed as he watched the many people passing by. There were indeed both humans and eshans here, and they seemed to be minding their own business, having little issue with their funny eared neighbors.

"Oi," a voice said suddenly next to Bashkim. "It's a beautiful statue, isn't it?"

Bashkim turned to see a man approaching him.

"Honestly, I'm surprised it hasn't been taken down yet," Bashkim admitted.

"You sound the same as you look, friend."

"Pardon?"

"Worn out. Distressed. I've seen a lot of faces in my time, but yours? Oh, yours could tell stories for days, couldn't it? I'll be honest, my good man, I'm not sure they're stories people would like to hear. You've had a rough go of it, haven't you?"

Bashkim narrowed his eyes and observed the man. He wore a working man's clothes, complete with patches and calloused hands. What stood out more, though, were the mismatched ears on his head.

"Can I help you?"

"Oh, I'm not the one that needs help," the man said. "Not by the look of it, anyway. I'm on my way to get a drink. Been working all day and it's time to recover with a pint or two or ten. Was the plan, anyway, until I saw that storm cloud hanging over your head. I seen that and thought to myself, sure would be a damned shame to drink all that goodness alone."

Bashkim remained silent and still, unsure of what to say.

"Look," the man said. "You're not from around here, that much is obvious. Handleson is a decent place. No need for trouble, and pardon me for judging, but you look like you've seen quite a bit of that. So how abouts as one hybrid to another, we split a nice cold drink and forget about all that, yeah? I've been here my whole life, so I can only imagine what it's like out there for one of us. But that *stays* out there."

"That's very kind of you," Bashkim said. "Is the Crossbreed Brew still here?"

"Oh, so you *have* been here before," the man said with a smile. "It's only the best tavern in the city, of course it still stands! Though we had a bit of a scare recently. The owner's son runs it these days, and he got a bit ill. Almost lost him. His wife though, what a gem. She went traveling to get some meds and healed him right up. That's how we do things around here. We don't give up."

"So it would seem."

"It's true! Even when that orphanage burned down. Oh, it was terrible. Terrible accident about twenty years ago or so. I was barely a man when it happened, but I remember seeing the remains the next day. Miss Angela made it out though, and she rebuilt that orphanage from the ground up with her own hands. Never missed a beat. Still raising them kids, too."

Bashkim remained silent and sighed slowly.

"Well, enough of that," the man said. "We're trying to get away from the storm clouds, right? Come on, let's get a drink."

"I'll meet you there later. I have a few things to take care of first. It...might take a little while."

"Gives me time to put on my drinking clothes," the man said, patting Bashkim on the shoulder. "Oh, by the way, my name's Henry."

"Bashkim," Bashkim said, shaking the man's hand.

Henry smiled and gave an energetic handshake, then bid him farewell.

"Remember!" Henry shouted and walked away. "Happy thoughts, my friend. Leave your troubles at Handleson's gates."

Happy thoughts, Bashkim thought to himself, watching the man make his way down the street. *Don't think there's going to be very many of those where I'm headed.*

By all means, Handleson should have made him extremely happy. A city that would simply leave him alone and let him live in peace. He could stay, settle down, and stop all the adventuring nonsense. He could just...live.

"Have you ever tried giving it a chance?" He heard Cynthia ask.

I used to have a home, Bashkim wanted to tell her. *Once...right here.*

Bashkim tilted his head back and closed his eyes, trying to contain himself. Every part of him would rather go toe to toe with a white dragon than do what he was about to do.

"You're running," he heard Rin tell him. "You've been running your entire life."

Not anymore, Rin, he told himself. *The running is going to stop.*

Bashkim took a quick breath and turned around. He made his way down the street and kept his face low out of habit. The roads hadn't really changed since his previous time here, and he knew exactly where to go. How could he forget?

The people he passed attempted to nod and say hello, to which Bashkim awkwardly tried to return the gesture. His instincts told him to keep a low profile, but in his mind he knew he didn't have to. The idea that hybrids were actually welcome somewhere failed to fully sink in with him.

Fewer stores and services stood on the sides of the road as he made his way farther down and were instead replaced with homes. Among them stood one particularly larger than the rest, with a large area of dirt and grass that hadn't been covered up with stone. Several children played in the yard near the home. Some of them pretended to battle with wooden swords while others were chased. A few of them even chose to be more relaxed and laid on their backs, pointing to the various clouds in the sky.

On the porch sat an older woman in a rocking chair, teaching the small child on her lap to read. The child didn't seem very interested with the idea, but the woman insisted that he learn. Bashkim's heart sank when he saw the woman and he froze in place. The woman saw him out of the corner of her eye and looked over, waiting for him to speak.

"Are you here to adopt or drop off?" she asked after a brief silence. "Judging by the sword I'm guessing drop, but I don't see one with you."

"Neither," Bashkim said, his voice nearly cracking as he made his way forward.

The lady closed her book and motioned for the child to join the others in the yard as Bashkim made his way up the porch's steps. The hybrid child paid him little mind, fleeing from the book and running to more entertaining activities with the rest of the children.

"Miss Angela?" Bashkim asked quietly.

The woman tilted her head slightly, looking Bashkim over as she brushed her hair back behind her pointed ears. Suddenly, her eyes widened as if she had seen a ghost, and her hands went to cover her mouth.

"Bashkim?" she gasped. "Is that you?"

"It's me," Bashkim said, taking a hard swallow.

"Praise the Light!" she said, jumping from her rocker and throwing her arms around him. "I'd recognize those green eyes anywhere. I thought we lost you in the fire with everyone else!"

Bashkim stood motionless, his arms trapped under Angela's embrace. The guilt crushed him like a boulder falling onto his shoulders. "No," he said. "I made it out without a scratch."

"Then where have you been?"

"That's...what I wanted to talk to you about. It's a bit of a story. Can we go inside?"

"Absolutely," she said, motioning him to the door. "Please, come in. Come in."

Angela opened the door and practically shoved Bashkim inside. "Would you like some tea?" she asked. "I made some earlier today."

"Only if you have enough left."

"You know," Angela said and grabbed two cups and began to fill them with tea. "There was an older gentleman that used to happen by here years ago. He told me there was always enough tea for two."

Angela brought Bashkim his cup and made him sit down. "Now," she said, taking a seat herself. "By the Arbiters where have you been? You were just a child the last I saw you. What happened?"

"I ran away," Bashkim said, staring down into his tea. "The night the fire happened. I ran away."

"But why?"

"Because I'm the reason the orphanage burned to the ground."

"How?" Angela asked, her voice surprisingly calm as she leaned back into her seat. "Was there an accident?"

"I want to say it was an accident," Bashkim tried to explain. "But sometimes it's hard to tell myself that. Some nights I wonder if I actually meant to do such a thing."

"I'm not certain I follow."

"Do you remember David and Je'luna?" Bashkim asked, taking a small sip of his tea.

"I do," Angela nodded. "Je'luna was such a sweet soul. That eshan couldn't hurt a fly if his life depended on it."

"That was the problem. David was bullying him."

"Well, that's no surprise. I always had trouble with that one."

"One time was worse than the others. It was late at night. Us kids were all in bed, and I assumed you were too. For some reason David decided to give Je'luna a harder time than normal. I tried to stop him, but no matter what I did, he just wouldn't stop. He kept pushing Je'luna around, and then he started hitting him. That's when I stepped in. David then decided to focus on me, and when he started hitting me...something happened. Something inside of me that I hadn't felt before. I'd had a fight or two before then, but that night was different."

Bashkim continued to stare into his cup, unable to look Angela in the eyes.

"It was magic," he said, after taking a moment to breathe. "It just...swelled up inside of me. At first it felt like bugs were biting me all over, then the pain got worse. I tried to stop it, but then there was fire in my hands. It jumped from me to David. Then he was...I had never used magic before that day. It just kind of happened."

Bashkim paused, unable to finish his story. Angela reached forward, carefully taking his teacup out of his hand and setting both his and hers down on a nearby surface.

"It's okay," she said, holding his hands. "Take your time."

Bashkim had fully expected wrath and fury from the woman, or at the very least a tremendous amount of disappointment. Instead, she showed kindness and understanding. The calmness in her voice only made things worse, causing a tear to fall from his eye.

"David wouldn't stop screaming," Bashkim whispered. "I tried to stop the fire, but whenever I did it just grew...and spread. Before I knew it, the floors started to burn, then our beds, the other kids...and Je'Luna."

Bashkim took another moment to catch his breath again and tried to collect himself so that he could tell the story.

"Two men came in," he said after a while. "One was your husband, and another an eshan I hadn't seen before. They tried to control the flames with their own magic, but it didn't work. I tried to help them, but when I did it only made it worse. I ended up trapping both them and the kids in the room. I knew it was me because I could feel the fire in my own hands. Yet no matter what I did, it just...I made everything worse. Since the fire wasn't hurting me, I thought I could pull them out...but..."

Bashkim stopped before giving too much detail. He remembered clearly what had happened when he tried to pull Je'luna out of the fire. The flames burned so hot that they instantly melted the flesh right off Je'luna's bones, leaving a pile of torched skin in Bashkim's hands.

"The whole place burned," Bashkim said after wiping his face against his shoulder. "I watched it, and it didn't just burn. Whatever those flames touched, they disintegrated and turned to ash. It wasn't just me accidentally starting a fire. It was me fueling the fire with magic, and all I could do was stand there and watch while they begged me to make it stop."

Even though he had been staring at the floor, Bashkim turned away from Angela, taking his hands back.

"I can still see Je'luna's face," he said. "And the absolute horror in his eyes. I can hear the others too. Their voices. Their pleas."

"Bashkim," Angela said softly. "You were a child. You knew nothing of magic. It's not uncommon for eshan children to discover their abilities in dangerous situations. They're just usually fortunate enough to be surrounded by those better equipped to handle it."

"Eshan children don't burn people alive."

"And an eshan child's magic is nowhere near as strong as yours was. You can't blame yourself for the absence of adults in your life as a child. That's on us. Had you known how to control it, you wouldn't have done it."

"Are you sure that's who I am?"

"I raised you, Bashkim," Angela said with a smile. "I know who you are, and I know you could never wrongfully hurt anyone. Not intentionally."

And then it hit him: the stabbing pain from a guilt coated knife that dug all the way through his entire chest. Bashkim felt as though all of his air had left him and he wanted to fall to the floor.

"How did you get out?" Bashkim asked, trying to keep the last few pieces of himself together.

"I was never there," Angela said with a small smile. "I had decided to stay the night with my mother to spend time with her, for she had fallen ill at the time. The man you saw was my brother. He had volunteered to help while I was away."

The knife in Bashkim's chest tore downwards, opening him up completely.

"I'm sorry," Bashkim said breathlessly.

Angela appeared unaffected for the most part by the memories, for she merely sat in her chair with her head tilted slightly, waiting for Bashkim to speak.

"I'm sorry," Bashkim said again.

"How long have you been running?" she asked, her eyes staying on him.

"What do you mean?"

"I might not ever leave Handleson, but even I've heard tales of a man named Bashkim. It was several years after the fire when I heard my first story. Deep down I hoped this mystery man called Bashkim was you, and now I know it was. You were a white knight even as a child. And just like you said, *you* ran away that night, but you never stopped running, did you? You've spent all these years trying to undo one mistake."

Bashkim finally looked over at Angela, his eyes red and watery as he tried desperately to find his words. His mouth attempted to move, but nothing came out. Angela leaned forward and grabbed both of his hands again.

"I need you to listen to me, young man," she said softly. "Nothing you do will bring those people back. You can't spend the rest of your life trying to repay a debt that can never be repaid, and I know I can't be the only one that's told you that."

Bashkim's eyes slowly fell to the floor as he thought of Rin.

"It's good to remember those that we've lost," Angela continued. "But we can't forget about those that are still with us. There're people out there that need a hero like you, Bashkim. You're an adventurer now, and a damned good one from the sound of it. Help those that are alive and here now. Focus on making a better future instead of trying to fix a broken past. Let the Light hold those we've lost."

Bashkim nodded his head slowly, still refusing to look at her.

"Now," she started, "why have you come back here?"

Bashkim shrunk inside of himself. He knew exactly what he wanted, but pulling the words out to actually say it took more strength than he thought possible. Angela rose from her seat, pulling Bashkim up with her.

"Look at me," she said softly, putting her hands on his face and wiping away his tears with her thumbs. "Look at me and tell me what you want."

Bashkim forced himself to look, despite every muscle in his body trying to turn away.

"I want to be forgiven," Bashkim barely managed to say.

Angela smiled, pulling Bashkim closer and kissing him on the forehead. She held him close, wrapping her arms around him. Bashkim sank into her embrace and buried his face into the top of her shoulder as his tears flowed freely.

"You *are* forgiven, child," she said. "Now, no more running."

No more running.

After taking the time to clean himself up and catch Angela up to speed on *some* of the events in his life, he decided to make his way over to the Crossbreed Brew. He found Henry waiting at the bar with an empty seat next to him, which Bashkim took.

"I thought you were going to change?" Bashkim asked, taking note Henry still wore the same outfit.

"That's the trick," Henry said with a smile, raising his eyebrows. "I'm always in my drinking clothes."

The eshan behind the bar stepped up to them, wiping his hands on a small towel. "You the one Henry's been waiting for?" he asked. "Boy's been sipping as slow as he can and taking up space."

"I apologize," Bashkim said. "Things took a little longer than planned."

"Aw, don't worry about him," Henry said. "People aren't exactly lined up to get in, are they? He'll be alright."

The eshan behind the bar balled up his towel and threw it at Henry. "Now," he said, "what can I get for you?"

"Ice cold bandleberry," Henry said, removing the towel from his face. "It's on me. The first one, anyway."

"Bandleberry?" Bashkim asked.

"Don't let the crowd fool you, it's the best damned ale around. If you've never had a bandleberry before, you're in for a treat. Bit sour, so be ready."

The bartender returned just a moment later with a large mug in his hands. A cold mist floated around it radiating from both his hands as he chilled the drink. He sat it down on the bar top with a thud and slid it over. Bashkim nodded his head in appreciation and looked down at the bright pink liquid inside.

The bartender reached under the bar and grabbed two perfectly round berries that just barely fit in the palm of his hand. They were a deep purple in color and smooth all the way around. "These are bandleberries," he said. "A crossbreed of two berries found around here. Extremely hard to get started but fairly easy to grow once you do."

"A hybrid fruit?" Bashkim asked.

The bartender winked and dropped the two bandleberries into Bashkim's drink, breaking the thin layer of ice on top. The eshan stepped back, crossing his arms as he waited.

"Go on," Henry said eagerly. "Give it a try!"

Bashkim grabbed the cold beverage and took a sip, jerking his head back instantly and squinting his eyes as the liquid made its way down him.

"Holy hell," he coughed.

"It's good, isn't it?" Henry asked.

"Yeah," Bashkim said, licking his lips. "Oddly enough."

"You going to be able to finish it?"

"Absolutely."

"Atta boy, Bashkim!" Henry laughed, slapping him on the back. "Come on, let's get some food."

"Lilly!" the bartender said loudly, and out from the door behind him came a woman.

"This gentleman and...*Henry*, would like some food."

"Oh hey, Henry!" Lilly smiled and stepped over to them but stopped dead in her tracks when she saw Bashkim. "You," she said, almost losing her breath.

Bashkim looked at the woman, almost not recognizing her.

"Oh," Bashkim said, not sure what to say. "Um...hello."

"You two know each other?" Henry asked, concerned.

"He was the one that saved me from those thieves I told you about," Lilly explained.

"That was you?" the bartender asked.

"Yeah," Bashkim said, retreating into himself. "That was me. It's uh...it's nothing. Don't worry about it."

"Don't worry about it?" the bartender asked loudly, then added more calmly. "Son, you saved her life and mine as well."

"Well...you're welcome?"

The bartender snorted. "You're not much used to appreciation, are you?"

"No, sir," Bashkim admitted.

"Well then, allow us to show you some. Whatever you need while you're in town is on us."

Henry's face lit up with a wide smile, but the bartender cut him short. "Whatever Bashkim needs," he clarified.

"Whatever Bashkim needs," Henry repeated in a sarcastic tone.

"Oh, shush, Henry," the woman said, gently slapping Henry on the shoulder. "Now tell me, what can we do for you? Other than food and drink. We also have rooms available if you're looking to stay a while."

"Perfect," Bashkim said with a nod. "I'll be needing one of those."

CHAPTER 14

A few days had passed since Bashkim's arrival in Handleson. Wanting to spend some time with Angela but also not wanting to miss Fandul, Bashkim spent only the first day at the orphanage. Naturally, Bashkim did his best to help where he thought he might be useful. At first, she refused the money he offered, but when she wasn't looking, Bashkim slid the purse of Rin's riches inside of a cupboard that she could find later. After that, she scolded him for continuing his journey of trying to repay her for what he had done in the past.

"If you're honestly just wanting to help from the goodness of your heart," she finally said. "Then be what you wish you had growing up."

Bashkim's shoulders dropped, and he let his head sink. He knew exactly what she meant. He turned to look at the kids outside in the yard and sighed as he rubbed a hand through his hair.

"Alright," he agreed. "I'll try."

Angela took her seat on the porch and watched Bashkim make his way out into the yard and gather the children around him.

"Let's talk about magic," he said, kneeling in front of them.

Bashkim briefly glanced back at Angela. A smile formed on her face as she watched. He knew full well that she could teach them plenty about magic without his assistance.

She's an eshan after all.

Bashkim worked with the children by summoning small, candle-sized flames and carefully sliding them into their hands. Others tried a colder approach and attempted to freeze the water inside of a small cup.

The human children also tried to summon magic but of course had little success. The failure, however, did little to deter them as they were convinced they had some magic "somewhere" inside of them.

After several brief small puffs of fire and the occasional frosty palm, Bashkim decided to give the children a break and instead told them tales of his journeys. He told them of climbing mountains, fighting goblins, saving damsels in distress and anything else he thought they might enjoy. As he shared his adventures, Angela quietly made her way back into the house and removed the allegedly hidden purse, placing it back in Bashkim's backpack on the table.

Bashkim spared his audience the stories of the white dragon, figuring ignorance would help them sleep better at night. He did, however, tell them of a mighty dragon named Rin.

"She had the most beautiful scales you'd ever lay eyes on," Bashkim explained.

The kids were blind to the emotions he kept buried underneath his storytelling, but Angela could not be so easily fooled. Seeing the struggle within Bashkim, she eventually decided to step in and started to round up the kids.

"Come on," she said. "Don't think you're getting out of going to the library today. Go on. Get ready."

The kids whined and groaned at the idea, one of them even stating that "nothing exciting ever happens in a library."

"You might be surprised," Bashkim said, ruffling the hybrid child's hair.

Bashkim spent the next couple of days in his room next to a window above the Crossbreed Brew's entrance as he waited for Fandul. He saw several eshans come and go in the meantime, but none of them were the soldier he had hoped for.

So strange, he thought while watching the humans and eshans coexist. *They make it look easy here. What makes it so damned difficult everywhere else?*

He knew he couldn't really answer the question, yet he oftentimes found himself trying to. He thought that perhaps the cities were to blame for raising people with the idea that "others" are not their equals.

But Simon has shown he doesn't feel that way. Nor does Fandul. But here...the circumstances are completely different, and the people act the same as those two.

Bashkim scratched his chin as he continued to watch the townspeople.

Then perhaps Simon was right. Maybe it isn't the circumstances of our birth that determine our future, but the choices we make each day as we build our own road.

He thought of the kings of Nennossen and Teasvanna and how readily they looked down on others. As he did, he couldn't help but remember Rin's parting words.

"In your eyes," she had told him, "all are guilty."

Maybe...but they haven't exactly given me a reason to see them otherwise.

As soon as he thought it, he could feel the foolishness of his own silent words.

After the things I've done, Fandul and Simon have little reason to see me otherwise.

Bashkim took in a long breath and let it slowly leave through his nose as the thoughts settled into him. It was a lot to take in, and he had lots of free time to work on it.

Finally, on one afternoon, Bashkim saw Fandul making his way towards the tavern with Treydola close to his side. Bashkim almost missed the eshan at first for he had arrived in regular clothes covered with a large cloak instead of his usual Teasvanna steel. Bashkim quickly got up from his seat and made his way down the stairs into the Crossbreed Brew's main room.

"Oh?" Lilly asked, feigning surprise with a smile. "Finally decided to join the rest of us?"

"Yes, ma'am," Bashkim said, heading for the tavern's door. "My friends have made it in."

Bashkim opened the double doors wide as Fandul and Treydola approached and motioned for them to come in. Fandul peered inside, observing the half-full tavern.

"It's safe," Bashkim said quietly. "I'm a man of my word."

"Very well," Fandul said as he stepped in and motioned for Treydola to follow.

Bashkim brought them to a table at the end of the room, away from prying ears. Lilly, however, came over quickly to assist.

"This is the first we've seen of ol' Bashkim since he got here," she said and patted him on the back. "He's been cooped up in that room staring out the window for days waiting for you two. You lot must be close."

"We get a little closer each time we meet," Fandul said with a half-smile.

"Aw," Lily said, oblivious to the sarcasm. "What can I get for you all?"

"Nothing at the moment," Fandul said.

"You sure?" Lilly asked. "Even you, Bashkim?"

"I'm fine for now, thanks. Give us a few minutes first. I imagine they've had a long journey."

"Alright," Lilly said, shrugging her shoulders and holding her hands up as she walked away.

Before anyone at the table could speak, Henry made his way through the tavern doors, wide eyed and surprised when he saw Bashkim at the end of the room.

"Oh, ho!" Henry blurted. "I see how it is! Forget all about ol' Henry you do. But when some cute little thing comes a struttin' around here, out you come!"

"Oh, leave him be," Lilly said, slapping him across the chest. "You know you're just here for the booze anyway."

"Yes!" Henry said, making his way over to the bar. "But you see, it's the principle."

"Making plenty of friends I see," Fandul said once things quieted down.

"A few."

"Well then. I'm eager to get this underway for Lady Tredyola has been awfully tight lipped the whole way here."

"Do you not trust Fandul?" Bashkim asked.

Treydola remained silent and kept her eyes locked on Bashkim.

"With all due respect, ma'am," Fandul said. "I've risked more than you realize by bringing you here. I think I've earned the right to hear whatever it is you have to say. I've let you have your silence, but this is where I draw the line."

"Are you sure you want to be involved in this?" Treydola asked.

"I'm already involved."

"For what it's worth," Bashkim added. "Fandul seems to be a cut above the rest. He's stuck his neck out for me too."

"Well, Mr. Bashkim," Treydola said with a single raised eyebrow. "It would seem you have friends everywhere you go."

Bashkim only shrugged his shoulders, unsure of how to take the comment.

"But I suppose you're right," she continued. "Fandul *is* a cut above the rest, for sure. And that's what makes it all the more difficult to get him involved. I feel guilty bringing someone like him into this, and I can't help but wonder if it would better to leave him in ignorance."

"Ignorance is never a better option," Fandul said. "We're all here. We've made our choice."

"So be it," she said and put her arms on the table to lean forward. "Tell me, Bashkim. What do *you* know?"

"White dragons and a wizard named Telanos were a problem a long time ago," Bashkim explained. "Ascura and his knights used kesshonite to fight the white dragons. In the end the dragons were defeated, and Telanos sealed away. About two hundred years later, Telanos is out, and a white dragon has returned."

"White dragons weren't the only thing Ascura fought against," Treydola noted. "He fought the king at the time as well."

"For what?"

"Unity. He wanted humans and eshans to continue to coexist together and to put an end to our differences. A vision that was ultimately his undoing."

"I take it the king in Ascura's time wasn't fond of the idea?" Bashkim asked.

Treydola sighed. "He was not. Nor was he fond of anyone that shared Ascura's goals and vision. With the threat of the white dragons gone, things returned to the old normal, and Ascura's legend was wiped away. As much as it could be, though there are still those that know of Ascura's vision and choose to continue to believe in it, albeit in secret."

"Kings only have as much power as you give them," Bashkim said. "Nennossen has recently learned that lesson."

"And what did they do?" Treydola asked, her eyes curious.

Bashkim hesitated. "They...currently don't have a king."

"I see. While I don't seek to hang my father from the gallows, there might be a lesson to be learned from the humans in balancing power."

"How many would you say know of Ascura's history?" Fandul asked. "And choose to follow his vision?"

"Very few, I'm afraid," Treydola said. "And it feels as those numbers only dwindle as time goes on."

"But we're here," Bashkim said. "That's two more than you had."

"I suppose you're right," Treydola said with a half-smile. "But where does that get us?"

"We know what kills the white dragons," Fandul said. "It's kesshonite. But what about Telanos? All that happened to him in the past was sealing him away."

Treydola held her tongue, and her eyes trailed down to her hands on the table.

"I feel as though catching him is going to be the hardest part," Bashkim said. "As well as finding him. He might be a powerful wizard but if he were to be found, I would doubt he could take on everyone. He did seal himself away after all, or so the stories go, when he was cornered. If it comes down to it, I'm fairly certain we could use the kesshonite. If it works on white dragons, surely it would work on him too."

Fandul crossed his arms and looked over at Treydola. "Do we still have any of the kesshonite?"

"Some of the kesshonite weapons remain, behind lock and key," she explained. "However, if what Ishmonyae says is correct, then I would be afraid to hand such a thing over to the humans. It sounds as though it would cause more harm than good if they're unable to control it without eshan support."

Bashkim nodded. "I agree. So the question is, how do we convince the eshans to help? Getting support from the humans shouldn't be too difficult considering some of the...*changes*...they've been through recently."

"Honestly," Treydola admitted as she twiddled her thumbs. "I was hoping you had a plan for that."

"Sorry to disappoint." Bashkim shrugged. "But I don't. And as long as we're being honest, I'm not sure if Ascura himself could convince them if he were here."

"Not behind bars, anyway," she said.

"Excuse me?" Bashkim asked, both him and Fandul shooting Tredyola a questioning look.

"Ishmonyae," she said. "The one you were in prison with. That *is* Ascura."

"What?" Fandul asked, leaning in closely and trying to keep his voice down. "Ascura and the white dragons were over two hundred years ago. No eshan lives that long. You and I would be lucky to see half that."

"He says he's had a little help," she insisted.

"A little help?" Fandul repeated and leaned back into his chair. "You'd need more than that to live that long."

"I believe him," Treydola argued. "How else do you think he knows about these things?"

"We're assuming they're all true," Fandul said.

Bashkim lifted his hand up. "No. He was right with what he told me. About the kesshonite's existence and about humans with their magic. I saw it. Even if he was lying about being Ascura, he definitely knows what he's talking about."

"I don't like it," Fandul scoffed. "There's some magic at play here that isn't right."

"But imagine if it's true," Bashkim said, his hand sliding down the side of his face. "I was sitting right next to Ascura the entire time. He wasn't telling me stories he had heard. He was telling me the stories he lived! He was there! Why didn't he tell me?"

"And what would you have done?" Treydola asked. "I spoke with him. You were willing to break him out when you didn't even know who he was. Look how much damage you caused simply escaping on your own. Now try to imagine what would have happened had you been dragging an old and frail man behind you. Had you known the truth, you would have likely blazed a path all the way to the front gate."

Bashkim held his tongue and let his head sink.

"Which...isn't completely a bad thing," Treydola added, realizing she might have overstepped. "Wanting to free a wrongly imprisoned man is far from an ill trait. Bullheadedness and blindly charging in, however, aren't the most desirable. Sometimes you must consider what your actions will do to those around you."

Bashkim glanced over at Fandul, remembering the incident with his ear.

"She does make a good point," Fandul smirked.

"Yeah...she's right."

Sensing the defeat in Bashkim, Fandul cleared his throat. "I think it's about time we get something to eat and drink," he said. "It's been a long trip and we still have a lot to discuss."

Fandul patted Bashkim on the shoulder as he rose to his feet. "Milady," he said with a nod before making his way over to the bar next to Henry.

"Ol' Bashy over there save your woman too?" Henry asked.

"Hm?" Fandul muttered. "Oh, no. Not yet, anyway."

"He's some kind of hero, isn't he?"

"Yeah," Fandul said, looking back over at Bashkim and Treydola. "Maybe one day the world will see it that way."

Back at the table, Bashkim remained silent. Treydola scooted herself closer and kept her voice low. "There's one more thing," she said.

"And that is?"

"Ascura wants you to come back. He didn't say why but insisted it was worth it. That said, I do have some concerns of my own."

"Such as?"

"I don't always agree with my father, that much you know, but Teasvanna *is* my home. Last time you were there your dragon destroyed the side of our castle. There are innocents to worry about, Bashkim, and it's only by the Light's mercy that nobody was killed last time."

"She knew what she was doing," Bashkim defended.

"It doesn't matter. It's not a chance I'm willing to take again."

"Then I guess it's a good thing you don't have to worry about it," Bashkim said as his eyes focused down on the table.

"Oh?" Treydola asked, realizing that she had apparently struck a nerve. "I'm...sorry? Did something happen?"

"She's fine. She's just...not around anymore."

"I see," Treydola said, unsure of what Bashkim meant. "Well, in that case, how do you suggest we get you back inside?"

Bashkim glanced over at Fandul and watched as he spoke with Lilly about their food and drink.

"Arrest me."

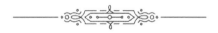

Reluctantly, Fandul agreed to the new plan and the trio began their journey back to Teasvanna. On the first night along the way, they found themselves surrounding a campfire, exchanging silent glances with one another.

"I'm going to lose more than an ear for this," Fandul sighed as he began to make his bed. "If the king catches wind I had his daughter anywhere near you, it will be my head that he removes."

"Should he hear such a thing," Treydola said. "I'll make sure he knows you were merely following my orders. Despite your best efforts to sway me, I forced your hand."

"I appreciate it, but you'll excuse me if I have my doubts as to how well that will work."

"He makes a fair point," Bashkim said. "Unless it's normal for you to leave Teasvanna for more than a few days at a time, questions are bound to be asked."

"We left under the ruse we were headed to a nearby village for a few days," Fandul explained. "Dasc is there waiting for us and covering while we're away."

"I don't suppose there's any way you can leave Teasavanna altogether is there?" Bashkim asked. "After we talk with Ishmonyae."

"I'm afraid not."

"How come?"

Fandul reached over to his belongings and pulled out something wrapped in a large cloth. He untied the thin rope keeping it closed and revealed an extra sword still in its sheath. He handed the weapon to Bashkim and told him to look at the design. Bashkim couldn't help but notice the similarities between Fandul's weapon and the one he bought from Cynthia.

"I'm a Senguan Knight," Fandul said, taking his sword back and wrapping it up. "A title that is not so easily acquired, and nigh impossible to walk away from."

Treydola's eyes widened as Fandul revealed the truth about himself. "I thought you were just a guard."

"What exactly is a Senguan Knight?" Bashkim asked.

"The king doesn't know who belongs to the Senguan, for starters," Fandul explained. "He only knows of the Senguan's existence. We work in secret all throughout the city, making sure it gets what it needs, and not what some king wants. It's a way that Teasvanna has attempted to balance power over the years. It's thanks to them that eshans haven't had an all-out war against the humans."

"So that's how you were going to get me out," Bashkim said.

"A member of the Senguan definitely has some strings they can pull." Fandul nodded. "But the power isn't to be abused. However, some things are worth its use."

"So, all of this, then?" Bashkim asked. "You feel it's worth it?"

Fandul casually laid down on his bedroll and stared up at the sky. "I do. Let's just hope I'm right."

"If the white dragons are even half as bad as Ascura makes them out to be," Treydola said. "Then I would say it is most definitely worth it."

"I agree," Bashkim said. "But I can also understand what it feels like to stick your neck out for someone else."

"It doesn't get any easier, does it?" Fandul asked.

"It does not. Yet here you are."

"Yeah." Fandul sighed. "Here I am."

Fandul closed his eyes and rolled over to his side and pulled his blanket over him. Treydola rose from her seat and followed Fandul's example by making her own bed and lying down. Bashkim soon found himself sitting by the fire alone.

His shoulders dropped as he sat in his seat and looked over at the two eshans. It felt nice to have them around, even if one had been somewhat reluctant. Handleson more or less required by law that you get along, but out here on the road? They made that choice on their own, and they had chosen him.

He couldn't deny it felt good, but he also couldn't deny the hole that remained inside of him large enough to fit a dragon.

The trio reached Teasvanna within about five days of leaving Handleson, having picked up Dasc along the way. Fandul covered Bashkim's head with a hood and slapped a pair of the magic nullifying cuffs onto his wrists. Dasc then picked up Bashkim and threw him over his shoulder as they approached the city's gate.

"What's with him?" one guard asked after banging on the door. "And the hood?"

"He touched me," Treydola said sharply, her eyes burning as she glared at the soldier.

The guard held his tongue and stepped aside, not wanting to anger the woman any further and let the group pass through. Fandul and Treydola led the way through the streets as quickly as they could and took them straight to the castle. Dasc's armored shoulder dug into Bashkim's chest, causing him great discomfort.

The city guards along the way were curious to see Treydola out and about, but after the glares she shot them coupled with the two escorting her and their prisoner, they decided to mind their own business. Even those within the castle walls merely bowed, and remained bowed until she had passed them, allowing them to move freely as they pleased. When they reached the underground of the castle, they found a single guard patrolling the dark hallway.

"Is he one of yours?" Treydola whispered as they stepped forward.

"No," Fandul answered.

Treydola nodded and stepped ahead of her escorts, coming up to the guard. "You. What are you doing down here?"

"Milady," the guard bowed. "Your father has requested for someone to remain posted here since the last escape."

"We require use of these cells."

"Well..." the guard said, a confused look on his face, "they *have* just been refitted due to the recent escape, but, with all due respect, milady, I'm not sure the king would like you to do that. He seemed very particular about our prisoner down here. We do have other cells—"

Treydola stepped right up to the guard as he spoke, cutting him short as she put her face directly in front of his.

"Did I stutter?" she asked quietly, her face so close that her nose almost touched the guard's.

"Uh, no, ma'am," the guard mumbled.

Treydola whispered something to the guard but kept her voice so low that neither Fandul nor Dasc could hear what she said. They could, however, see the absolute look of terror on the guard's face, along with the sweat that began to form. Bashkim tried to move his head to hear what took place but failed to hear anything. The guard suddenly bowed and quickly left the hall. Treydola put her hands on her hips and looked at her escorts with a dangerous smile on her face.

Fandul shook his head. "I'm not even going to ask."

"I am," Dasc said.

"No. You're not."

The group made their way through the wooden door into the room with the cells, and Dasc sat Bashkim back on his feet. Fandul removed the hood, as well as the enchanted cuffs, and hung them on the cell's bars.

"We're back," Treydola said as she closed the wooden door behind her. "And we'd like to speak with you."

"Very good," Ishmonyae said from his corner, sliding a key forward.

Bashkim kneeled and grabbed the key but hesitated. He looked at the three eshans behind him, and Treydola motioned with her head for him to proceed. Bashkim took a small breath and slid the key into the lock. He gave it a short twist, and the latch snapped open. The door slowly creaked forward, creating an entry for Bashkim.

"You've returned," Ishmonyae said. "I had a feeling you would."

"How could I not?" Bashkim asked as he stepped inside. "Are you really Ascura?"

"That I am. Not much to look at, is it?"

"But how? How could you be kept alive for so long?"

"Very carefully," a new voice said from behind them.

The trio turned around in surprise and saw an eshan man standing behind them in an old brown robe that hid his arms. Long white hair dripped down past his shoulders, pairing well with the wrinkles on his face. Riding purely on instinct, Fandul attempted to draw his sword. The weapon went flying out of his grip and into the hand of the stranger. Reacting the instant his sword left him, Fandul had also started to summon fire in his off hand. The enchanted cuffs hanging on the bars shot towards him and clasped themselves shut around his wrists and choked his magic.

Dasc reached out to grab the man, but just before he could touch him, he felt a crushing weight on his shoulders pushing him down. Dasc fell to his knees, grunting as he tried to resist the pressing force against him.

"And," the stranger said, unbothered as he stepped into the cell, "with a little help from magic that has been kept hidden, and probably for good reason."

Bashkim took a step back and put himself between the stranger and Ascura, hovering his hand over his sword.

"You're early, Telanos," Ascura said with a smile.

"Telanos?" Bashkim asked.

"Yes," Telanos said. "It's me. And yes, I'm early. Bashkim has been a very busy little boy."

"I told you he would come back," Ascura said with a wheezing laugh.

"And I did not doubt you, old man," Telanos said, casually handing Fandul his sword back.

The cuffs snapped open and fell to the ground. The mysterious force crushing Dasc vanished as well. Dasc slowly got up to his feet and rolled his neck and shoulders with several pops as he readjusted. With a scowl on his face, Fandul begrudgingly took his sword and sheathed it.

Ignoring the glaring eyes, Telanos simply stepped past Bashkim towards Ascura, handing over a vial that he had pulled out from inside of his robe. Ascura took the vial and popped the topper, drinking the contents in a single gulp.

"I'm sorry, Treydola," Telanos said as he took the empty vial once Ascura had finished. "There were so many times I wanted to speak to you before. I saw you down here so often speaking with Ascura, and I applaud you for finding the truth when others attempted to keep it hidden. However, I felt if you never saw me with your own eyes, then you would at least have plausible deniability should something happen."

"And now?" Fandul asked, crossing his arms. "Now we've all seen you."

"Well, now it really doesn't matter, does it?" Telanos asked. "At least one white dragon has returned, and with it, no doubt, whatever evil it is that controls them."

"We thought that was you," Bashkim said. "How did you get out?"

"I've been out for quite some time now," Telanos said. "If you must know, I was only in that seal but for a few minutes."

"So where have you been this whole time?"

"Hiding," Treydola chimed in. "And keeping Ascura alive. Everyone was more than happy to believe Telanos was responsible, but nobody ever had any proof. Over time it just became accepted that he was to blame for the white dragons."

"I don't get it," Dasc said, rubbing the top of his head.

"Come!" Ascura said, motioning all of them forward and for Bashkim to sit next to him. "Sit! There is much to explain."

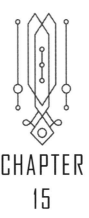

CHAPTER
15

<u>242 Years Ago</u>

A much younger Ascura made his way to a small shack next to the mine's entrance. The rest of his fellow soldiers had all left the previous day, and the diggers the day before that. However, by the order of Telanos, he had been instructed to remain behind. He stopped as he passed the mine's entrance and stared at it.

The torches hung on the walls but provided no light, having long been snuffed out and leaving the tunnel too dark to see down. It felt odd seeing it so abandoned. He had only been posted at the mine for a few days before the order to return to Teasvanna came, but he had already grown accustomed to the sounds coming from within. The striking of picks, the singing of the workers as they hauled carts of stone and dirt, but now? Now it just sat there, silent and still.

Ascura shook his head, putting the mine's entrance behind him and continuing to the makeshift shack. He started to knock on the door, but it suddenly flung open on its own and revealed Telanos sitting in a chair next to a desk.

"Come in!" Telanos said with a smile, realizing he had somewhat startled Ascura.

"Sir," Ascura said as he stepped inside. "Everyone else has packed up and returned to Teasvanna as you ordered. I know you requested I stay behind, but may I ask what you want me to do? I've yet to receive any direction."

"Would you like to know what I'm doing here?" Telanos asked and leaned back into his chair.

"I'd be a liar if I said I didn't, sir. I asked the king's scribe before we headed out, but his answer was convoluted at best."

"Well, it's really quite simple. We're digging!"

"And Teasvanna needs soldiers for this? As well as their most powerful wizard?"

"You flatter me, boy." Telanos chuckled, then got to his feet once he saw the unsatisfied look on Ascura's face. "Come. Let's go for a walk."

Ascura stepped to the side and let Telanos pass, then followed him outside the shack. With a little help from Telanos's magic, the door shut itself as they left.

"I assume you're familiar with Forrandi and her falling?" Telanos asked as they made their way towards the mine.

"Yes, sir. She tried to steal the power of the other Arbiters and was banished."

Ascura started to reach out with his hand to light one of the torches on the wall, but Telanos had beaten him to the punch, igniting all of them without so much as moving a muscle.

"That is correct," Telanos said while leading Ascura farther down the tunnel. "What most people don't know though, is that buried within the ancient texts is the suggestion that she succeeded and stored those powers in something. Some sort of device that allowed their power to be used at her command. Deeper, yet, is the suggestion that the devices with the stored power fell with her."

"And you think those devices are here? Where we've been digging?"

"I don't think that at all."

Telanos led Ascura farther down the tunnel through a series of smaller shafts until they came to a more freshly dug out room that hadn't any torches on the wall. Telanos summoned a ball of light in his hand and let it float above them until it clung to the ceiling.

"I *know* they're here," Telanos said, his tone more serious. "Do you feel it?"

"No, sir," Ascura admitted. "I'm afraid I don't feel anything other than a little claustrophobic."

"I didn't either at first. I've passed through this area more than once, as have many other eshans. But one day I felt something. It was strange. It was as if several voices were calling out to me. I was curious at first, but as I reached out, I could feel something far greater. A power well beyond anything I could ever hope to achieve. At first I sought to leave it alone, but I'm afraid my own curiosity got the best of me."

Telanos held his hand out and faced his palm towards the wall in front of them. Slowly, the stone and dirt turned to dust and fell to the ground in a pile. As the wall gave way, the tip of a purple crystal poked through, causing Telanos to stop. Telanos turned his hand over and used his magic to carefully pull the crystal out of the wall and into his hand.

"Only the Light knows how much time eshans have spent over the years trying to find these," Telanos said, taking a small breath.

"A crystal, sir?"

Telanos smirked and handed the crystal over to Ascura. "Here. Take it."

Ascura hesitated and looked at both Telanos and the crystal in his hand. He slowly reached out to take it, but once his hand neared it, Ascura withdrew and stepped back.

"Now you feel it, don't you?" Telanos asked.

"I do," Ascura said, keeping his distance. "What is that?"

"What you felt in your hand is what I can feel all around us. This mine is full of these things. I don't know what's awakened it, but I believe these crystals hold the power of the Arbiters that Forrandi captured."

"In that?" Ascura asked, nodding towards the crystal.

"Not the most convenient device, is it?" Telanos asked, holding it up in front of Ascura. "Go on. Take it."

"I'm not sure that's a wise idea, sir. You're more in tune with magic than any of us, so I can understand how you would have the ability to handle it, but I question my own."

"You give me far too much credit," Telanos chuckled, then wagged the crystal in front of him. "Go on. I insist."

Reluctantly, Ascura carefully grabbed the crystal and held it. "By the Light," he muttered. "That's...incredible."

"Feels like the whole world in the palm of your hand, doesn't it?"

"Yeah...or at least, I think. I definitely feel something, but it feels so far away somehow."

"Try to use it."

"Excuse me?" Ascura asked, surprised.

"The power. Try to use it. Pull it out if you can."

"With all due respect, sir, that's a terrible idea."

"Do it," Telanos said, his voice stern this time.

Ascura took a hard swallow and attempted to connect with the power he felt inside of the crystal. He could feel his own magic spinning wildly inside of his chest. Whatever the crystal contained, his magic wanted to be a part of it and swam through his body to try and get closer. Once the magic reached his fingers, however, it vanished in an instant.

"What the..." Ascura mumbled. "Wait. Let me try again."

Ascura made another attempt to connect with the crystal, but the results were the same.

"I don't understand," Ascura said. "I can feel it right there in my hand."

"It's almost like trying to hold oil, isn't it?" Telanos chuckled as he took the crystal back. "The harder you try to grab it, the more it slips between your fingers."

"Are you able to use it?"

"I'm afraid not," Telanos said. "It would seem you and I are equals when dealing with these things."

Ascura frowned as he looked at the crystal in Telanos's hand. His eyes then wandered to the rest of the room as he looked at the walls around them.

"You said this place was full of them," Ascura said. "Just how many are we talking about?"

Telanos smiled and put the crystal in his pocket. He turned his back to Ascura and held both his hands out and closed his eyes to concentrate. The walls slowly started to deform and turn to sand like granules that fell to their feet. As the walls sank backwards, Ascura could see more of the crystals start to emerge. His mouth dropped and his eyes widened as he watched the events unfold before him. Standing in the rubble were giant chunks of the purple crystals that spread and reached out as though they had been growing like a tree's roots. Telanos lowered his hands and took a deep breath.

"By the Arbiters," Ascura whispered.

"It's quite the sight, isn't it?"

"Yes, sir."

Ascura stared at the crystal conglomeration, trying to process what he saw.

"The others," Ascura finally said, breaking the silence. "The diggers and the other soldiers...they don't know, do they?"

"No," Telanos said. "Before they dug too deep, I told them the dig was a failure and to return home with the unfortunate news."

"Then why me?"

"Do you remember a few years ago, the humans that were brought to Teasvanna?"

"Yes, sir," Ascura said. "They were accused of plotting an attack on the city."

Telanos turned to face Ascura. "And if memory serves, instead of hanging them outright without question, you saw to it that they received a proper investigation, despite what the king wished."

"Yes, sir. We discovered it was some of our own framing the humans to push their own agenda. I remember it clear as day."

"And despite the king's willingness to execute them, you defended them. Why?"

"Because it was the right thing to do, sir."

Telanos smiled. "And that's why you've been chosen. I've been watching you ever since that day. You're a good soldier and a good man. I could use someone like you on my side."

"Your side? Sir, I don't even know who we're against."

"Not who, but what."

"Sir?"

"The powers of darkness, of course. Or more simply put, a lack of integrity. If we can use these things, then we've discovered enough power to change the world."

"You don't think the people can be trusted with this power? Or the king?"

"I would doubt most mortals could be trusted with this."

"And you?" Ascura challenged.

"Also mortal, I'm afraid."

"Then what do we do? I'm just a soldier. I haven't near the power you do, sir."

"Sometimes," Telanos said, taking the crystal out of his pocket and handing it over. "One man is all it takes to set in motion a change the world requires. Tell nobody, and keep this one to yourself. I'll take a few samples as well, and when I return I will inform the king that it is all I found. I will see to it that the mine is sealed before I leave. Should things get out of hand, we'll at least have one more piece on our side."

Ascura grabbed the crystal and held it. The crystal didn't weigh much itself, but he couldn't help but feel the weight of the burden that Telanos had placed on his shoulders.

"You really think this is the right thing to do?" Ascura asked.

"If we don't try to use it first, then somebody else will. Who do you trust more than yourself?"

Ascura looked down at the crystal in his hand. The weight of the burden increased tenfold.

"What do we call these things?" Ascura asked.

"Kesshonite."

"So there's more of this stuff?" Fandul asked as he crossed his arms. "Buried underground waiting for someone else to discover it?"

"I saw to it that it was a little more than buried," Telanos said. "But yes. And if there is some to be found there, then most likely there are other places in the world it can be found as well."

Fandul looked across the cell at Telanos, frowning. He kept silent and leaned against the cell's bars as he waited. Bashkim remained seated by Ascura, and Treydola had taken a seat of her own nearby. Dasc and Fandul were unable to relax as much as the others and kept some distance between them and the wizard.

"Did you guys figure out how to use it?" Bashkim asked, ignoring the tension between Telanos and the soldiers. "When you got back to Teasvanna?"

"Not quite," Ascura said. "There were some other events that had to take place first."

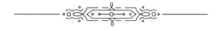

241 Years Ago

Back at Teasvanna's castle one year after the kesshonite's discovery, Telanos found himself sitting in a chair hunched over his workbench once again. A few small pieces of kesshonite lay in front of him, as well as an assortment of equipment. Tiny picks, hammers, and other small hand tools sat on his left, and a handful of alchemical brews stood on his right.

Ascura approached the doorway to the room but decided to wait before knocking to prevent startling the wizard.

"It's alright," Telanos said without turning around. "You can come in."

"It's late," Ascura said, joining Telanos at the table.

Telanos continued to focus on the kesshonite in front of him. "Indeed, it is. So why are you out?"

"I have the nightshift for now. I'm on my way to the main gate."

"Well then, do be careful."

Ascura snorted as he pulled up a stool and sat down. "You've been at it for a year. I know you're the best wizard Teasvanna has but...even you need sleep, right?"

"Yes." Telanos chuckled and slid his chair back away from his work. "Yes, I do. And more of it."

A heavy sigh left Telanos as he rubbed his face and scratched his chin, followed by a distant look.

"Still no luck?" Ascura asked.

"I'm afraid not. Truth be told, I don't think we're any further along than the day we started. Thankfully, there haven't been any accidents, but I'm beginning to wonder if that's because these things can't actually do anything. Not with our magic, anyway."

"What do you mean?"

"We've been trying to connect with the kesshonite using our magic. It's that very magic that lets us feel the power that's inside these things, or so we believe. What if instead of our magic being the connection that we assumed, it is instead a wall that separates us?"

"We have the means to nullify magic in people. Have you tried that?"

"I did. The results were the same. I'm inclined to believe that no matter what we do ourselves, there will always be a trace of magic in us."

"Well, I don't think you're going to find an eshan completely without magic any time soon."

Telanos grinned. "I suppose not."

Ascura remained silent, fidgeting as he readjusted the two swords on his hips.

"What really brought you down here?" Telanos asked.

"I've been hearing mixed things," Ascura admitted. "Some say you're leaving. I would like to believe you would have told me such a thing if it were true."

"Yes, if it were true, I would have. I'm not leaving, or, at least, not entirely. I'll still be here in the castle doing my work on the kesshonite, but some new responsibilities have arrived. My brother suffered from an accident recently that I'm sad to say cost him his life. To make things worse, he had a child he was caring for by himself. My wife is unable to bear children, and now that we're both old enough to be having grandchildren, we volunteered to take the child as our own."

"So, you'll be in the city then?"

"No. My brother wanted dearly to raise his child outside these walls, but his work kept him here. There are some farms on the outside. I am taking my wife and the child there. It would be our new home."

"Since when do wizards become farmers?" Ascura asked.

Telanos snorted. "It's more so farmers adopting a wizard. Considering they're outside the walls, I'm sure they'll feel a lot safer having one around."

Telanos paused for a moment, then reached out to the table and started drumming his fingers against it. "I could have helped him," he sighed. "I could have pulled some strings and set him up outside the city, but he refused to take anything I offered him. 'No handouts', he said. My brother was a stubborn fool, but he wanted to show his son how to make it on his own, for he knew his boy would one day outlive Uncle Telanos."

Ascura remained silent and waited for Telanos to continue. Telanos stopped drumming his fingers and instead laid his hand down flat on the table.

"Maybe," Telanos said distantly. "Maybe if I had spent more time learning about how to use magic for healing, we'd be having a very different conversation right now."

"I'm sorry," Ascura said. "I've not thought of it that way before."

"Hmm. Some all-powerful wizard, right?"

<u>235 Years Ago</u>

Ascura slowly made his way down the castle's halls six years later, stopping once he passed the entrance to Telanos's workshop. His face frowned as he stared at the closed door.

"Something wrong?" a voice from behind him asked.

Ascura turned and saw his captain. "Sir!" Ascura said and snapped to attention. "No, sir."

Ascura's captain crossed his arms and stared at him.

"Perhaps, sir," Ascura admitted. "Telanos is late. I was told it was because his wife fell ill, but it's been five days since he was supposed to return, sir. Has nobody gone to check on him and his wife?"

"Actually, that's what I've come to talk to you about."

"What is it, sir?"

"Telanos's wife isn't sick. She's dead. As is the child."

"Sir?" Ascura gasped. "What happened?"

"The farmers found their bodies in the house. They were murdered. It was a robbery gone wrong."

"Then where is Telanos?"

"That's where things get difficult. You and Telanos were close. Would you defend him?"

"I would, sir," Ascura said without hesitating. "With my life if I had to."

"And that's why I'm coming to you. Now, let's go speak with the king."

Ascura's captain, Menosa, brought him into a small room at the end of a hallway where the king waited for them. The king sat at the only table in the room and eyed Ascura curiously as he entered.

"Captain?" the king asked.

"I thought it wise to bring him, sir," Menosa said. "He's a close friend of Telanos."

"Is he?" the king asked, oblivious to Ascura's entire existence.

"Yes, my lord," Ascura said, closing the door behind him. "Me and Telanos have been working together for some years now."

"I see," the king said as he drummed his fingers against the table. "Do you know where he might be now?"

"No, my lord. Telanos has always been punctual. Very rare for him to be this late, sir. Especially with no word."

"And what do you know of his family?"

"Not much, my lord," Ascura admitted. "He has a wife, but I've never met her as she stays on the farm. He also adopted his late brother's son about six years ago. If he has any more family than that, I'm afraid I haven't heard of them."

"Has Menosa told you of the accusations?"

"No, my lord."

"Telanos," the king said as he leaned forward onto the table. "Has been reported a killer."

"A killer?" Ascura asked. "Surely you don't mean the thieves that murdered his family?"

"I would happily overlook the death of thieves," the king said. "But he let one of them live, and that thief came to us. To say he was rattled is an understatement. The man acted as though he had seen the ghost of his own ancestors. If what this man says is true, not only did Telanos kill these men, he killed them in ways that were beyond necessary."

"Even so, my lord, you can't hold that against him. His family was murdered for Arbiter's sake!"

"No. I would never hold that against a man. If I had Telanos's strength, only Arbiters know what I would do in his position. My concern is from one small detail in this man's story. Telanos had a creature with him, and according to the thief's confession, it seemed to be under Telanos's control. This creature was a white dragon."

"A dragon?" Ascura asked.

"A *white* dragon," Menosa corrected.

"What's the difference?"

"We received word just a day ago," Menosa explained. "Between us and the humans, nearly an entire platoon's worth of men was slaughtered by it just last week. Right on our borders."

"An entire platoon's worth?" Ascura asked. "Just how big is this thing?"

"It's not the size," Menosa said. "It did something to the soldiers. Instead of fire, it breathed a black mist on them. More than half the soldiers turned on their own. At first it was eshans against humans, then it was eshans against eshans and humans against humans. They killed each other, Ascura. Their own brothers in arms. The humans even volunteered to return with our soldiers to vouch for this story, as did our own to Nennossen. I'm no dragon expert, but I've never heard of those overgrown lizards doing anything like this. This sounds like magic, and a dark magic at that."

"And you think Telanos did it?"

"It doesn't look good for him," the king admitted. "You know as well as I do that if anybody in this city was powerful enough to control something like this, it would be him. Our soldiers were slaughtered by this beast, and only days later it was by his side. What am I to believe?"

Ascura held his tongue, trying to find a counter argument.

"Did he ever tell you what he was working on?" the king asked.

"The kesshonite?" Ascura asked.

"Yes," the king answered, none too pleased with Ascura's response. "A questionable decision to tell you about such things, but perhaps something good can come of it. Tell me, did you ever notice a change in his behavior?"

"I don't understand, my lord."

"In Telanos. He's been exposed to the kesshonite more than any of us. I wonder if, perhaps, there was something in it that even he could not handle."

"You think the kesshonite drove him mad?"

"It's a possibility," the kind admitted. "We're dealing with the unknown. Anything is possible at this point."

"With all due respect, my lord," Ascura said. "If Telanos could be driven mad by the kesshonite, don't you think we would have too even with our limited exposure?"

The king's eyes narrowed at Ascura.

"He makes a good point, my lord," Menosa said. "It's no secret Telanos has powers well beyond our own. If the kesshonite can wear him down in such a way, I'm inclined to believe the rest of us would have fallen victim too."

"I'll admit Telanos is not to be underestimated," the king said as he leaned back into his chair. "But we have to be careful not to overestimate him either. I don't like the idea any more than you do, Ascura, but this sudden change of behavior can't be ignored."

Ascura crossed his arms. He wanted to tell them about the kesshonite Telanos had given him to try and prove the wizard's innocence, but he couldn't quite convince himself to do it. Not yet anyway.

"I don't like it either," Menosa said, seeing Ascura's frustration. "But try to see it from our point of view. There's a trail of dead bodies and a witness describing Telanos in ways that I would never think possible. This thief has little to gain from lying to us. In fact, this man is so afraid that he practically begged us to lock him away for his own safety. Had he gone about his own life, none of us would have been the wiser."

"If the white dragon hadn't been there," the king added. "His innocence would be a lot easier to believe. But right now, that creature is the bloody dagger, and it's in Telanos's hand."

234 Years Ago

One year later, Ascura stood alone in Telanos's workshop where dust had laid claim to the wizard's belongings. Everything remained in their place as he had left them, patiently waiting for their master's return. Not a single clue to his whereabouts had been uncovered.

Ascura had dealt with death before, but his loss always came from something more powerful than himself, such as disease or even time itself. But to lose to someone to a mere thief, murdered for nothing more than a few trinkets and coins, left a feeling inside of him that he struggled to shake.

He had little doubt that Telanos made the thieves pay for what they did, but he refused to believe that the man had a hand to play in this white dragon business. They had already lost several eshan soldiers to the beasts, and he couldn't figure out for the life of him what Telanos had to gain from such a thing. The king still held the theory that the kesshonite had driven Telanos mad, but Ascura knew better than that.

You were with the white dragon, Ascura thought. *They said you were controlling it. I just can't bring myself to believe it. I refuse to believe that you turned on your own. There's something else going on.*

A gentle knock on the workshop's door broke him from his thoughts, causing him to turn around.

"Sir!" Ascura said, snapping to attention once he saw Menosa.

Menosa stood in the doorway and held his hand up. "At ease, soldier."

"Yes, sir," Ascura said and sat back down on his stool. "Thank you, sir."

Menosa casually joined him and took his own seat. "I had a feeling I might find you in here," he said.

"Yes, sir. It's quiet here. Good place to gather my thoughts."

"And what have you gathered?"

"Permission to speak freely, sir?"

"Of course," Menosa said, leaning onto his elbow on the table.

"Not shit, sir. Not much of this makes sense. We're fighting a losing battle against these things. The white dragons have beat us at every turn. We've done nothing but lose good men, and we've yet to kill a single dragon. It's only by dumb luck they haven't struck Teasvanna yet, and we're just sitting here waiting."

"And what would you have us do differently?"

"We're fighting alone, sir. When the dragon first attacked, it was both humans and eshans. There were at least some survivors that day."

"Meaning?"

"Why not cooperate with them? The dragons threaten them just as much as us. It's foolish to fight alone when we're so clearly out powered."

"I agree."

"You do?" Ascura asked, surprised.

"I have my own reservations about the king's methods for handling this."

Ascura hesitated and watched Menosa carefully. "Why are you telling me this?" he asked.

"Several years ago," Menosa explained. "Telanos expressed to me his own concerns about resting the entire city on one man's shoulders. He doubted any man could handle such a power and concluded that such a thing should be handled by many, instead of one. We needed people that could work in secret, connected throughout the city from mere peasants to the king's most trusted. We are the Senguan."

"The Senguan? And you're one of them?"

"I was the first."

"Why didn't he tell me any of this?"

"I often asked the same question," Menosa admitted. "He said you had a different role to play. But he never explained what."

Ascura sighed. "That would have been too easy. I don't guess he ever got the kesshonite working and didn't tell me about that either, did he?"

"No," Menosa said. "Despite the many experiments, everything seemed to come out the same. I think the only thing we haven't tried is putting it in a human's hands."

Ascura looked at Menosa with curious eyes. "Sir?"

"Telanos had a theory that our magic might be what's keeping us from using the kesshonite. It's one of the few things we couldn't test. Not like we have humans around to ask. Even if we did, the king would never agree, and the kesshonite is behind lock and key."

Ascura hesitated, considering his next words carefully. "Not all of it, sir."

"Pardon?"

"At the original dig site, Telanos gave me a piece to keep safe in case something ever went wrong. I've been holding onto it ever since."

"Really," Menosa said, almost smiling and lacking surprise. "No wonder you were so quick to disagree with the king's theory."

"Yes, sir."

Menosa tapped his fingers on the table and weighed his options before getting back up to his feet and casually sliding the stool back under the table. "As Captain," he said. "I cannot order you to travel to Nennossen. However, as a member of the Senguan, I can request that you help us do whatever is necessary to save this city."

"Yes, sir. And thank you, sir."

"Don't mention it," Menosa said and turned to leave. "Seriously, don't."

CHAPTER
16

<u>234 Years Ago</u>

After several days on the road, Ascura reached Nennosen with the sun at its highest point. A pair of armed guards stood their posts by the city's main gate and pointed their spears forward as the eshan in Teasvanna steel approached. Ascura had already dismounted his horse by this point and continued forward on foot with his arms up.

"That's far enough," one of the guards said. "What's an eshan soldier doing all the way out here, and alone?"

"Some things are better handled alone," Ascura admitted. "I've come to speak with your king about white dragons."

The first guard kept his eyes on Ascura and paused. With narrowed eyes, he took a slow breath and gently put the butt of his spear on the ground. "You must be Ascura," he said.

"I am," Ascura answered. "But how did you know?"

"We received word an eshan would be coming to us. The letter was a bit ominous, really. Signed by "The Senguan". Said a soldier would be coming to Nennossen to speak with us about white dragons, as well as a potential solution."

The Senguan move fast, he thought as he slowly lowered his hands.

"It's true," Ascura said.

"Then I have to ask," the same guard said. "Has Teasvanna fallen?"

"Not yet. Though I fear for its safety. I'm glad to see Nennossen also still stands."

"The front puts up a good show," the first guard started to say, but stopped as he looked at the soldier next to him.

The second guard still had his spear out, clutching it tightly and keeping it pointed at Ascura.

"Oh, put that thing away, Jr," the first guard said and pushed the spear away.

"But, sir," the much younger guard said.

"Put it away," the first one ordered.

Ascura watched curiously as the two argued. The younger soldier reluctantly withdrew his spear and put its butt on the ground.

"They started with the farms outside the walls behind the city," the first guard continued after giving the other one a dirty look. "Then about ten days or so ago a bigger one showed up and decimated the back of our city. I don't know if I should tell you this or not but at this point I don't really care. It took everything we had to defend ourselves. Arbiters only know how many people we lost. And so long as I'm being honest here, I'll add that I'm surprised it hasn't come back to finish the job."

"Then I wish I had come sooner. This isn't a battle we should be fighting alone."

"I'm glad to hear you say that, but it begs the question: how do eshans fare against it?"

"Our losses haven't been as severe yet, but our city hasn't been directly attacked either. Unfortunately, in the encounters we've had, we've yet to kill a single one."

"Yeah," the guard said, his head dropping. "Same here. I'm beginning to think that maybe the end times are upon us. Some beasts come to devour the world and all that."

"I'm not willing to believe that just yet," Ascura said. "Which is why I'm here. We should be fighting these things together."

"I appreciate your positivity, but having seen what one of those things can do, I'm inclined to believe we would only die together."

"Then would it not be better to die together, than apart? We might be different, but in the end we're both soldiers."

"Die next to an eshan?" the guard snorted. "Not exactly how I thought I'd go out. But then again, I never thought I'd be fighting dragons either."

"Even if we don't make it," Ascura said, and held his hand out to the guard. "We can at least give it one hell of a fight before we go."

The guard looked at Ascura's hand and considered the offer. He took a deep breath and let it out in a short huff through his nose.

"Ah, Arbiters be damned," the guard said and shook Ascura's hand. "If I'm going to die, then I'm going out the same way I came in."

"Kicking and screaming?"

"And covered in blood."

Ascura smiled. "What is your name?"

"Jason," the guard answered as he took his hand back. "Now tell me, what is it that you've got up your sleeve that you think might help?"

"May I?" Ascura asked, motioning towards his satchel.

Jason nodded, and as Ascura reached for the kesshonite inside of his satchel, he could see the younger guard tensing up.

"What's the matter, son?" Ascura asked. "Don't trust an eshan?"

"Can't say that I do," the younger guard said.

Jason instantly brought his hand up and smacked the backside of the guard's head, causing his helmet to fall over his face.

"Enough!" Jason barked. "Go on and tell the king I'll be bringing him a soldier from Teasvanna shortly. Now get out of here."

"But, sir," the younger man argued.

"I said get!"

The other guard growled and saluted quickly before leaving. Jason sighed once they were alone and apologized for the soldier's behavior.

"He's practically a child," Jason said. "We've been recruiting them awfully young lately due to the dragon attacks. I'm afraid things are getting desperate."

"Fighting dragons is a task no man should have to face, young or old," Ascura said as he reached into his satchel again. "But I'm hoping this can at least help us out."

"A rock?" Jason asked once Ascura unwrapped the small cloth in his hand.

"We call it kesshonite. It's a discovery we made some years back."

"And that's supposed to help us with the dragons?"

"I'm hoping so. We've been attempting to tap into its power, but we've had little success."

"Is this a religious thing or something?"

"No," Ascura said with a small chuckle. "Though it may have started off as such, there is a tangible power in this thing."

Jason looked down at the kesshonite curiously, then back at Ascura. "You're pulling my leg."

"I promise you, I am not."

"Let me see it," Jason said and held his hand out.

Ascura hesitated, staring down at Jason's hand.

"You're wanting to present this to the king," Jason said, still holding his hand out. "As curious as I am, I still have to inspect it before bringing it behind our walls. Surely as a soldier you can understand that."

"Fair enough," Ascura said and slowly handed the kesshonite over.

Jason reached for the crystal, but as his hand neared it, he quickly jerked back right before he touched it.

"By the Arbiters," Jason gasped. "What was that?"

"Did you feel it?"

"I felt something alright. What is that thing?"

"That's the power we've been trying to tap into. It's inside the kesshonite. If you can feel it, then perhaps you can see what I mean when I say it might be able to help us against the white dragons."

Jason leaned his head against his spear, looking down at the kesshonite. "I don't want you to take this wrong way but...I don't really understand anything about eshan magic. I'd wager none of us around here do. I can tell you I felt something, but I can't tell you *what* I felt."

"This isn't eshan magic," Ascura said. "This is something beyond us. Some of us even think it's possible our magic is what keeps us from using these things."

"Then that's why you've brought it here? To experiment?"

"Partly," Ascura admitted. "But also to share."

"Well, if it helps kill those damned things, I'm game." Jason said, then motioned with his hand for the kesshonite again. "I still need to see it though."

"Are you sure?"

"Yeah," Jason said and bounced his shoulders as he prepped himself. "Let's try it again."

Ascura held the kesshonite up in front of him and waited. Jason's head moved side to side. He flexed his hands, then took a quick breath and held it as he yanked the kesshonite from Ascura's grip.

"By the Light," Jason whispered, having only paused for a second before staring down at the crystal in his hands.

Much to Ascura's surprise, a faint glow started to radiate within the kesshonite.

"Are you...doing something?" Ascura asked.

"Just holding it. I think. Though I can definitely feel something inside of it. It kind of feels like there is something moving around in my hands."

Ascura quickly looked around him to make sure they were still alone. He then held his hand out near the kesshonite.

"Well, that's certainly something, isn't it?" Ascura asked, keeping his palm faced towards the kesshonite. "It's never felt that way before. It's always slipped between my fingers but now...now I think I can hold it."

Ascura attempted to take hold of the power growing within the crystal, but as he did, the glow diminished.

"Is it working?" Jason asked.

"No," Ascura said and took his hand back. "I still can't get it. I can feel it, but if I try to connect with it, it runs away."

"Weird," Jason said, watching the faint glow return. "I can feel it too."

"Do you think you can grab it somehow?"

"I can try."

"Carefully," Ascura said after a moment of consideration.

Jason took a few quick breaths as he prepared himself. His eyes narrowed as he tried to focus, but little seemed to happen.

"It sure is a strange feeling," Jason said after a few attempts. "It feels like I can grab it, but trying to feels so awkward. It's like trying to write with my offhand."

"Take it slow," Ascura reassured.

Jason continued to focus on the kesshonite. Eventually, the glow within it pulsed slightly.

"You're doing it," Ascura whispered in excitement. "I think."

Jason didn't respond. Instead, he continued to stare at the crystal in his hand with a blank expression on his face. The glow within the kesshonite stopped pulsing, and instead remained steady, growing in intensity.

"Jason?" Ascura asked.

Jason didn't respond.

"Jason?" Ascura asked again and waved his hand in front of him.

Feeling the power rise within the kesshonite, Ascura quickly snatched it out of Jason's hand. The glow diminished almost instantly. Jason took a sharp breath and blinked his eyes several times as he regained himself.

"What happened?" he asked.

"I think you just made more progress than eshans have in the past five years."

"I don't understand. Eshans are magic users. Shouldn't..." Jason tried to find the words but could only vaguely gesture towards the kesshonite. "*This*, come naturally to you?"

"That's what we originally thought," Ascura said, wrapping the kesshonite back into the cloth and putting it in his satchel. "Turns out we were wrong. Can you tell me what you felt?"

"I don't have the words," Jason said and patted his chest. "But I could feel it here. Felt like something was swimming right through me."

"I could feel the power being drawn out of the kesshonite," Ascura said. "It's more than I've felt before. I'd like to think this means we're on the right track to something great, or at the very least, a way to stop the dragons."

Jason nodded. "I think it's time we have a chat with the king."

Jason posted two guards at the front gate to take his place and marched Ascura through the city streets. The citizens looked at the eshan curiously, whispering amongst themselves and theorizing why one might be in their city.

"I wonder if Teasvanna has fallen?" one of them would ask.

"Not even their devilish magic could save them against those beasts," another would add.

Ascura ignored their whispers and stuck close to Jason all the way to the king's war room within the castle. Inside stood a long table with the king at the end, as well as several soldiers who reached for their swords when they saw Ascura.

"Settle down, gents," Jason said, holding his hand out as he closed the door behind him.

The king narrowed his eyes and leaned against the table with his chin against his thumbs. His glare locked onto Ascura.

"You bring an eshan before me," the king said, surprisingly calm. "A spell caster, unbound."

"I have not come to harm," Ascura said.

The king paused, slowly sinking back into his chair. "I believe you," he finally said. "If you had come to kill me, then the deed would already be done."

"Yes, my lord," Jason said. "But saying as how we're all still kicking, do you think you could spare us a few minutes? It's awfully important."

The king sighed. "I'm assuming your insolence is backed with good reason?"

"I'd like to think so, my lord," Jason said as he approached the table ahead of Ascura. "I realize just how out of line I am, and you can hang me if you want, but if you're going to, then I suggest you hurry it up and do it while there's something left to hang me from. Your city is being destroyed, your majesty, and you've been reduced to children watching the gates these days. That's why I highly encourage you to hear what this man has to say. He's come on his own accord, and he brings something that I think you might be interested in."

"I'm listening," the king said. "Though don't think I haven't considered your offer for a hanging, Jason."

"Never a doubt, my lord," Jason said with a bow and a smile, then motioned Ascura forward.

"You're not alone in your struggle against the white dragons," Ascura explained. "I care very little for whatever petty differences there might be between our two people. What I care for is the safety of Teasvanna, as well as the rest of the world we share. These white dragons threaten just that. And the eshans, much like yourselves, have failed all attempts to kill them. It's clear we do not stand a chance against these creatures alone."

"You would have us form an alliance?" the king asked curiously. "Why has your king sent merely a single soldier to request such a thing? I would think he'd send a member of his council accompanied by several armed guards. Unless, they've been consumed by these monsters?"

"No, sir. It's because he doesn't know I'm here. If he knew of my plans, he would have me locked away."

"And why is that?"

"Because pride and arrogance aren't unique traits to humans."

The king snorted. "You come here alone. You insult me. My own guard disrespects me, and you expect me to help you? Do all eshans behave as you?"

"No, sir," Ascura said. "But you've lost part of your city, and many of your men. The time for pleasantries has passed. We face a dangerous threat and death is at our very doorsteps. I beg of you, please, do not follow Teasvanna's example and be too proud to accept help."

The king laid his arms on the sides of his chair, drumming his fingers slowly as he watched Ascura. "You're a bold one," he said. "That's for sure."

"I act for the safety of my people. Not my king's pride."

"And if I agreed to this request? What do you expect to happen to my people when they show up at Teasvanna without the king's permission, or knowing? They would be attacked on the spot."

"There are those within the walls that are aware of what I'm doing here. They would see to it that such an alliance would be kept. King or no king."

"That sounds a lot like treason."

"Far less treasonable than a king damning his people, sir. He won't have much to rule over if we're all dead."

"You're just the gift that keeps on giving, aren't you?" the king asked with a faint smile.

The king crossed his arms and pondered for a minute. He scratched his beard and weighed the situation before him while keeping an eye on Ascura.

"Fine," he finally said. "What is it that you've brought?"

"If I may," Ascura said. "I have something in my satchel that I would like to show you."

The king motioned for Ascura to continue. "Slowly."

"I assume you are aware of our Arbiter's falling?" Ascura asked as he pulled the cloth covered kesshonite from his satchel.

"I am," the king answered.

"Some eshans believed that before she fell, she created some devices that held the power of the other Arbiters. When she was outcast, those devices fell with her."

Ascura unwrapped the kesshonite and carefully set it on the table. "We have since found those devices. We call it kesshonite."

"A crystal?" the king asked.

"Yes, sir," Ascura said. "We've been trying to tap into its power for some time now, and eshans have had little luck. Jason, however, made tremendous progress just moments before coming here to see you."

"Humans are not users of magic," the king said. "You know we do not partake in your sinful ways, yet you chose to experiment on my people without my knowing?"

"I've been sinning since before I could walk, my lord," Jason said. "Not only did I volunteer for it, I had to make him do it."

"To be fair," Ascura added. "He was trying to keep your city safe. He wanted to make sure I wasn't some devilish eshan come to do harm."

"Sharp as a knife, aren't you?" the king sighed. "So what happened with this...kesshonite?"

"That thing is jammed full of power, my lord," Jason said. "Or something. It started glowing when I held it, but it felt like I could draw something right out of it."

"As a magic user," Ascura noted. "I can assure you that was indeed a magical power he felt, and a lot more than even our strongest wizards have had in the past. Though the stability of it is in question. It seemed to keep rising as Jason held it until I took it away from him."

"You grabbed it?" the king asked. "Did you not think it would harm you?"

"If I've learned anything over the years, it's that eshans are extremely good at making kesshonite *not* work. And besides, better me than him."

"Your behavior continues to amaze me," the king said.

The king slowly got out of his chair, and as he did the other soldiers in the room came to his side. He quickly waved them away, signaling that he required room to move. The king made his way over to Ascura at the other end of the table, close enough for arm's reach.

"Hold it," the king said, nodding towards the kesshonite.

Ascura grabbed the crystal and held it in his hand close to the king. The king slowly reached out with his own hand but paused before he could touch the kesshonite. His eyes widened briefly, and he gently brought his hand back.

"Sir?" Ascura asked.

The king took a slow breath. "With your experience, how dangerous do you think it is? For us?"

"Hard to say, sir," Ascura admitted. "As I mentioned we've been unable to tap into it. Jason's had more luck than all of us combined. When he held it, I felt more power coming from it than I do now holding it in my own hand."

"And that power continued to rise?"

"Yes, sir."

"If this power were to escape, and you couldn't control it, what kind of damage are we talking about? What do you think would happen?"

"That's a big question, sir. We're dealing with the unknown. I'm a soldier. I've used steel and eshan magic my whole life. Not this. But from what I felt earlier, I would highly recommend a large and empty workspace should we be allowed to experiment further."

"How large?"

"Outside the city, sir."

The king decided to let Ascura and Jason experiment with the kesshonite before making any final decisions on the alliance. With plenty of guards, the two soldiers were escorted through the back of the city. There Ascura could see the destruction for himself. Flattened homes and roads ripped from the ground lined their path. Even the city's walls had fallen, crushed into nothing more than a pile of broken rocks and dust covered rubble. Large trenches big enough for Ascura to fall into lined the ground, dug from the monster's massive, clawed feet. He swallowed as he pictured a beast large enough to do such a thing.

What lay beyond the wall's remains fared no better. Several farms had been either abandoned or destroyed, and little of the ground remained flat. Ascura and Jason decided to take one of the abandoned farmhouses for themselves to set up shop. The other guards waited outside, keeping a generous distance from the experiments.

"I'll be honest," Jason said as they sat down at the remnants of a table, looking outside through where a wall used to be. "From what I felt inside of that thing, I don't think we're far enough away from the city if something goes wrong."

"Nor do I," Ascura admitted. "But I'm afraid going any farther would only rouse suspicion."

"Well at least we can't make this spot any worse. Now. What do we do?"

"Try again, I guess," Ascura said, pulling the kesshonite out and setting it on the table.

Jason only looked at the kesshonite.

"Something wrong?" Ascura asked.

"Maybe," Jason answered. "You know how I said I could feel it in my chest? Back at the gate?"

"I do."

"Well, that never really went away. It's still there."

Ascura looked over at Jason curiously. "Does it feel like a muscle in your body?"

"Kind of," Jason shrugged. "It's hard to explain."

Ascura looked around them calmly, trying not to catch the attention of the guards outside. "That sounds an awful lot like eshan magic," he whispered.

"But I'm not eshan."

"You certainly don't look like one, but you did do something with the kesshonite. Perhaps it has done something to you as well. Here. Hold out your hand."

Jason held his hand out with the palm facing where a ceiling normally would have been. Ascura did the same, only a small flame suddenly appeared in his. Caught off guard, Jason flinched from the sudden display of magic.

"It's okay," Ascura said and dismissed the flame. "I want you to try and do the same thing."

"I don't even know where to begin to try and do something like that."

"With what you feel in your chest. Try to use it. Think about the fire in your hand and try to use that new muscle to make it happen."

"I think I liked the idea of getting blown away by the kesshonite better," Jason said and closed his eyes to concentrate. "Didn't think I was going to be turned into something."

Jason took a deep breath as he tried to focus. His face twitched randomly, and his fingers bounced up and down as he tried to summon a flame. However, his hand remained empty.

"Easy," Ascura said. "Not even eshan children start big. They start with flames no bigger than a candle's light. You should be no different."

"Yeah, except eshan children are a bit more familiar with magic."

"They're born with the magic, not the experience."

Jason opened one eye briefly and looked over at Ascura. He chuckled and closed his eyes again as he tried to focus. "Damn eshans," he said with a grin.

Ascura smiled, watching Jason's hands closely. Jason's fingers tapped forward and backwards as he tried to reach for the mysterious new feeling inside of him. Much to Ascura's surprise, the tiniest fire he had ever seen suddenly popped into existence in Jason's palm. Jason's eyes opened the instant it appeared, causing him to jump in shock. As a result, the flame vanished instantly.

"By the Arbiters," Jason gasped. "What's happened to me?"

"You used magic," Ascura said as he tried to contain his excitement. "I saw it!"

"Gods alive. It felt like something inside of me was about to jump out...like it was coming out of my own skin."

"That was magic you felt."

"But how?"

Ascura looked down at the kesshonite. "Call me crazy, but I think I have a theory."

Ascura took the kesshonite and held it in his hand. "Go on," he said, keeping the kesshonite away from Jason. "Try it again."

"To make fire?"

"Yes. But keep it small."

Jason hesitated for a moment at first but eventually took a short breath and agreed. He held his hand out and closed his eyes again. Within just a few seconds another small flame appeared in his palm, causing him to flinch once more and accidentally snuff it out.

"Again," Ascura said, still keeping the kesshonite to himself.

Jason followed the order and attempted with the fire several times more, each ending with the same result.

"I can't seem to hold it there," Jason said, aggravated. "It's like it keeps slipping away."

"That's okay," Ascura said and slid the kesshonite over. "Now try holding onto this when you do it this time."

Jason looked down at the kesshonite. "Are you sure?"

"I'm sitting here watching a human use magic. I'm not sure of anything anymore. Just...try to keep it small. I'll be right here."

"You're going to get us both killed," Jason sighed and put one hand on the kesshonite.

Jason closed his eyes again and held his free hand out, palm facing upwards. The kesshonite began to glow as soon as Jason started to focus. Ascura's eyes widened as he watched the veins beneath the skin of Jason's hand start to give off a faint light.

Feeling the power grow rapidly within the kesshonite, Ascura quickly snatched it out of Jason's hand. Jason opened his eyes in confusion, but as he did, a blast of fire erupted from his hand. Although extremely brief, it managed to startle both of them enough to make them fall to the ground while singeing the exposed edges of the open ceiling.

"By the Arbiters!" Ascura exclaimed, holding his hand out and forming ice over the scorched wood.

Jason remained on the ground, coughing and trying to catch his breath. Ascura came to his aid and helped him back to his feet.

"Okay," Jason wheezed. "That was something."

"Are you alright?"

"Yeah," Jason said, taking a deep breath. "Just a little winded...and confused."

A couple of the other guards had run over to them to investigate but Jason waved them away, insisting that he felt fine. Jason made his way back over to the table but as he took his seat, a loud bell began to ring from the city.

"The dragon approaches!" one of the men from outside shouted.

"Quick!" Jason said as he jumped to his feet and drew his sword. "Give me the kesshonite. We'll end this here and now."

"No," Ascura argued and stuffed the kesshonite into his satchel. "That's too dangerous. Look at what it just did to you."

"Look at what that dragon has done to this city! It's going to tear through us."

"Better the dragon than the kesshonite I delivered," Ascura said, drawing both of his swords and stepping out of the house.

Ascura's eyes widened as they fell upon the beast in the distance. The dragon flew in a straight line and headed right towards them. By the time the first of the reinforcements had arrived, the dragon had already closed the distance. Down it came, slamming its massive feet against the ground as it landed. The impact shook Ascura's entire body and several of the soldiers lost their footing and toppled over one another.

The dragon reached out with the hand on the crook of its wing and slapped the ground with its massive palm, crushing several of the fallen soldiers. Its horned head reared back like a snake before shooting forward with its jaws open. The dragon's mouth grabbed one of the soldiers, and its teeth tore through the steel armor. The soldier screamed for his life, but the sounds were quickly drowned out by the crunch as the dragon closed its mouth completely.

The dragon tossed the mangled body to the side and eyed the rest of the soldiers as they started to surround it. Ascura could feel the low growl of the beast inside of his chest, and the air passing through its large nostrils blew against him. The dragon's eyes looked over the soldiers, scanning through them individually as though looking for someone specific.

The yellow eyes fell on Jason, and its claws gripped the dirt as it prepared for a strike. A quick fireball from Ascura struck the side of the dragon's face and stole its attention. The dragon roared, its many teeth showing as it snarled at Ascura. Ascura gripped his swords tightly, bracing for the beast's strike. The muscles along the dragon's neck rippled as it reared back for another attack. The dragon opened its mouth wide and lunged forward. Ascura dragged both swords against the side of the creature's face as he dodged, each blade failing to cut through the scaled hide. In one clean motion, Ascura summoned fire on the blade in his right hand and took a second swipe near the eye.

The dragon roared in anger, and Ascura could see that he had barely managed to inflict any damage. The dragon swept its tail wide in retaliation, a limb far too large and fast to avoid. The numerous spikes growing out of the creature's body skewered several of the soldiers while the mass of its tail crushed even more. Those that survived the blow were thrown to the ground, including Ascura. His body tumbled and slid across the ground, and he could feel the snap in his arm as it twisted and broke. He quickly looked down, spotting his satchel that had been torn away from him during the slide. The kesshonite had spilled out of it and lay on the ground out of his reach. Jason, having stood just outside the tail's arc, made a mad dash for the kesshonite.

"No!" Ascura shouted, trying to force his body back to its feet.

Jason grabbed the kesshonite, causing it to glow brightly. The dragon turned and refocused on Jason. The kesshonite started to glow even brighter, and Ascura could feel the power flowing from it into Jason's body.

"You're holding too much in!" Ascura shouted as he reached out with his hand to try and stop the kesshonite. "Let go!"

With the kesshonite in his left hand and a sword in his right, Jason's body became the conductor as the power flowed from end to the other. A blinding light formed around the blade and created a beam that extended beyond the weapon's original length. Jason started to scream as the kesshonite's intensity grew, and the dragon took a step forward.

"Let it go!" Ascura shouted, trying to pull back the kesshonite's power.

The dragon's head shot forward straight for Jason. He swung the sword wildly against the beast, barely dodging the blow as he fell to the ground. The dragon's head crashed down next to him, its eyes still open. A line from the corner of its mouth up to the back of its skull formed, and black blood began to pour from the wound as the head separated into two pieces. Jason remained on the ground, clutching both the kesshonite and sword while screaming uncontrollably as smoke rose from his body.

"Gods!" he shouted. "Make it stop! Make it stop!"

Ascura quickly crawled past the dragon's corpse as fast as he could to get to Jason. He yanked the kesshonite from Jason's hand and tossed it to the side. Next he went for Jason's sword, which had become a blackened and mangled mess, twisted and bent in every direction. The deformed weapon fell to the ground and Ascura held Jason close as his own arm dangled next to him. He could feel the raw power flowing through Jason's body, as well as *see* the glow beneath the soldier's exposed skin.

"It burns!" Jason cried.

"It's okay," Ascura said and patted Jason's back. "I got the magic now. I'm stopping it."

As Ascura tried to force the power out of Jason's body, he couldn't help but notice the kesshonite on the ground still glowing. Keeping Jason propped up, he reached out with his hand, magically taking hold of the kessonite's power. As he held it, he could feel his grip slowly loosen as the power thinned and slipped between his fingers. The kesshonite's glow faded, pulsing a few times before completely disappearing.

"We did it," Ascura said, feeling the raging energy within Jason fade. "*You* did it! You killed the dragon!"

Jason breathed rapidly, trying to catch his breath as he stared wide eyed into the distance. Ascura carefully laid him on the ground on his back and looked him over. Jason's hands had both been burnt badly, and Ascura summoned a thin layer of ice over the wounds as Jason stared at the sky above them.

"It hurt so bad," Jason panted, his eyes empty. "I could feel myself...in the kesshonite. In the sword...coming out of the sword. I was everywhere...my body..."

Jason's words grew quieter as he spoke, and his breaths slower.

"Just hang in there," Ascura said. "We'll get you fixed up."

"You were right," Jason whispered, his eyes closing. "That shit is dangerous."

Nearly two whole days had passed since the attack. Ascura refused to leave Jason's room and stayed by his bed with his own arm in a sling. The others had already been patched up and sent home to recover, and the less fortunate had been buried. Jason, however, lay unconscious the entire time.

The king entered Jason's room one afternoon, holding a small satchel and taking a seat next to Ascura. "Still here?" he asked.

"Yes, sir," Ascura said. "I can't help but feel his condition is my fault."

"Had you stopped him, I think a lot more of us would be much worse off."

"You might be right, sir, but I'm not sure if it makes me feel any better."

"I've lost a lot of good men to those dragons," the king said. "Women and children, too. Not only did you save lives, but you gave the people hope in a time they had none. *That* should make you feel better."

"Yes, sir."

The king sighed and shook his head. "You know what's really a shame?" he asked.

"What's that, sir?"

"You told me not all eshans behave like you. I can only imagine the world we'd live in if they did."

Ascura remained silent, unsure of what to say. Instead, he looked down at the ground.

"Here," the king said, handing the empty satchel over. "Since yours got ruined in the fight."

"Thank you, sir."

"I've agreed to the alliance. You have plenty of volunteers ready and willing to march with you back to Teasvanna."

"Glad to hear it, sir. If possible, I'd like to borrow a wagon so that I can cart the beast's head back as proof."

"Of course," the king said. "But there's something I want you to tell me."

"What is it?"

"The kesshonite. Is this going to be the cost every time?"

"The kesshonite is definitely wild and unstable, sir," Ascura admitted. "But I've been thinking about it since the fight. I think eshans might be the key to containing it. When Jason used the kesshonite, I could feel it. Normally I can't get a hold of the kesshonite's power on my own, but when he released it, I was able to, sir. I was able to pull it back some. With a little practice, I think between the two of us, we can learn to control the kesshonite."

"Then it would seem if we are to survive, we will need to work together, won't we?"

"It would seem so, sir."

"We're living in strange times, aren't we?" the king asked.

"Sir?"

"A human king and an eshan soldier are in the same room and sharing the same concerns."

"Yes, sir. Strange times indeed, sir."

The two sat in silence, both looking over at Jason.

"Can I ask you something?" the king asked, still watching Jason.

"Yes, sir."

"Do you think it's possible for man to unlock and use the power of the Arbiters?"

"For our sake, I hope so, sir. I don't see us surviving any other way."

The king slowly nodded his head. "I can only imagine what that kind of power would do to a man."

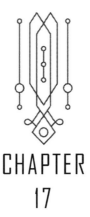

CHAPTER 17

"So that was the first white dragon killed?" Bashkim asked. "What happened to Jason?"

"Oh, he woke up after a couple of days," Ascura said. "He was more confused than anything."

"Then what about the kesshonite? I'm assuming you figured out how to use it safely?"

"That turned out to be simpler than they imagined," Telanos said.

Telanos lightly waved his hands, and several stones gently lifted themselves from the walls and floor. The stones floated smoothly towards him, all coming together and forming a chair for him to sit on.

"All they had to do was cut the kesshonite down into small enough gems and embed them into their weapons," Telanos explained as he sat down. "Once there, a human could wield said weapon and draw out the power directly, channeling it through their own body and back out."

"And it worked?" Fandul asked, sitting in the opposite corner of the cells next to Dasc.

"Like a gift from the gods," Ascura said. "Thought it wasn't as easy as Telanos makes it sound. A human could draw the power out well enough, but an eshan had to be nearby to keep it from overflowing. The good news is that it made short work of those dragons."

"So long as an eshan was nearby," Fandul noted. "I'm assuming that part didn't always go as planned."

"Unfortunately, you are correct," Telanos said. "There were some casualties in the beginning. If too much power was drawn before an eshan could stop it, it would rise beyond their control. The result was an explosion large enough to decimate an entire white dragon and everything around it. It's a delicate balance, and if it's not kept, there will be nothing but a crater left."

"To make matters worse," Ascura added. "Those accidents did little to strengthen our relations in the beginning. Luckily, we learned to avoid such things the more we practiced, but it was still a deadly risk each time."

"What about humans and their magic?" Bashkim asked. "Jason had it, but did it happen with everyone that used the kesshonite?"

Ascura nodded.

"The kesshonite drew magic out of every human it touched," Telanos said. "As though it had been in them the whole time, just waiting to be awoken. We never got to see much progress with those abilities in our time. Those that touched the kesshonite were soldiers and they were kept on the battlefield, not at home for study and practice. What we saw was far from eshan levels of magic but had the kesshonite been kept around and the abilities passed down to future generations, then perhaps they would have gotten close."

"Amazing," Bashkim said, taking a breath as he let all the new information sink in.

Bashkim looked over at Ascura sitting next to him, a sudden and curious look on his face. "Wait a minute," Bashkim said. "None of that explains how you ended up in here."

"Things got a little complicated," Telanos said once he saw the grin forming on Ascura's face.

"How so?" Bashkim asked.

"Women!" Ascura said happily.

Telanos snorted. "Yes. The city's mighty hero, Ascura, fell to man's oldest threat: a woman."

"And I'd do it again," Ascura said with a wide smile on his face. "And again, and again, and again. Her name was Rachel, and by the Arbiters...what a woman. Left me speechless when I first met her. She was what really got me thinking about the relations between our people. For you see, Rachel was a human."

"Oh?" Fandul asked. "I'm guessing that didn't go over well with the locals."

"We kept it a secret," Ascura said. "Jason was in on the whole thing from the beginning. Hell. He was the one that encouraged me to introduce myself to begin with. I fought it tooth and nail because I knew I of all people couldn't be caught with her. Teasvanna had already begun making an icon out of me, saying I was an example of "eshan power", all the while ignoring my goals of removing the rift between us and the humans. If they were to find me with Rachel...well, you know how people are. It wouldn't have been good for us, or the entire relationship between humans and eshans."

"But that didn't stop you, did it?" Fandul asked.

"Not a chance," Ascura said with a wheezing chuckle. "And with enough time in a hidden relationship, I suddenly found myself with a whole new problem."

234 Years Ago

Ascura sat in a chair in Rachel's house late one night, his face in his hands. On his left stood Jason, and on his right sat Rachel.

"Are you sure?" Jason asked.

"I haven't bled for nearly a full season," Rachel said. "And I've been nauseous for several days. I think it's safe to say I'm sure."

"What have I done?" Ascura moaned.

"We'll make it through this," Rachel soothed as she rubbed Ascura's back. "We can be strong."

"I've no doubt we can," Ascura said as looked at her. "But what of the child? They have yet to be born and I already feel guilty for bringing them into the world. There's nowhere for a hybrid child to go."

"We can find a home somewhere outside the city," Rachel said. "By ourselves. Nobody would have to know."

"That's awfully risky with the white dragons still around," Jason said. "Granted, we've done well to thin their numbers, and they're getting harder to find with each hunt, but we do know they're still out there. I wouldn't want to be caught alone out there with one."

"He's right," Ascura said. "it's still too dangerous."

"Although," Jason said, snapping his fingers suddenly. "You know about Handleson, right?"

Ascura nodded his head, but Rachel spoke up. "I don't," she said.

"There's a place halfway between our two cities where they meet for trade," Ascura explained. "It's seen a lot of support over the years from those that would like to see us cooperate a little more. If I'm not mistaken, the supporters have made a more permanent stance of late and officially established their own village there."

"That's them," Jason said. "They've got a little of both there, along with some hybrids. And considering what happened when you two got in the same city, there's bound to only be more hybrids on the way."

"I've no ties to Nennossen," Rachel said, "If this Handleson village is as new as you say, then I've little doubt that work would be hard to find."

"It might work," Ascura said. "Thing is though, our hunts haven't led us out that way yet. Neither of us could break away from the other knights long enough to get you there safely and traveling alone is out of the question."

"We've got the entire city fooled," Jason said. "Everyone thinks she's with me. There's no reason she can't stay until the child is born, right? How hard can it be to hide a hybrid baby? Just put a sock on its head so nobody sees the ears."

Ascura managed to find a chuckle within himself. "The eshans would be able to sniff them out, surely."

Jason crossed his arms. "Yeah. About that. Do you honestly think they're going to stick around when all this is over?"

Ascura sank into his seat and deflated with a defeated sigh. Rachel grabbed his hand and gave it a gentle squeeze.

"Then it's settled," Jason said, slapping his hands together and rubbing them. "Rachel stays here until the kid is born. Me and you can take rotations on the hunts so one of us is always here with here. When the kid comes along, we put a sock on it and head to Handleson and everyone lives happily ever after. At the rate we're going, the white dragons will probably be gone by then too."

Ascura thought it over for a moment and looked at Rachel. "What do you think?"

"If being in Handleson means we can stop hiding, then I'm all for it. I can wait here until it's time."

A smile came across Ascura's face as he slowly started to find some hope in the situation. The three shared a cup of tea and pondered what life in Handleson would be like, as well as the hybrid child. Once their cups were dry and their eyes heavier, they decided to head their separate ways for the night. Rachel hugged Jason and kissed Ascura goodnight before sending them on their way.

The two walked in silence for the most part as they made their way back to the barracks, but Jason eventually broke.

"Part of you kind of wishes the white dragons would stay," Jason asked. "Doesn't it?"

"As bad as it sounds, yes. They seem to be the only thing keeping our people together. I hate the idea of using fear in such a way, but I think we both know why the eshans are really here."

"They want to figure out how to use the kesshonite themselves?"

"Most likely. Whether they can or not, they're going to pull out eventually either way once this fight is over."

"So damned stupid," Jason grumbled and stopped walking. "Look at what we've done together. Those dragons were kicking our asses like it was nothing. And now? Now we've got them on the run. When we started fighting back, we could find four or more a month easily. Now they're hiding and we're coming back from hunts empty-handed."

"I agree," Ascura said. "Clearly, we're better off together, and who knows what else the kesshonite could do for us if we *continued* to work together. But there's something else, isn't there?"

Jason crossed his arms and huffed as he looked down at his feet. "Yeah. What's going to happen to the rest of us when this is over?"

"What do you mean?"

"Us human soldiers," Jason said, gesturing towards himself as he looked back at Ascura. "Those of us that touched the kesshonite. We're...different now. Not everybody accepts that. While my momma might be proud of me for finally doing something with my life, others haven't been so fortunate. Some won't even have a home to go to when this is all over."

"I didn't realize," Ascura started to say, but Jason cut him short.

"Not all humans like magic. There's a fair number of them that contribute it to some kind of witchcraft or devil worship. Or some other stupid shit."

Ascura held his tongue, unsure of what to say.

"Bah," Jason said after a brief silence and waved his hand as if pushing something away. "It's not your fault. I'm just...I like the way things are too. I mean, the white dragons aren't great, but eshans in Nennossen?

That's something fantastic. And knowing I can go to Teasvanna without getting arrested on sight is also pretty nice. Pa was a woodworker when he was still around. He would have loved to have seen the carpentry Teasvanna has."

"To be fair," Ascura said once Jason fell silent. "We are just assuming the eshans will pull out. We don't know for sure what's going to happen."

"No," Jason said, his eyes trailing back down to his feet. "Nennossen is doing their own part to make sure this doesn't last. The king has noticed a decline in the white dragons and has already begun to fear losing the kesshonite. He requested that we start...well, stealing it, basically. He wants to make sure he has plenty in reserve when the eshans pull out."

Ascura put his hand against his face and pinched the bridge of his nose. "By the Arbiteres," he groaned. "What does that damned fool think he's doing?"

"We just received the orders today before I met up with you to see Rachel."

"The eshans are going to notice, and when they do, it could be enough to start a war."

"As much as I'd like to, I don't think we'll be able to stop them completely. I wasn't the only one that received the order."

Ascura crossed his arms and scratched his chin. "So now it would actually be a good thing if the eshans pulled out, and the sooner the better."

"It'd be a lot better than starting a war, or us accidentally killing ourselves with the kesshonite once they're gone."

"Fortunately, we're already fairly limited on kesshonite weapons. It's going to be hard for some of those to walk away. We'll just have to make sure it's even harder now."

Jason shook his head and groaned. "As if smuggling hybrid babies wasn't enough."

Ascura only shrugged his shoulders.

"Alright," Jason said, taking a deep breath. "Alright. Then we'll just wait for the eshans to pull out and try to keep the weapons safe. If that's what we've got to do, then that's what we've got to do."

Jason started to continue his walk towards the barracks but noticed Ascura remained in place.

"You not coming?" Jason asked.

"A little later. I was planning on walking a couple more laps before turning in. Might need a few more now."

"Fair enough. Just don't get caught sneaking back to Rachel's."

"I'm not heading that way," Ascura chuckled. "But hey...thanks."

"For what?"

"For telling me."

"What was it you said when you first came to Nennossen?" Jason asked. "You're here for your people, not some king's pride? That stuck with me, and I'd like to think I'm doing the same. If we're going to not only survive, but progress as a people, we need eshans, and eshans need us."

Ascura smiled and nodded. "Thanks," he said again.

Jason waved goodbye and made his way down the street towards the castle barracks. Ascura continued down a different road, slowly walking along in the dark as he contemplated the delicate situation he had found himself in. Luckily, everyone had long since retired for the night and left the roads empty, minus the occasional patrolling guard. As he rounded a corner, he heard a man's voice gently call out for him.

"Ascura?" the voice asked.

"Yes?" Ascura asked, turning to see a cloaked and hooded figure behind him. "Can I help you?"

"I believe so," the man said and pulled his hood back to reveal a familiar face.

"Telanos?" Ascura gasped and stepped back while placing a hand on one of his swords, then added in a quiet voice. "What the hell are you doing here? Where have you been?"

"Lost, I'm afraid."

Ascura's hand stayed on his sword, but the blade remained sheathed as he locked his eyes on the wizard.

"Please," Telanos said. "I mean you no harm. You know that."

Ascura took in a slow breath and stood up straight, slowly taking his hand away from his weapon. "I'd probably lose that fight, anyway. So, tell me then, what's going on? What happened to you?"

"I went to hunt down those that murdered my family as I'm sure you are aware. And yes, I killed them. I chose to let one live, but Arbiters know I cannot call it mercy. I wanted him to live the rest of his days in fear."

Ascura crossed his arms. "Well, you succeeded. Poor bastard begged to be locked away so he could get away from you."

"I'm not proud of what I've done."

"It's understandable, Telanos. Your family was murdered. I'd be more worried if you *didn't* react in such a way. But what doesn't make sense is that the one you let live said there was a white dragon with you."

"Yes." Telanos nodded. "When I left my house to hunt the thieves, the dragon was sitting just outside as though he had been waiting for me. It made no motion to attack, and I thought it nothing more than a regular dragon until I felt a...connection."

Ascura looked at Telanos with raised eyebrows. "What does that mean?"

"I could feel its thoughts," Telanos said. "Or at least, I thought I could. As strange as it sounds, I think that thing was drawn to my own bloodlust at the time."

Ascura kept his arms crossed and continued to stare the old man down.

"I might be Teasvanna's best wizard," Telanos said. "But there is plenty in this world that even I don't understand. When I was hunting those thieves, I was connected to that dragon somehow. I could feel it. It became my ally, or so I had believed. Once I killed the thieves and took the time to properly mourn my loss, I realized what I did to those men was not vengeance, but merely revenge. I was out for blood for my own satisfaction. My family had nothing to do with it. As I realized this, the bond between me and the dragon became broken and unstable."

"How so?"

"The beast's thoughts became wild and sporadic. It felt as though it were in my head, screaming and trying to claw its way out. The dragon turned violent, and I barely managed to get out alive. I don't think we're dealing with just dragons, Ascura. There was something else going on with that creature. I could hear it. Sense it. Almost *see* it in my mind."

"You think someone is controlling the dragons?"

"Someone," Telanos said. "Or something. There's a magic at play like nothing I've ever seen before."

"Magic?"

Telanos slowly rolled up his left sleeve, revealing his arm and a black substance that covered it from the tips of fingers to slightly above his wrist.

"By the Arbiters," Ascura whispered, holding his hands out and taking a step back.

The black on Telanos's hand slowly shifted and swirled beneath his skin, worming around as though it were alive.

"I may have made it out in one piece," Telanos said and rolled his sleeve back down. "But the dragon left a mark. It tried to turn me, but I was able to stop it. I've managed to keep it contained for now, but I don't know if I can keep it there forever. My theory is that whatever *that* is, is the same thing controlling the dragons, which means they aren't the main threat."

"Who has that kind of power?"

"That's what I've been trying to find out, though I'm afraid I haven't had much luck in my search."

"Why didn't you come back before? We could have used you."

Telanos smiled, slowly rolling the sleeve far enough forward to cover his entire hand. "You didn't need me. Look at where we are. We're two eshans standing in Nennossen. *You* did that. The white dragons were terrorizing our two cities, and you've got them on the run. On top of that, you even learned how to use the kesshonite."

Ascura put his hands on his hips and slowly looked down towards the ground. "I could have used you."

"You still give me far more credit than I'm worth. You're standing on your own feet just fine. You should be proud."

"Maybe," Ascura said distantly and looked back up at Telanos. "But why *didn't* you come back sooner?"

"The damage had already been done by the time I got myself back together. Proving my innocence would have only slowed down my work, and you never would have taken the plunge to go to Nennossen."

"So why now?"

"I've come to help you and your child. I'm assuming neither you nor Jason know anything about delivering a newborn?"

Ascura's eyes widened, and his mouth opened but words failed to come out.

"It's a boy," Telanos said.

Ascura ran a hand through his hair. "A son?" he said quietly. "How do you know?"

"I'm a wizard, Ascura."

"Right. Right. And that also means you're a doctor now?"

"A master wizard has many uses," Telanos said. "I've been in the women's chamber for more than a handful of births in Teasvanna."

Ascura shook his head and paused. "A son, huh?"

Telanos nodded.

"Alright," Ascura said with a deep breath. "What's your plan then?"

"I'll continue my studies in secret as I have been. Only now, I'll stay nearby to keep an eye on Rachel. When the day comes, I will be there."

"Can you do that? Hide in the city, I mean?"

"This is Nennossen. The odds of running into someone that recognizes me here are extremely low."

"But not impossible."

"I'll be careful. I always am."

Ascura crossed his arms, then looked down at Telanos's hidden limb. "What about...*that?*"

"If it starts to become too much, I'll let you or Jason know."

"And what are we to do about it?"

"The safest thing would be to put me down."

"You want me to kill you?" Ascura gasped. "I can't do that. You've been a friend and a mentor to me. Hell, you're trying to help me bring my son into the world!"

"And it pleases me greatly to hear you say that," Telanos said and put his unaffected hand on Ascura's shoulder. "I know I've been gone, but I'm grateful for our friendship. However, deep down, you know I can't be allowed to turn. If I were to keep my powers after turning, then who knows what damage I would do before I was stopped. I have little desire for such destruction or to bend to the whims of whatever it is controlling these beasts."

Ascura sighed and his head dropped. "I just...I don't know if I have the strength to do something like that."

"You do," Telanos said with a smile. "Because you know it would be the right thing to do. That's why I picked you when we discovered the kesshonite."

"Well, if it's all the same to you, don't make me prove you right."

Though shocked to hear about Telanos's return, both Rachel and Jason agreed to the plan. Ascura had often spoken highly of Telanos to the both of them even before he made his return. Ascura defended

Telanos more than once and had always refused to believe that he had been behind the white dragons, so it came as no surprise that Ascura would vouch for the wizard. All of them in agreement and keeping themselves on the same page, each of them performed their parts.

Ascura and Jason rotated their hunts so that one of them would always remain behind with Rachel. This also allowed them to keep an eye on things in Nennossen to make sure the kesshonite weapons were all accounted for. Telanos also made a regular appearance at Rachel's home to check in on his patient.

"He's very strong," Telanos would tell Rachel during the checkups. "And healthy."

As time went on and the child inside of Rachel grew, Ascura had to make some small changes to their plans. To keep things believable, he kept Jason in Nennossen as the pregnancy came closer to an end so that he may witness the birth of what the city believed to be his son. Meanwhile, the real father would be absent.

It's safer this way, Ascura told himself. *For everyone.*

One evening after nearly an entire day of labor, Rachel found herself on her bed in a tremendous amount of pain.

"Where is that damned wizard?" Jason asked frantically.

"Right behind you," Telanos said, entering Rachel's house.

"Thank the Arbiters," Jason sighed. "What do we do?"

Telanos stepped into the kitchen briefly and returned with a small hand towel. "*We* remain calm."

Telanos rolled the small towel up and came to Rachel's side, handing her the towel. "Here. Bite on this."

Rachel gladly took the rolled towel and sank her teeth into it as it muffled her cries. Telanos watched carefully, taking note of the swelling in her forearms.

"Cover the windows," Telanos said, keeping his eyes on her.

Jason ran to each window and closed the curtains. Rachel continued to bite into the towel as hard as she could, her face having long ago turned red.

"Does that help?" Telanos asked gently.

Rachel nodded and continued to bite. The towel eventually slipped, and a not-so-muffled scream escaped. Jason ran to assist and grabbed the small towel.

"Now what?" Jason asked as he handed the towel back to her.

Telanos remained silent and his stare looked on past Rachel.

"Someone heard the scream," he eventually said.

"How do you know?"

"Because they're at the door."

Jason turned to look at the closed door to the house, and as soon as he did, he heard a knock on the other side.

"Hello?" the voice shouted. "I heard screaming. Are you alright?"

"We can use him for our benefit," Telanos said. "Tell him to wait outside and keep an eye out to make sure more people don't come in."

Jason made his way to the door and opened it, quickly explaining to the man Rachel's situation. The man's eyes widened in shock, but he readily agreed to Jason's request to remain outside once he saw Rachel.

"Now what?" Jason asked after closing the door.

"Now it is time," Telanos said. "Grab that chair and bring it over here."

Jason did as instructed and set the chair in front of him and waited for the next order.

"Good," Telanos said, then motioned towards Rachel. "Take her. Sit on that chair and hold her in front of it just on the edge. Keep her up straight."

Awkwardly, Jason followed Telanos's instructions and grabbed Rachel. He kept his arms curled just under her shoulders, making sure she sat up straight.

"You're going to feel something grab you," Telanos said calmly. "Do not be afraid. It will only be my magic to aid the process."

Tears running down her face, Rachel nodded repeatedly. She could feel something slowly wrapping around her ankles as Telanos waved his hand, but she could see nothing. The invisible force gently grabbed her but refrained from squeezing. It did, however, have enough strength in its grip to lift her legs off the ground and keep them spread, gently angling her back into Jason.

"You're doing great," Telanos assured. "Now push."

Rachel suddenly started shaking violently.

"Telanos?" Jason asked as he struggled to keep her in place.

Telanos waved his hand again and his magic grabbed hold of Rachel by the shoulders to help keep her still. Jason looked at Telanos with questioning eyes. Keeping his own eyes locked on Jason, Telanos slowly shook his head from side to side as Rachel stared up at the ceiling.

"What do I do?" Jason whispered.

"Just hold her in place the best you can."

The shakes from Rachel stopped. Her head came back down and dropped the towel in her mouth.

"That's fine," Telanos said as he used his one arm to prepare a few other towels for the coming child. "We don't need it anymore. We have a friendly neighbor posted outside to help. Scream as much as you'd like."

Rachel did indeed scream as she pushed. She also reached down and squeezed Jason's legs. Her fingers dug into his skin nearly hard enough to draw blood. Jason winced in pain but did his best to retain his composure, ignoring the burn both in his legs and his ears from her screams.

"That's it," Telanos said, kneeling down in front of her. "Just keep pushing and breathing. Your son is on his way."

A wince suddenly came across Telanos's face as he flinched.

"You okay?" Jason asked.

"It's nothing," Telanos said. "Keep her steady."

Rachel continued to scream loudly and did everything she could to push the child out of her. The baby soon came out and slid his way into Telanos's hand. He quickly laid the child down and cleaned him up while ordering Jason to return Rachel to her bed. Jason rose to his feet and gently carried Rachel with him. As he laid her down on the bed, she started to shake again.

"Telanos?" Jason asked as he tried to hold her down.

Telanos came to her side and handed the child and towels over to Jason. He held his hand out and used his magic to force her still again. She continued to shake but eventually started to calm once more. She stared emptily at the ceiling, trying to speak.

"Ba..." she muttered, but the words could not be heard.

Telanos leaned in closer and put his ear next to her mouth so that he might understand.

"Yes," Telanos said as she spoke and put his hand on her shoulder. "he's here. Alive and well."

Jason came over with the newborn child, but Rachel only stared at the ceiling as if she could no longer process what took place around her. Her lips slowly moved as she tried to form words.

"Rachel?" Jason asked but received no response.

Jason looked at Telanos, confused. "What's going on?"

Telanos gently waved his hand over Rachel's face. Her eyes remained fixed and unblinking. Telanos pulled his hand back and lowered his head.

"Turn the child away," Telanos whispered.

Jason hesitated, but after seeing the empty stare in Rachel's eyes, he slowly turned the crying baby away from his mother. Telanos reached out with a hand and used his magic to pull the rolled towel from earlier towards him. He rolled it tighter, gently placing it into Rachel's open mouth.

Keeping the baby facing away, Jason watched as a violent seizure suddenly whipped through Rachel. Her mouth clenched down onto the towel, and her head bounced from side to side as her arms slammed against the bed. Nearly as soon as it had started it came to a chilling finish. Rachel opened her mouth and the towel fell out as she took a sudden gasp of air and held it, freezing in place.

Telanos breathed in through his nose slowly and reached his hand out. He gently slid his hand down over Rachel's face, closing her eyes for the last time.

"She's gone."

"But how?" Jason asked as the baby cried even louder. "And why?"

Telanos pulled a blanket over Rachel to cover her completely. "Sometimes the cost of life is another life."

Jason kept the baby close to him and stared at the covered body. He shook his head, struggling to accept what had just happened. The two stood in silence as they listened to the newborn's cries. As the wailing grew louder, Telanos winced and grunted as though something had hurt him.

"Something wrong?" Jason asked.

"My arm. It's getting worse. Rapidly."

"What? How?"

Telanos pulled his sleeve back and revealed the darkness on his arm. It had progressed almost all the way up to his elbow. The black substance looked as though it had thickened as well, and it thrashed about violently as if it were trying to escape.

"I don't know what's happened," Telanos admitted. "It began to burn once Rachel started giving birth. I kept quiet so as not to make her nervous."

"Can you contain it?" Jason asked, slowly taking a step back and reaching for his sword.

The baby started to shriek even louder. Telanos hunched over, grasping his arm and grunting in pain. Jason drew his sword.

"Telanos?" he asked. "Don't make me do this if I don't have to."

Before Telanos could answer, a soldier burst into the room happily with several more behind him. "We hear that baby! Congratulations, Jason you're a—"

Before the soldier could finish, he stopped dead in his tracks when he saw Jason with his sword out. Telanos instantly took advantage of the situation. He quickly snatched the child and used his magic to sling Jason against the wall at the far side of the room. Telanos summoned ice from the ground and used it to lock Jason in place. Seeing the assault, one of the soldiers lunged at Telanos with their sword drawn and came down hard with the blade.

Telanos held his darkened arm up to defend the baby. The blade cleaved completely through the bone in one fell swipe near the elbow. The severed limb fell to the ground with a thud, and the darkness spewed from the open wound up from the ground and towards the soldiers. They jumped back and swatted the swirling black mist, but it did them little good. The darkness swept over them, turning them against their own.

During the confusion, Telanos kneeled while still holding the baby. A transparent barrier started to form over him, staring from the floor and working its way over his head. Just before the magical barrier closed, he looked at Jason who remained pinned against the wall. Telanos nodded at Jason, and the ice shattered into pieces.

"Telanos!" Jason shouted as he stumbled over, but the barrier closed itself shut.

Jason looked at the soldiers in disbelief, watching as the turned were struck down. Black blood poured from their wounds and spilled across the floor as their bodies collapsed. The darkened soldiers snarled even with their last breaths. It wasn't until their wounds started to bleed red did they come back to reality. A point at which they were well beyond saving.

As the last turned soldier fell, Jason looked back over towards Telanos. He could see through the barrier, finding a wizard frozen in place, for not even his eyes moved. Jason also took note that Telanos had kept the baby hidden underneath his robe and out of sight. Before Jason could attempt to come up with a decent story, a familiar voice could be heard outside the house.

"What's going on?" he heard someone demand, and pushing themselves through the remaining soldiers came Ascura.

"Jason!" Ascura shouted when he entered the room but stopped suddenly when he saw the bed with a covered body on it.

"It was Telanos!" Jason blurted without hesitation as he forced tears to his eyes. "I didn't know who he was! I thought he was just a normal eshan. He showed up and said he was a doctor. Rachel was giving birth, and he said he could help. I...I panicked! I didn't know what to do! I thought he was going to help us!"

"What happened to Rachel? And where's *your* child?" Ascura asked, trying to keep himself together.

"He took my son!" Jason bellowed and threw a chair across the room. "He took him! He turned him into that dark mist! He's gone, Ascura! Him *and* Rachel!"

Ascura grabbed Jason and held him close, going along with the act while trying to look as though he had not been affected. He took Jason away from the house and instructed the other soldiers to clean up the mess.

Several days passed after the incident. Jason got to fully explain to Ascura what had truly taken place, admitting that he didn't know the fate of Ascura's son. Telanos remained in the strange crystal-like barrier but the soldiers had hauled him out of the house. The eshans were quick to construct a sarcophagus to contain the wounded wizard, filling it with the magic-negating nectar.

For the first time since Rachel's death, Ascura finally had a moment to himself. The funeral they gave her didn't even allow him to mourn properly, for he had to remain under the lie that Jason had taken the greater loss. He rarely got to go to Rachel's house on his own without Jason's assistance, but now that she was gone, there wasn't much need for the charade.

He sat at the foot of her bed. As he let everything fall into place in his mind, he took a long and much-needed breath. It felt as though he had pretended *not* to be hurt for so long that he almost didn't know what to do or how to process the emotions. As he sat there alone and with no need to pretend, the feelings quickly taught him what to do. Tears formed in his eyes and slid down the sides of his face as reality revealed its face. Rachel was gone, and his son's fate unknown.

A hand suddenly touched his shoulder, causing him to jump.

"You!" Ascura said with gritted teeth once he saw Telanos. "What did you do?"

Telanos held his arms out beside him to show that he meant no harm, as well as revealing his missing limb.

"Your arm," Ascura said.

"It's gone. The good news is, so is the darkness that was in it."

"Where is my son?"

"He is safe. Sleeping peacefully inside the barrier I made."

"Then how are you out?"

"How did I escape my own barrier?" Telanos asked with a small grin on his face. "Or how did I escape that pathetic contraption they thought could contain me?"

Ascura refused to smile at the wizard's attempt at humor.

"Your son is alive and safe," Telanos said more gently and took a seat next to Ascura at the end of the bed. "Nobody knows I've escaped, and your son remains hidden. For now, it's as if he is frozen in time. When we take him out, it will seem to him as though no time has passed at all."

"And when do we do that?"

"That's up to you."

Ascura remained silent as he considered his options.

"Not now," Ascura said after thinking. "I don't think I can bring him into this world just yet. It's not ready for someone like him. I've still got work to do on that."

"As you wish," Telanos said with a small bow. "What is your plan, Master Ascura?"

"The white dragons...we have to kill them. All of them. If we can do that, then whoever is controlling them will be without power, hopefully. Or at least, they won't have their beasts and the cities will be safe from their attacks."

Telanos nodded. "Very well."

"Can you help us track them?"

"I can. As barbaric a treatment as it was, removing the arm seems to have done the trick. I should be able to focus all of my power on the tasks at hand now. In secret, of course."

"Good," Ascura said and stood up. "Then let's get started."

Telanos remained seated and gently grabbed Ascura's arm. "Wait," he said, pulling Ascura back down. "Sit for a moment."

Telanos took a deep breath as he collected his words. "When I found my family," he said, then paused as he recalled the images of his own wife and child. "When I found them in the house, all I could think about was finding those responsible. I wanted them to pay, and I wanted them to pay in blood. I took it upon myself to hunt them down and collect what was owed. I failed to take time to properly mourn the death of my family, and as a result, I lost myself. You can see the price I've had to pay for my mistake."

"Rachel wasn't murdered."

"No. But you're still looking to make someone pay for it. You can take your swords and be a soldier tomorrow, but tonight, you mourn."

Telanos put his hand on Ascura's shoulder and gave it a slight squeeze. Another tear found its way down Ascura's face as he closed his eyes. He nodded and slowly leaned forward. Telanos patted him on the back and got to his feet to leave Ascura alone.

"What did she name him?" Ascura asked as Telanos opened the door to leave.

"Bashkim."

CHAPTER 18

<u>Present Day</u>

Bashkim paced back and forth inside the cell as he processed all the new information. "Alright. Hold on," he said and held his hands up as he stopped pacing and stared down at Ascura. "You're telling me that you're my dad? I'm the son of *the* Ascura?"

"Indeed, you are," Ascura said with a smile. "And words cannot express how happy I am to finally meet you as such."

"And you've been down here the whole time?" Bashkim asked as he looked back and forth between Ascura and Telanos several times. "How'd you end up down here? What happened to me? How long was I sealed away?"

Telanos held his hand up and motioned for Bashkim to relax. "One question at a time, child. After our little incident, the soldiers continued to hunt down the white dragons and finish them off. In the meantime, the eshans remained in Nennossen to study the humans. They never figured out how to extract the power of the kesshonite on their own and considered it a loss. The humans played their part as well, seeing to it that some of those kesshonite weapons went "missing". The humans were accused but never proven guilty, and the eshans were accused of their selfish motives but could also not be proven guilty. In the end, things returned to the way they were before the white dragons arrived. Humans stayed out of Teasvanna, and eshans stayed out of Nennossen. The relationship was stable so long as it was far apart."

"And the white dragons?" Fandul asked as he rose to his feet and leaned against the cell's bars. "All of them were gone?"

"All that we could find," Ascura said. "We thinned their numbers greatly, which made them harder to find each time we went out." Ascura chuckled and coughed. "You'd almost think they forgot the white dragons even existed as quick as they were to get things back to normal. Who knows? Maybe they did forget."

"Whether they did or not," Telanos said. "With the threat no longer around to remind them of why they were together in the first place, the rift between humans and eshans returned."

Ascura attempted to form his limp hand into a fist and shook it. "I fought to keep them together. I pleaded with our king, but the damned fool would hear nothing of it. I kept in touch with the humans, secretly training them how to use the magic they had acquired. It wasn't long before I was found out. The king confronted me, and I confessed."

"You did more than confess," Telanos noted.

"I proudly told the king I had befriended the humans! On top of that, I told him about Rachel. That was what finally broke him. He couldn't stand the idea of his icon of "eshan power" bedding a human. He said if I couldn't see the difference between our two people, then I didn't need eyes."

"He took them?" Bashkim asked in disbelief.

Ascura sighed and calmed himself down. "Yes. I was hauled away, my eyes removed, and in the cells I went. While I was locked away, that which I had truly been fighting for was swept under the rug."

"The world was led to believe that Ascura had gone into hiding to avoid the publicity," Telanos said. "Most people believed it and chose to respect it and let him live in what they thought peace, just as the king had hoped. As time went on, Ascura and his vision was forgotten."

Telanos turned to Treydola, who had remained sitting on the floor for the entire story. "But there were those that refused to believe Ascura would just suddenly disappear, and they chose to pursue the truth in secret."

"Then it would seem not much has changed in the past two hundred years," Fandul noted, grateful the current king had taken *only* part of his ear.

"Not everyone wants the world to move forward," Telanos said. "Especially those in a position that benefit from where it currently stands."

"Makes sense," Bashkim said, then turned to Ascura. "So you've been down here ever since then?"

Ascura chuckled. "Yes. I made Telanos promise to keep us both alive until I felt like it was safe enough to bring you into the world. After outliving so many kings, I started to doubt it would ever be safe and feared I may have waited too long."

"About that," Dasc chimed in, pushing his head against the bars from the outside. "How *did* you both live so long? And how come Telanos has aged so much better?"

Telanos leaned back into his stone chair. "That secret dies with me."

"Surely you can understand why we're curious," Fandul said. "Two hundred years is an awfully long time."

"There is more to the magic of our world than merely manipulating a couple elements. The kesshonite should be proof enough of that. There are magics that have been lost, forgotten, and even hidden. All for good reason. So surely *you* can understand why I don't want to pass it on."

"Well, at the rate we're going," Fandul sighed. "The rest of us will probably be lucky to even see forty anyway."

"You're more likely to if you stay away from such things," Telanos said, then turned to Bashkim. "Now, as I was saying. Your father did eventually agree to have you released. I pulled you out and took you to the orphanage in Handleson, as it was our best option."

Bashkim rubbed both of his hands through this hair, slowly pulling it back as he went. "That means I'm over two hundred years old."

"Technically. But you weren't exactly aging while you were in there."

"The sarcophagus then, when it was leaking. What was that?"

"Natural causes. That nectar is no normal substance. It's unsurprising it lasted all those years and eventually found its way through the cracks. But...there is one other thing."

"What's that?" Bashkim asked.

Telanos leaned forward in his chair and put his chin in his hand. "The darkness from my severed arm filled the room. It overcame several of the guards and was right in front of me. I'm afraid I might not have protected you as well as I thought I had."

"What do you mean?"

"There's a chance some of that darkness made it into the barrier with us...with you."

"With me?"

"Yes. I didn't know it at the time, nor two hundred years later when I pulled you out. As promised to your father, I kept an eye on you even after I dropped you off at the orphanage, but it wasn't until the fire that the idea occurred to me."

"The fire?" Bashkim asked. "You were there?"

Telanos kept his eyes on Bashkim. "I was. I tried to stop the fire from outside. Your magic overpowered *mine*, and you were but a child. Considering some of the nights you've had recently, I was hoping you could shed some light on the situation."

"You've been watching me?" Bashkim asked, taking a small step backwards.

"Since the day you were born."

Fandul and Dasc slowly positioned themselves upright, discreetly moving their hands closer to their weapons. They watched Bashkim closely, waiting to follow his lead.

"You hear a voice," Telanos said. "Don't you?"

Bashkim hesitated for a moment and kept his eyes on the wizard. "I do," he finally said and sat back down next to Ascura.

"So could I," Telanos said, leaning back into his own seat. "When my arm was infected, I could hear a faint whisper of a language I did not recognize. Towards the end as the darkness's power grew, the voice became louder."

"I spoke with this voice. It's Mykenebres, and he controls the White Dragons."

Telanos remained silent, and his eyes stayed locked on Bashkim as he sat still as a statue in his stone chair.

"I wondered why you called for that name in the forest," Telanos finally said. "Are you sure that's who it is?"

Fandul and Dasc looked at one another, confused. "Is there something we should know?" Fandul asked.

"Mykenebres is the same as Umbra," Bashkim said. "And yes, Telanos, I'm sure. At first, I thought it was the white dragon speaking to me and I was losing my mind. But eventually it spoke directly in a way I could understand."

"If you're losing your mind," Telanos said. "It's because somebody else wants it."

"But why?" Bashkim asked, throwing his hands up in the air. "It can't be just because we were stuck in that seal together. And how could you just sit by and let me go on like this when you knew?"

"Son," Ascura said and put a hand on Bashkim's shoulder. "We didn't know. Honestly we *still* don't know for sure what's going on."

Bashkim glanced over towards Fandul and Dasc, his shoulders dropping when he saw the questioning and concerned look on their faces. He could easily see their uneasiness, and he could hardly blame them. Bashkim had questioned his own sanity in the past, so why should they feel any different about him? He wanted to ask if they still trusted him but feared their answer. Fandul and Dasc only looked at one another, with Dasc eventually nodding his head.

"I've witnessed this struggle before," Fandul said, turning back to face Bashkim. "When you were surrounded during your escape. At the time I thought it was only us you were fighting against. Now that I can more clearly see the struggle that was really taking place, I believe it's safe to say that it's Umbra that has chosen you and not the other way around. However, it begs the question: are we expected to fight the devil himself as well as the white dragons?"

"We're in trouble if so," Telanos admitted. "This fight of ours seems to be less and less of one for mere mortals. If we're lucky, all *we* have to fight against are the white dragons."

Fandul crossed his arms. "Doesn't strike me as very lucky."

"Considering the alternative, I'd count my blessings."

"We know the kesshonite can kill the dragons," Bashkim said. "So if we have to fight Mykenebres too, then maybe it can also help with that."

"That's a lot of faith to put in the kesshonite," Fandul said. "And right now, all we have is that dagger of yours."

Fandul, Bashkim, and Dasc all turned to Treydola who had just checked the door to make sure they were still alone.

"Those weapons are locked away good," she said, closing the door. "It won't be easy to get them, but I won't say it can't be done. However, I'm afraid there's only a few weapons remaining from those days."

"You forget," Telanos said as he pulled a purple crystal out of his robe. "I know where the source is."

"Then we'll make new ones," Bashkim said. "You two remember how it's done, right?"

Telanos started to nod his head as he put the crystal back in his robe, but the sound of a loud bell suddenly rang through the prison cells.

"We're under attack," Fandul said, him and Dasc both standing up straight.

"And by the sound of that bell," Ascura said, listening to the pattern. "It's a dragon."

"You're right," Fandul said, and motioned for Bashkim to get up.

"You said your dragon wouldn't come for you," Treydola snipped.

"That's not her," Bashkim said. "That's something else."

"What are the odds it's a white dragon?" Dasc asked.

"How many dragons have attacked Teasvanna in your lifetime?" Telanos asked as he stood up, his chair disassembling itself and the bricks returning to their places.

Dasc shrugged. "None."

"Then I would say the odds are quite high."

"We might actually be able to use this to our advantage," Fandul said. "We can slip you out in the chaos."

"And run?" Bashkim asked. "If it's a white dragon I can help fight it! We have some kesshonite with us, plus the dagger. I'm half human, so maybe that'll be enough to make it work."

"That's too risky and you know it," Fandul argued. "It might have worked for Jason when him and Ascura were attacked but we're not taking that chance with you. If people see you here at the same time as a white dragon, you'll be no better off than Telanos. Let the eshans handle this one."

Bashkim motioned to Ascura. "And what about him? I can't just leave him here."

"Yes, you can," Ascura said. "I've been down here for well over a hundred years. Another day won't kill me. Besides, I would only slow you down. That dragon would have me before I could even think about getting to the gate."

"This isn't right," Bashkim growled. "I can't run away like this."

Telanos took a step towards Bashkim. "This isn't running. You're preparing for an even bigger fight. I know you're used to fighting for other people, but today's battle is not yours. Today belongs to the eshans."

"Come on," Fandul said, gently pushing Bashkim along. "Before I take offense to the idea that you think we can't handle our own."

Bashkim looked down at Ascura, then back at Telanos. "Fine," he said, stepping out of the cell. "But I'm coming back for him later."

"I would be shocked if you didn't," Telanos said. "Now go. I will acquire more of the kesshonite and we will rendezvous at a later time."

As everyone left the cell, Treydola closed it and locked it behind them. "Be safe," she said. "I'll be able to make it to my quarters unnoticed."

Fandul and Dasc took Bashkim out to the hallway and paused to let the guards on the floor above them run to the city streets. Fandul carefully poked his head out through a barely open door, watching the soldiers run past. They failed to notice him, many of them still strapping their helmets on as they made a blind dash towards the castle's exit.

"If it is a white dragon," Fandul whispered. "And those tales are true, then we are going to lose a lot of men tonight."

"Then let me help," Bashkim said.

Dasc reached out and put his large hand on Bashkim's shoulder. "We don't need to lose you too."

"But—" Bashkim tried to argue, but Fandul cut him short.

"You have a bigger role to play."

"We are the ones that fight tonight," Dasc said, taking his hand back. "We may die, but we're soldiers. Sometimes that is our role to play. So let us do our part so that you may do yours. Don't let us die for nothing."

Bashkim's hands tightened into fists. "I want to help," he said quietly.

"You have helped," Fandul reassured. "More than you realize."

Fandul motioned for the two of them to follow as they trailed behind the commotion, keeping Bashkim hidden between the two of them. The trio rushed through the castle's main entrance and continued into the streets. The sun had long since set, and a heavy rain fell on top of them, soaking Fandul's lengthy hair nearly instantly. Above them they could see the beast approaching through the storm, its wings spread wide as it swooped down. A slew of lightning bolts shot up from the city streets as the soldiers cast their magic against the creature, failing to slow it even the slightest. The dragon slammed its feet down as it landed, crushing several homes and buildings as it made room for itself. There it stood, tall and proud, roaring as it revealed all its white-scaled horror.

"By the Arbtiers," Fandul gasped as he watched the creature completely flatten the structures.

"It's time for you to go, Bashkim," Dasc said, pushing him along.

"Wait," Bashkim argued, pointing at the dragon. "Your men! They're too close!"

The dragon's feet gripped the ground as it reared its head back and puffed out its chest. Its mouth opened wide, and its head shot forward towards the soldiers. A black mist spewed from the monster's mouth, swirling and spreading as it swam forward. The mist wrapped around several of the soldiers as they frantically tried to avoid it by swinging their swords and casting fire. The soldiers fell to the ground, coughing and gasping for air as they clutched their chests.

"They're going to turn," Bashkim said.

The soldiers slowly loosened their grips on their chests and pushed themselves back up to their feet. They grabbed their weapons and snarled as they pointed them towards the other soldiers that had survived the attack. They lunged at their own and put their fellow soldiers to the blade. Fandul and Dasc stared in disbelief, watching their brothers in arms strike themselves down.

I can't just run away from this, Bashkim thought. *I have to help them. They don't know what they're dealing with.*

"Damned thing is right in our way," Fandul spat. "We'll have to chance it with the main gate."

No, Bashkim told himself, carefully taking an unnoticed step away from his escorts. *We fight.*

Fandul went to push Bashkim along in the right direction, but he had already jumped away and ran straight towards the White Dragon.

"Bashkim!" Fandul shouted.

Bashkim ignored the cries, making his way towards the beast while pulling the dagger from his pack.

Come on, he begged to himself. *Please work.*

The dragon saw Bashkim approach and fixated its eyes on the dagger as Bashkim tried to grasp the kesshonite's power. He could feel it in his hand, just waiting to be used. All he had to do was grab and take hold of it. While focusing on the kesshonite, Bashkim nearly failed to see the dragon's reaction to his approach. The dragon swiped one of its hands wide across the remains of a home and hurled debris of stone and timber towards Bashkim.

Bashkim quickly dropped to his knees and summoned a thick layer of ice to cover his front. The house's remnants smashed against his frozen barrier, but the ice held true. Bashkim focused more magic into his icy protection, struggling to keep it intact. The house behind him had caught most of the debris. The structure groaned as its supports failed and the home came crashing down over him, pinning him to the ground.

Bashkim yelled in pain as the debris crushed him, and he found himself unable to break free. Fandul and Dasc called for him, begging for him to get up, but the white dragon came between them as it approached Bashkim. He could see the dagger beside him, just out of his reach. The white dragon stepped up to him, extending its neck out and placing its head close to Bashkim. Once right in front of him, Bashkim could finally see the monster up close. Seeing the gouged eye on the dragon's face, Bashkim recognized it as the same one him and Rin had encountered before.

"You," Bashkim groaned. "What did Mykenebres do to you?"

A low and slow growl came from the white dragon, and Bashkim could feel its pungent breath blowing against him.

Bashkim stared into the yellow eye of the beast. "I'm not afraid of you. Not anymore."

The dragon's eye narrowed, and it slowly pulled its head back as if the retort had satisfied it. As it did, something suddenly struck the side of the white dragon and sent it crashing into the nearby structures. Another dragon had attacked it and sank its teeth into the white one's neck while flailing their claws like a wild animal. The white dragon roared in pain as its scales were ripped from its body and the streets painted with its black blood. Bashkim focused his eyes on the second dragon, his heart nearly stopping when he saw the light-blue scales.

"Rin?" he asked in disbelief.

The white dragon snarled and rolled itself back up to its feet. It lunged at Rin, using its massive body to shove her backwards. The city crumbled beneath the two dragons as they brawled. Homes were completely leveled as the tails swept wide and the stone roads ripped apart as their claws dug into them. The ground shook as they slammed one another against it, jarring Bashkim's broken bones. Rin blew her icy breath repeatedly, forming a heavy fog that fell over the entire city and hindered Bashkim's view.

Even though a thick layer of ice had already begun to form on the white dragon's body, it pushed forward. Rin reared back for another blast and took a different approach. A blaze of fire came spewing from her mouth, splashing against the white dragon and blackening its scaled hide. The rapid change in temperature only made the fog worse, making it nearly impossible to see them fighting.

The soldiers fled the scene, unable to see Bashkim within the fog and rubble. He could hear Dasc and Fandul calling for him, and he started to shout for them, but through the fog came one of the darkened soldiers, a sword driven into its side. The darkened soldier crawled on the ground, pulling its crippled body closer to Bashkim while it still clutched its weapon. Bashkim tried again to reach the dagger, but the collapsed house kept him pinned. The soldier snarled as it slowly crept forward, its eyes whitened and glazed over.

"Stay back," Bashkim shouted. "I don't want to hurt you. I know you're not in control."

The soldier ignored him, still pulling itself forward.

"Please stop," Bashkim begged.

Admitting to himself that the soldier could no longer understand him, Bashkim moved his hand the best he could and summoned a single spike of ice that shot up from the ground beneath the soldier, lifting it and skewering it through its chest. Black blood poured from the soldier's wound and slid down the ice spike. The soldier continued to growl and reach for Bashkim as though it hadn't even noticed its wound. Much to Bashkim's surprise, red blood began to come out of the wound instead. As it did, the soldier's eyes returned to normal, and he began to cry for mercy, begging for his life. Bashkim could only watch in horror as the last few breaths left the soldier, and his body hung lifelessly on the spike he had created.

"I'm sorry," Bashkim whispered.

The monstrous sounds of the dragons fighting continued to fill the city. Bashkim could feel the cold sweep over him whenever Rin used her icy breath. The dragons thrashed with their claws against one another, and every so often when Rin blew fire, the fog would light up where he could see their silhouettes fighting. The two dragons eventually came stumbling back into view, allowing Bashkim to see Rin fight like he had never seen before.

She's scared, he thought, watching her tear into the white dragon's hide. Fire and ice beamed from her mouth, sometimes appearing as though they came at the same time. Each blast sounded as though she roared at the top of her massive lungs, her voice echoing through the entire city. While still in view, the white dragon tackled Rin by smashing its entire shoulder into her and pushing her into the fog where Bashkim could no longer see.

The ground continued to shake, and Bashkim could hear the jaws snapping at one another. Another blast of fire came from Rin, briefly revealing the dark figures within the fog. Rin lay on her back, pushed down with the white dragon towering over her. The fire faded, taking the light with it just as the white dragon's head shot forward to strike Rin, leaving nothing but the dense fog. He could hear Rin roaring briefly, but the silence that followed left him in panic.

Get up, Bashkim told himself. *Please get up.*

The commotion had stopped, and what little of the buildings around him remained finished collapsing. He could hear a dragon's footsteps approaching him. A shiver ran through this body as the white dragon emerged from the fog. The monster approached, putting its head directly in front of him. Unable to free himself, Bashkim could only look the beast in the eye as the rain dripped down its scaley face.

"Go to hell," Bashkim groaned.

Surprisingly, a voice answered Bashkim that didn't belong to Mykenebres. "I'm already there," it said.

Before Bashkim could even process what happened, Rin's hind foot dropped from above and grabbed the dragon's head and smashed it against the ground with all her weight and slid it away from Bashkim. Keeping the white dragon pinned to the ground under her foot, her jaws shot down and clamped over the area of the gouged eye. The White Dragon shrieked and flailed its limbs wildly as it tried to break free, but Rin's grip held true. Her jaws squeezed as hard as they could and her teeth tore into the monster's face, ripping the entire area around the eye away as she jerked her head back. She shoved the white dragon farther down the street, allowing it to push itself farther away and for her to grab Bashkim.

"We're leaving," she said, carefully clearing the debris and scooping him into her hands.

"We can't," Bashkim coughed, his bruised body cursing him as he moved.

"The eshans can handle it from here," she argued, jumping up and flying away. "You've done enough for today."

Bashkim tried to speak but she had already taken to flying at full speed. Instead, he only watched as Teasvanna became smaller and smaller, quickly fading away into the distance as Rin sped through the air. He hid inside of her hands, protecting himself from the strong winds as they flew. The adrenaline gradually left his body, and he could feel himself slowly slipping away and his vision growing darker.

When Bashkim finally woke up, he found himself lying in a pile of furs and luxurious coats within a cavern covered in ice. He blinked his eyes several times, trying to adjust to the dim moonlight as well as recall what all had happened. He looked over and sighed in relief once he saw Rin deeper in the darkness of the cave. As he did, it felt like spears drove into his skull.

"Are we all the way back to your mountain?" he groaned, rubbing his head.

"We are," Rin said quietly, sounding rather winded. "I wanted to put as much distance as possible between us and that thing."

"How?" Bashkim groaned in pain as he tried to sit up. "That's too far. You can't fly that much in one go...unless...how long have I been out?"

Rin ignored him and instead stepped farther into the cave. With a grunt and plenty of pain in his bones, Bashkim forced himself to his feet, slowly limping his way over to her as he tried to find his words.

"I'm sorry," Bashkim said, unable to think of anything else to say.

Rin remained silent and rummaged through her pile of treasures. There were so many things he wanted to tell her, so many things he had *planned* to tell her if he ever had the chance to. Now that he had that chance, his words abandoned him, leaving him to be nothing more than a silent fool. He opened his mouth to try and speak, but Rin slowly turned and came over to him, pushing a sword along the ground with one of her claws.

"I think you dropped this during our first encounter with that white dragon."

"My sword," Bashkim said, wincing as he grabbed the weapon.

"How did you manage to find it?"

"I've had a lot of free time recently," she said simply, stepping out towards the entrance of her frozen cavern and laying down.

"Are you alright?"

Rin laid her head on the ground. "Yes. I just need some rest."

Lacking an extra sheath, Bashkim gently laid the sword down on the coat pile and limped his way over to Rin. He ran a thousand lines through his mind as he tried to decide on what to say, but nothing felt good enough.

Rin broke his thought, taking a small pause for air as she spoke. "I'm pleased to see...that I have rescued Bashkim and not the one that has been posing as you."

Bashkim remained standing in place slightly to the side of her head. "You came back for me. I...can't thank you enough."

"I never left your side, Bashkim. It was you who abandoned yourself."

"Never again," Bashkim said, a tear sliding down his cheek. "I stopped running, Rin. I went to Handleson. I spoke with Angela. I told her everything. She...she forgave me, Rin."

A smile came across Rin's scaled face. "Oh, Bashkim," she said with another breath. "You were born a soul with wings but bound to the body of man."

Rin grunted but remained in place. "Do you remember," she asked. "What I told you about the Final Flame?"

"Yes," Bashkim said quietly. "But why?"

"It falls to you," she said, her voice gradually fading to a whisper and her face wincing with each word. "For I can think of no one better, nor closer. You are my friend. My family. My Deneethwen...Delso mesh...Deneethwen."

"Rin," Bashkim said breathlessly. "What are you saying?"

Rin did not answer. Bashkim ignored his own physical pain and quickly limped his broken body over to the front of her. His eyes widened in terror when he saw the several cuts and gashes along the underside of her body she had tried to seal shut with ice.

"No," Bashkim said, falling to his knees and crawling over to her. "No. No. No."

Bashkim pulled himself over to her head and gave it a small nudge. He could no longer feel the icy breath coming from her nostrils.

"Rin?" he asked, pushing against her large snout. "Rin! Don't leave me, Rin. Please don't leave me."

Tears welled in Bashkim's eyes and streamed down his face. He pushed against her head as hard as he could, trying to wake her up. Pain shot through his broken body as he forced it to move but he refused to stop. He continued to push, but Rin did not respond. Bashkim brought his hands together, summoning the magic inside of him. It sparked to life within his chest and shot out through his entire being.

This is my magic, he told himself. *Not yours, Mykenebres.*

Pillars of ice sprung up all around them, rising from the ground and reaching up taller than Rin's body. Holding his hand up, Bashkim then attempted to freeze the very air around them.

"Come on!" Bashkim cried, lowering the temperature even more. "Is this not cold enough for you?"

Bashkim waved his hand, creating even more layers of ice around them and chilling the air. His body began to shake uncontrollably from the cold, and he could feel the tears on the sides of his face freeze in place before they could fall.

Bashkim lowered his hands, getting closer to Rin. "Please. Please don't leave me. I lost you once already. I can't do it again."

Bashkim reached out and held as much of Rin's head as he could and buried his face against hers. A fierce wind howled as it blew past the cave. He could feel the cold piercing his body and cutting its way down to his bones.

I can't let you go, he wanted to tell her, but his mouth could not move. *I can't do the Final Flame. You have to come back. I'm not strong enough for that.*

Snow piled over him and Rin. His vision became blurry, and his shivering stopped as he his eyes slowly closed.

You're my family too. I'm sorry, Rin.

The howl of the wind got quieter, eventually falling completely silent and replaced only by his own heartbeat. It thumped slowly against him, the pause between each beat growing.

"Not like this," a man's voice said calmly.

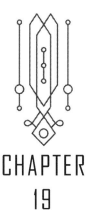

CHAPTER
19

Bashkim slowly opened his eyes and slid his hand across his face. He found himself on his back, seeing nothing but white. He blinked several times, rubbing his eyes as he tried to adjust his vision.

Why can't I see? he thought, looking to both sides.

The whiteness seemed to go on forever, having neither a beginning nor an end. He held his hand out in front of him and moved his fingers back and forth.

Not blind, he thought and started to sit up.

As he sat himself upright, he realized his body felt different. He patted himself repeatedly in several places but felt none of his previous bruises and broken bones.

Healed? Wait...Rin!

Bashkim put his hands down on what felt like solid ground and pushed himself up to his feet.

"Rin?" he asked, his voice echoing into the void as he frantically looked around.

"She's not here," a man's voice said calmly. "Not yet."

"Where are you?" Bashkim asked, looking around him.

"Behind you."

Bashkim whipped back around and saw a figure draped in a black cloak, his face hidden within a hood. Next to the mysterious stranger sat a large white wolf, its head about level with the man's waist. Bashkim narrowed his eyes and looked the two over curiously.

"Am I dead then?" Bashkim asked.

"No."

"Are you Mykenebres?"

The wolf whined at the mention of Mykenebres. The stranger gently stroked the top of its head to calm it.

"I am not," the man said.

"Then who are you, and what do you want? I've not prayed to an Arbiter since I was a child so I can't imagine one has come to pay me a friendly visit. Or perhaps you are one and you've finally decided to step up and help?"

"On the contrary," the man said while continuing to scratch behind the wolf's ear. "It is I that needs help. I need you to kill one."

"Excuse me?"

"Though deities they may be, they are not without their own faults."

Bashkim shook his head in confusion, then leaned forward as he tried to see the stranger's face. "Arbiters aren't perfect?"

"No. Some of them are even young, and as the young often do, they make mistakes. Some cross the lines of the duties given to them by the Light. One might even say they share a similar trait as you, Bashkim."

"And what's that?"

"The drive to do what you believe is right while neglecting the potential consequences, either to yourself or those around you."

Bashkim held his tongue and tightened his fist. "I couldn't just leave them at Teasvanna," he said eventually. "I had to try."

The stranger said nothing. Instead, he stood there in silence without movement.

"Is that why you want me to kill an Arbiter?" Bashkim asked. "Because he tried to do something that you don't approve of?"

"He made a mistake that has cost him dearly. Death would be a mercy to him."

"How?"

"His actions have trapped him into a life of never-ending torment and suffering. Mykenebres has darkened him, and death is the only way to set him free."

Bashkim crossed his arms and tapped his foot against the ground though it made no noise. "So Mykenebres is stronger than Arbiters? How is that possible?"

The cloaked figure lifted his hand and motioned for Bashkim to look behind him. As Bashkim turned, the whiteness surrounding him faded and he found himself in a completely different place. He stood in a garden filled with flowers nearly tall as him, and out beyond it rested several trees that surrounded them. He looked up and saw a bright blue sky. Bashkim turned back to face the stranger, but in his place rested a small cabin. The white wolf happily made its way over to the door and waited for someone to open it as it wagged its tail. The cloaked stranger casually walked past Bashkim, making his way to the cabin.

"Is this your home?" Bashkim asked.

"No," the man said, opening the door and letting the wolf in. "This is hers. She helps make sure souls can find their way home safely."

The stranger motioned for Bashkim to come inside, but as Bashkim followed the small path through the flower garden he noticed something. All the flowers looked as though the wind had blown them, but they remained frozen in place as if time had completely stopped. Even the several butterflies floating around nearby hung motionless in the air. Bashkim gently reached out, barely pressing against one of the flowers. It bent in the direction that Bashkim pushed and remained perfectly in place where he left it.

"Souls, huh?" Bashkim asked, looking back at the stranger. "So why are we here if I'm not dead?"

The man stepped inside the cabin, leaving the door open for Bashkim. "I thought you might like to know who would be there when Rin crosses over."

Bashkim's eyes fell to the floor as he stepped inside, a small pain striking his chest. The cabin's interior housed nothing more than a couple of rooms, containing only a bed on one side, and a table with a pair of chairs in what one might call a kitchen. The wolf quickly jumped onto the bed and curled up to sleep as the stranger made his way over to the stove.

A tea kettle sat on the stove, the small amount of steam coming from it frozen in place. As the stranger grabbed the kettle, the steam regained its motion, floating and disappearing into the air. The man grabbed two small cups and sat down at the table, motioning for Bashkim to do the same.

"There was a time when Mykenebres stood closer to the Light than any other," the man said as he filled the two cups. "Before your world's creation, he was once the leader of what you now know as

Arbiters, and he was a leader they respected and loved. It was the creation of man that broke him."

Bashkim took his seat as well as the cup offered to him, a confused look on his face. "How?"

"With the creation of the world came new orders. Mykenebres and those under him were to become Arbiters. Their job was to keep the world balanced. Anything from the waters to the animals, as well as all races of this world, including humans and eshans. Even the technologies and romances formed by the people were under their care. All was created by the Light, and all was to be watched by the Arbiters that the Light had assigned.

"And that broke him?" Bashkim asked and took a sip of his tea.

"He took the new orders of caring for mere mortals as betrayal and an insult to his service. He rebelled, forming an army of his own. As a result, a holy war broke out between the Light and Mykenebres."

"Unless I'm mistaken, it doesn't seem like Mykenebres won considering people are still around."

"No," the stranger said, wrapping his hands around his cup on the table. "But there was still loss. The wars of your world were to be kept in balance by two brothers, Crimson and Wynn. Those responsibilities fell fully on Wynn, however, as Crimson was lost in the war. He landed a sacrificial blow to Mykenebres that knocked him from the heavens and sealed him away. Unfortunately, Crimson went with him. Nothing remained of Crimson but his sword."

"And Wynn?"

"He carried on with his responsibilities after the war, but the pain of his loss never left him. Many years later, when Mykenebres began to corrupt your world, Wynn refused to sit idly by and watch. He took the fight to Mykenebres himself."

"He broke the seal?"

The stranger reached up with a single hand and pulled his hood back, revealing his face as well as the lengthy bright white hair tied behind his head. "No," he said, taking a sip of his tea. "He never made it that far. Mykenebres's power overwhelmed him before he ever had a chance. Wynn became the white dragon you've faced and began to wreak havoc upon that which he was supposed to watch over."

Bashkim tried to quickly observe the man's face without making it obvious. His ears came to a point, similar to an eshan, and for just a brief moment Bashkim thought that he might be dealing with one. However, the nearly glowing orange eyes told him otherwise.

"And the other white dragons?" Bashkim asked, taking note of the scar that ran across the stranger's face, suggesting either mortality, or that he had perhaps experienced it at some point in his life.

"A twisted creation from a mixture of his own powers along with Mykenebres."

Bashkim tapped his fingers against his cup slowly, absorbing the new information. "So why me? I feel like Arbiters would have a much better chance of dealing with Wynn than me. Do they fear Mykenebres's power that much?"

"An Arbiter's responsibility is no small feat. Those duties come from a higher power than you and I. The Arbiters are to fulfill those duties and those duties only. No more, no less. An Arbiter also risks a lot more by getting involved."

"You mean they have more to lose."

"You know the story of Forrandi. Why do you think she was cast out instead of killed?"

"I'm not sure."

"Arbiters are tied to this world, some so closely that they have become interwoven into its very being. Forrandi is the Arbiter of eshans. If she were to be killed as penance to her crime, she would not be the only one who suffered. The eshans would share the same fate."

Bashkim's eyebrows raised. "They'd die?"

"Each and every one of them, which is why Forrandi has instead been forced to roam your world until the end of time so that those she was meant to care for will continue to live."

"Then what about Wynn? If he's killed, then there's no more wars, right?"

"There would be nothing but conflict without him. Have you forgotten the constant struggle between humans and eshans? Due to Wynn's condition, that balance has been broken and constantly teeters over the edge of war."

"So do you want me to kill him or not? It seems whether he lives or dies the world is screwed."

"A plan has been set in motion to ensure things are kept in balance, but it requires you to do your part. The slate *must* be wiped clean."

"But why me? Why don't the Arbiters do something about this? Are they all so scared of Mykenebres that they can't make an appearance once in a while to sort things out?"

"And what would you have them do?" the stranger asked, his voice growing sterner. "Instead of answering the call to you, you would instead risk your world? You would have the Arbiters neglect their Light given duties and turn their backs on that which they were sworn to protect? You would have them march into a battle that they cannot win? Knowing what I have just explained to you, what do you think would happen?"

Bashkim held his tongue and shrugged his shoulders.

"Should the Arbiters fall," the stranger explained. "The oceans would run dry. The trees would wither and fade. The beings of this world and those you've come to know would die. Should that happen, who would be there when it comes time for Rin to cross to the other side? You have fought hard to make this world a better place, Bashkim. Why are you so willing to turn your back on it now?"

Bashkim banged his fist against the table, startling the wolf on the bed. "I'm only mortal!" he growled.

The wolf barked, ready to jump. The stranger held his hand out, calming the wolf.

"Yes," the stranger said calmly and took another sip of tea. "A mortal with nothing left to lose."

Bashkim kept his fist on the table and tightened it, growling under his breath.

"You also have something that Arbiters don't," the man added.

"And what's that?"

"A resistance to the darkness."

"How?"

"When Telanos sealed you away, you were trapped with a small part of Mykenebres. Inside of that barrier, his darkness attempted to take root in you, but it was weak. The two of you have struggled for control your entire life, yet you have always remained victorious."

"Not always," Bashkim said, sinking back into his chair.

"The fire at the orphanage?"

"And those people in the forest. And in Teasvanna when I hurt Rin."

"The darkness may have won those battles, but it is you who continues to win the war."

Bashkim looked down at the table. "Doesn't feel like it."

"Nobody said the road to victory was a pleasant one."

Bashkim rubbed his arm and mulled the whole thing over. The stranger remained in front of him, calmly drinking his tea as he waited for a response.

"Fine," Bashkim said. "What do you want me to do?"

"Wynn may have been darkened, but his life still clings to what is left of him. He keeps the dragons dormant in the Forest of Anderwood. Go there and finish the fight."

The man put his cup down then reached into his cloak and pulled something out.

"The Arbiters aren't completely out of this fight," the man said, placing a green gemstone on the table. "You have their power in the kesshonite, after all."

Bashkim grabbed the small gemstone and held it up to look at it, but as he did, the cabin and everything around him had returned to white, causing him to fall to the ground as his chair vanished.

"Now go," the voice said, echoing around him. "Give her your last words while you still have time."

Bashkim blinked his eyes several times as the world around him transitioned from the empty white to the interior of a cave. He could feel the cold again, and as he looked behind him, he saw Rin with her head still on the ground. The walls of ice he had summoned before had vanished, and the wind had stopped. Bashkim quickly crawled over to her and put his hand on her head. To his surprise, he could feel her breathing again.

"Rin?" he asked, tears instantly filling his eyes.

Rin did not speak. Instead, she pushed her giant head against Bashkim, nearly knocking him over. Bashkim threw his arms around her snout, holding her as close as he could to his tiny body.

"Surely you're not cold," he said, trying to smile.

Bashkim gently rubbed the side of her face, pushing his head against hers. He had a hundred things that he wanted to tell her. He wanted to apologize, he wanted to praise her, he wanted to tell her that there might actually be hope in winning against the white dragons, but his words kept silent. As he listened to her breaths, he realized that he still held the gem in his hand that the stranger had given him. He opened his hand just enough to see the green gem.

"I found one," he said, attempting to smile through his tears. "A green gem. Just like you wanted."

Rin remained silent and continued to nuzzle as far as she could into Bashkim. He could feel her breaths getting slower. His time to speak was running out.

"Thank you," Bashkim whispered, forcing the words out as he kept his head pressed against hers. "For being my family."

A smile slowly stretched across Rin's scaled snout, and her head gradually rolled over to the side. Bashkim closed his eyes, tears streaming down the sides of his face as Rin's breaths stopped.

"Goodbye, Rin."

Bashkim slowly let go of Rin and sat down on the ground in front of her. He tried to collect himself but instead fell over to his side and rolled on his back next to Rin. As he did, his eyes fell upon a large, but familiar red dragon that sat quietly and watched him.

"I remember you," Bashkim said, wiping his eyes. "In the forest on our way to Nennossen, back when we started this white dragon nonsense."

The red dragon nodded his head slowly. Bashkim took in a deep breath, exhaling as he stared up at the ceiling. "She's gone."

The red dragon said nothing. He sat silently as he watched Bashkim. Bashkim slowly got to his feet, pocketing the green gem as he looked over at Rin. His hands formed into clenching fists as more tears ran down his face.

"She's gone and it's my fault," he muttered under gritted teeth.

The dragon ignored his blubbering and simply reached out with a single clawed finger and pulled Bashkim back towards him.

"It's my fault!" Bashkim yelled, pounding his fists against the dragon's scaled hand. "If I hadn't lost control, she wouldn't have left! She wouldn't have had to come back and save me!"

The dragon kept Bashkim inside of his hand, letting him punch and pound it repeatedly. Bashkim's knuckles began to bleed as he struck the armored hide, and the dragon eventually closed his hand, gently holding Bashkim in place.

"It's my fault," Bashkim whined.

Bashkim tried to catch his breath, but every time his eyes fell on Rin his emotions overcame him. The dragon carefully opened his hand and gave Bashkim his space.

"Jinkear Deneelsah," the dragon said, motioning with his head to Rin.

Bashkim looked over at her, wiping his face clean. "Right," he said, taking a breath. "Right. The Final Flame."

Bashkim stopped, unable to take a step forward. Instead, he looked up at the red dragon.

"Deneethwen," he said, pointing a claw to Bashkim.

"What if I'm not strong enough?" Bashkim asked. "What if I fail her *again?*"

The dragon said nothing. Instead, he pointed his claw to Rin, motioning for Bashkim to proceed.

"But what if I—" Bashkkim started to say, but the dragon cut him short.

"Jinkear Deneelsah!" he said loudly, a roar in his voice.

Bashkim summoned a ball of fire in his hand, narrowing his eyes at the dragon. The dragon met his gaze, refusing to budge in the slightest.

"I just want to get it right," Bashkim said quietly, turning his back to the dragon.

Bashkim approached Rin and set the ball of fire down next to her. He summoned several more, laying them all on the ground in a ring that circled Rin. When he came back around to the front of Rin, he put the last flame down and went over to retrieve his sword. As he grabbed the weapon, he paused as his eyes fell upon the many riches within the cave. Coins, gems, jewels, coats, armors, weapons, just about anything that had value to it she had collected and hoarded. A small smile almost made its way onto his face as he pictured her bringing it all back home, one piece at a time. As he turned to make his way back to Rin, he saw the red dragon looking at him curiously.

"She gave this to me," Bashkim said, returning to the dragon. "I'd like to keep it if that's alright. Something to remember her by."

The red dragon nodded. Bashkim slid the blade down into his belt next to his other sword and held his hands out towards Rin and the small flames.

"You know I don't like fire, Rin," he said, closing his eyes to focus. "But for you, I'll make the brightest fire you've ever seen."

The magic built up inside of Bashkim, swirling around in his chest and out through his limbs. He could feel his connection to the fires, each and every one of them reaching out to him. He took hold of them, rotating his hand to face the palm upwards as the fires grew in size. He lifted his hand, and as he did the flames rose up higher than Rin's body. His fingers curled inwards as the magic intensified. The fires widened and engulfed Rin's body. His hand and arm began to shake as he made the flames burn hotter.

Bashkim raised his other hand, making the fire grow even more. He could feel the heat beating against him, as well as the thump of his heart against his chest as he tried to hold the magic.

It's not enough, he told himself. *It has to burn hotter.*

Bashkim's arms began to shake even more as he struggled to keep them up. He gasped for air, grunting and groaning as he forced more magic through his body.

You're in control now. This is you. This is your fire.

The beat of his heart grew louder, and he could feel his body weakening. He yelled as he tried to reach down into himself for more magic. Blue flames flashed within the fire briefly before fading and leaving the original orange color. Bashkim gasped for air and fell to his knees.

"No!" he cried as he opened his eyes and saw the fire start to shrink.

Still on his knees, he kept both hands out and reached forward, keeping his grip on the fire.

"No, no, no!" he said, trying desperately to hang on.

This is the best I can do, Rin...I'm sorry. I'll hold it for as long as it takes.

"Trakear untadda meshta," he heard the dragon say behind him.

The dragon firmly planted his front feet down on both sides of Bashkim, gripping the ground with his claws. The dragon reared his head back and drew in a massive breath. His neck reached out directly over Bashkim, and out from his mouth came the most brilliant flame that Bashkim had ever seen. He could feel the creature's gigantic muscles rippling all around him, and the dragon's roar rained down over the entire mountain.

Bashkim squinted from the tremendous amount of light in front of him but retained his grip on his own magic. Rin's body steadily turned to ash as the fire continued to flow from the dragon's mouth. The ice that covered the cavern melted rapidly, forming a steady stream of water on the ground. The dragon's flames blasted through the entire cavern, consuming all of her hoarded treasures and melting them down to a liquid that mixed with the flowing water.

Within the flames consuming Rin's body, Bashkim could just see the silhouette of a cloaked figure, and a wolf. The figure bowed then turned to leave, him and the wolf fading into the fire.

See you on the other side, Bashkim said to himself, and let go of the fire.

As he did, the dragon also stopped. Before them stood a pile of ash and charred bones, collapsing in on themselves and crumbling into dust. The flowing water shimmered as the moonlight bounced off the melted gold, and Bashkim watched as it carried Rin's ashes away down the mountainside.

"Greneeshtah," the dragon said, lowering its head. "Kaldea shala deen tumos, Rin."

Bashkim stood silent for a moment, watching the flowing water as he recovered his breath.

"I don't know much about dragons," Bashkim said after a while, looking over at the red dragon. "But I do know that Rin had some history she wasn't fond of with the rest of you. If I had to guess, you probably didn't care for her lifestyle. But I want you to know...I want you to know she was the best damned thing that ever happened to me. You might not think she was a good dragon, but she was a good...she was good to me. She meant a lot to me and if it weren't for her, I don't know where I'd be today. It may not mean much to dragons, but it means the entire world to me."

The red dragon reached towards Bashkim with his hand, gently tapping him with a single claw. "Trakear."

The dragon took his hand back and lowered himself flat onto the ground, motioning with his head to the back of his body.

"You want me to...ride?" Bashkim asked.

The dragon nodded his head and waited for Bashkim to mount. Hesitantly, Bashkim stepped over towards the dragon and gently put his hand on the red scales.

"Okay," Bashkim said, taking a deep breath. "Okay."

Bashkim carefully crawled up the dragon's side and got onto his back, holding on tightly to the spikes along his backside. Once positioned, the dragon slowly rose up and pointed down the mountainside.

"Tel...esa," the dragon tried to say, his face looking as though it were in great discomfort. "Esa...aruh."

"Telscara?" Bashkim asked.

The dragon nodded.

"It really does hurt, doesn't it?"

"Mustah."

CHAPTER
20

It took the red dragon little time to swoop down to the bottom of the mountain. To avoid detection, the dragon stayed out of the moon's glow and on the opposite side of the mountain until he reached the bottom. Once there, he proceeded on all fours, silently carrying his massive frame along until Telscara came into view. He stopped and motioned for Bashkim to dismount and finish the trip on his own two legs.

"Thank you," Bashkim said as he slid down the dragon's side and patted him on one of his muscular arms. "Are you going to stay nearby or go back to where we originally met?"

The dragon pointed a claw at the ground, signaling that he would remain. Bashkim nodded in understanding and approached the village's gate. As expected, the guards pointed their spears forward as Bashkim approached.

"You're out late," one of them said. "What do you want?"

"Shelter," Bashkim answered plainly. "I'm tired and need rest."

The guard eyed the two swords on Bashkim's belt. "You're not going to cause any trouble, are you?"

"No, sir. I'm the one that came to aid in Telscara's dragon problem not long ago."

"You?" the guard asked, almost laughing. "A dragon hunter? You don't exactly look the type."

"That's because I don't *hunt* them."

"And what do you do? Talk to them and ask them to go away?"

By this point the second guard had gotten a good look at Bashkim. "Hey, wait a minute. I remember you. Yeah. You were here before, and you *did* have a dragon with you. Gave the whole town a good scare. Especially the day shift. I think the fools soiled their armor. I reckon it's no coincidence you're here and that we just heard a dragon a moment ago."

"He had a dragon with him?" the first guard asked, looking back and forth between the two. "You guys are pulling my leg."

Before Bashkim could respond, a low and slow growl came from behind him. The guards jumped and looked past Bashkim into the darkness. Bashkim casually stepped to the side and motioned behind him. A sudden but small puff of fire ignited from the dragon's mouth, providing just enough light to show part of his massive head.

"By the Arbiters," the first guard muttered. "Is it...yours?"

"He doesn't belong to me," Bashkim answered. "But he is *with* me. Now please, may I come in?"

The first guard continued to stare out into the darkness where he had seen the dragon. Bashkim glanced at the second guard who had recognized him and waited for an answer.

"Well, I'm not going to argue with somebody who can tame dragons," the second guard said. "And neither is he by the looks of it. Come on, I'll show you to the inn."

The guard proceeded through the gate and motioned for Bashkim to follow him. As Bashkim stepped through the gate, he could just barely hear the dragon chuckle to himself as the other guard watched him disappear into the night.

"I wasn't at the gate the first time you arrived," the guard explained. "But I did see you leave Cynthia's. If you're the one Telscara hired, then would I be correct to assume your name is Bashkim?"

"It is."

The soldier stopped walking once he got a bit farther from the gate and its remaining guard. He turned to face Bashkim. "Would this also be the same Bashkim that attacked Nennossen's king?"

Bashkim straightened his posture, carefully sliding a foot backwards and watching the soldier's hand on the spear. However, the soldier made no motion to attack.

"If you are," the soldier continued after Bashkim's silence. "Then I would like to thank you."

"Excuse me?"

The soldier calmly reached a hand behind the armor on his chest and pulled out a small piece of cloth.

"I chose to be stationed out here in Telscara," the man said, also pulling a small waterskin from his belt and dampening the cloth. "After I locked someone up for attempting to study magic, I requested an immediate transfer. Simon didn't even argue. I'm pretty sure he knew why I wanted out."

The guard handed the damp rag over to Bashkim. "Here. Your eyes are as red as can be. You must have had one hell of a night out there."

"Thanks," Bashkim said, taking a breath as well as the cloth.

Bashkim used the damp cloth to rub his eyes and face, attempting to clean himself up. The guard waited patiently, even as Bashkim's eyes trailed off to Cynthia's house. Bashkim's hand slowly tightened, squeezing water from the rag.

"Something wrong?" the guard asked.

Bashkim wadded the cloth and wrapped his hand around it. He continued to stare at Cynthia's house, and steam began to rise from between his fingers, as well as from the drops of water on his face.

"Cynthia has something I need," Bashkim said, still looking at her house. "A scabbard. It belongs to my sword."

The guard looked at Bashkim curiously. Bashkim turned back to face him, opening his hand and revealing a completely dried cloth.

"It's very important to me," Bashkim said, handing the cloth back to the guard. "It belonged to somebody extremely close that I've recently lost."

"I'm sorry to hear that," the guard said as he took his cloth back. "But...can it not wait until morning?"

"They're the reason my eyes are red."

The guard held his tongue, looking down as he folded the cloth and put it back under his armor.

"Alright," the guard sighed. "But she's not going to like this. And she's got some heavy hammers if you catch my meaning."

The guard escorted Bashkim to Cynthia's house and knocked on her door.

Please answer, Bashkim thought. *I need that scabbard back. It's all I have left of her.*

After a couple of minutes, the guard lifted his hand to knock again, but the door suddenly creaked open, barely enough to reveal Cynthia with bedridden hair and a blanket wrapped around her. She squinted and blinked several times as she tried to focus.

"Greg?" she asked. "What in the blue blazes are you doing? Is something—"

Cynthia stopped short once she realized Bashkim also stood next to the guard. "Oh," she said. "It's you. Almost didn't recognize you, green eyes. What with it being the middle of the night and all."

"I apologize, Cynthia," Greg said. "Bashkim here has a request that he feels is rather important."

Cynthia looked at Bashkim, waiting for an explanation.

"I..." Bashkim started to say, fumbling for his words. "That scabbard I left with you. Do you still have it? I got the sword back that it belongs to."

Cynthia looked down at the exposed weapon on Bashkim's hip, then back up at him. She shook her head in confusion with narrowed eyes.

"Are you mad?" she asked while keeping her voice quiet. "Is it really that bloody important to you that you need to wake me? Could it not have waited till morning?"

"I have money."

Cynthia looked back at Greg, desperate for an explanation.

"It is that important," Greg said.

Cynthia looked back at Bashkim and watched as a single tear formed under his eye and slowly slid down his cheek. She paused, taking a slow breath as she tried to put the pieces together.

"Alright," she said. "Yeah. I should still have it here somewhere. Come on in."

Cynthia opened the door all the way and motioned Bashkim inside. Bashkim stepped into the house, as did Greg.

"I'll take it from here," Cynthia said, stopping Greg and pushing him back. "Don't you have a gate that needs guarding?"

"But—" Greg started to say, but Cynthia had already started closing the door on him.

"I'll take it from here," Cynthia said more sternly and closed the door all the way.

Bashkim stepped to the middle of the main room, his eyes trailing to the floor as he waited. Cynthia quickly made her way past him, telling him to wait just a moment while she got the scabbard from another room. She returned only a few minutes later, this time without the blanket and what seemed hurriedly brushed hair and warmer clothes. The scabbard rested in her hands, but she hesitated before handing it over. Bashkim looked at her, confused.

"Who'd it belong to?" she asked.

"Excuse me?"

"The last time I saw a man with that look in his eyes, my father was burying my brother."

Bashkim turned away and hid his face. "Rin," he whispered, trying to keep himself together. "Her name was Rin."

"Oh," Cynthia said, her eyes also trailing down to the floor. "You two must have been close. Was she an adventurer too?"

"Rin was the dragon I was with when I last saw you."

Cynthia pursed her lips, standing in silence as she tried to figure out what to say. Bashkim almost chuckled, realizing how confusing it must be for the smith.

"Rin gave me the sword a long time ago. She was quite the hoarder. Now that she's gone, I'd like to keep it close by. It's the last thing I have of her."

Cynthia stepped to the front of Bashkim and handed him the scabbard. "I'm sorry. Losing someone is difficult. I can only imagine what's out there that could stop a dragon."

Bashkim gently took the scabbard and stared at it. "It was me," he said quietly. "I got her killed."

Cynthia looked at Bashkim curiously as if she had misheard.

"She died because of me," Bashkim said. "She believed in me until the end, and she paid for it with her life."

Bashkim turned away again and made his way to the door. "I need to go."

"Wait," Cynthia said and put her hand on his shoulder. "Grieving is good but grieving alone can be dangerous."

Bashkim tightened his grip on the scabbard, trying to hold himself together. "Do I even have that right?"

"To grieve? Of course you do. Come, sit down."

Cynthia put a hand on Bashkim's back and gently pushed him towards a chair, motioning for him to sit down. She pulled out another chair for herself and put it directly in front of him and sat down.

"Now," Cynthia said, putting her hands on the scabbard that Bashkim held on his lap. "You said she believed in you. Could you two communicate?"

"Yes," Bashkim said while staring down at the floor. "She could speak our language. She was very well spoken."

"So, Rin was strong *and* proper spoken?" Cynthia asked with a smile on her face. "She must have been something extraordinary."

"She was. And she was all I had."

"And she cared for you, no?"

"She did."

"And you cared for her?"

"I did."

"Then grieve."

Bashkim shut his eyes tight, trying to hide himself as tears flowed down his face. He lowered his head and squeezed the scabbard hard enough to whiten his knuckles.

"It's okay," Cynthia said gently. "Take as long as you need."

"I can't," Bashkim argued. "I still have work to do. We were trying to stop the dragon that attacked Telscara. It's the same dragon that..."

"And you can tell me all about it *tomorrow*," Cynthia said as Bashkim's voice trailed off. She let go of the scabbard and leaned back into her seat. "But for now, let's remember Rin."

Cynthia kept Bashkim in her home for a while, allowing him to properly mourn as he told her more about Rin. He spoke highly of her as he pushed his way through the tears. Eventually, Cynthia told him he had said enough for now and helped him clean himself up. She sent him off to the inn, letting him know that she would be around tomorrow and wanted to hear more about what Bashkim planned to do with the white dragon, but she wouldn't listen until they both had gotten some decent rest.

Feeling the heaviness in his eyes and the ache ringing through his head, he didn't argue. The guard had already spoken with the innkeeper and a room had been prepared for Bashkim, waiting for him to occupy it. Bashkim thanked the innkeeper for his hospitality and made his way to his room. He slowly removed his two swords and leaned them against the wall near the bed. As he did, somebody spoke from the hallway outside his door.

"I think she likes you," a familiar voice said.

Bashkim quickly whipped around and reached for one of his swords. In the doorway to Bashkim's room stood Telanos.

"How?" Baskim asked.

"Easy. It's late, she's alone, she invites you in—" Telanos started to say, but Bashkim cut him short.

"How did you get here?"

"I'm a wizard, Bashkim."

"I've seen wizards before, and none of them have been able to travel that amount of distance in such a short time. Not to mention live for over two hundred years. Why are you always so mysterious about where your power comes from?"

"We've all done things we're not proud of," Telanos said, slightly more seriously this time as he stepped into the room and closed the door behind him. "While you may be willing to air your sins in search of forgiveness, I long to take mine to the grave so that no other may stumble. But I can at least tell you this: an eshan's ability to control fire and ice pales in comparison to the other magics of this world. There are magics that could turn this room into dust with the snap of one's finger. We might have only discovered kesshonite recently, but it has already changed our world drastically, and will only continue to do so as time goes on."

Bashkim looked at the wizard and narrowed his eyes. "Could you have gotten us out of Teasvanna?"

"I could have, but had you followed the plan, I wouldn't have needed to."

Bashkim's hands tightened into fists, causing his knuckles to pop slightly. He knew he couldn't argue against him. The wizard was right, but he still didn't like it. If Bashkim had only followed the original plan, tonight would have gone far differently. Instead of trying to argue, Bashkim calmly took a breath and leaned his sword back against the wall, then laid down on the bed on his back.

"Rin is gone, isn't she?" Telanos asked after a moment of silence.

"She is," Bashkim sighed, staring at the ceiling. "The wounds from the white dragon were too much."

"I'm sorry to hear that. You two shared an extremely strong bond with one another. But what of you? Surely you did not walk away from the fight without wounds of your own."

"My entire body was wrecked, but when we got back to Rin's cave I...met an Arbiter."

"An Arbiter?"

"I think it was. He didn't specifically *say* he was one, but he definitely wasn't like us. He took me somewhere strange. It was all white at first, then we were in a field with a cabin. Everything was stuck in place like time had stopped."

"Did he have a white wolf with him?"

"He did."

"It sounds like you died."

"I thought the same thing, but no, apparently he wanted to talk."

"About?"

"He wants me to kill an Arbiter."

Telanos held his breath and paused before asking for clarification. "Did I hear that correctly?"

"You did. Do you know the name of the Arbiter of War?"

"There were two from the texts I've read. Crimson and Wynn, but Crimson fell in the early days of our world."

"Yeah. Then it was just Wynn. Apparently, Wynn became the white dragon that we've been chasing."

"And that's who he wants you to take down?"

"It is."

"Any particular reason he has chosen you for such a task?"

"I have you to thank for that. When you put me in that seal with a part of Mykenebres, it apparently caused me to develop some kind of resistance to his darkness."

"Something tells me that thanking me is not what you want to do."

A sigh left Bashkim as he continued to stare at the ceiling. "It's not your fault. Hell, you lost your arm trying to keep me safe."

"Arm or no arm, the blame still falls on me."

"Well then we can both feel guilty about past decisions we can't change, so let's just focus on what needs to be done."

Telanos nodded. "Very well. I can retrieve the kesshonite as planned. I can also rendezvous with Fandul at Teasvanna. I imagine things will be in a bit of disarray for the next several days."

"Good," Bashkim said, not bothering to move. "Do you think Fandul will be able to get any support from Teasvanna?"

"After what just happened to their city, I think more than a few people would be willing to listen and stand up for the cause. The tales are going to be hard to hide now."

"I think the humans are ready to step up too. After you speak with Fandul, I need you to go to Nennossen and find Simon. Tell him everything that has happened and that we need soldiers."

"And where would you have all these soldiers go should they volunteer?"

"Here. In Telscara. The man said Wynn keeps the white dragons dormant in Anderwood which is only a couple days ride south of here. Nennossen will be on the eshans' route here, so they can meet first then travel as a single unit."

"And what will you do in the meantime?"

Bashkim slowly reached into his pocket and retrieved the green gemstone. He held it up in front of him, looking it over on every side. "Whatever that man was, he gave me this. He said it was more kesshonite that could help us."

"Are you going to try and use it?" Telanos asked, eyeing the gem carefully.

"No. Not by myself anyway. I'd rather play it safe and wait till more eshans are here to tone it down in case things get carried away."

Bashkim then held the gem between his thumb and finger so that Telanos could better see. "Is this about the size and shape the kesshonite needs to be?"

"As far as we know, the shape doesn't matter. The size however, yes, is fine. If anything, it's a little bigger than what we used."

"Alright. Then I'll speak with Cynthia tomorrow and see if we can't prepare some weapons for more kesshonite while we wait for reinforcements."

"Then it's settled. I will head out in the morning for the kesshonite."

"In the morning?" Bashkim asked, sliding the gem back into his pocket. "You can't just magically appear over there like you do everywhere else?"

Telanos chuckled. "I may be a powerful wizard, but even I have limits. I need rest, for I may have pushed myself too far chasing after you. Besides, I want to hear the full story of you and this Arbiter over some breakfast."

Telanos made his way to leave but paused as he opened the door. He half turned to face Bashkim. "This isn't just some random quest to help somebody in need anymore. You've been recruited by the gods to kill one of their own. Are you ready for that?"

Bashkim continued to stare at the ceiling as he paused to consider the question. "If I don't do anything," he sighed. "Then I'm single handedly throwing the world into chaos, right? So I don't really have much choice, do I?"

"I suppose not."

Bashkim woke the next morning to a knock on his door. Telanos had decided for once *not* to mysteriously appear next to him and instead used the door like a normal person. Bashkim invited him in and got himself cleaned up for the day. From there they went to get some breakfast and Bashkim explained in detail all that the mysterious man had told him. About halfway through his story telling, the ring of a hammer striking metal could be heard in the distance. Cynthia had begun her work for the day, and each blow of her hammer called for Bashkim's attention.

"Eager to go somewhere?" Telanos asked once they had finished their meal.

"Cynthia is waiting for me to come back and finish my story about the white dragon. I don't want to keep her waiting."

"Such a gentleman," Telanos said, pulling some coins out of his pocket and setting them on the table. "It's just as well. I don't think our host is very fond of having an eshan around. Go. Be with her. I'll get the kesshonite and rendezvous with Fandul."

The two said their goodbyes, and Bashkim made his way to Cynthia's. She stood near the stone furnace, watching it as it heated a piece of metal.

"Ah, so you've come back," Cynthia said, still focusing on the metal. "I'm glad you did. Most men would cower away after showing tears like you did."

Bashkim stood silent, unsure of how to take the odd greeting.

"My fire doesn't seem to be hot enough this morning," she huffed, trying to pump more air into the pit. "Makes working the metal a bit more difficult."

"I can help with that," Bashkim said and stepped over with his hand out.

As he reached his hand closer to the furnace, the glow from the coals became much brighter. A wave of heat radiated from the furnace, causing Cynthia to pull her head back slightly.

"Well, you're handy to have around, aren't you?" she asked.

"There are *some* perks to being a hybrid," Bashkim said with a small smile.

Cynthia put her hands on her hips as she watched the furnace. The orange glow of the heating metal steadily grew, slowly reaching farther up the piece.

"So," Cynthia said, keeping a close eye on the metal. "Are you going to tell me about this white dragon now?"

"Actually, I was wondering if I could ask you something first."

"Oh?"

With one hand still reaching out and controlling the furnace's heat, Bashkim reached into his pocket with his other hand and pulled out the green gemstone.

"Can you put this into the handle of a sword?"

"Sure," Cynthia said, readjusting the metal in the furnace slightly. "A little something for Rin's sword?"

"No. Well, yes, but for different reasons."

"Well, whatever the reason, it's not a difficult task."

Satisfied with the heated metal, Cynthia pulled it out of the furnace and took it to her anvil where she started to pound it with a hammer. Bashkim let go of his magical grip and watched the sparks bounce from her hammer strikes.

"Could you put similar sized gems into several other swords?"

"What? Are you planning on going to war?"

"Yes."

Cynthia stopped hammering and looked at Bashkim. "There's more to this dragon business, isn't there?"

"It's a bit of a long story."

Bashkim spent a better part of the day recapping his entire adventure, starting with the day he had come to Cynthia's shop and sparing no details. Cynthia continued to work as she listened, often asking for Bashkim's assistance to either hand her a tool or hold something in place. Her hair had become drenched in sweat by the time he reached the end of his story, and grease and grime covered her arms.

"I've been a smith for most of my life," she said once he had finished. "Grew up in Nennossen, then came out here to make my own way. It's a quiet life, and I quite enjoy it. This talk of Arbiters and dragons and magical stones, it's all a bit much for a girl to handle."

Cynthia put her hands on her hips and stared at the ground. "Should the people answer your call, what makes you think I can supply an army? I am but a single woman."

"You have an entire collection of eshan weapons," Bashkim said with a smile. "I haven't forgotten. We can prep them for the kesshonite while we wait for the soldiers to arrive."

Cynthia snorted, her muscles flexing as she crossed her arms. "Nennossen soldiers armed with my eshan styled weapons? Never thought I'd see the day."

She shook her head, wiping away the sweat from her face and smudging it in the process. "It's still work to cut out the handles for a kesshonite piece. I will need help."

"Of course," Bashkim nodded. "I will do whatever I can."

Bashkim spent the next several days with Cynthia learning to chip away at the weapon handles. They would start early in the morning and find themselves working at night by only the light of a candle. When they had made their way through the eshan weapons, they began to cut into her next shipment of swords for Nennossen.

During this time Bashkim learned both about Cynthia and working metal. She spoke of her family and her upbringing, how she missed her brother, and about what her mother had expected her to be instead of a smith. Most of the concepts were foreign to Bashkim as he had lived on his own for the most part, but he enjoyed listening to her whether he understood it or not. As she spoke, his mind would often recall what she had asked him the first time they met.

"Have you ever tried it giving it a chance?"

He caught himself drifting from time to time, watching her as she chiseled out the wooden handles.

Is this what it would be like? He wanted to ask her. *When this is all over, could I just work as a hired hand somewhere? Could I work here, in Telscara?*

"What about you?" Cynthia asked him, catching him off guard.

Bashkim didn't know how to respond. Most of his upbringing involved little more than simply staying alive, save for the first years of his life at the orphanage. He chose to instead focus on speaking highly of Angela and his time with her. From there, he told her more tales of Rin, recalling the memories fondly.

This time Cynthia stopped working and watched Bashkim as he reminisced about his dragon companion. His eyes trailed to the end of the room, and the smile on his face tried to grow. However, it faded with the end of each story as he came back to reality.

"Here," Cynthia said after one of his stories and took his hand. "Let me show you something."

Cynthia took Bashkim to the furnace where a piece of metal rested within it. The heated metal had the basic rough shape of the beginnings of a blade. Cynthia grabbed a pair of thick leather gloves and handed them to Bashkim as well as a hammer.

"This metal has a lot to be worked out before it can be a proper blade," she said, nodding towards the metal. "Take it and hammer it on the anvil over there."

Bashkim put the gloves on, looking at Cynthia questionably. He grabbed the cooler end of the heated metal and made his way to the anvil and stared blankly as he had no clue how to forge metal.

"The work is done while it's hot," Cynthia said. "You can't shape cold metal."

Bashkim continued to stare at the glowing metal, holding the hammer in his other hand and hesitating.

"Just hit it," she said. "You'll figure it out as you go."

Bashkim raised his hammer up and brought it down against the glowing metal. Sparks flew from the strike, and he could feel the vibration course through his body.

"There you go," Cynthia said with a smile. "Again!"

Bashkim struck the metal again, his body vibrating once more. He continued to strike with the hammer, and slowly but surely, he could see the metal start to take shape. It might not have been the shape of a blade, but it was at least a shape.

"Tell me more about Rin," Cynthia said, taking a seat nearby.

Bashkim continued his stories about Rin while trying to shape the metal. He told her how they had first met, how she interacted with the red dragon, and he even told her of Rin's own upbringing with the farmer. As he recalled the memories his focus steadily shifted away from shaping the metal and more towards Rin. Bashkim even found the courage to explain to Cynthia the Final Flame and its importance to dragons. As he did, his hammer strikes started to hit harder, and the sound of clanging steel rang louder through the village. Cynthia only watched as Bashkim worked his way through both the stories and his emotions while beating the metal to a pulp.

"You're working cold steel," she eventually said, the metal's glow having long ago faded.

Bashkim stopped hammering and looked down at the mangled work as he breathed rapidly. He could feel his heart thumping against his chest wildly, and sweat had started to drip down his face.

"It's okay," Cynthia said, coming up beside him and taking the hammer. "Sometimes when I miss my brother, I come out here to work through it. Nobody is the wiser since I'm out here banging metal all day anyway."

Bashkim removed the leather gloves and sat down on the ground, looking up at the sky as he caught his breath. Cynthia carefully sat down next to him, also looking upwards.

"What was flying like?" she asked.

Bashkim thought about it and tried to find how to put it into words. "I've never felt anything else like it. It's...freeing. All your problems are beneath you when you're up there. But when you come back down..."

Bashkim's voice trailed off and his head slowly lowered as his eyes looked back down to the ground. "Do you think any of them will come?"

"The soldiers?"

"Yeah. Do you think we'll be able to work together? With the kesshonite?"

"If we want to survive, I think we'll have to."

Bashkim nodded. He started to lean backwards to lay down on the ground, but a booming voice echoed through the town.

"Bashkim!"

Bashkim and Cynthia quickly perked up, getting to their feet and stepping out into the main road. Much to their surprise, several soldiers dressed in steel marched through the village with Fandul and Dasc leading the way.

"Fandul?" Bashkim asked in surprise as he ran to him.

"We came as fast as we could," Fandul said.

"Aye!" Dasc growled, grabbing Bashkim and looking him over several times. "Telanos told us your wounds were healed, but even though I see it, I can hardly believe it! That white dragon had you pinned."

"I would explain if I could, but I'm afraid you know as much as I do."

Bashkim then looked past the two eshans and down the long line of soldiers, seeing a mixture of both eshans *and* humans. "But, what's all this? These people?"

"You requested soldiers, no?" Fandul asked, motioning to the militia behind him.

"I did. I just...didn't expect this kind of turnout."

Dasc slapped Fandul on the back. "Fandul can be pretty convincing when he wants to."

"Perhaps," Fandul said, straightening himself back up. "But the white dragon showing itself to the entire city as well as Bashkim's display of willingness to fight it head-on certainly helped turn a few hearts."

"And Nennossen?" Bashkim asked, again looking at the mixture of soldiers. "They agreed?"

"We needed little convincing," a familiar voice said, and out from the troops behind the two eshans came a most welcoming face.

"Simon!" Bashkim exclaimed. "I'm glad to see you're still around."

"Likewise. You've done Nennossen a tremendous service."

Though he had been smiling since he saw Bashkim, the look on Fandul's face grew more serious and he put a hand on Bashkim's shoulder. "We were told of your dragon's fate. You have our condolences. We owe her a great deal. Not only did she save you, but in doing so, she has most likely saved us all."

Bashkim's head dropped at the mention of Rin, and Cynthia to step closer to his side.

"Oh?" Fandul asked, taking his hand back. "And who is this?"

"This is Cynthia. She is the smith I told you about that made my sword and the other eshan weapons. We've been prepping them for the kesshonite."

"Is that so?" Fandul asked, his eyebrows raising. "It was you?"

Cynthia nodded her head several times, unsure of what to say.

"Then may your hands forge many more," Fandul said with a polite bow. "Your craftsmanship is fit for the Arbiters."

"Oh," Cynthia said, her face turning red. "Are all eshans as charming as you?"

Fandul grinned as he rose back up. "But of course. Surely you've noticed the eshan side of Bashkim."

"Well, he does make for good company around the shop," Cynthia said, nudging Bashkim with her elbow.

"I'm sure he does, and I've little doubt that your blades will see us home safely."

Fandul then turned to Bashkim and stepped to the side so that Bashkim could see the troops behind him. "Bashkim, you have Teasvanna's soldiers as well as the Senguan at your service."

"Nennossen's army is also at your command," Simon said. "You need only to lead the way, for we will follow."

Bashkim took in a deep breath and held it, nearly not blinking as he looked over the long line of men and women. Most were dressed in steel, but even the citizens of both cities had volunteered themselves, bringing their own assorted tools and equipment. The row of people stretched out past Telscara's gate, and as Bashkim stared at them, he realized some of the people had both human *and* eshan ears.

Hybrids? He thought, just before someone stepped out of line.

"We may not have an army, but Handleson stands with you as well!"

Out from the crowd came a man, making his way to Bashkim.

"Henry?" Bashkim asked in disbelief. "What the hell are you doing here? Do you even know how to use a sword?"

"No. But now is one hell of a time to learn!"

Bashkim put his hand to his head, sighing. "You're going to get yourself killed, Henry."

"Maybe. But I brought bandleberries!"

Bashkim snorted. "Are they any other surprises?"

Fandul and Dasc didn't answer. Instead, they just motioned with their heads for Bashkim to look behind him. Bashkim and Cynthia turned around and found Telanos standing behind them. Cynthia jumped in surprise, but Bashkim refused to budge.

"Of course," Bashkim said with a small grin. "Were you able to get the kesshonite?"

Telanos reached into his robe and retrieved a large, purple crystal. "I have brought this and more."

"Is that the kesshonite?" Cynthia asked quietly to Bashkim. "It looks different than yours."

"It is," Bashkim nodded.

"Then that's everything you need, right?"

"Yeah," Bashkim said, turning back to look at the long line of soldiers. "That's everything."

"Then what is the order?" Fandul asked.

Bashkim stood silent, unable to fully believe what he saw before him.

"We've been preparing weapons for the kesshonite," Cynthia said, then gave Bashkim a small nudge.

"We have," Bashkim added. "But we didn't expect this many people. We'll need to prepare more now. The kesshonite will also need to be cut down to size."

"Then for now we will lay down our swords and take tools instead," Fandul said, turning to Cynthia and motioning behind him. "Lady Cynthia, choose any and all that you require to aid you in your work. We will follow your instruction."

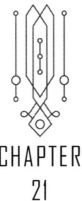

CHAPTER 21

Cynthia wasted no time forming an assembly line to produce the weapons needed for the upcoming battle. With the help of Dasc, several workstations were quickly set up and ready to go. She put the volunteer craftsmen to work carving out the sword handles, as well as preparing spear heads and even war hammers for kesshonite. With the basics set up and the selected people put to work, Cynthia requested that Telanos show her exactly how to cut the mysterious gemstones. He reassured her that they were no different than any other gemstone she had worked with before, and that her current tools would do just fine.

"Ordinary?" she asked doubtfully while waving a piece of kesshonite in front of Telanos. "I don't know about you, but I've never felt like I had enough power to destroy cities when holding an *ordinary* ruby or emerald."

"It will cut the same," Telanos explained calmly. "Just don't reach for the power yourself and everything will be fine."

"Then you won't mind sticking around and making sure, will you?"

Cynthia left Telanos with little choice. He stayed with her as she worked through her first couple of pieces. Only when finally satisfied, she began to prepare more workstations for cutting kesshonite. As she and Dasc got things set up, Fandul approached Bashkim outside the work area.

"You left something in Teasvanna," Fandul said, holding up a familiar dagger in his hand.

Bashkim looked down at the jeweled weapon. "Oh, I don't really need it anymore. I think it's served its purpose."

"More than you realize. We've been using it to practice with on our way here."

"Were there any accidents?"

"None. Telanos was there to make sure things went smoothly. Some of them learned to balance the kesshonite's power, but there's still plenty that need training since we only had the one weapon and limited time."

Bashkim turned to face Cynthia's workshop and watched as she worked with Telanos. "I imagine we'll have plenty to work with soon enough."

Fandul gently tapped the dagger's handle against his hand. "Are you not curious how the hybrids handled it?"

"Extremely," Bashkim said. "But I'm also a little scared to ask."

Fandul patted Bashkim on the back. "It works. Better than you might have imagined."

Bashkim sighed in relief and let his shoulders drop. "Good. I wish I could say I hadn't dwelled on it much, but I'd be a liar if I did. I've been worried that when it finally came down to it, I'd be unable to do anything. But...what do you mean it's better?"

Fandul called for Telanos and motioned for him to come over. Once Telanos joined them, Fandul led the two of them away from the work crew.

"What's going on?" Bashkim asked.

"Hybrids can draw power from the kesshonite on their own," Fandul explained. "Though, unlike humans, it takes a bit of effort on their part. The good news is that seems to allow them to contain it on their own as well."

Bashkim looked back and forth between Telanos and Fandul. "Then why are we stepping away from everyone?"

Fandul lowered his voice. "Because we don't know how kesshonite reacts to *you*. In case you've forgotten, you have a little something extra inside of you. I've seen with my own eyes what can happen with that magic of yours, and I didn't think you'd want us bringing that up around others."

"No. We probably shouldn't. But what do I do? Do we try it here?"

"Better here where we're available than on the battlefield when your life depends on it," Telanos said.

Fandul handed the dagger over to Bashkim, who reluctantly took it.

"It's okay," Fandul said, putting a hand on Bashkim's shoulder. "We're here."

Bashkim took a deep breath. "Alright."

Bashkim wrapped his fingers around the dagger tightly. He could feel the kesshonite within the weapon and the power it contained. It seemed to be right in front of him, waiting to be grabbed. He closed his eyes and held his breath, carefully trying to reach out with his own magic to connect with the mysterious gemstone. However, as he reached out, there seemed to be something blocking him. It didn't feel as solid as a wall, but more like an incredibly thick liquid that he *might* be able to push through.

"I can feel it," Bashkim said. "But I think you guys are holding it back too much."

"We're not doing anything," Telanos said. "The hybrids said there's a bit of resistance for them and that they have to push through on their own."

Bashkim opened his eyes and looked at both the dagger and the two eshans next to him. "Interesting."

He took another breath but kept his eyes open. The barrier between him and the kesshonite remained, but this time he tried to focus his magic more to make it pierce through as he pushed harder. A glow started to flicker inside of the kesshonite.

"The hybrids said the more they pushed, the more resistance they felt," Fandul explained. "According to them, there's a "breaking point" to push through. It's like pushing your hand through a thick cloth. Once it starts to tear, hold back so you don't fall through under your own weight."

"Alright," Bashkim said, rolling his shoulders as he gave it another go.

He focused his eyes on the kesshonite and watched the glow flicker randomly. He pushed against the mental barrier and tried to feel for the "tear" as he pushed harder into it. His eyes narrowed. It felt as though a liquid flowed through his veins from his chest and out through his arms while something with hundreds of tiny legs crawled under his skin. As he tried to connect with the kesshonite, he could feel its power working its way back inside of him, mixing with his own magic.

"Push a little harder," Fandul said quietly.

Bashkim grunted as he tried to push more. Suddenly, he felt a jolt from the kesshonite shoot through his arm and directly into his chest. He jerked back and took a sudden breath but kept both his physical and magic grip on the weapon. Bashkim looked down at the dagger. The kesshonite had a consistent glow to it. He no longer felt the resistance of the barrier, as if he had torn through the aforementioned cloth.

"I think that's it," Bashkim said, breathing easier as he carefully moved the dagger around. "It's...strange."

"Does it feel like it might get out of control?" Fandul asked.

"No. If anything, it feels...maybe limited? When I hold the kesshonite itself, it feels like a world of power, but now that I've tapped into it, I feel like there is only so much I can pull out on my own."

"That's about how the others explained it too. It's still far more than the rest of us can do on our own."

Bashkim held the dagger in front of him and watched the kesshonite glow. He could feel the kesshonite's power passing through him as if he were nothing more than a conduit for it. Though he could much more easily hold his connection to the weapon now that he had broken through, he could feel the continuous drain it had on his body as he held it.

"It seems safe *now*," Bashkim noted. "But how do we know it will stay that way for me?"

"We don't," Telanos said. "But we do at least know you seem to be able to use it like the others."

Bashkim let go of his connection to the kesshonite and its glow faded as the power left his body "That's better than nothing. So now what?"

"We introduce you to some of the other hybrids that have already been trained," Fandul said and took the dagger back. "They can better bring you up to speed. Once Cynthia gets some weapons finished, we'll get the others trained up too. Arbiters only know how much time we have."

"Agreed," Telanos said with a nod. "I imagine Wynn can only keep the white dragons dormant for so long. Considering his behavior."

"Behavior?" Bashkim asked. "What do you mean?"

"Nennossen was attacked," Fandul said. "Just a couple days before we arrived."

"How bad?"

"Similar to Teasvanna. Their eastern wall was destroyed as well as several homes. I'm not sure how, but the humans managed to drive it away before any more harm could be done. On the bright side, the attack may have helped convince them to join us."

More than happy to share what little they knew with Bashkim, the hybrids readily brought him up to speed so he could help teach the rest that had yet to be trained. Cynthia saw to it that her production line kept pace with the fast-moving soldiers and had them equipped to train with several kesshonite weapons within the first day. Telanos stood close by and made sure to be present for each pair's first attempt to draw out the kesshonite's power. Simon stayed with Telanos, also keeping himself present for the first timers. Much to Bashkim's surprise, he discovered that Simon had stepped up days ago as the first volunteer for the kesshonite tests, but his explanation made sense.

"I am their captain," he told Bashkim. "I will not ask them to do something that I myself am not willing to do."

Fandul and Dasc spent their time teaching basic swordsmanship to the civilians they had acquired. They bumbled about with their weapons, but their willingness kept them trying. Fortunately, most of them already had skills with a bow, some even surpassing their soldier counterparts.

Over the next couple days, Telscara didn't sleep. The entire group worked in shifts, practicing with their weapons and magic. They worked into the night, the glow of the kesshonite and magic keeping Telscara alight. The soldiers pushed both themselves and the civilians to their limits as they prepared themselves for the battle to come.

One day, while taking a small break, Fandul approached Bashkim to check in on him.

"You seem concerned," Fandul said. "Something on your mind?"

"I'm used to a lot of this," Bashkim said while catching his breath. "But what about the others? Don't you think we're pushing them a little hard right before sending them to a fight?"

"They'll have time for rest. It might not be as much as they want but it'll be as much as they need. We're on borrowed time, remember?"

"Yeah. I remember. It just seems like working with this kesshonite is more draining than you'd think."

"It is, but we're at war, Bashkim. I'm afraid we can't wait. Now tell me, what is it you're *really* concerned about?"

Bashkim snorted and grinned as he unhooked Rin's sword from his belt and handed it over. "What can you feel when you hold this?"

Fandul grabbed the sword, taking note of the green gem in the weapon's handle. "This is the kesshonite from our mysterious stranger, correct?"

Bashkim nodded.

"It feels similar to the other kesshonite," Fandul said as he focused on the weapon. "But at the same time...there's something oddly familiar about it. Like I've felt it somewhere else before. I can't quite seem to place it though."

"That's more than I get," Bashkim said, taking the sword back. "I barely feel anything from it."

"But it works, right?"

Bashkim held the sword where Fandul could see it and made the green gem glow. "I can tap into this one much easier than I can the others."

"The man gave it to you specifically, so that's not too surprising."

"Maybe," Bashkim said and hooked the sword back onto his belt. "If kesshonite is power pulled from the Arbiters, I'm curious as to which Arbiter this one belongs to."

"Well, when this is all over, maybe you'll have the chance to ask him. It would be awfully inconsiderate if we went through all this trouble for him and he couldn't even bother to stop by and say thank you."

Bashkim's shoulders shook as he chuckled. He paused and gently scratched the side of his neck. "I guess we're really doing this then, aren't we?"

"Aye. Heading out first thing in the morning just like we planned. Are you prepared?"

"Can anyone be prepared for what we're about to do?"

"For what the rest of us are doing, yes. But the rest of us haven't been tasked with killing an Arbiter."

Bashkim sighed, his gaze finding its way to the dirt beneath them. "I'll admit. All of this is a little difficult to accept. If you had told me just a few days ago that eshans and humans would be working together, I would have called you a damned fool. I wanted it to happen, but I question whether or not I believed it ever would."

"If you didn't believe it could happen, I don't think you would have chased after it so hard. We're all here because of you."

Fandul slapped Bashkim on the shoulder. "And in case you didn't know, we're celebrating tonight. That should help put you at ease."

"We are?"

"Aye. Dasc has made sure of it."

Dasc did indeed make sure they celebrated that night. It took all the tavern's ale and some more to provide for the soldiers, but with a little cooperation and a little magic, they managed to all score at least a couple drinks. Only a few days had passed since they originally arrived in town, but the soldiers and volunteers were more than ready for a night off. Not only had it been a long journey to Telscara, they had worked nonstop since the moment they arrived. When they weren't making weapons, they trained with them, and when they weren't doing either of those, they practiced magic. Three days might not have been a long time, but they were more than willing to forget for just a few moments what waited for them in Anderwood.

Even the citizens of Telscara had chipped in to help where they could, providing food, water, and other helpful services. A white dragon had attacked their town too, so they were plenty eager to help get rid of it. They were also plenty willing to take part in the festivities that night.

As the people played their instruments and sang their songs, Bashkim remained a safe distance away from most of it, taking a seat in front of one of many campfires next to Simon and Telanos. He enjoyed watching the eshans amuse the humans with their magical talents by summoning small fires in their hands or even chilling their drinks for them. Even the humans tried to use their newly awakened magics, much to the eshans' entertainment. A smile found its way onto Bashkim's face as he watched one eshan summon a flame on the tip of his finger to light a pipe for the human he shared a drink with.

"You're not much for celebration, are you?" Simon asked.

"Not really," Bashkim said as he got more comfortable. "It's good that they do, but it's just a little more crowded than I'm used to."

Telanos grabbed a teapot and held it up for Bashkim to see. "Care for some tea?"

"Sure. If you have enough to spare."

"Ah, there is always enough tea for two," Telanos said, then glanced at Simon. "Or three in this case."

Bashkim narrowed his eyes as he watched the wizard. Telanos sat both the teapot and a cup on the ground, using his magic to pull the liquid out from one container to the other.

"I can understand why you're not used to such things," Simon said. "But I'm still a bit surprised by your lack of emotion. This is what you wanted, isn't it? A celebration between humans, eshans, and hybrids?"

"It is," Bashkim sighed as he took his cup. "I'm just worried it won't last."

"You think history will repeat itself?" Telanos asked.

"Yes. I'm afraid the same thing that happened to you and Ascura will happen again. People tried to hide what you guys fought for. I almost feel like it's kind of foolish to think it'd be any different this time around. We're even fighting the exact same enemy as before."

"The enemy is the same," Telanos agreed. "But this time we know where it is, and *who* it is."

"Maybe. But even if we kill Wynn, there's still Mykenebres."

"I don't think that's our fight," Simon said. "I believe for that, all we can do is shine a light where the darkness tries to reach."

Bashkim frowned and took a sip of his tea. He rested the cup on his knee, tapping his finger against it slowly as he watched Cynthia in the distance. She had been dancing with some of the eshans when Bashkim had sat down, but now she had taken to arm wrestling them instead and winning.

"Why do you not go to her?" Simon asked.

Bashkim turned to face him. "Excuse me?"

Both Telanos and Simon laughed at him. "It doesn't take a wizard to see you have eyes for the smith," Telanos said.

"Assuming I even come out of this alive," Bashkim said as he looked down at his tea. "Why would I put her at risk like that? Hybrids are accepted today, but what of tomorrow?"

"I think that's a risk she just might be willing to take," Simon said. "And who knows. Maybe this time it will be different."

Bashkim looked back towards Cynthia. She had just won another match and rose from her seat, posing to flex her muscles in victory. As she did, her eyes crossed paths with Bashkim's, prompting her to pause and smile at him.

"Go," Telanos said, a small wave of his hand taking the cup away from Bashkim and forcing him up to his feet against his will.

Bashkim awkwardly stood up and stumbled his way to the rest of the party as he tried to regain control of his own legs.

"Oh ho, ho!" Dasc shouted loudly as Bashkim joined the crowd. "Look out, ladies! Here comes Bashkim, the great slayer of white dragons!"

Several of the people raised their drinks and cheered, making things all the more awkward for Bashkim. He knew half of them were too drunk to even know what they cheered for, but it didn't help any.

"I knows that man," Henry said, stumbling towards Bashkim. "It's true, I tell you. Every word. Poor bastard didn't even know what a bandleberry was when I met him. Mmhmm. Sad!"

Bashkim tried to ignore Henry and instead made his way straight to Cynthia. However, when he got there, Dasc came to his side.

"Oh, I see, I see. I see what's going on here," Dasc said in a not-so-subtle whisper of ale-coated breath as he wrapped his arm around Bashkim's shoulders. "Now, you listen here, tiny. Me and Henry here can clear out one of these tents. Clean it up real good-like. Flowers, blankets, the works."

Dasc then tried to give a wink but struggled to move his face the way he wanted. "You just give us the word, and Dasca Montilli will save the day."

"A tent?" Henry asked loudly. "Not for Bashkim. No, no, no. We'll give him the entire tavern! They can drink as much as they wish!"

"Are you daft?" a woman from the crowd asked. "The tavern is out here. There's nothing left in there!"

"What?" Dasc asked, whipping around. "Outside? You humans are a strange lot. Who has taverns outdoors? What if it rains?"

Henry shrugged his shoulders. "Don't look at me. I'm only *half* human."

Bashkim groaned and rubbed a hand over his face. Luckily, Fandul came to his rescue.

"Gentlemen," Fandul said and put a hand on each of their backs. "We're in a bit of a bandleberry crisis."

"A travesty," Henry cried.

"Yes. We seem to have run out over here, but the good news is, I hear Telanos has a basket full of them at his campfire."

"Ah ha!" Henry said with a wide smile as he grabbed Dasc. "Come, my oversized friend. There are bandleberries in need of a rescue. It's time to put all this training to use!"

Unlike Bashkim, Cynthia had quite the giggle from the whole thing as she watched the two stumble away. Fandul politely and sarcastically bowed before following the bandleberry saviors.

"Telanos doesn't have any, does he?" she asked once they were all out of earshot.

"Not a single one."

Cynthia held her hand out. "Well, then. Would you like to dance?"

Bashkim hesitated, unsure of what to say or do as he looked down at her hand.

"Or we could arm wrestle if you prefer?" she asked.

Bashkim grabbed her hand. "I'll try the dancing first. But...I don't know how. I've never really had the opportunity."

"Then I'll show you. Wouldn't be the first thing I've taught you."

Cynthia took Bashkim's hands and placed one of them on her hip while holding the other. She brought herself close to Bashkim, and he reactively stepped back.

"Sometimes, I think you're more scared of me than you are that dragon," she joked.

"Sorry," Bashkim said, trying to hide his face.

One of the humans from the nearby group grabbed his lute and started to slowly strum its strings. An eshan next to him grabbed a flute, carefully listening to the notes to know when and how to accompany the human. After a couple of tries, the two found themselves playing together rather well and filled the area with a soft tune.

Cynthia kept her focus on Bashkim, leading him through a slow and simple dance. His feet shuffled clumsily, frequently running into themselves as he tried to stand upright.

"It's just me and you," Cynthia whispered through a smile. "No fancy footwork or swordplay. Just dancing."

Bashkim took in a slow breath and held it before nodding. He tried the dance again and forced his feet to move slower as he tried to follow Cynthia's lead and ignore those around him. After a few tries, he learned to follow her movements and stay in step with her.

"You're a fast learner," she smiled.

"Maybe you're just a good teacher."

"Is that you talking or the ale?"

"I think it's the eshan half."

Cynthia grinned and nodded in approval. "There you go."

The human and eshan continued to play their music as the two danced. A few others grabbed their drinks and joined in song. The singing didn't go over quite as smoothly as the music, but through the power of ale they managed to work their way through. Bashkim and Cynthia laughed to themselves and continued to dance.

"See?" Cynthia asked, patting him on the back. "It's not so bad, is it? Sometimes you just got to give it a chance."

"Yeah," Bashkim said distantly and looked at everyone around them. "Not bad."

When Bashkim awoke the next morning and left his room in the tavern, he found the soldiers already well into packing and preparing for their journey. He quickly made his way past them and found Telanos, Fandul, Dasc, and Simon gathered together.

"Everything alright?" Fandul asked.

"Yeah," Bashkim said, somewhat distracted. "I'm just a little surprised to see everyone up and around so early after celebrating."

Fandul chuckled. "There was only so much booze to go around. If Dasc hadn't drank all of it, you could have had some more and maybe enjoyed yourself a little bit."

"Might have helped your dancing skills too," Dasc said as he nudged Bashkim with his massive elbow.

"Like you even remember anything," Bashkim huffed.

"I remember being lied to about bandleberries so you could have a little alone time with your sweetheart."

"It's not like that."

"Right," Fandul said. "And we're all off to pick daises in Anderwood."

"About that," Bashkim said, trying to shrug off the whole thing. "How long do you think it will take to get there with a caravan this size?"

"That's what we were just discussing," Simon said. "Dasc predicts a three-day journey if we want to be in any kind of fighting condition when we get there."

"Three days?" Bashkim asked. "We've already spent that many getting ready."

"Are you worried the dragons will move before we get there?" Fandul asked.

Bashkim crossed his arms. "It's a concern. The man said Wynn is keeping them there, but he didn't say for how long. What if Wynn loses his control and they leave?"

"Then we'd have to hope your Arbiter friend would tell us not to waste the trip," Telanos said. "This whole fight is hinging on faith. I'm afraid all we can do is trust what we have and go from there."

"And how does everyone else feel about that?" Bashkim asked.

Simon smiled. "Let's go find out."

Both Simon and Fandul began to muster their troops, yelling loudly enough for all of Telscara to hear them. The soldiers instantly stopped their preparations and formed a row outside along Telscara's walls. The once civilians took a little longer to get in formation, but followed the soldiers' leads and fell into formation easily enough.

Fandul, Simon, and Telanos stood in front of the men and women and brought Bashkim along with them. Simon stepped to the front, pausing and looking over the volunteers as he took a slow breath and contemplated his next words.

"I discussed this with all of you before we left Nennossen," Simon said loudly, but calmly. "You've seen the enemy. You know what it is capable of. We face what was once an Arbiter that has since been damned by Umbra and darkened into an uncontrollable beast. But what we didn't see for years prior was the silent killer that roamed freely within our own walls. A monster much more terrifying than any white dragon."

Simon took another breath as he looked over the many soldiers. "Brothers and sisters, it's time we bring an end to that monster, as well as this white dragon. I can't pretend to know what the heavens have in store for us, but I do know that they've tasked Bashkim with putting this fallen Arbiter to rest, and *we* are his army."

Simon lowered his tone and spoke more softly. "I'd be a liar if I said we're all coming home from this. For some of you, this will be your final journey. Your road *will* end here, and you will wake up in the arms of the Arbiters. If you're not prepared for that, then now is the time to step back. You will not be judged, nor will you be shamed."

Before Simon could get another word out, the entire group of men and women took a single step forward in almost perfect unison. Bashkim's heart jumped and forced him to take a sudden gasp of air.

Simon's shoulders shook as a chuckle escaped him. "Then today is a good day. History is being made at this very moment, and I'll be damned if it gets erased this time. We know that humans and eshans have fought together in the past, and today, they will do so again. Our ancestors fought for this, for what we see right here and now. Let us not disappoint them."

The men and women threw their hands up high, cheering and whistling. Simon took a step back, letting Fandul have his turn. Fandul held his arms out and motioned for everyone to calm down and listen.

"You've had this drilled into your heads for days now, but we'll go over it again," Fandul barked. "These white dragons will use our own against us. Most of you have already witnessed this personally. The beast breathes a dark mist, and if you are touched by it, you will lose yourself. Your own brothers and sisters will attack you without restraint. Death is their only cure, and it is up to you to grant them that mercy. But know this: this is the *only* reason a sword should ever be raised against our own, be it eshan, human, or hybrid. Do I make myself clear?"

The soldiers all saluted, followed by a "yes, sir."

Fandul turned to face Simon and held his hand out. "Then today we stand united, Captain."

Simon grabbed the eshan's hand and gripped it firmly. They both then turned to Bashkim and saluted. Bashkim started to take a step back, but Telanos kept him in place with a slight push from his hand. Bashkim slowly brought his hand up, unsure if he should mimic the eshan salute or the human. Instead, he fumbled between the two and found himself somewhere in between. As he did, Fandul and Simon returned the same gesture, and turned so that the soldiers may see the new salute. The soldiers in turn copied the motion, letting out a triumphant cry.

Just as the soldiers started to break away and finish their packing, Bashkim could hear Cynthia pounding metal in the distance. After exchanging a few words with Fandul and Simon he left to go pay her a visit. When he got to her shop, he found her outside standing over her anvil and striking the metal with her hammer.

"Heading out?" she asked without bothering to turn around and face him.

"I am."

"Well then, I would say Arbiters be with you, but I'm pretty sure they already are all things considered."

Bashkim chuckled, a grin barely forming on his face. "Before I left, I wanted to make sure I said thank you."

"For what?"

"For helping me with Rin."

"Oh. Think nothing of it."

"No. You could have just given me the scabbard and sent me on my way, but you didn't."

Cynthia continued to beat the metal, her strikes becoming heavier and more aggressive, yet her tone remained the same. "You were broken, green eyes. Anybody with a shred of decency would have done the same."

"I've had a hard time finding those shreds."

Cynthia hesitated her next strike for just a brief second, nearly making her miss. At that point, Bashkim realized the metal lacked an orange glow and that she beat no particular shape into the metal.

"Thinking of your brother?" Bashkim asked.

Cynthia stopped hammering and looked down at the anvil. "Something like that, yeah."

"Didn't you tell me grieving alone is dangerous?"

Cynthia chuckled, resting the head of her hammer on the anvil. "I did, didn't I? I guess you had better make sure you come back then, hadn't you? And besides, you owe me quite a bit of money for all those swords you're taking."

Before Bashkim could respond, a panic suddenly spread through Telscara.

"Dragons!" the people shouted, everyone grabbing their weapons.

Bashkim ran towards the gate, eyeing the approaching creatures. Three dragons headed straight towards Telscara.

Wait a minute, Bashkim thought, eyes locked onto the dragon in the lead.

"Stand down!" Bashkim shouted, waving his arms as he stepped in front of everyone. "Stand down! Put your weapons down!"

"Are you sure?" Fandul asked, coming to Bashkim's side.

"I'm sure."

Both Fandul and Simon repeated Bashkim's order to make sure their soldiers stood down. The three dragons closed the distance between them and Telscara and landed directly in front of the village. Their wings blew a massive gust of wind over the people as they landed, forcing them to shield their eyes. A familiar red dragon stood in front, tall and proud. Behind him stood two more, one a dark blue and the other a vibrant orange.

"What's going on?" Fandul whispered.

"It's okay," Bashkim said calmly as he stepped up to the dragons. "He's with me."

The three dragons stared down at Bashkim as he approached.

"I'm glad to see you again," Bashkim said from below the dragon. "But who are they? Are they friends?"

"Delso mesh Jungadda. Wesht ahn kraken meshta. Trakear."

"You know I can't understand you." Bashkim smiled.

The red dragon pointed to himself and then to the others behind him. "Trakear."

"That word...you called me that before. Does it mean friend?"

The red dragon winced as he struggled to move his mouth to form the proper word. "Fuh-me. Fah. Heelee."

"Family?" Bashkim asked.

The red dragon nodded, then used the tip of a single claw to gently touch Bashkim. "Trakear."

The three dragons then all lowered their heads, bowing before Bashkim.

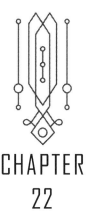

CHAPTER
22

While Simon and Fandul led the caravan, Bashkim and the red dragon flew on ahead to scout, as well as keep an eye on the Forest of Anderwood. They kept their distance from the forest, but they made their camp close enough to keep an eye on it, or at least a dragon's eye.

"You feel it, don't you?" Bashkim asked, watching the red dragon's muscles twitch.

"Mustah," the dragon said, nodding and trying to relax.

"You and me both," Bashkim sighed. "At least we know they're still in there. Hopefully Wynn can hold out until the soldiers arrive."

Bashkim started to put together the beginnings of a campfire but stopped as he watched the dragon get more comfortable.

"You know," Bashkim said. "It'll be a few days before the others arrive, and if we're going to wait here for them, it wouldn't hurt to know your name."

The dragon looked at Bashkim and spoke a single word that he couldn't even begin to hope to repeat.

"How about Red?" Bashkim asked.

A deep chuckle escaped the dragon, and he repeated the word "red" to the best of his ability.

As they waited, the blue and orange dragon took turns meeting with them and reporting their findings to the one who remained with the caravan. To Bashkim's surprise, both the blue and orange dragon came to them on the third day. As Bashkim looked between the dragons curiously, Red gently grabbed him and lifted him up. Once there, Bashkim could see in the distance the line of soldiers approaching with the sun already starting to set.

Bashkim found himself by a small campfire that night with Fandul and Simon. The rest of the soldiers, despite being awake, were awfully quiet. Much quieter than the last time Bashkim had seen them in Telscara.

"For some," Simon said as he watched Bashkim observe the soldiers, "tonight will be the last time they ever see the stars. It is only natural to be afraid."

"I understand that. I've faced a few battles of my own I didn't think I'd be able to win, but I was also alone. Would speaking to them not help?"

"No. Tonight they need to be alone in their prayers."

Bashkim frowned and stared at the fire. Simon grinned, amused by Bashkim's desire to help.

"I would normally consider myself an experienced soldier," Simon said once he grew tired of the silence. "Mostly due to my years of service. But when I look at you two, I feel like I might be coming up short. Bashkim has traveled more than those even my age. And you, Fandul, you lead with as much experience as I, yet you are so young."

"I am young," Fandul chuckled. "But I've already been in service for a good bit longer than most my age. I was brought on early, and when I became a member of the Senguan, I was exposed to a lot more. Some things a soldier might not see in his entire career. It tends to make a person grow and adapt a lot quicker."

"Telanos told me of the Senguan. I admire the idea, and respect those that carry the burden."

Fandul took a sip of his drink. "Thanks. Though my career as one might be over after this. Not sure I'll even be allowed back in the city should I survive tomorrow."

"What do you mean?" Bashkim asked.

"After the white dragon attacked Teasvanna, I approached the king with a few Senguan Knights. I informed him that I had willingly brought you into the city. Treydola then came forth with everything she knew and revealed what had been going on behind the scenes. We told everyone that was present. Soldiers, Senguan, even the commoners. We told them of the kesshonite and the history he had been trying to keep hidden. Needless to say, the people were not pleased to hear their king had been keeping not only an innocent man, but a hero, behind bars."

"Did they at least let Ascura...dad, out of jail?"

"Your old man refused to budge. Said he'd wait until you came back. The good news is, his living conditions are better at least."

Bashkim lowered his head, unsure of what to say. Trying to lighten the mood a little, Simon jumped in.

"I think you're becoming a bad influence," Simon said. "You've got Fandul outing his king in front of everyone too."

Fandul half smiled, having already heard Bashkim's story from Simon. "The king might have been furious and wanted me dead, but he was cornered. Not only did I have the Senguan on my side, he couldn't exactly hide the fact a white dragon had just attacked the city. Though I'd be a fool to think he wasn't trying to figure out a way to keep us out now that we're gone."

"Did you bring all of the Senguan with you?" Simon asked.

"As much as they wanted to come, no. We had to keep a fair number of them within the city should we not make it back. Since I had already been digging my nose into the whole affair, I was assigned to lead the fight with but a handful of them."

"Promotion?"

"Temporarily, at least."

"Well, here's hoping it sticks."

Fandul held his drink up. "Here's hoping we live long enough to make it stick."

The soldiers rose with the sun the following morning and stared at the forest in the distance as they geared up. The three dragons stood in front, ready to lead the way. The soldiers and volunteers stayed silent, but none of them showed signs of second guessing their decision.

"You still sure about this?" Fandul asked as Bashkim came up beside him.

"What? You think I'm going to back out now?"

"Oh, I don't know," Fandul said with a grin. "I think there might be a certain someone back at Telscara looking pretty tempting right about now."

Bashkim scowled at Fandul who only laughed as he made his way to the front of the camp.

"This is it everyone!" he shouted. "Anderwood is in sight. We don't know how many of those things are waiting for us, so make sure you keep your designated kesshonite partners close. We will march from here on foot. The last thing we need are horses running in the wrong direction."

The soldiers acknowledged with a resounding "yes, sir" as they strapped their helmets on and tightened their armors.

"Looks like you've got yourself an army," Simon said as he stepped to Bashkim's side.

"It's you two they follow, not me."

"Ah, but we follow *you*."

Telanos joined them as well, putting a hand on Bashkim's shoulder. "All eyes are on you, much like your father all those years ago."

Bashkim sighed, nodding his head as he turned to lead the march with Simon and Fandul. "No pressure."

The dragons stayed in front of the group to position themselves between the soldiers and the Forest of Anderwood. Sweat dripped from the faces of the men and women, and their adrenaline rose as they neared the forest. They flinched every time the wind blew, expecting something to come flying out of the massive trees. Fandul suddenly held his hand up and motioned for everyone to stop. He narrowed his eyes, looking between the dragons in front of them at what stumbled its way out of the forest.

"Arbiters help us," he muttered.

Out from the forest came a large formation of people. They stumbled over their own feet, dragging their weapons along the ground. Both soldiers and common folk stood in their ranks, some of their bodies starved and frail but still forced to move by the dark magic controlling them. Among them were both eshans and humans, as well as some races that Bashkim had never seen before. Some wore Teasvanna steel, while others wore Nennossen's. All of them, however, had glazed over eyes and snarled as they slowly made their way forward.

"I think the Arbiters are sitting this one out," Bashkim said.

All three of the dragons gripped the ground with their claws and stretched their necks out. Fire shot forth from all of them, clearing out the approaching force by disintegrating them within seconds. The flames went on past them and set the trees ablaze. The intense fires quickly rose up the trees, spreading throughout the forest.

The soldiers watched in silence as the men and women burned to nothing more than a pile of ash in front of them. They held their breaths and waited for the beasts responsible for the massacre to show themselves. Bashkim's eyes widened as a familiar voice came to him.

"You can stop this," Mykenebres said. "Come to me and accept my offer, and I will spare your people."

Fandul took note of the changed look in Bashkim's eyes. "What is it?"

"It's Mykenebres."

"What should we do?"

Bashkim hesitated and weighed his options.

"You can save them," Mykenebres said. "All of them."

Bashkim could feel the magic inside of him start to move.

No, he told himself. *I'm in control.*

Bashkim rested his hand on the handle of the sword with the green kesshonite. As he did, it glowed faintly. He could feel a second source of magic growing inside of him.

"We're with you until the end," Fandul reassured.

"Then we move forward," Bashkim said and started walking.

"So be it," Mykenebres said angrily. "Your hands will be stained with their blood."

The dragons in front of the troops shot their necks upright as if something had caught their attention. Not a second later, several white dragons emerged from the thick smoke of the burning forest and flew towards them.

Fandul raised his sword high and yelled at the top of his lungs. "Attack!"

The allied dragons leapt from the ground and took to the skies as the soldiers charged forward with their weapons and war cries. The white dragons varied in stature, ranging from half to equal in size of the allied dragons.

Where is Wynn? Bashkim wondered as he drew his own two blades, thankful that none of the other white dragons were as massive as the Arbiter he hunted.

Fire filled the air as the dragons attacked the white abominations, ripping and tearing into their flesh with their claws. Bloodied scales rained down onto the battlefield, the occasional limb or chunk of flesh landing with a loud crash. More of the white dragons came bursting out of the burning forest, launching from between the trees and heading straight for the soldiers. They held their weapons high and made the kesshonite glow brightly. The enchanted blades tore through the white dragons' scales with ease, and black blood spewed from the gaping wounds. The white dragons roared in pain and fury, slashing and flailing about like wild animals.

"They move slower than I expected," Fandul shouted to Bashkim.

"I think Wynn is still fighting against them," Bashkim yelled back. "We need to find him before he loses what control he has."

Though the weapons proved effective, and the beasts moved slower than their colored counterparts, it still didn't promise a victory. The jaws of the white dragons claimed several men and women, as did their claws. When the massive tails spun wide, they crushed all that stood in their path and hurled the bodies across the battlefield. The beasts charged into the groups of soldiers recklessly, sometimes even crossing paths with one of their own. The near collisions nearly broke out into brawls amongst themselves as they fought over their prey.

What Bashkim could only assume were the more mature of the white dragons raised their heads, breathing their dark mist over the soldiers and forcing them to fight their own. Tears fell from Bashkim's eyes as he drove his blades into the men and women that had chosen to follow him into battle.

"Stay strong!" Fandul shouted beside Bashkim. "I pray you will have the strength for me when my time comes."

"Yes," Mykenebres said in Bashkim's head. "Stay strong, Bashkim, as your friends die by your hands."

Bashkim gritted his teeth and tightened his grip on his weapons. The green kesshonite's glow intensified, and Bashkim could feel a small burning inside of his chest.

Try all you want, Mykenebres, Bashkim thought. *Today's fight is mine.*

Another white dragon made its way to the center of a large group of soldiers and reared its head back as if to spew the dark mist. Just as it started to shoot its head forward, it locked in place, shaking as it struggled against an invisible force. Among the group in front of the white dragon stood Telanos, his hand extended towards the beasts. The white dragon's head slowly started to turn, twisting around to face behind itself.

Telanos's fingers bent and curled as if he were grabbing hold of something, and his hand slowly rotated as the muscles in his arm tightened. The white dragon clawed the ground frantically, trying to push itself forward towards Telanos even though it couldn't see. Telanos stood his ground as the beast slowly came forward. The white dragon shrieked as its neck started to twist past its limit. The giant bones inside of its lengthy neck could be heard cracking, forcing the beast to cry out in pain before falling to the ground lifeless. Telanos dropped to a single knee to catch his breath as the soldiers covered him.

The white dragons became faster and more aggressive as the fight continued, overwhelming the soldiers and scattering them in multiple directions. The groups of soldiers became smaller, and many of them found themselves without support, rendering their weapons useless. Dasc also found himself separated and alone, face to face with a smaller one of the beasts.

"Just you and me, big guy," Dasc said with a smile as he held his massive sword at the ready.

Dasc swung the giant blade wide, but the dragon only grabbed it between its teeth, holding it in place and narrowing its eyes. Dasc wasted no time. He instantly let go of his weapon and grabbed two of the dragon's larger front teeth and used every muscle he had while screaming loudly to yank them right from the dragon's mouth. The white dragon roared and pulled away, dropping the sword. Dasc retrieved his weapon and swung it repeatedly against the side of the creature's skull.

"Incoming kesshonite!" a voice shouted, and a spear came flying past him, straight into the white dragon's chest. A bright light came from the spearhead, the intensity growing at a rapid rate and burning its way through both the dragon and the spearhead the kesshonite rested in. Dasc quickly reached out with an open hand to grab and calm the kesshonite's power.

"It's getting out of control!" Dasc said, now running for the weapon instead.

Dasc grasped the glowing remains of the weapon with both hands. Smoke rose from his grip as he screamed, but the kesshonite's glow began to fade. Once the kesshonite fully stopped, Dasc quickly stepped away. The human who had thrown the spear ran to his assistance to help remove the heated gauntlets.

"That was close," Dasc said with heavy breaths.

The battle in the sky had taken a turn for the worse. As the white dragons seemed to grow even stronger, they pushed the allied dragons down to the ground, forcing them to be more careful with their fire breaths. The white dragons had swarmed the orange one, pinning him down and tearing into his scaled hide like hungry dogs. He roared and cried out in pain for help. The other two dragons rushed to his assistance, but the damage had already been done. The orange dragon roared with a new burst of strength that struck fear in the white dragons as well as the soldiers.

With a heavy swipe of his claw, he caved in the skull of a white dragon and lunged at another, forcing it to the ground. The white dragon snarled and bit, but the orange dragon only roared back and spewed fire down onto the white dragon's face. Nothing but the neck with a charred tip remained and lay lifelessly against the blackened ground. The orange dragon didn't stop. More fire came from his mouth, prompting the soldiers to jump for cover as the blast mutilated another white dragon's wing. The orange dragon lunged forward to his wounded target and clamped his jaws on its neck while ripping its chest open with his claws.

The black blood rained over the soldiers and forced them to raise their shields to cover themselves. Several of the white dragons turned their focus to the orange dragon and jumped on him all at once, covering his entire body. The orange dragon stood strong, ripping limbs from his attackers and biting his way through. Red and the blue dragon stayed by his side and did what they could to tear the beasts away from him. The orange dragon began to slow, struggling under the overwhelming odds as the bodies piled high next to him. He eventually buckled and collapsed. Red and the blue dragon frantically tried to pull the white dragons away, but they were too late. The orange dragon lay on the ground, motionless. The white dragons started to back away, one by one.

Red and his companion roared loudly, crying for vengeance for their fallen brother. The blue dragon's tail came crashing down and broke one of the white dragon's necks. As Red dealt with two white dragons of his own, he noticed something in the corner of his eye. The orange dragon started to move again, sluggishly trying to get back to his feet with glazed over eyes. Red instantly came to his side and stomped his hind foot down on the orange dragon's head, shoving it back down to the ground. He squeezed tightly and drove his claws into the skull of the orange dragon and put him out of his misery. Red roared so loudly that fire dripped from his mouth and burned his own scales.

He became enraged and lunged into several white dragons at once. He swiped and clawed, stripping the flesh right off their bodies. He clamped his jaws down on one's neck near its torso, fire coming from his mouth as his teeth pierced and burned all the way through to sever the neck and head from the body. A larger white dragon approached him and readied its own breath attack. Red's head quickly shot forward and bit down on the white dragon's snout before it could open. The white dragon's jawbone crunched under the immense pressure as it tried to cry out. The white dragon squirmed to break free, but Red grabbed it by the neck and threw it to the ground. With a back foot on the white dragon's neck, Red reached down with both hands and gripped its head, making sure to keep the broken jaw shut. Keeping his foot firmly planted, Red pulled upwards on the white dragon's head and tore it from the neck that held it.

Bashkim watched with wide eyes as Red turned to face the approaching white dragons. He roared at them, proudly displaying the head he had taken and crushing it between his hands. As the remains fell and the blood dripped between Red's fingers, the white dragons slowly took a step back.

We can't keep going like this, Bashkim thought. *Wynn is losing his grip. They're getting stronger by the minute.*

Not only were they getting stronger, it seemed as though their numbers failed to dwindle, despite several of them lying on the ground dead. The soldiers did well enough to handle the kesshonite weapons, but their army was thinning. Not only that, but the battlefield had also become so hectic that Simon and Telanos found themselves fighting side by side despite having started on nearly opposite ends. As a white dragon approached them, Simon dropped his sword and reached for a dagger from his belt.

"Telanos!" he shouted, charging up the kesshonite in the dagger. "Guide me!"

Simon hurled the charged dagger forward and instantly retrieved his sword from the ground and ran forward. Telanos guided the blade through the air and kept the kesshonite's power stable as the small blade sank into the monster's chest. The dragon roared and lowered its head to bite Simon, but the captain's sword sliced cleanly through the monster's neck, downing the beast in an instant.

"Not bad for an old man," Telanos said.

"Give me a couple hundred more years," Simon said while catching his breath. "Then I might be as good as you."

Bashkim and Fandul had their own hands full as they tried to hold their ground against the dragons approaching them.

"If you're going to kill an Arbiter," Fandul shouted. "I suggest you do it quickly while we're still able to support you!"

Bashkim pulled his swords from the chest of a downed dragon and scanned the battlefield. As he searched for Wynn, another white dragon came up behind him and reared its head back.

"Bashkim!" Fandul yelled.

Bashkim turned around just in time to see the white dragon open its jaws wide. The black mist shot from its mouth and spilled over Bashkim as he held his arms out in front of him.

"No!" Fandul screamed and waited for the inevitable.

The mist slowly dissipated into the air, and Bashkim blinked his eyes several times over.

Am I turned? he wondered, looking down at the weapons in his hands.

The kesshonite in them still glowed, and as far as he could tell, he still had control of himself. Even the white dragon seemed confused and tilted its head as it stared at Bashkim. Fandul gripped his sword and shield tightly, waiting for Bashkim's next move. Bashkim swiped the weapon holding the green kesshonite across the dragon's neck, and the black blood poured from the open wound. The dragon gurgled and choked, falling to the ground within seconds.

Fandul held his ground. "Bashkim?"

Bashkim stared down at the green kesshonite, watching it shine. The burning in his chest grew, its intensity seeming to match the kesshonite's glow. As the kesshonite's power flowed through him, it felt as though it burned something away inside of him.

"It's okay," Bashkim said in disbelief. "It didn't work!"

But how? Bashkim wondered. *And what is this pain?*

"Don't celebrate just yet, Bashkim," Mykenebres said. "Your friends won't be so lucky."

Bashkim's eyes widened in horror as he looked to his side. Henry stood before a white dragon, alone. The white dragon blew the dark mist over him, knocking him to the ground.

"No!" Bashkim shouted, running to Henry's aid.

Bashkim's swords glowed brightly, and he swiped both of them wildly against the dragon, cutting it down to his level and finishing the job. Henry clutched his chest and coughed as he struggled to get to his knees. He turned to face Bashkim with a defeated look in his eyes.

"I guess I didn't make a good soldier after all," he struggled to say, trying to smile.

"Don't," Bashkim pleaded. "Please don't."

Henry coughed again, droplets of black blood splashing against the ground. "Do it!" Henry shouted between coughs.

Just as his eyes started to glaze over, Bashkim summoned a spike of ice from the ground that shot upwards and drove through Henry's heart. Bashkim shut his eyes and turned away, unable to bear the sight as the black blood eventually flowed red.

"You could have saved him," Mykenebres said. "All you had to do was accept my gift. Come to me while there's still hope for the others."

Bashkim gritted his teeth, ignoring the voice as he looked back at Fandul. Simon and Telanos had joined up with him and called Bashkim over. Dasc was on his way as well from Bashkim's side of the field, but as they regrouped, they noticed a white dragon nearby frantically kicking and screaming on the ground with a sword stuck in its side.

"That kesshonite is going to overload!" Dasc shouted.

Telanos reacted in an instant and dropped down to a single knee. A dome barrier started to form over him, large enough to shield those near him. The transparent protection formed in pieces, molding themselves together as it slowly worked its way to the ground and left an opening big enough for Bashkim and Dasc to pass through.

As the white dragon flailed on the ground, multiple rays of light started to beam from the kesshonite. The rays varied in size, some no wider than a sewing needle, while others were wide enough to blast an entire trench out of the ground they shot across. Some of the thinner rays curled and twisted, thrashing from the kesshonite like an uncontrollable whip. One snapped through a white dragon, leaving only a thin, heated line across its body as it fell to the ground dead.

"Come on!" Simon and Fandul yelled, motioning for Dasc and Bashkim to hurry over to the barrier.

Bashkim and Dasc ran as fast as they could as several of the light rays shot past them. One of the rays lashed out and whipped directly towards them. Dasc pushed Bashkim out of the way just in time, almost knocking him over as they ran.

"You can lie down when we're done," Dasc said as he grabbed Bashkim and pulled him upright.

Dasc kept his hand on Bashkim's back as they ran, guiding him forward. The two of them ran through the opening in the barrier and crashed to the ground inside as it closed behind them, just as the kesshonite fully overloaded. A thunderous boom rattled what seemed the entire world and shook the ground they stood on. The light from the kesshonite grew with such intensity that they were forced to cover their eyes.

They could hear the destruction taking place outside their protective dome. Chunks of the ground flew up against their shield, and the rays themselves blasted against it. Telanos's arm began to shake as he struggled to keep the barrier up, groaning as he pushed the magic through his body. The light outside began to dim, allowing them to see the destruction that had taken place.

Several white dragons lay dead on the ground, some torn into several pieces, others thinly pierced in a multitude of places. Trenches and holes stretched across the battlefield, many of them filled with soldiers. An enormous, smoking crater rested where the kesshonite had overloaded, leaving no trace whatsoever of the dragon it had been in, nor anything unfortunate enough to be nearby.

Telanos released his magical grip on the barrier and allowed it to fade as he collapsed and gasped for air. Bashkim turned to aid the wizard but realized that Dasc had never stood back up.

"Dasc!" Bashkim gasped.

Fandul looked at Dasc, his eyes widening. A thin, red-hot line ran diagonally across Dasc's chest armor. Dasc rested on his knees, a calm, but distant look on his face.

"Dasc," Fandul said breathlessly, getting down on his knees and grabbing him. "What happened?"

"I didn't make it," Dasc said simply. "But...I kept him safe, sir...I did my part."

Dasc's eyes slowly turned to Bashkim. "Time for you to do yours."

Dasc tried to swallow before continuing but struggled to do so. He looked at Fandul who shook his head as he refused to accept the truth before him.

Dasc slowly raised his arm up, mimicking Bashkim's salute one last time. "It's been a pleasure…friends."

Dasc's arm went limp and fell to his side as the rest of him slowly slid forward into Fandul. Before any of them could mourn, a wounded white dragon approached them from behind and made its way to an exhausted Telanos. Blood poured from the dragon's missing arm, causing it to move clumsily. Simon quickly put himself between the dragon and Telanos and raised his shield up.

Unable to properly keep its balance, the white dragon attempted to strike with its teeth. The jaws crushed Simon's shield, as well as the hand that held it. Simon yelled in pain, quickly driving his sword into the side of the dragon's jaw. The dragon pulled back, but not before Bashkim could jump on it and drive his own two swords into the top of its head. The dragon's body fell to the ground dead.

Simon dropped to his knees, trying to overcome the pain. Telanos quickly crawled his way to Simon and used his magic to tend to the wound as best he could, as well as tear his robe to create a makeshift bandage.

"I'm supposed to be the only one-armed old man here," Telanos joked as he tied the bandage. "There's no need for two of us."

"What can I say?" Simon asked through gritted teeth as Telanos worked. "I want to be like you when I grow up."

"Only a couple hundred more years to go."

Bashkim returned to Fandul, watching as he gently laid Dasc down.

"How many will you let die?" Mykenebres asked. "Come to me. End this suffering."

"I'm going into the forest," Bashkim said.

"Is that you talking, or Mykenebres?" Fandul asked, recognizing the look on Bashkim's face.

"The white dragons came from the forest, and considering we haven't seen Wynn, I'm beginning to think he's in there waiting."

"I don't think Wynn is the only thing waiting for you."

"Probably not, but we're losing out here," Bashkim said, looking down at Dasc. "I've let you do your part, now let me do mine."

Fandul started to argue but held his tongue. "Good luck, Bashkim. We'll do what we can out here."

Bashkim looked back towards Simon and Telanos. The two of them nodded, also wishing him luck. Bashkim turned and ran into the burning forest, using his magic to push the flames and smoke away and keep himself safe. He weaved between the trees and progressed deeper and deeper into the forest.

"Come closer," Mykenebres whispered in his head.

Bashkim ran farther into the forest, the flames still surrounding him. He stopped suddenly, feeling as though he were no longer alone. He held his swords out and prepared himself.

"Do you think the blades of a mere mortal can strike me down?" Mykenebres asked. "Or does your faith in the kesshonite lead you to believe it has the power to slay that which you cannot even see?"

"I'm not here for you. I'm here for Wynn."

"Ah, yes," Mykenebres said, sounding amused by the idea. "The Arbiter of War."

Bashkim looked to his side, and through the burning trees beside him he could see Wynn approaching. The white dragon circled around him and came to his front to stand before him. As the beast towered over him, Bashkim couldn't help but notice the many scars Rin had left on the dragon's body.

"You have come to kill him, no?"

"I have," Bashkim said, tightening his grip on his swords.

"And once you do, you will take his place. *By my side.*"

"I will not."

"Oh, ho, dear Bashkim. You don't have much choice in the matter. You believe you were sent on some divine quest, but they sent you here to die."

"I was sent to kill Wynn."

"Yes, you were. But then what? They never told you what would happen once he was gone, did they?"

Bashkim remained silent, watching the yellow glow of Wynn's eye.

"The Arbiter must be replaced," Mykenebres said. "And right now, this one belongs to me. If you strike him down, then you assume his position."

"No," Bashkim said, looking directly at Wynn. "Nobody belongs to you."

"You both belong to me. I am Mykenebres. I am what the light cannot touch, and you, children, have strayed far from its reach."

"Light or not, I can resist the darkness. The other white dragons have already tried and failed."

The voice in Bashkim's head chuckled. "And why, little Bashkim, do you think you were able to resist?"

"Because of what Telanos did. By being trapped with a small part of you, I am able to resist you."

"You have been deceived," the voice said, and as it did, the magical pressure in Bashkim's chest increased several times over. "The darkness is already *in* you."

A sharp pain in Bashkim's entire body suddenly shot through him, causing him to gasp and lose his concentration on his magic and be briefly burned by the surrounding fires. Wynn stood motionless in front of him and watched with a single narrowed eye. The pain in Bashkim's body grew. The magic inside of him felt as though it could simultaneously spiral out of control *and* snuff itself out.

"Thanks to Telanos, I've been a part of you ever since you were in the womb. The old fool kept me as close as I needed to be. You belong to me, Bashkim, and you have since the day you were born."

"No," Bashkim said, shaking his head and pushing the flames back. "I've resisted!"

"And just what have you resisted? Look around you. There's a fire left in every step you take, and death follows you like a slave to its master. I've seen you, Bashkim. You've ripped people apart, limb from limb. You want to give them what they rightfully deserve. You've put those you care about in harm's way to see that your justice was carried out. Even children have burned by your hands."

Bashkim's arms began to shake, and he fell to his knees. His chest tightened and he coughed violently as he dropped his swords. He looked at his hands, his eyes widening in terror. Darkness began to form under his skin, and thick, black lines crawled up his arms like veins.

"It wasn't me," Bashkim choked.

"Oh, but it was. Those fires came from you, Bashkim. Not I!"

Bashkim gripped his chest, coughing up black blood into the palm of his hand.

"It wasn't me!" he cried in a hoarse voice.

"It may not be who you *want* to be, but it is who you *are*."

Bashkim looked up at Wynn. The dragon remained completely still.

"No," Bashkim groaned, locking eyes with the dragon. "It's not who I am. And it's not who you are either, Wynn."

Wynn drew back ever so slightly and narrowed his eye. Bashkim reached for his sword with the green kesshonite gem and used it to prop himself up to a single knee.

"But," Bashkim barely managed to say, "you're right about one thing. I do leave a trail of fire wherever I go."

The kesshonite in his sword began to glow brightly, and the pain in his chest extended out through the rest of him. Fire erupted all around him in a single burst and engulfed his entire body. The green of Bashkim's eyes started to glow, and as they did, the flames surrounding him snapped to blue.

"There's a fire in all of us," Bashkim said, slowly getting back up to his feet. "And I won't let *you* condemn mine."

Wynn made a motion to attack but froze in place as if something had suddenly stopped him. To Bashkim's surprise, a different voice came to him this time. The same voice that had spoken to him at Teasvanna when Wynn had him pinned.

"Strike me down," the voice said, sounding as though it were struggling through immense pain.

Bashkim reached out with his hand and formed several whips of blue fire to lash out from the ground and wrap around Wynn's neck and arms. The magical whips yanked Wynn down to the ground as he struggled to break free and forced his head down to Bashkim's level.

"Do it!" the voice begged, despite the body trying to escape.

Bashkim lifted his sword high and drove it into the dragon's skull. The blue fire from his body wrapped around his weapon and swam over Wynn, spreading across the entire dragon. The fire grew in intensity, reaching higher and higher. Bashkim yelled as he pushed his magic and kesshonite to their limits. The crystal cracked under the strain and shattered from the overload. He fell backwards and shielded himself from the tremendous light he had created. The voice came back to him again, fading and getting farther away as it spoke.

"Thank...you," it said.

The giant fire in front of Bashkim rapidly increased in brightness twice over, the blue and white light almost blinding him. Then, just as it grew, it started to settle back down, leaving nothing more than a pile of brittle bones burned beyond recognition, as well as a deformed sword. Bashkim started to cough again and yelled as the pain ripped through his chest. Black blood continued to spit from his mouth, and he crawled across the forest floor on his hands and knees. The cough wouldn't stop, and he soon found himself unable to crawl any farther away and collapsed onto the ground. He watched in horror as the darkness in his arms grew, reaching farther up his body.

He rolled over to his side and waited for the encroaching fires of the forest to consume him. He closed his eyes. The magic felt as though it were tearing him apart from within. It riddled through his entire body and made each one of his hairs feel like a knife being driven into him. Then after what felt like his chest being ripped open, he screamed loudly and hacked up a large splash of blood. *Red* blood.

He tried to catch his breath and watched in disbelief as the darkness in his arms began to fade. He continued to cough as he tried to get back up to his feet, this time without blood spitting from his mouth. As he looked up, he realized all the fire and smoke had been stuck completely still. Even the ash and embers floating in the sky hung in place while still retaining their glow. Bashkim lowered his head and attempted to chuckle as much as his broken body would let him. He let all of his air out at once and collapsed onto his back. He stared upwards and saw a familiar man in a large black cloak standing over him and looking down.

"I did what you asked," Bashkim said, staying on the ground. "Would it be too much to ask of you to save the others? There's no need for them to die."

"With Wynn defeated, the other dragons will fall soon enough. You have already won the battle for them."

Bashkim took in a long, slow, and well-deserved breath. "Well then...how about that?"

The stranger lightly smiled and reached his hand out. Bashkim took the stranger's hand and let himself be pulled back up to his feet. He brushed himself off somewhat and looked back at the charred remains of Wynn. He paused to let it all properly sink in before turning to face the stranger. "Mykenebres was right, wasn't he? Wynn has to be replaced."

"If there is no Arbiter of War, then there is only chaos."

"But why me?"

The cloaked figure motioned for him to follow and led him through the motionless fires. The two returned to the battlefield, and Bashkim stared at the soldiers all frozen in place like statues.

"These people fight for you," the man said. "They believe in you and what you did. It is because of your example they are together today. You were the catalyst for a much-needed change in this world. A change that was long overdue. War is inevitable, Bashkim, but one such as you watching over it will ensure a balance is kept."

Bashkim frowned and took a slow breath as he weighed the stranger's words.

"Lest you forget," the man added. "You also survived Mykenebres's grip. Where Arbiters have fallen, you have remained standing. A power such as that might be what we need to fight against Mykenebres one day."

"A holy war?"

"Perhaps. But that is for another time. Today is the day you make a decision."

"An Arbiter," Bashkim said distantly. "I just...what would happen to me? Would I just leave and never see anyone again?"

"Deities aren't usually in the habit of revealing themselves, but it's not unheard of."

Bashkim slowly made his way over to Fandul. He held a human in his arms, pulling the wounded man to safety. A defeated sigh left Bashkim, and his eyes trailed to the ground.

"I had just found friends. I thought that maybe...maybe I could finally stay somewhere. With Rin gone, I didn't have anywhere else to turn, and now that I do, it's going to be taken away from me."

"They cannot force you," the man said. "But you should know that all of them agreed you were the best choice."

"And if I say no?"

"Then the Arbiters will have to find someone else."

Bashkim looked over the several soldiers, a thousand questions and concerns storming through his mind.

"I *hoped* there was somewhere I could go. But I suppose in all honesty, I really didn't have a home to go to, did I?"

"I believe there is someone in Telscara that eagerly awaits your return."

"Yeah," Bashkim said, staring at the ground as his eyes began to lightly water. "Yeah...there's that, isn't there?"

"The decision is yours, and yours alone."

Bashkim sighed as he sat down on a motionless white dragon's tail. He thought it over the best any human, eshan, or hybrid could. He could become an Arbiter. He could be a force that would change the world for the better. Mykeneberes had tried to tempt him with a similar offer before, knowing how much it would entice him. However, even with the offer coming from the Arbiters themselves instead of Mykenebres, things were different now. He knew Simon and Fandul stood by him. He knew his father. He knew who waited for him back at Telscara.

You were born a soul with wings that should fly, he remembered Rin telling him. *But bound to the body of man.*

Bashkim gently tapped a loose fist against his leg.

At least I won't be leaving you behind.

Bashkim faced the cloaked stranger. "I'll do it."

The man stepped to the side and revealed a sword stuck in the ground behind him. "Then you will be needing this."

Bashkim eyed the weapon. The handle had been made from a bright, white metal, and its blade dyed red.

"What is that?"

"It is Crimson's sword," the man said, pulling the weapon out and handing it over. "It is a symbol the people of this world recognize. Wynn saw to it that the world knew of his brother instead of himself. Crimson is the Arbiter they know, and the one you will become."

Bashkim carefully took the sword. The blade weighed a bit more than his own swords, but he felt confident he could make it work.

"By taking this weapon, you accept your duties as the Arbiter of War. You will bear the name Crimson, and you will watch over any and all wars of this world, from now until the end of time."

Bashkim thought the words over as well as his mortal mind could and stared down at the sword. He slowly nodded and slid the sword into his belt. "I accept."

"Then allow me to introduce you to your new partner," the man said, motioning for Bashkim to look behind him. "Or might I say, your old partner."

Bashkim turned around and much to his surprise, Rin stood before him.

"Rin!" Bashkim gasped in disbelief. "How?"

Rin lowered her head down to his level, allowing him to throw his arms around her. "How?" he repeated. "You were...I saw you. Me and Red, we were both there. We did the Final Flame."

"You did," Rin said gently. "I didn't expect to be passed onto the next life by an Arbiter. You've come a long way, Bashkim."

Bashkim buried his face into Rin's snout, still not believing what stood before him.

"Come on then," Rin said, raising her head. "I believe we have work to do. You've an entire world to watch over now. Not some two measly cities."

Bashkim happily crawled up Rin's side and onto her back. However, once he got up top, he paused as he looked down at the stranger.

"Something on your mind?" the stranger asked.

"Yeah. Just one thing. Whose power was in the kesshonite you gave me?"

The stranger grinned. "Yours."

CHAPTER
23

"Stay with me!" Fandul ordered as he dragged the human to safety. "Stay with me and you'll be fine."

The soldier moaned in pain, clutching the half of his leg that remained. Fandul shouted for assistance, and another eshan rushed to wrap and tie off the wound to stop the gushing blood.

"Look out!" a voice cried from afar.

Fandul half turned to look over his shoulder. A white dragon rushed towards them, baring its teeth. Fandul put himself between the dragon and the wounded soldier. He brought his shield up to protect himself only to witness the dragon's head slam into the ground forcefully enough to shoot rock filled chunks of dirt forward. Fandul peeked from behind his shield as the debris bounced against it, trying to catch a glimpse of what had taken place. The light-blue scaled foot of another dragon gripped the white dragon's head and held it down.

"Rin?" Fandul muttered.

When he lowered his shield, he saw only the white dragon, dead, with its skull collapsed in on itself.

"Did you see that?" Fandul asked, turning to the eshan assisting the wounded.

"The dragons are falling on their own," the eshan soldier said and pointed to the other side of the battlefield. "What is happening?"

Fandul stared in disbelief. The white dragons had become sluggish, struggling to move as though something held them back. Those in the air dropped to the ground. Some tripped over themselves as they landed while others came down with thunderous crashes that nearly knocked the soldiers over. Amongst the chaos, Fandul spotted a familiar figure. The man swiped a sword horizontally with two hands, a wide streak of blue fire trailing behind the blade that opened a white dragon's neck.

"Bashkim?" Fandul whispered.

Black blood spewed from the dragon's wound and blocked Fandul's view. When the corpse fell and rolled out of the way, the man had vanished.

"Sir?" the assisting soldier asked. "What do you see?"

Fandul shook his head then shouted to all who could hear. "We have the advantage! Close in before we lose it!"

The soldiers swarmed the winged beasts and tore them to pieces with the kesshonite weapons. The allied dragons took their share as well, crushing the skulls under their massive feet. The white dragons cried in pain and attempted to flee. Within minutes, black blood coated the battlefield and white dragon corpses piled high. The soldiers showed them no mercy and pushed forward until the last white dragon fell.

Fandul frantically scanned the battlefield for Bashkim. The soldiers stood still, processing what had happened for only a moment before dropping their weapons and running to assist their wounded. Dust kicked up from the battle slowly began to settle, but Fandul saw no Bashkim. Confused, his gaze eventually turned to the still burning forest.

"Quickly!" Fandul ordered, gathering several eshan soldiers. "Bashkim might still be in the forest. Help me douse these flames."

The eshans ran to the tree line with Telanos in the lead, grabbing the fires with their magic and pulling them down to the ground to snuff them out. Smoke rose high into the sky, and the blackened branches fell to the forest floor with an ash-rising crash. The trees cracked and groaned as they threatened to collapse.

Telanos reached out with his hand and covered the weaker trees with a layer of ice. The frozen grip held the crumbling trees in place and helped cool the area. As the ice wrapped itself up around the trunks, Red stepped in front of the group to lead the way into the forest.

"Easy," Fandul said. "If Bashkim is still in there, he might be on the ground wounded. I need you scouting from the sky, not down here knocking over trees."

Red nodded and launched himself into the air.

"I'm going too," Simon said from behind Fandul.

"You'll need to leave this to the eshans. It's too hot in there. Our magic will keep us safe."

"I can keep us all safe," Telanos said.

Fandul glanced at Simon's bandages, where part of his arm used to be. "Are you sure?"

"Let's go get Bashkim," Simon said, tightening his grip on his sword.

Fandul nodded and led the way into the forest. More volunteers followed behind. Telanos continued to wrap the trees in ice as they pushed farther in and held them in place. The heat from the burned forest and cold from the frozen trees beat against the soldiers as they searched, resulting in a mixture of sweat and chill. The soldiers ignored the strange conditions and continued forward, spreading out and covering as much ground as Telanos's magic allowed. Before long, they found the charred, ashy remains of Wynn, and stopped dead in their tracks.

"By the Light," Simon muttered. "Is that Bashkim's doing?"

"I've seen Bashkim melt steel in an instant when cornered," Fandul said as he wiped the sweat off his face. "I don't doubt he could manage this."

Simon stuck the blade of his weapon into the ground and kneeled in front of the dragon's remains. Within the dragon's skull rested a sword. As Simon took Bashkim's weapon, the brittle bone collapsed on itself, sending up a cloud of dust and orange embers. Most of the blade crumbled with it, leaving little more than the hilt in Simon's hand.

"I found the other one," Fandul said, kneeling to pick up Bashkim's second sword.

As he grabbed the sword, he spotted the red and black blood spatters on the ground. Fandul remained kneeled, crushing the weapon under his grip.

"When Bashkim explained magic to me," Simon said once he joined Fandul. "He told me it's possible to push yourself too far, even to the point of death."

"It's true," Fandul said in a lowered voice. "And having seen how far Bashkim can push his magic, as well as how willing he is, I can't help but think that—"

"I'm not sure it was his magic this time," Telanos said, stopping Fandul short.

Fandul rose to his feet and turned to face the wizard. Telanos stepped toward them and held his hand out. In his palm rested a few small shards of a green gemstone.

"These look like the remains of the kesshonite he had in that sword," Telanos said, nodding to the hilt Simon held. "The power has been completely drained. I feel nothing in these."

"You think he overloaded it?" Fandul asked.

Telanos nodded and let the shards fall to the ground. "Possible, though, if that's the case, it clearly didn't cause the same reaction we saw earlier. But we can't ignore that those remains are well beyond burned."

Fandul cursed to himself as he stared at the ash pile.

"If he did consume himself," Telanos added. "He won the war doing so. It seems safe to assume these are the remains of Wynn. It would explain why the battle turned in our favor so quickly."

"He did a lot more than win a damned war," Fandul said, then motioned for the soldiers to move forward. "We keep searching."

The group continued their search and covered more distance than they even thought reasonable. They found nothing and hung their heads low as they returned empty-handed. Red landed in front of the tree line and waited impatiently for news, looking down with narrowed eyes at the soldiers. Fandul only shook his head in shame. A defeated breath escaped the dragon. He nodded and joined the blue dragon in carefully pulling their orange brother away from the battlefield.

Fandul's gaze made its way towards the soldiers. Nearly all the wounded had been rounded up by the time Fandul returned from his search. Limbs were broken or severed, armors crushed, cuts, gashes, bruises, burns; the wounds seemed to go on forever. The soldiers stood tall and proud as they could though, confident they had made the world a better place. Even the wounded that knew they wouldn't survive the trip home had a smile on their faces, content they had played their part as they prepared to cross to the other side.

Fandul's head drooped once more. His eyes were drawn to Bashkim's sword in his hand, and a painful sigh of acceptance left him. He knew the odds of survival hadn't been in their favor. He had even accepted that he might not make it back himself, but he had sure as hell hoped Bashkim would. Fandul looked back, watching as Red and his companion cleared the area around their fallen kin. He went over to them, and Red turned to face him as he approached.

"Bashkim told me what you did for him," Fandul said. "With Rin. Are you about to do the same now?"

Red nodded, eyeing Fandul curiously.

"If it's alright, I would like to pay my respects as well. Most of my life I thought dragons to be nothing more than oversized beasts. Wild and uncontrollable. But you fought for us. You believed in us. You protected us. And one of you paid the ultimate price for that. I still don't know much about dragons but, for a soldier...for anyone, there's not much greater one can do than that."

Both Red and the blue dragon looked at one another. Their eyes did the talking at first before they finally exchanged a few short words with one another. They turned to Fandul and nodded. Red motioned with his head for Fandul to step forward. Fandul looked at the dragon curiously, unsure of what to do. Red breathed a small, brief puff of fire, then motioned towards the body of the orange dragon. Fandul held his hand out, palm upward, and summoned a small flame, waiting for the dragon's approval. Red nodded, again motioning Fandul forward.

Fandul slowly made his way to the orange dragon's body and kneeled, placing the small flame in front of him.

"Thank you," Fandul said, barely above a whisper. "Thank you for giving us your strength, your protection, and for putting your life on the line for our cause."

As Fandul spoke, his eyes fixated on the dragon's wounds. The white dragons had stripped several of the scales from his body and shredded the flesh underneath. Accompanying the destruction wrought by the claws were bite marks that removed chunks of the dragon's body. Fandul held his breath, trying not to imagine the pain of being eaten alive as the dragon made his last stand.

"Your sacrifice will not be forgotten, nor will the service of your kin."

Fandul remained kneeled and waited for the tear to finish sliding down his face. He slowly rose to his feet and returned to the two dragons. Both Red and the blue dragon lowered their heads. Once Fandul had moved to the side, the two dragons stepped forward. They dug their claws into the ground and stretched their necks out. Fire blasted from their mouths and their roars bellowed across the field. Fandul shielded his eyes at the sudden burst of heat and light. The dragons blew fire until the orange dragon crumbled into a pile of ash and brittle bone. Eventually, the flames thinned, and the dragons pulled back.

"Greneeshtah," they said in unison and lowered their heads. "Kaldea shale deen tumos—"

The two dragons paused and looked at one another. Red then repeated himself, struggling with the last word. "Kaldea shala deen tumos...*Orange*."

Fandul watched as the dusty remains gradually blew away.

"Can I ask you something?" he asked, squeezing Bashkim's sword.

Red nodded.

"Toward the end of the fight, when the battle swung in our favor, did you see...or feel, Bashkim and Rin?"

The two dragons looked down at Fandul curiously.

"Right when things turned, I thought I saw them. I know it doesn't make sense but...it seemed so clear."

Fandul looked up at Red hopefully. "Did you see them?"

Red slowly shook his head.

"Then I must have been seeing things," Fandul said, his grip on the weapon loosening.

The dragons gave each other a glance then stepped past Fandul. They then began to carefully collect the fallen soldiers and lay them next to one another. The able-bodied soldiers soon joined once they realized what the dragons were doing. A chill ran through Fandul as he watched the line grow.

Once the last of the fallen had been placed, Red gave Fandul a gentle nudge with his claw.

"Pograk," Red said gently, motioning with his head towards the bodies.

"I don't understand," Fandul said.

Red tapped his mouth with his claw, then gestured with an open hand as he spoke. "Pograk."

"You want me to speak?"

Red nodded.

Fandul smiled, shaking his head. "We're a little different than dragons. We mourn in silence."

He motioned towards the quiet soldiers standing near the fallen. Some stood with their heads bowed. Others put treasured belongings or trinkets on the bodies of their friends.

"Our silence speaks in ways we can't," Fandul said before making his way down the line.

Fandul's heart grew heavier with each step. He knew most of the eshan soldiers by name, and a knife pierced his chest as he envisioned telling their loved ones of their departure upon his return. One by one he pictured it. He knew each mother he'd have to give the news, or wife, or husband, or child. For some, their only home was the barracks. Their bunks would be emptied, eventually refilled by others willing to lay down their lives like those before them should duty call.

Even the humans and hybrids he had come to know in the past handful of days stung in their own way. Though the burden of delivering the news of their fate to loved ones didn't fall on his shoulders, their loss still weighed heavily all the same. He had come to not only know them in the past handful of days, but to trust in them, rely on them, and to call them brothers in arms against a common evil.

The knife in his chest sank deeper when he came to Dasc's body. In front of him lay a soldier, a Senguan Knight, and a close friend. A tear slowly pushed its way out of Fandul's eye and slid to the bottom of his chin, eventually falling to the blood-stained ground. Simon approached his side, keeping a respectful distance between them.

"Two hundred years," Fandul said quietly. "Only two hundred years ago and we managed to forget all of this had already happened."

"I believe there were forces at play that made sure we forgot," Simon said.

Fandul slid the back of his hand across his chin. "We still failed. Kings or devils, I don't care. We all failed to remember. We *chose* to forget. And because of that, we had to fight this war a second time."

"Then *we* should see to it that it does not happen again," Simon said and put a hand on Fandul's shoulder. "We must all tell our families, our children, and our children's children. Everyone here fought today so the rest of the world can have a better tomorrow. For those of us that survived, it's our duty to make sure the world doesn't forget. For those that didn't, we should pray that the Arbiters welcome them with open arms."

"I'd like to," Fandul said as he stepped away from the line of bodies. "Only I can't help but remember one of those Arbiters is the reason so many *didn't* survive."

The two dragons stepped up to the line of fallen soldiers, and Fandul motioned everyone to stand back. Red looked at Fandul and waited for his approval. Fandul took a slow breath and looked at Dasc one last time.

"Do it," Fandul whispered.

"Extu mesh vondeerenz Keesheer," Red's voice boomed with his eyes locked on Fandul. "Kaldea shala deen tumos, Jungadda."

The dragons each drew in a large breath and blew fire over the bodies. The flames didn't burn as intensely as when they burned their orange companion and allowed Fandul to more easily see. The armor on the soldiers glowed a bright orange and melted as the bodies turned to ash. Fandul watched with narrowed eyes, clutching Bashkim's sword.

"I'll see to it personally that Nennossen never forgets," Simon whispered once the dragons had finished.

"If this gets swept under the rug again," Fandul said as he walked away. "Arbiters help me, I'll bring the white dragons back myself."

The survivors packed their things and made sure not to leave a single kesshonite weapon behind. A few days later, they arrived in Telscara. The townspeople celebrated their return and praised their victory while providing plenty of food and drink. Fandul, Simon, and Telanos stood at the town's gate, staring at the ground as they listened to Cynthia's hammer strikes in the distance. The high-pitched ring of each blow drove right through them, piercing their hearts.

"Who is going to tell her?" Telanos asked.

Fandul took Bashkim's sword from his belt and looked down at it. "I'll do it."

"Are you sure?" Simon asked. "I can come with you if you'd like."

"I can as well," Telanos offered.

"No. I'll take this one."

"Very well," Telanos said. "Then if it is alright with you two, I will take my leave. I've an old friend I need to check in on."

"Will we see you again?" Simon asked.

"Perhaps. But you must remember, I have lived well beyond my natural years. It will be time for me to go soon."

"In that case," Simon said, offering his hand, "thank you for your service, and everything else you've done. Not just for us, but for the world."

"It was my pleasure," Telanos said as he shook Simon's hand before turning to Fandul. "Fandul...I wish you the best of luck."

"Thank you," Fandul said, also shaking the wizard's hand.

Telanos said his goodbyes and left the two soldiers, vanishing from sight the instant they looked away.

"Still sure?" Simon asked after a solemn silence.

"Yeah," Fandul sighed. "I'm sure."

Simon pulled the remnants of Bashkim's second sword from his belt and handed it over. "Then may the Light be with you."

Fandul nodded in appreciation then made his way to Cynthia's home, trying to keep his head up. Each step felt heavier than the last, and each blow of her hammer felt as though it shoved the dagger in his chest deeper. She stood over her anvil, pounding the metal as always. When he saw her, the lump in his throat grew twice over.

"Cynthia," Fandul said, gently.

Cynthia turned to him, but her expression shifted rapidly when she saw the swords in Fandul's hands. Her face went from curious to shocked, then to hurt, and ended with a feigned acceptance. Neither one of them spoke. They stood in silence as the emotions swam over them, and Cynthia returned to her work.

"I'm sorry," Fandul said, lowering his head.

"He was an adventurer," Cynthia said with a sudden elevation in her voice. She cleared her throat before continuing. "He rode with dragons for Arbiter's sake. That kind of life...it was bound to happen."

"Bashkim is the reason we won the war."

Cynthia's strikes grew heavier. She raised the hammer up higher before each swing, grunting with each metal-crushing blow.

"He's the reason the rest of us are alive," Fandul said, then motioned with his hand towards the mixture of soldiers. "Look around you. He's changed our entire future."

A tear mixed in with her sweat as it slid down her face, and her jaw began to tremble.

"Then I supposed as a smith," she said between blows, refusing to look up. "I should be proud such a hero used my steel."

Fandul remained silent, trying to keep his own tears contained. Somehow, Cynthia's strikes became even heavier. With a soul-shattering cry, she raised her hammer as high as she could and brought it down with enough force to break the metal into two pieces. The clang echoed in Fandul's ears, and her cry silenced the entire village. The ruined metal fell to the ground, as did her hammer as she let go and leaned against her anvil.

Her hair drooped down over her face, swaying back and forth as she shook her head. She straightened herself up and pulled the hair out of her face. With a small huff, she placed her hands on her hips and looked directly at Fandul. Holding her breath, Cynthia nodded several times then retrieved her hammer and ruined metal from the ground. She put the broken material back on the anvil and gently tapped her hammer against it as though she could still work with it.

Fandul watched as she let both the hammer and metal fall back down to the ground. One hand on the anvil, and one hand back on her hip, she took another breath and held it. Fandul gently laid Bashkim's weapons down and went to her. He wrapped his arms around her, holding her close. Finally, her tears ran freely.

More than once in his career had Fandul reported the death of a soldier to their lover, but this was the first time he wondered who it hurt more.

Back at Teasvanna, Telanos made his way, unnoticed as always, to Ascura's cell. The old man smiled from his new bed in the corner once he felt Telanos's presence. Telanos retrieved a small bottle from inside of his robe, but Ascura held his hand up to stop him.

"Not anymore," Ascura said. "I've lived long enough. You've held your end of the bargain."

Telanos's eyes widened and he froze in place.

"It's alright," Ascura reassured.

Telanos took a slow breath and stared into the contents of the small bottle. A chuckle eventually escaped him.

"I've been telling myself for years this day would come. But of all those times, I don't think I ever truly believed it. A part of me believed we would live forever. Or perhaps, I had hoped."

"We have to go sometime," Ascura said with a smile.

Telanos rolled the bottle in his hand. "I suppose you're right."

Telanos looked at Ascura, trying to pick his next words carefully. "I need to tell you about your son."

"What about him?" Ascura asked, sounding confused. "Is that not him with you?"

Telanos turned around to see Bashkim leaning against the prison bars from the outside, next to the open cell door.

"Don't like it when people sneak up behind you, do you?" Bashkim asked with a grin.

Telanos smiled, silently admitting he had been bested, and slid the bottle back into his robe. "You're standing taller than I last saw you. What happened?"

"I was approached by that man again after I killed Wynn."

"And he gave you Crimson's sword as a trophy?" Telanos asked, nodding at the new sword hanging from Bashkim's belt.

"I am Crimson now."

Telanos paused and kept his eyes on Bashkim. An abrupt, but gentle, chuckle escaped him, and he shook his head. "I suppose I should have seen it coming. The Arbiters approach you and give you a gift. It seems natural you would fill the void they asked you to create. So, Crimson, what happens now?"

"I stay here with my father for a while. Then I have duties to attend to."

"Such as?"

"How does Simon and Fandul becoming kings sound to you?" Bashkim asked as he stepped into the cell and came to Ascura's side.

"It certainly sounds nice, but I'm afraid Teasvanna's current king has a handful of years left."

"I think his rule will be coming to an end sooner than the people think."

"Well then," Telanos said with a smile. "In that case, I think my work here is done. Ascura, as always, you have been an inspiration, as has your son. It's been an absolute pleasure."

With Bashkim's assistance, Ascura got out of his bed and made his way to Telanos. He wrapped his old, frail arms around his friend, holding him tight.

"Likewise, old friend," Ascura said. "I can't thank you enough for what you've done. I think it's safe to say you changed the world."

"The real change started with you, old man," Telanos said, patting Ascura on the back.

Telanos guided Ascura back to his bed and gently sat him down.

"Crimson," Telanos said and held his hand out. "I suppose congratulations are in order. Good luck in your new life."

"Thank you, Telanos," Bashkim said, shaking Telanos's hand. "For everything."

Telanos waved goodbye and slipped through the wooden door, closing it behind him before vanishing from sight. Bashkim unhooked the sword from his belt and leaned it against the wall before taking a seat on the bed. Ascura rested his head on his pillow and waited patiently as the two of them searched for their words.

"Well," Ascura said, taking the lead. "I knew you would be a special child, but never did I imagine you'd become an Arbiter. I think it goes without saying that your father is quite proud."

"Thanks, dad," Bashkim said, for the first time in his life.

Ascura chuckled, causing himself to cough. "Now tell me all about how it happened."

Bashkim recapped his entire adventure for his dad, starting all the way back with his climb up the mountain to make sure Rin hadn't been eating the locals. He told him all about Rin, Cynthia, Fandul and Simon, Dasc, and even Angela and Henry from Handleson. He spoke of his own failures with the king of Nennossen and the thieves in the woods, as well as Rin's rescue from Teasvanna. Bashkim told his story in full, including his visit from the cloaked stranger and every moment of the final battle he had witnessed up until Wynn's death. Ascura listened intently and made sure Bashkim spared no details.

"Crimson," Ascura said distantly. "Just wait till I tell your mother."

Bashkim tried to smile, knowing his parents would be reuniting soon enough. The two remained silent, enjoying their time together.

"Tell me about mom," Bashkim eventually said.

Ascura's face lit up as he remembered his lover from so long ago and described her as though he had met her the previous day. He spoke of her laugh, her wit, her humor, and even the plans she had for Bashkim if they had made it to Handleson.

"She was as sharp as a spear," Ascura said. "Sometimes I think the world wasn't ready for her."

He sounded as though he could go on for days, but he eventually began to tire and fade. Bashkim held back his tears as the old man's voice lowered and his words grew further apart. Ascura's voice eventually drifted into a soft whisper as he reminisced about the days of old. He kept a smile on his face all the way to his final breath.

Bashkim lowered his head. With his father's voice gone, silence filled the cell.

"Goodbye, dad," he said.

A familiar figure draped in a black cloak stood at the cell's door, waiting.

"It's time," the man said.

Bashkim rose to his feet and strapped the sword back to his belt. He carefully slid his arms under Ascura and lifted to carry the legend. The cloaked man stepped aside, motioning with his hand for Bashkim to lead the way.

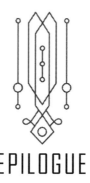

EPILOGUE

With Wynn and the white dragons defeated, Bashkim took Crimson's sword and willingly accepted his new role as the Arbiter of War. The humans and eshans remained united thanks to a change in leadership. Guero Orenzen's rule over Teasvanna came to a swift end and Fandul took the throne. The citizens of Nennossen elected Simon as their new king whether he liked it or not. Together, the two soldiers did everything in their new power to make sure the cities stayed together.

Within only a few seasons, the first eshans learned to call Nennossen their home. Shortly after, humans started to take up residence amongst the eshans. With eshan guidance, humans were allowed to bond with the kesshonite in order to unlock their magical abilities. As the years progressed, a "coming of age" ritual was established for humans that wished to acquire and learn magic. Humans openly practiced magic, and with the eshans' guidance, some of them were even good at it.

The citizens of both cities erected a statue of Ascura, Telanos, and Bashkim standing beneath Rin's wings, as well as a wall that held all the names of those that had fallen that day. They kept the stories alive of what their heroes had accomplished. They remembered the dragons, the soldiers, and all that had been sacrificed. The taverns sang songs of them, the scribes wrote their tales for future generations to learn, and the memories continued to thrive.

Fandul did everything he could as a king, a knight, and a gentleman to take care of Cynthia. In doing so, a bond formed between them over the years leading to Cynthia bringing three hybrid children of their own into the world. Despite being married to a king and a mother of three, she continued to forge some of the best steel Fandul had ever seen for both Nennossen and Teasvanna's soldiers.

Fandul also donated a large amount of time and resources to the study of kesshonite. Simon put in his own equal share as well, eager to find a use for the strange crystals other than destruction. Much to their dismay, they discovered nothing. As far as they could tell, they could use the kesshonite for nothing more than making their weapons more deadly. Disappointed, Fandul and Simon both agreed that it might be for the best to keep the kesshonite on lockdown and to stop their studies. Politically, the decision was not well received. The citizens began to fear their new kings would follow the footsteps of those before them and hoard the power for themselves. Despite their reassurances, Fandul and Simon could not convince their people.

Due to the political pressure, Fandul continued the studies in Teasvanna despite Simon's concerns. To Simon's horror, an accident occurred with one of Teasvanna's experiments. A piece of kesshonite overloaded and destroyed itself, as well as all the other kesshonite within the city. The chain reaction shook the land, and nothing but a massive crater remained of Teasvanna. Upon learning the news, Simon immediately outlawed kesshonite in Nennossen as well as wherever his authority could reach.

He personally took the kesshonite from the city and buried it, making sure nobody knew where. He left only a single piece in Nennossen so that the people could still acquire their magical abilities once they became of age. Had Simon known what actually caused the "accident", I imagine he would have reacted quite differently.

However, despite how much it pained him to do so, he had made up his mind. The world wasn't ready for kesshonite. Not yet.